Falling AT THE Barre

LOVE IN FAIRWICK FALLS

BOOK FIVE

ELISE KENNEDY

I

ALSO BY ELISE KENNEDY

***Love in Fairwick Falls* Novels**

Accidentally in Bloom (Rose & Gray)

Wallflower in Bloom (Violet & Jack)

Conveniently in Bloom (Lily & Nash)

Unexpectedly Bookish (Pearl & Reed)

Falling at the Barre (Olivia & Luca)

Book 6 - Summer 2026 (Allison & Wells)

~

***Cozy Nights in Vermont* Novellas**

Fall Inn Love

Falling in Vermont

~

***Only One Cozy Bed* Novellas**

Pumpkin Spice & Pour-overs

Apple Cider & Subterfuge

Hot Cocoa & Mistletoe

Snowed In & Snuggle Weather

For those who made a home
where no one yells

AUTHOR'S NOTE

Please note: despite the cute cover and the deceivingly slow burn, this is a very **spicy** book! You can double check content and trigger warnings at elisekbooks.com.

Happy reading! 😉

Chapter One

OLIVIA

Welcome to Fairwick Falls.

Olivia Maroo nearly cried. Relief wasn't a strong enough word for what she felt as her ancient Honda puttered past the welcome sign for her hometown.

It was eight o'clock in the morning, and she'd driven all night to Fairwick Falls, Pennsylvania—her refuge for the next four months.

Hay bales and pumpkins sat in front of local businesses as she drove through town. It had been decades since she'd been home during fall, her favorite season. Every fall, like clockwork, she'd been trapped in endless rehearsals of *The Nutcracker* as a dancing rat or background snowflake.

She'd spent the last fifteen years as a professional ballet dancer around the country in small ballet companies. She'd been a ballet corps member, a thankless job in the background ensemble. They danced endless hours in nearly every number and their primary job was to not be noticed while not missing any steps.

Until her contract was quietly not renewed last spring after eight years with the Salt Lake City Ballet.

She sniffed. *But I can still fouetté with the best of them.*

Even though months had passed, she still found herself checking her email to see if they'd realized their mistake.

The shame roiling in her stomach made her nauseous.

She'd been an outstanding dancer as a kid, but as she became a professional, she went from star to perfectly adequate. She'd dreamed of being a soloist or even ballerina, dancing a principal role like the Sugar Plum Fairy or Odette in *Swan Lake.*

Now, I just dream of employment.

A hard pill to swallow even now.

Audition season started in January, which meant she needed a rent-free place to live for four months.

She decided to admire the golden, turning fall leaves in the morning sunshine rather than let the tears win again.

She slowed to a stop at the new (and only) stoplight in her tiny hometown and rested her head on the steering wheel.

The fifteen-hour overnight drive had made her loopy. The hilariously tiny salary of a ballet corps member meant she'd counted every single dollar for the past fifteen years. There hadn't been enough dollars for a non-murdery hotel last night, so she'd hit the road after her last day of her off-season teaching job at a ballet intensive in Sarasota.

She'd openly sobbed through the state of Georgia. A concerned fellow traveler had mouthed *Are you okay?* as they drove down I-95. One couldn't exactly yell back, *I've wasted the potential everyone thought I had, and now it's too late. I'm too old, and I have no other options.*

So instead, she'd given them a tearful thumbs-up as she scream-sang to "Part of Your World."

She dragged a heavy eyelid open to peek at the stoplight. In her feeling-sorry-for-herself monologue, she'd let the light go green.

Shit.

Just as she sat up, the light turned back to red.

"Fuck. My. Life." She hit her forehead against the steering wheel of Baby, her ancient trusty car, with each word.

One stoplight later, she turned into the cute, historic neighborhood of her childhood.

Her breath hitched at the canopy of trees arching over the cobblestone street. Golden morning light broke through the dewy leaves tinged already with orange and yellow.

Small pumpkins lined the neighboring cottage steps. *It might even be fun to be here during fall*, she thought as she parked. The creak of her car door matched the one in her bones as she got out.

The front door flew open. Her tiny, seventy year old mother in a sparkly neon green robe and fuzzy, hot pink slippers shuffled quickly down the front steps.

"You're here, I was so worried," her mom called, practically dancing over to her for a hug. Martha Maroo-Canon was about a hundred pounds soaking wet, usually wearing neon or rhinestones, and Olivia's favorite person on the planet.

A heavenly cinnamon scent wafted under her nose as her mom tugged her inside. It smelled like home—that cinnamon-sweet apple smell she remembered from her childhood.

The welcome sight of her stepdad at the stove greeted her. "Hey, kid. How's my girl?" Pop said in his gravelly, low voice that always made her feel at home. He wiped his hands on a towel and gave her a rib-crushing hug that she returned right back.

Pop Canon had been a cornerstone of her childhood, despite only being her stepdad for about a year. Every day after school, she, her brother Wells, and her mom would sit at the corner booth in Pop's diner working on homework, eating fries and the occasional apple slice he'd make them eat. The entire town had called him Pop, but Olivia felt a secret joy at knowing Pop was *her* family now.

He'd apparently been silently in love with her mother for thirty years and had *finally* done something about it. Olivia had been thrilled—not just because it kept her in apple-pie pancakes when she was home, but because her mother hadn't beamed like this *ever*.

"I still can't believe you wouldn't let me pay for a hotel room," her mother said, pouring a giant cup of coffee in Olivia's favorite mug and handing it to her.

"*Eh.*" Olivia slung down her bags. "You know I don't like staying alone in a strange place. I'm very tossable," she grumbled.

"I still can't believe that those bastards didn't renew your contract."

"Mom"—Olivia rolled her eyes—"it's fine. It was time for me to go anyway. I was tired of Salt Lake City. Do you know how hard it is to find a good cocktail there?"

"Food's ready," Pop said, plating the syrupy, caramel-apple goodness.

Olivia made a conscious effort not to drool as she took the plate. Normally she wouldn't indulge in something so carb-heavy. Being a professional dancer meant her body was her livelihood. The macros of what she ate, how she moved, how she stretched, how she hydrated, everything was a precise science to make sure she was at her best at all times.

But now, *fuck it*—she was eating the whole plate. She had four months before her auditions, and with how hard she was going to work, one giant stack of cinnamon-dusted pancakes dripping with syrup and caramel would be easily burned off.

"I am *starving*. I need coffee, carbs, and then fifteen hours of sleep," she said through a mouth of pancakes.

"How about we make that five?" her mom said with a twinkle in her eye.

"Five... cups of coffee?" Olivia said, sipping the weak, watered-down coffee her mother always made.

Her mother's arched eyebrow meant business. "Georgia wants to see you."

Olivia smiled. Georgia Papadopoulos, Olivia's first dance teacher and owner of Fairwick Falls dance studio The Barre, was like an aunt to her.

The kind of aunt that yelled at you to sit up straight and had no problem punishing you while your parents weren't there.

Still, she was full of mischief, and Olivia owed everything to her. She'd been the first to make Olivia's parents take her talent seriously.

She caught up on the town gossip with her mom and Pop. A new bookstore had opened since she'd last been here, including an allergen friendly pop-up bakery. The Firefly Festival had gone off without a hitch thanks to her mother's fearless leadership (so said her mother), and Pop talked about how odd it was to be retired. He'd sold his family's diner and given the keys over to a new company, wanting to maximize his time with her mother now that they were married.

Her belly finally full of pancakes, Olivia dragged heavy legs and heavier eyelids upstairs to her childhood bedroom.

She pushed open the door and was greeted by the ghost of her potential.

Every award, every ribbon, every picture from her childhood dance recitals still hung on the wall.

With one new addition that took up most of the room.

"Um, Mom?" she called down the stairs. "What is my barre doing in here?"

Her six-foot practice barre loomed large in the small room.

Her mother leaned on the banister. "We had to make room for Herbert's things in the basement. I can have him move it to the dining room for you."

"No, don't worry about it." Olivia waved the idea away. The last thing she wanted was her eighty-year-old stepfather manhandling equipment down a flight of stairs.

But where on earth am I going to practice?

She turned around in her old room, taking it in.

It was a shrine to her old potential, one she'd never fully reached. She'd plateaued once she'd hit twenty-one and felt like she'd just been... *hanging* on in the background ensemble ever since.

Her mom had added framed news clippings that had been featured in local papers from her past. "Eighteen Year Old Ballet Phenom Goes Big Time," said the *Elliotsville Gazette*.

It hung next to the mirror, where Olivia looked at her own reflection.

She was thirty-three, young by modern standards, old by ballet standards.

Ancient according to this mirror, she thought, examining the duffel-sized bags under her eyes.

She flopped on her back, stretching out her hips, relieving some of the constant pain.

Could she keep going?

Once she left ballet, that would be it. There was no going back, professionally. Keeping her muscle tone and agility was a full-time job already. If she took a break, no one might want her again.

She laughed to herself, feeling empty. *No one probably wants me now anyway.*

But lieu of marketable skills for any other job, she'd just

buckle down and try harder. *Discipline got me this far, it can last me a few more years.*

She'd prepare a new audition. Get even sharper, even stronger. When audition season opened in January, she'd be ready. This time she'd finally get what she'd always wanted: a soloist position before the final curtain dropped on her career.

I have one last shot, and I'm going to work my damndest on it.

As she closed her eyes in her childhood bedroom, it became very obvious she needed three things to get through the next four months: money to support herself, a place to practice, and somewhere to stay that wasn't wallpapered in her lost potential.

LUCA

"AB, come finish your breakfast!"

Luca Bishop could *hear* his daughter ignoring him. The living room floor thudded from her jumping to death-metal Disney covers.

A hastily scrambled egg sat rapidly cooling on a unicorn plate.

"Annabelle, let's go!"

This was not the day to oversleep. He'd been up late last night researching the complicated permitting system for Fairwick Falls' business zoning, and had fallen asleep looking for "cute kid lunches."

Now, where the hell are those cookie cutters? He rummaged through his kitchen drawers.

"Five bites," he called as she ran into the kitchen.

Annabelle, his first grader, love of his life, chaos goblin, and the sweetest human he knew, didn't walk anywhere.

She grimaced at the egg. "How about four?"

"How about five?" He pulled out the last drawer in his kitchen. All the small cookie cutters were shoved in the back.

Aha, finally.

He grabbed two. "Star or heart-shaped cucumber slices today?" He held them up for inspection.

He watched her eat two bites. It was two more than he thought he'd get.

She stabbed another bite with a grimace. "Hearts are gross. Stars."

He agreed. Hearts were gross. He'd stayed far away from anything that looked like love for a long time.

They were going to be late, but other parents sent their kids to school with cute-ass lunches. He didn't want Annabelle to feel left out.

"I want to wear my teal unicorn shirt today," AB said to no one in particular.

Luca spied it on top of the pile in the laundry room.

"Ehh, let's do purple." This girl had a unicorn shirt in every color.

"Teal is my favorite!" she said, stomping her foot.

"I'll wash it tonight, but you gotta wear something else, kid."

"No," she said, slamming her body against the chair.

"Annabelle," he said sharply, and then caught himself. Tears started to form in her eyes.

Mornings had been hard, emotion-filled things since his sister had moved out.

I should be able to handle this on my own. Thousands of single parents did mornings all on their own with no help from anyone, so he would too, damnit. Since AB's mom had died five years ago, he'd relied too much on his sister's help. This was him proving he could do this all on his own.

And I'm failing miserably.

"Hey." He crouched down by her chair and glanced at his watch. It was only 7:30—*ah fuck, 7:35*—in the morning, and somehow it had already gone to shit. He hated seeing her cry. "I'm sorry. Mornings are hard for both of us."

"I don't wanna go to school. My stomach hurts," she said, resting her head on the table.

"What kind of hurt? Throw-up hurt?"

"No. Maybe."

Oh, god. He hated throw-up hurt. "Is it nervous-hurt, like when you go to the doctor?"

"Yeah," she whispered. Her little lip trembled.

Annabelle was full of chaos and energy, but his favorite thing about her was it never occurred to her to lie.

He always believed her. "What's making it nervous-hurt?"

She shrugged her shoulders.

Lately, she just needed extra time in the morning. He rubbed her back. "There have been a lot of changes, and you've been handling them like a champ. Being in first grade is really hard."

"I have to be there *all* day this year," she whined. "And I miss AP."

It was week three of him being a completely solo parent, and frankly, it wasn't going so great. AP was Annabelle's nickname for his sister Pearl. She'd moved out a few weeks ago to finally focus on her own life, and he was happy for her. She was in love and about to launch her own business. Plus, he'd depended on her for way too long. She'd already sacrificed so much for him and Annabelle.

The first year after Marcy had died, he'd barely been able to get himself together at all. Missing her had eventually turned into a dull ache, like a hangnail that only caught sometimes.

He just needed to get the hang of balancing childcare and his own business.

"I know you miss AP." He pulled AB into a hug, picking her up and swaying as he stood. He ignored the clock ticking to 7:37. "You love her a lot."

"Mm-hmm," Annabelle said through a sniffle against his chest.

"You're going to see her after school today, okay?"

Annabelle smiled and wiped her eyes.

Light of my fucking life, that little smile right there.

He'd run back to Fairwick Falls, grab AB from school, and drop her off at story time at *Bookish* for an hour where Pearl would be working. He'd have just enough time to run back to his body shop, lock it up, and go back to pick her up. "And you can get any book you want in the bookstore."

"Really?" She lit up.

"Now"—he put her down—"how about the purple unicorn shirt just for today?"

"No!" she said, digging her heels in.

His temper flared, but he tried not to lose his cool. "Annabelle."

"Dad, I don't want to!" Her temper flared.

He knew where she got it. "You're just like your mom, you know that?"

She smiled, knowing what he was about to say. "Pretty—"

"*And* stubborn," he finished for her. "How about wearing your blue plain shirt and you can put unicorn stickers all over it?"

Her eyes lit up with glee. "Yeah?"

"Have at it, kid." *Small victories.*

At least he didn't give in to her wearing a dirty shirt.

How was he so bad at this? She was just one kid, who he

loved, who he'd been in charge of, *technically*, for six whole years.

But getting four hours of sleep every night after he planned out how to move his body shop to Fairwick Falls, then getting himself up, her up, her ready, her lunch packed, him out the door, her to school, and him to work forty minutes away all before 8:00 AM seemed like an impossible task.

Then there were the constant running messages on his phone: two clients asking where their cars were, which was fair, but they didn't have to be such assholes about it, and one of his guys calling out sick.

His eyes caught on a clock on his phone: 7:40. *Shit*, they were definitely going to be late. He made the best out of her lunch that he could.

Annabelle had a deathly wheat allergy, and she sat at a separate table in the lunch room with her friend Sophie, who also had an allergy. He wanted to make sure Annabelle never felt too different.

Not like he had when he was a kid.

He'd been the kid whose mom didn't care if he wore dirty clothes. Who had *never* packed a lunch for him.

He was determined AB would never know what it felt like to be forgotten.

They rushed out the door, and Luca had to admire her artistry of placing stickers every-fucking-where on her shirt.

Feeling quite proud of himself for only being two minutes late to drop-off, he pulled up to Fairwick Falls Elementary School and got Annabelle out of her booster seat.

He hugged her to his leg. "Hey, you're going to have a good day, okay?"

She smiled up at him with that sweet angel face that made it all worth it. "Can I have my lunchbox?"

He looked in the passenger seat.

Empty.

Fuck.

He sighed. "Go, I'll leave it at the front office."

She ran to the door as the bell rang.

Already late and now I have to double back. Fuck.

A text pinged on his phone as he pushed the upper speed limit back to the house.

ANGIE (BODY SHOP)

Hey…anybody here yet?

Shit. Luca was the only one with a key to open the body shop in Elliotsville, over forty minutes away.

He voiced to text, "Running late" and stepped on the gas.

Chapter Two

OLIVIA

Hours later, feeling like an over-caffeinated zombie, Olivia walked to meet her mother and Georgia.

Little pokes of red and orange shone through the trees, despite it only being September. She enjoyed stretching her legs as she rounded the town square, which already had hay bales around the gazebo.

An unusually crisp wind fluttered her long hair as she walked past Pop's old diner. He'd sold it to a large, faceless company—his only offer—and retired a month ago. She was happy for him, but it had been the end of an era.

The pang of nostalgia was interrupted by a series of *pings* from her phone.

BESTIE LIL

Your mom said you're in town

YAYYY

I can't wait to seeee youuuu

Hellooooo

Are you alive?

If you die right as you get home, I'm going to be BIG MAD at you.

It's been 1,000 years since we've been in the same state, let alone the same town.

Helloooooooo????

Are you friend-breaking up with me??

And after all we've been through.

We have shared deodorant TOO MANY TIMES for you to ghost me

WHY DONT YOU LOOOOVE MEEEEE

oh my bad I was on airplane mode

Come seeeeeeee meeeeeeee at Bloom.

OLIVIA

Alive

But barely

Be there in 1 min

BESTIE LIL

Dolphin noises!!!

Olivia smiled at their old inside joke. Her face felt weird.
Ohmygod, has it been that long since I've smiled?
She looked at her reflection in the hardware store windows in surprise.
Add that to my list of things to do more.
She crossed the square to Bloom and spied Lily setting up a new window display. Her pretty face burst into a grin, and Olivia heard her whoop from ten feet away.

A cackling, tiny bullet of blonde hair ran out the door of Bloom and launched at her.

"You're here!" Lily said as she jumped onto Olivia and wrapped her in a spider monkey-like hug. Olivia squeezed her best friend back hard, so happy to see her. They'd been inseparable as kids and had rarely gotten to see each other in the last fifteen years due to work schedules.

"Warning, the Guild is here," Lily said, climbing down and looping their arms together.

The Gossip Guild was the ladies' auxiliary in Fairwick Falls her mother had founded ages ago. They did a lot of good for the town.

While talking a *lot* of shit.

"All of them?" Olivia grimaced, bracing herself for the invasion of the aunties.

Lily opened the front door for her. "They rented out the shop for an afternoon tea to plan the fall festival."

The scents of chrysanthemums, lilies, and roses wrapped around Olivia as she walked into Lily's pretty flower shop, Bloom.

Ladies she'd known all her life who were basically her adopted aunts waved at her with bright, beaming faces.

"What a sight for sore eyes," Georgia said, walking to her with dramatic open arms. Her old dance teacher looked like if a museum gift shop was a person. "My star student ballerina back in Fairwick Falls!"

Olivia opened her mouth to correct her. "Well—"

She crushed Olivia in a bone-breaking hug.

"Oh, good, you're here," her mother said, dancing with happiness as Olivia gasped for breath. "Georgia has exciting news."

Georgia let her go but wrapped an iron hand around Olivia's upper arm, which was code for *You will listen, now.* Her bangles and layered wooden necklaces clanked against each other with each movement. "Your mother said you need a place to practice while you're here this fall."

Olivia blinked, still groggy and playing catch up. "Yes—"

"I insist you use The Barre between classes for your practice. Also, my cottage isn't being used right now." Georgia wiggled her eyebrows. "Your mother might like some *alone* time with her new hubby and *I* have taken a lover—"

Olivia felt a wave of awkwardness crush through her. "Oh, I don't need to know—"

"—so I insist you stay at the cottage. Give you your own space. I need a house sitter anyway. Here are the keys," Georgia said, shoving them into Olivia's hand.

Olivia looked from her mom to Georgia, waiting for the catch. They smiled at her placidly, but she didn't trust that something wasn't afoot.

Access to a great studio and some space away from her childhood potential? Yes the hell please. "I don't think I can pay you, though. For the space."

Georgia waved a hand, clanking her bracelets. "No cost, of course. You're practically family. The gold key is for the house, and the other is for The Barre. You'll have plenty of time to practice uninterrupted."

"Perfect." Olivia smiled at last, feeling a weight lifting off her shoulders.

She could practice every hour possible, have her own space, and still only be a quick drive away from her mom and Pop.

Things are looking so up.

"Thank you. This is...just thank you."

"You're welcome, my dear," Georgia said, patting her hand and *finally* releasing her arm. "Now, don't forget, the tots class starts at one PM sharp today."

"Uh..." Olivia had a sinking feeling. Like she'd just been

hoodwinked by a fae into an unbreakable bond. "What was that?"

Georgia picked up her purse and waved to the other ladies as she walked to the front door. "The kids will be *so* excited you're their teacher. A real ballerina. They always ask about you."

Not a ballerina. "But—"

"And you'll need to go to Bookish and do the story time at four today. We've got to recruit for the new fall season of classes. Do you have a tutu with you? Oh, of course you do, what am I talking about? You're a professional ballerina! Make sure to wear your sparkliest one. We need to *really* impress. I've been hyping it up to that handsome owner of the bookstore. *Oof*, if I was thirty years younger... hell, if I was *ten* years younger," she snorted, elbowing Olivia as she walked past. "Don't forget—four PM. Today."

Olivia looked at her phone. *Shit, that's in a few hours.*

Georgia walked toward the door. "The class schedule's on—"

"But—" Olivia called.

"—the front desk. Please make sure to water my plants in my *beautiful* house that you will, I'm sure, take *excellent* care of."

Aha, *there* was the guilt trip.

My old friend, we meet again.

Olivia forced her lips into a pained smile. "Sure thing."

Studio space and a place to live in exchange for teaching *very* small children.

"Now." Georgia turned with a dramatic flair as she opened the door. "Please do *everything* I would do, especially with any amorous callers." She winked as she walked out.

Olivia's mom kissed her cheek before she walked off to her friends. "So good to have you home, dear."

Olivia stared at the keys in her hand.

Well, shit.

Nothing like being hoodwinked by the people who love you most to make you feel right at home.

❦

LUCA

LUCA SLAMMED the mallet into the side of a bumper, trying to pop out a stubborn dent one of his guys couldn't get.

He'd founded an auto body shop, and it had grown like crazy in the last four years. He had a couple of good guys working for him, but he still liked being hands-on.

Everything had to be right for his clients. He didn't want someone feeling like they got ripped off. People worked hard for their money, and they deserved the best that his team could give them.

Despite being the owner, sometimes he stepped in on a job. He knew it irritated the shit out of Angie, his office manager. Sometimes, he could just take five minutes and make everything better.

"*Goddamnit*," he muttered, whacking the bumper again.

Putting a little more oomph behind it, he tried to find the sweet spot. Hard enough to pop out the bumper so it was round again, but light enough not to fuck it all up.

Ritchie and Cam stood watching him. "Not so easy, is it, boss?" Ritchie said with a smirk.

There. He hit it just right and the bumper popped out.

"Yeah, pretty easy," Luca said, smirking back as he handed the mallet to Ritchie, who rolled his eyes. "This one has to be finished today."

"I know, boss," Ritchie called back in annoyance, stepping over the bumper and finishing out the small dings.

Their bread and butter was fender benders, bumps, and scrapes. Every once in a while, they'd get some young guy in who wanted his Nissan to look like a street racer, and they were starting to get more clients who wanted expensive custom paint jobs. Business was looking up.

"Boss," Angie called over from the garage office. "Somethin' won't shut up on your phone. Come get it or I'm tossin' it in the fuckin' bucket of car shampoo."

Luca grabbed his handkerchief from his back pocket and wiped the grease off his hands. He'd told the staff last week that they'd be moving the shop to Fairwick Falls soon and everyone was still pissed at him. He'd offered them a raise for the extra gas and trouble, or a great reference, and they'd all decided to make the move with him.

He couldn't deal with ten more years of forty-five-minute drives to and from Fairwick Falls. They'd moved because Annabelle needed a school that would take her allergy seriously. He'd do anything for her, including piss off his favorite employees.

Because maybe, if he fixed her childhood, he'd somehow fix his, too.

He grabbed his phone and saw his alarm had been going off for twenty minutes.

Fuck. Late again.

SHE-DEMON SISTER

Story time's almost over.

AB can hang out with Reed and I at the store if you're running late.

"Got to go," he said, grabbing his keys.

"You want us to leave the door unlocked?" Angie said, swirling around in her chair.

He grabbed his wallet from his desk. "I'll, uh, come back, later."

Angie rolled her eyes. "See you then."

LUCA

Be there in 40

Thirty-six minutes later, he slammed his SUV into park in front of Bookish, the Fairwick Falls bookstore where his sister worked part-time.

He'd been forty minutes late to pick up last week too. Annabelle played it off like it was no big deal, but he knew it hurt her feelings.

Luca threw open the big, ornate door into the bookshop and was hit in the face with a bunch of dangling fall leaves that he swatted out of the way.

Fuck. He was disoriented, trying to untangle himself. *What a terrible idea.*

As he shook his hair free of the remaining strings, he glanced up to look for Annabelle.

He froze as his heart stopped.

A beautiful, sparkling ballerina slowly turned on the bookstore's small stage in the warmth of the setting sun.

Strawberry blonde hair caught the golden afternoon sun as it streamed through the back window, spotlighting her.

She stood on tip toe mid-pose, like she'd been plucked out of a music box. She gracefully moved elegant arms as she gently hovered in those classic ballet shoes with ribbons on her ankles. Her light pink tutu glittered like diamonds in the filtered beams of sunshine.

Am I...hallucinating?

But the thing that had made his heart stop?

The beaming, gorgeous smile she shared with his Annabelle.

AB stared at her, entranced, like she was an angel that had fallen from the sky.

The ballerina's wide pretty eyes were filled with kindness and humor. The apples of her cheeks curved delicately to a princess-perfect jawline. Her elegant neck looked like it was spun from fine glass as it sloped down to the gentle curve of her throat.

As he took in the rest of her—a strong dancer's body, adorable earlobes, elegant hands, full lips in a mischievous smile—a stunning realization hit Luca with all the subtlety of a Mack truck honking its horn at full volume.

I am going to marry her.

Chapter Three

OLIVIA

"Why do your shoes look like breadsticks?"

"But *why* do you dance on your toes?"

"Does it hurt?"

"Then why do you do it?"

"How do you make your skirt stick out?"

"Can *I* make *my* skirt stick out?"

And for her seventh question, the perfect, angelic little girl sitting criss-cross applesauce in front of Olivia asked, "Do you barf when you spin real fast?"

That...is a new one.

Olivia bit back a laugh. It was an honest question, and she liked honest people. "Thankfully, no." She explained how she picked a spot on a wall when she turned so she wouldn't get dizzy.

She turned gently en pointe on the small stage in Bookish, the new bookstore in her hometown where she'd wrapped up story hour a little while ago. The class sign-up had been a success after she'd read *Baby Bunny Ballerinas* and answered about ten thousand questions.

Olivia slowly turned. "This is called a pirouette. I have to do lots of them in a row sometimes, but I also like turning slowly."

Olivia slowly expanded her arms back and forth, as if she was swimming as she slowly came out of the pirouette.

Her eyes drifted to the bookstore entrance, and she was shocked to find a hulking man seething at her.

Something made her chest ache as she looked at him. *Jeez, did someone punch me mid-pirouette?*

He was handsome, if a little…*terrifying.*

A lock of longish dark hair fell across his forehead, looking like he'd run his hands through it in frustration a thousand times that day. His beard was a sexy dark stubble along his jaw. His give-no-shits punk band t-shirt hugged tight around bulky, thick muscles, and a chain ran from his belt to his wallet. Heavy work boots complemented his car grease-stained gray jeans. He had an aura of an everyman who worked with his hands.

His nose was a little crooked—*from a fist fight, maybe?*—that gave way to thick eyebrows furrowed at her. There was a thick brutish quality about him. Muscular thick thighs, arms that didn't look defined in a gym but rather by necessity. He was manly, and raw, and really, *really* hot.

Jagged, complex black tattoos covered his thick arms. Skulls and metal band logos were etched into his skin. They ran down his hands and onto his thick knuckles and up onto his neck. Like his armor against the world was slowly growing all over his body. Spiky vines and thorns to keep others the fuck out.

At least he could handle commitment.

He crossed his arms, scowling deeper, still staring at her.

Is he here to rob the store?

Is he here to rob me?

He looks like he's literally growling under his breath.

She'd never been into bro-y posturing.

Maybe he's here to beat the shit out of someone.

Or maybe he's here to give me my secret fantasy.

Visions of what he might look like shoving her against a brick alley wall with a thigh between her legs, pinning her arms above her head and using those muscles to give her the biggest orgasm of her life made her squeak with wanting.

Wait. She dropped her heels down to the floor. She'd seen him before. *Somewhere.*

He stood out from the cute seasonal decor and quaint Victorian architecture in Fairwick Falls. Like he'd taken a wrong turn from Bushwick and decided to stay.

He doesn't look like a wreath-hanging, small-town-festival kind of guy.

She couldn't stop *staring* at him.

His deep brown eyes went molten at her. Apparently he had the same problem.

What is with me?

His scowl broke though as he talked to Reed, the bookstore owner, as if they were friends.

Okay, so he isn't *here to kick over a trash can and shout "Punk's not dead" before setting a small anarchist trash fire.*

Olivia turned her attention back to the adorable chatterbox in front of her who was in the middle of a monologue about unicorns.

LUCA

He laughed—a humorless, despondent, and desperate sound.

Oh, no.

Oh, god.

No, no, no, no.

He wiped a hand down his face in desperation.

That's my future wife? The fuck?

Those thoughts had never occurred to Luca before.

He'd never once in his goddamn life looked at anyone and thought, *You know what? Why don't I marry you, stranger. You're the other half that completes my soul.*

Or some shit.

Frankly, if someone had told him he would *ever* think *anything* like that, he'd have decked them.

Love at first sight was bullshit.

Until it smacks you across your dumbass face with its bull-shittery.

He couldn't deny it. The woman on the stage was meant for him—and he for her. As certain as the sky was above and the ground below his paint-stained boots.

His hand rubbed at his chest as he stared at *her* in utter bewilderment.

Who *was* she?

She crouched down, laughing with Annabelle. Her reddish blonde hair was twisted into a bun, and she wore a small tiara on top of it. She gingerly took it off and set the tiara on Annabelle's head, gently moving the hair out of her face.

Had he *ever* been that gentle?

Oh, fuck me, he cursed at his bad luck.

His eyes couldn't stop drinking her in.

He needed to ask Pearl what the hell was going on.

Why was there a ballerina in the middle of the goddamn bookstore?

And why wasn't she wearing something warmer? Her long arms were bare, and she only wore tights and a bodice thing.

Why do I feel protective and territorial over her? Christ.

His life felt like it was on a tilt-a-whirl right now, making him dizzy with the idea of her.

Maybe I forgot to eat lunch, and this is just some weird psychosis as a result.

"Hey, man," Reed called, waving from the checkout counter. Luca nodded a greeting at his best friend without taking his eyes off of the ballerina.

Reed held up a stack of books as he walked to Luca. "You missed story time, but AB hasn't even come up for air. She and Pearl picked these out. Apparently, ballet is her new favorite thing. The top one is the one that Olivia read."

"So you see her, too?" Luca said, his eyes never leaving the ballerina talking with Annabelle.

Reed chuckled. "She's here promoting the new kids' dance classes in town."

"Huh." Luca went back to staring, bewildered, at the woman.

Reed placed a hand on his shoulder. "You okay? You look like you need to lie down, or take a shot."

"Probably," Luca said with a disconcerted sigh.

He had a strict no-dating rule until Annabelle graduated high school. He couldn't risk losing anybody again. He'd been a shell of a person after Marcy had died, and he was going to do fucking better than that. His entire focus needed to be on making sure AB had the perfect childhood. He only had one shot. He was struggling enough as it was.

Romance was not even on his radar.

AB saw him and ran over. "Dad, Dad! Ms. Olivia said I could be a ballerina."

His heart lit up. It never got old, her calling him Dad. *Top five sounds of my whole life.*

She'd been talking nonstop since she'd turned one, but still. Never got old.

He hugged AB to his leg, catching the tiara falling off her head.

Annabelle stared up with pleading eyes. "Can I take classes, please? Please? Please?"

He hadn't seen Annabelle this obsessed since she'd first discovered the existence of unicorns two years ago.

He opened his mouth. "W—"

"Please?"

"Annab—"

"*Please*? Come here, come here." AB pulled him over to the ballerina.

Oh...fuck.

Oh my god.

He *had* seen her before. She was *the* woman, the one he'd seen last Christmas. There had been a Christmas thing at the diner that Pearl had dragged him to, and he'd been caught up in a business discussion. He hadn't been able to take his eyes off of this woman—this...*Olivia*—but she'd disappeared.

She stood and looked as bewildered as he felt.

Olivia. He rolled the name back and forth in his head.

He could already feel the grooves of how it belonged there.

"Hi," she said warmly, softly. As if they were picking up from an old, lost conversation.

"Hi," he whispered. He felt like he'd practically screamed, *Oh, it's you. The other part of myself I didn't know was missing.*

AB pulled on his hand. "So can I take classes? I'll be a ballerina. And then—wait. Do we get to wear tutus?" she asked suddenly, tugging on Olivia's tutu.

"Hey, ask nicely," Luca reminded her.

Olivia leaned down, crouching into an impossibly small folded bundle so she was eye to eye with Annabelle. "It's a little while before you get to wear a tutu like this, but we get really fun costumes and fun ballet slippers." Her warm, indulgent smile at AB was going to make him pass out from wanting. "You get to dance and have fun and move your body and feel good."

"And wear a tiara?" AB asked with excitement.

"Sometimes, yes," Olivia said with a laugh as she stood, introducing herself. "I'm Olivia. I'm the new *temporary* dance teacher."

He memorized every movement as she spoke. The graceful curvature of her lips, her animated and bright eyes.

"Yes," Luca said, feeling lightheaded from how perfect she was.

Wait, that doesn't make any sense.

"Yes, I'm Olivia?" A pretty look of confusion contorted her face and her big blue eyes grew wider.

No, not blue, sapphire.

He liked the way her lips moved when she talked, as if they were part of her dance—smooth and luscious.

Hell, he'd go to war for this woman's earlobes—they were that fucking cute.

"Yes. I mean, the classes," he said, gulping.

Oh. My. God. I am fucking this up so badly.

"Okay," she said with a nervous smile. "So that's a…yes to the classes."

He gulped again.

"Yes."

AB tugged on his hand. "Dad, it starts this week."

"Okay," he said, his eyes never leaving Olivia's face.

He was making an absolute mess of this.

Olivia.

He rolled the name around in his head again, comforting himself. It was perfect and lovely, and it suited her.

"I'm so excited we have another student joining us," Olivia said, winking at AB, who beamed at her. Annabelle's face might crack in two from her smile.

"How about"—Olivia leaned over on her knees, now standing flat-footed in her heavy toe shoes—"you keep that tiara." She winked as Annabelle gasped and clutched the plastic tiara to her heart.

Annabelle shrieked, throwing her body at Olivia's legs and almost knocking her over.

Luca grabbed Olivia's flailing arms, and his hand went to her back to steady her. Olivia burst out laughing and patted Annabelle's back.

Olivia's eyes caught his with humor, and she aimed a grateful smile up at him. Gorgeous.

"Our girl loves hard," he said to Olivia.

He'd meant *our girl*—his and Pearl's and Reed's and everybody who loved Annabelle. But as the sentence reverberated between them, an insane, truly nuts part of him instinctively thought, *Maybe someday…?*

No, it's too much to hope for. A ridiculous thought.

He'd just met this woman. She could be married. Maybe she didn't even like men.

But maybe.

Maybe in some alternate universe, where happy endings blossomed and good things happened to good people…maybe there could be a *we* between him and this woman who'd somehow crawled under his skin in a matter of milliseconds and set up shop in his left ventricle.

Olivia rustled through her bag and handed Luca a piece of paper.

He was staring at her dumbly, trying to memorize every single hair on her head and freckle on her face.

Eight across the bridge of her nose.

Six on each cheek.

"This is a list of things to order for your first class. You can buy them at the studio's front desk or wherever you get your ballet essentials."

Her teasing smile was now his new favorite. It was full of humor and intelligence.

And maybe witchcraft? What is wrong *with me?*

He just nodded at her.

Say something, you ass. Any minute now. She's staring at you.

Instead, all he could muster was a panicked thumbs-up.

The blood returned to Luca's brain as he stepped away to pay for Annabelle's ballet books.

Reed smirked at the checkout counter like a *smug* mother-fucker. "Need help rolling your tongue back into your mouth, or can you handle it?"

Luca gave his best friend the middle finger as Pearl walked up.

"Don't flip off my boyfriend, dickhead." Pearl gave Luca a middle finger back as she kissed Reed's cheek with a sweet peck.

Luca rolled his eyes, but a very large part of him was beaming because his sister was so happy with his best friend.

"Uncle Reed, I'm gonna be a ballerina," AB said, peering over the counter and hopping up and down.

Reed smiled at her, delighted. "Hey, Anna the Bell-breaker. Yes, I saw your tiara. You're practically one already."

Then the reality of adding something else to his schedule hit him.

How the fuck am I going to manage another thing on our schedule?

Annabelle already had Girl Scouts. He had work far away. For some idiotic reason, school times didn't line up with busi-ness times. He was moving his business to Fairwick Falls, which was a full-time job itself.

He absolutely hated depending on Pearl, who was launching her own bakery soon in addition to working at Bookish. He'd already depended on her too much and wouldn't rope her into childcare again.

He needed to handle this on his own.

Annabelle danced in the open space of the bookstore, mimicking ballet moves.

"Thanks again, Reed!" Olivia waved as she walked to the front door.

She'd changed into sneakers, removed the tutu, and had thrown sweatpants on over her tights. *Good, she's warmer.*

She still looked like the most beautiful woman—*like his*—Luca had ever seen.

"Annabelle, I will see you at our first class next week!" She gave AB a high five, and if he wasn't mistaken, her eyes sparkled as she smiled directly at him.

He watched her walk out, not losing sight of her until the door of the bookshop clicked shut.

I know in my bones… I just saw the woman I'm supposed to marry.

And now I'm going to have to see her once a week and not *muke a fool of myself.*

OLIVIA

"And then he just gave you a thumbs-up?" Lily said with a scrunched, confused face.

"Yes!" Olivia said in exasperation, hauling another box from her car. They carried moving boxes up the small stone front steps of Georgia's cottage. "That's weird, right?"

"And *what* did you say he looked like?" Lily said in confusion, hefting a box onto her hip as she opened the screen front door.

"He was *huge* and hot," Olivia said as she walked into the cute cottage. "Like maybe he could be an asshole who would get in a bar fight, but then also he was fucking ah-dor-able with his little girl. My ovaries melted out of my body."

Georgia's cottage was stuffed full of keepsakes and tchotchkes. Floral couches, lamps dangling with gems, and scarves were everywhere.

The clutter was going to drive her nuts for the next four months, but all the better reason not to get too comfortable.

"He had a little girl at the bookstore. I think she knew your brother?"

"Oooooh," Lily said slowly, setting the box on a small wooden table in the kitchen. "Did he have scary neck tattoos? And biteable biceps the size of my head? *Literally?*"

Olivia pointed emphatically at her. "Yes, exactly his energy. I *probably* want to fuck him, but also he might shake somebody down for their wallet right after."

"That," Lily said, unpacking the box of Olivia's sewing supplies, "is Luca. He did some great work on the Bloom farmer's market van. And though I am *happily* married"—she wiggled her finger with an enormous rock on it—"I totally get the appeal."

Olivia unpacked her matcha powder, in its perfect container, and set it in the perfect spot on her countertop. She put her favorite mug beside it, and then put the rest of her supplies into an empty spot in the well-worn, jewel-toned cabinets in the kitchen.

"I just felt like I'd sorta been...shot in the chest when I met him."

Lily gasped. "In a...like, good way?"

"In a *scary* way," Olivia admitted.

"Oh, no."

"In a 'I think I just saw my future flash in front of my eyes and he made me orgasm' way."

Even that is an understatement. She'd read the word thunderstruck in the past, but now?

She'd lived it.

Seeing the wall of dark, brooding, tattooed man with a body that looked like it'd been carved from every one of her late-night fantasies walk toward her had been an out-of-body experience.

And when that hard-as-nails exterior turned into a pile of soft squishy mush when he saw his little girl?

Forget the EMTs—call the coroner. She'd been *dead* from cuteness.

Lily danced as she hopped down the steps back to the car. "Ooh, maybe you'll stay here forever as he sexes your brains out."

"*No*," Olivia said, yanking open the creaking front passenger door to grab the last bits of her stuff from her cross-country trip. "Only here for four months, the end."

"It's just so nice to have you home after all this time. I've barely seen you for a decade and a half. I want a permanent girls' weekend. In between the classes Georgia asked you—"

"Hoodwinked me," Olivia corrected.

"Into teaching." Lily grimaced.

Olivia groaned and leaned against her car. The warmth of the September sun hit her face and contrasted with a light, crisp breeze in the air. "I'm kind of dreading the classes. I've taught summer intensives for years, but those were semi-professional young dancers. Incredibly serious, incredibly determined."

"Probably not a lot of fingers up their noses," Lily said with a snort.

"Exactly," Olivia laughed.

"Miss Olivia," a tiny voice shouted.

Olivia turned to see the adorable little girl she'd met at the bookstore.

She'd felt a kinship with her immediately, with how completely obsessed she'd gotten with ballet in a matter of seconds. She'd asked smart questions as she waited for her dad to pick her up.

Her hot, no-wedding-ring, holy-fuck-he-could-toss-me-across-the-room fantasy, dad.

The little girl's backpack bounced as she ran across the grass from the house next door.

"Annabelle," a deep, growling voice called from the house next door. "Don't run toward the road."

He rushed out the door but stopped suddenly as he saw Olivia.

Olivia's pulse jumped at the unexpected realization.

Oh god, they live next door.

She was going to live next door to the ravage-you-then-cuddle-you combo that apparently was the secret to her vagina.

"Hey, AB." Lily gave her a big high five. "That is a very cool unicorn backpack."

Luca was busy locking the door, so Olivia let her eyes linger on him. It was rare for her to experience intense initial physical attraction. She normally was attracted to men after she got to know them more, but there was just something about Luca that made her feel like a magnet, drawn to him.

The fine lines on his arms twisted around skulls and wrenches. His chest was large, and pillowy. It curved down to what looked like a gentle, soft stomach, and she actually felt herself clench at the thought of putting her head there.

She felt her arm being tugged.

"So can I?" AB asked.

She'd been completely lost ogling the man who was apparently her next door neighbor. "I'm sorry, sweetie," she said, kneeling down to eye level with AB. "I was distracted."

A loud snort came from Lily that Olivia was going to ignore.

"Can I show you my gifts from the crows? They gave me decapitated doll heads," AB said with excited delight.

"...Sure," Olivia said, completely thrown off by the dark side of this adorable little girl.

AB tugged her to a pile beside their front tree.

Luca slowly walked toward them.

"Hi," she said softly. *Am I...breathless right now?* "I'm your new next-door neighbor." Her eyes traced the thick muscles moving inside his black T-shirt.

He nodded, staring at her with bewilderment.

"See this one"—AB held a mangled Barbie head with one missing eye and a half a head of hair—"I got on my birthday because I gave the crows snacks. And then—"

"Annabelle, we've got to go, we're late," Luca said, still never taking his eyes off of Olivia.

Olivia gulped. She liked the feeling of his eyes on her, but it made her skittish—like she was near a precipice, and she didn't know what was on the other side of it.

"I don't want to," AB whined.

"Come on," Olivia said, holding out her hand. "You can tell me all about it until we get to the car."

AB grabbed her hand and jumped as they walked across the rolling front lawn. "And sometimes I get earrings, and sparkly rocks from the crows. AP, that's my aunt Pearl," she clarified, "taught me how to be friends with them. When do we dance?"

"The first class starts in a few days," Olivia said, squeezing AB's hand.

"Thanks," Luca said quietly to Olivia. "Hop in, AB." He opened the car door and lifted her onto a small booster seat.

"Oh." Olivia spied a lunch box beside the front door. "Don't leave." She squeezed Luca's thick, hard forearm as he shut the car door. He stilled under her touch.

Okay, maybe that was an unnecessary grab, but come on. *So fucking hot.*

She dashed across the front lawn, taking the stairs two at a time, and grabbed a lunchbox.

"I think this is important, right?" she said with a smile.

Luca wiped a hand down his face and laughed. "Yes. The lunchbox is my nemesis. Thank you," he said quietly as she handed it to him.

His cologne wrapped around her as she stood next to him. It was musky and smelled expensive, like a cashmere man cave.

Do not sniff this man's chest right now. But something in her needed it, like he was the sole supplier of a nutrient she'd somehow forgotten to consume for thirty-three years.

Annnnd I look disgusting right now, she thought, having carried boxes in for over an hour. She pushed flyaways out of her face. "Any time, neighbor."

Luca licked his lips. A shy smile was on his face that was in total contrast to the menacing skull peeking out of his shirt collar.

Why did the contrast of it all make her dizzy?

His lips were plush for a man. She bit her own bottom lip, thinking about what it might be like to bite his.

Ridiculous. He could have a girlfriend or partner or something.

"You moved in next door?" he said suddenly, his eyes soft. The fall breeze played with the strands of dark hair over his forehead.

"I'm borrowing the cottage from Georgia until December. She has a *lover*." Olivia wiggled her eyebrows.

"Lucky Georgia," he said with a slow smile, his eyes tracing her face.

The sentence formed in her head: *Do you have one of those?*

But luckily, her mouth was smart enough to stop it before it got there.

"What happens in December?" he asked.

"I audition and then move wherever they need a moderately talented ballet dancer."

He nodded, fiddling with his keys. He started to say something but stopped himself. "I should go," he said, gesturing with the lunch box. "Big day ahead. Buying my first pair of ballet shoes," he added, giving her another one of those shy smiles.

Holy shit, he is so cute. "I don't know if we carry your size," Olivia said with a laugh.

He huffed out a laugh in return as he hopped into his SUV. The warmth from his smile radiated around her, glowed under her skin.

She waved at AB as they drove away, and it was at that moment that she noticed Lily doubled over in laughter

"What," Olivia said accusingly, knowing *exactly* why she was laughing.

"I just haven't seen you smile this big in a long time," Lily said, giving Olivia's arm a squeeze. "It's nice."

"I smile," Olivia said defensively, playfully pushing Lily.

Lily wrapped an arm around her. "You've had this haunted Victorian child aura. Seems like it's faaaaaading," she said with a teasing tone.

"Probably just all this fresh fall air." Olivia shrugged, laughing with Lily at the obvious lie.

"Hot as *fuck* fall air that is really cute with his little girl, more like," Lily said with a wink, opening the cottage door and walking in.

But for some reason that made no sense, the world felt a little bit brighter that morning. Her circumstances hadn't changed. She was still here to pick up the scraps of her career and braid them into something stronger.

Maybe it was because she could hang out with her best friend. Maybe it was because she'd been able to give Pop a kiss on the head as she left, knowing she'd get to see him tomorrow for dinner.

But, ridiculously, unbelievably, and so impossibly illogically, she had a feeling it had to do with the SUV at the end of the block turning out of sight.

Chapter Five

OLIVIA

"All right, class." Olivia clapped twice. "Let's go to the barre."

The gaggle of first grade girls continued to wreak chaos around the room.

Was I ever this little or this free?

They were making funny faces in the mirror, twirling around in their new outfits of ballet pink tights and black leotards. They leapt awkwardly—*adorably*—and giggled with abandon.

Additional sharp claps did nothing to deter them from their shrieks of laughter as AB wiggled her hips from side to side and attempted a cartwheel.

This was not how Olivia had imagined her first class. She had a whole barre routine for them to go through.

Olivia leaned down to the first little girl, Harper. "Can you do me a big favor and go hold your hand over there?" She gathered the next one with her and shooed her next to Harper. "Hey, AB," she called. "Can you come help me over here at the barre?"

AB ran like a crab on all fours with two little girls trailing her.

"Let's put our bubbles in," Olivia said, puffing out her cheeks. That was her trick she'd used when babysitting preschoolers. They all mimicked her as they stood staring—*blessedly*—silently.

"Let's put our right hand on the barre. Your other right," she said, gently patting an errant hand.

"Let's blow out our bubbles"—they all let out a dramatic sigh, a few of them giggling—"and now, let's go to first position." Olivia set her feet so they formed nearly a straight line side to side.

They silently stared at her with confused faces. The tall one in the back picked her nose.

The nose-picker raised her hand. "Is that like first base?"

Olivia puffed out her own bubble, puffing her bangs away from her face in frustration. Parents who had paid good money for a ballet lesson looked unsure as they peered through the waiting room window.

Ten minutes into the first class and they hadn't even started the barre routine, the most important part of the warm-up that every ballet class started with, no matter the age.

"Who knows the ballet positions?" Olivia said, raising her hand.

They cocked their heads to the side in confusion.

"I can do a cartwheel," AB said, cartwheeling away from the barre.

"Thanks, AB. Let's go back to the barre now," she said, gently correcting her.

She'd always made sure to be a kind teacher during the summer intensives. Olivia had been called horrible things by every ballet master she'd worked with, but that abuse stopped with her.

She wouldn't teach by fear, but she did need to teach them *something*. Their parents were paying, after all.

Olivia mentally pulled up the class schedule. She had planned to start with the barre and then basics of *demi plié* and *tendu*.

That was before she realized how unrealistic that was.

Nuke the whole plan. Start from the scratchiest of scratches.

"All right," she said, rolling her shoulders. *I can do this.* "Who can count to four?" They all raised their hands.

"Great. We are going to learn four positions today." She methodically went through all four positions at the barre, with them following her.

Olivia corrected each girl until they were perfect before moving on to the next position. That took approximately twenty-five minutes, and after her correction on the last fourth position, the girls' attention spans were waning.

Three girls were hanging on the barre like they were monkey bars, and one stared up at the ceiling, lost in thought.

"Are we going to dance?" AB asked sadly.

Olivia looked over her shoulder again at the parents who were whispering to each other.

Shit. Totally screwed this up.

This was a dance class after all, right? What would Georgia do? *End on a strong note, and leave them wanting more, darling.*

"Sure, let's dance." Olivia grabbed her phone that was connected to the ancient speaker in the studio, and two seconds later, "Under the Sea" started pounding through the speakers.

The girls' faces instantly lit up.

"Let's have some fun to close it out. Dance out all your feelings," Olivia said as the girls had already started moving their bodies.

The girls jumped at the barre and then started running around the room, full of the energy that had been so absent two minutes earlier.

"Are you gonna dance, Miss 'Livia?" Sophie asked as she and AB swayed side to side.

Olivia found that she didn't remember exactly what to do with her body. How did one just dance for *fun* in a ballet studio?

It wasn't something she'd had permission to do in a long time.

The girls' faces lit up as they all danced in a circle, jumping up and down, swaying adorably, not even a little bit gracefully.

It had nothing to do with the first four positions of dance, but they were having fun. It seemed to be important for them to want to come back.

One by one after the class, parents stood at the door as they coaxed their kiddos out of the studio.

Harper's mom was the second to last to pick her up. "I'm so excited for what you're going to do at the festival!" she exclaimed to Olivia, holding out a hand for her daughter.

"The...what?" Olivia said, her smile waning.

"You know, the fall festival, the kids always do a nice performance. My older girl was in it last year."

Uh oh.

Harper's mom gushed at the memory. "The costumes that Miss Georgia had were adorable. They were all little pumpkins, but of course, one accidentally fell over. It was absolute chaos, but it made for really cute pictures."

"Right. Pumpkins," Olivia said, trying to catch up. She had to do a fall festival performance on top of everything else in her life?

She waved Harper and her mom out, and finally it was just her and AB.

AB followed her like a shadow, asking constant questions.

"Will I get to wear toe shoes next time?" she said, hopping

up and down, spinning on the flat leather soles of her little ballet slippers.

Olivia wiped down the barre, catching a sticky patch from someone's candy-covered fingers. "Maybe in a few years if you keep dancing."

"We didn't really dance." AB spun in circles as she talked. "Can we dance more next time?"

"Learning positions at the barre is important if you want to be a ballerina," Olivia said, sitting down on one of the tumbling mats at the side of the studio.

"I do, I do." AB hopped around and twirled in front of her.

Luca was running late, it seemed. But Olivia didn't mind chatting with ballet's newest number one fan.

AB climbed onto the large stack of tumbling mats. She lay on her tummy, flipping her ballet shoes back and forth. "How long does it take to be a ballerina? I have lots of things I need to do."

Olivia burst out laughing. "What things? Filing your taxes? Finally getting that timeshare in Boca?"

AB giggled with her. "I'm gonna be a monkey rescuer and I need to be a ballerina. I'm gonna find the first ever unicorn. Then I'm gonna bake cakes like my Aunt Pearl." She'd listed each one on her fingers, like the weight of the world rested on her shoulders.

"That's a lot of things, kid."

She flopped over with dramatic exhaustion. "I *know*. So I need to dance more," AB said, as if trying to explain a very simple concept to Olivia.

All right, let's dance more.

"Name your favorite song, and we'll dance while we wait for your dad," Olivia said.

"'Let It Go,' but I want the screamy one."

"…Screamy?" Olivia cocked her head.

"Like German death metal," AB said with authority.

Olivia rolled her lips together, stifling a laugh. "How do you know what German death metal is?"

"I'm just really smart, I guess," AB said as she stared at the ceiling.

Olivia typed in "*Death metal Let It Go*," and sure enough, there was a great cover. As the screaming rang out, Olivia laughed, and they danced like maniacs in the mirror, jumping and slamming their heads to the guitars and the drums.

It was oddly freeing, screaming and thrashing around.

When the second chorus hit, she looked up from head-banging and jumping in circles with AB and saw that Luca was standing in the doorway of the studio.

"Oh, my gosh." Olivia gasped in surprise, clutching her chest. She'd been so lost in the music she hadn't looked up.

He leaned in the doorway with his thick arms crossed and a delighted smile on his lips. He waved at her, but his face lit up when AB saw him and ran toward him.

"Hey, goob." He caught AB as she flung herself at him.

Olivia was about to turn off the loud music, but she saw AB headbanging like a professional punk rocker in the mirror. Luca joined in, jumping up and down as he mouthed the words and thrashing his arms a little with AB.

Luca looked like an intimidating guy at first. Dark hair and eyes, menacing skulls on his triceps. Until he looked at AB and became a puddle of mush. She loved seeing the glimpse of him switching into dad mode, that soft, sweet side where his eyes lit up.

Olivia turned off the loud music. "Sorry," she laughed. "We got a little caught up."

She couldn't take her eyes off him as he smoothed AB's hair down. AB chattered up at him about their dancing, and his face practically glowed. AB's aunt had dropped her off, so this was the first time Olivia had seen him since that morning outside.

His black t-shirt hugged his thick arms, and his gray jeans had streaks of oil on them. His scruff had grown out, and his hair was mussed, like he'd been pulling at it.

Even hotter than I remembered. She filed away the way his chest and arms curved, how big his hands were, the knowing smirk of his smile. *The perfect complement to my vibrator tonight.*

"Go get your backpack, kiddo," he said, swatting AB into the hallway to grab her stuff. "Sorry I was late. Ran into cow traffic on the way back from Elliotsville."

"Were they un*mooooo*ved by your car horn?" Olivia said, unable to help herself. She liked seeing him smile.

He bit the inside of his cheek, chuckling at her. The way he stared at her felt like he could see into her soul. Like he was trying to figure her out. "You could say that. Still, I'm sorry. I don't like being late and I should have planned better."

She waved him away as AB joined them. "Oh, it's fine. We had fun." She could feel him getting ready to say goodbye as AB put her jacket on. Something inside her begged, *Please don't go. Please stay. I like it when you're here.*

Like a sixth sense that felt better when he was around.

"We can walk you to your car?" he offered. AB's tiny hand was now enveloped in his, and the sight made her want to cry.

She's so little and he's so big, but so gentle. Don't tear up. Ohmygod, am I about to get my period or something?

She shook her head and grabbed toe shoes out of her bag by the door. "Now my work starts, unfortunately." She held up the shoes by their ribbons, already sewn and broken in from her practice yesterday.

Olivia sat down, pulling on her shoes and lacing the ribbons around her foot and ankle.

AB's eyes lit up. "Can I stay and watch?"

Luca's eyes closed as if to say, *I'm sorry.* "Let's leave Miss Olivia so she can focus. We gotta go to Pearl and Reed's anyway for dinner."

AB's face fell. "Just for one minute? Please?"

Olivia stood up, toe shoes now laced, and slowly rolled to her toes. AB's eyes lit up at the magic of seeing her hover on tiptoe.

Almost makes the dull pain worth it.

"I wish all my audiences were as excited as you."

AB tugged hard on her dad's hand. "Please!"

"Just one warm-up routine?" Olivia asked Luca, now on AB's side.

"You guys are ganging up on me now?" He laughed in surprise. "Sure, but then we'll get out of your hair."

Olivia turned the music to her favorite warm-up track and danced gently, moving through positions that felt like home, doing what her body needed to start to warm up.

Developpé, pique, into pirouette. The Chopin melody got faster and more exciting. She danced and moved in her own world, enjoying the feeling of finally expressing all the things that had been trapped inside her body that day. A running grand jeté, leading into a lingering arabesque, then turn and turn and turn. She jumped and extended one limb, then another, letting all her feelings out—frustration, need, anger, joy.

She finished in fourth position as the music ended, her heart finally connected with her body.

And with a roar that would rival Wimbledon Stadium, an enormous, tattooed man and a little girl wearing her backpack became Olivia's smallest, loudest audience ever.

Chapter Six

LUCA

As Luca tripped over a pile of air hoses, he was nearly hit in the face by his terrible mistake.

He'd trusted somebody.

Like an idiot.

It had nearly cost him the business he'd built over the last eleven years.

At eighteen, he'd started building an auto-body business piece by piece, sometimes sleeping in the shop. At nineteen, he'd hired his first guy. At twenty, he could finally rent a two-bedroom and move Pearl out of the trailer and away from their mother.

He didn't need much, but needed to make sure the people he loved were taken care of. He'd come from a long legacy of white trash and needed to scrub the stink of it off of himself every day. He'd wanted parents who showed up at spelling bees and school talent shows. Like a fool, every year until third grade he'd look in the audience to see if his mom had showed up when she said she would.

Later, she'd always insisted she'd been there; he just hadn't seen her.

But Luca finally believed his own fucking eyes. He knew she'd *never* been there.

AB was his whole world, and he was going to give her everything he'd never had for himself. It was a small fucking thing, but she'd never gone to bed hungry. She'd never had the power or water turned off. She never worried about where her next meal was coming from.

The thing he was most proud of? She wasn't afraid of him. *No yelling in my house.*

He was determined that the pattern would stop with him. He would *will* the life that he'd wanted for AB with his own bare hands.

He'd be the parent that would go to spelling bees and school programs and any fucking thing. Be a room parent. *Whatever that is.*

He'd taken an unusual leap of faith over the summer to give AB an amazing memory. They'd spent six weeks in Florida to visit Marcy's parents, AB's only real grandparents. It had nearly kneecapped his business, but he'd do it all again in a heartbeat to see her eyes light up at Disney or the beach or the alligator habitat.

Every day though, his stupid mistake of trusting the wrong person over the summer haunted him in the form of supply piles in his auto body shop, late work, and constantly fixing leftover issues. Today he'd finally fired the guy who'd fucked everything up.

He rubbed a hand down his face, thinking about everything ahead of him. He needed a babysitter ASAP to focus on setting up the shop in Fairwick Falls.

Thick black coffee slowly slid from the cracked shop pot to his cup. Ritchie, his go-to guy, taped a chassis for a custom paint job.

"You have kids," Luca said, matter-of-fact.

"Yep," Ritchie said.

He couldn't shut up about the Steelers ten minutes ago, but now *he's tight-lipped?*

"I need a babysitter recommendation." Luca peered over his shoulder and spied Annabelle coloring at his desk, a door away.

Ritchie shrugged. "We got a couple of good ones, but we're over in Cooperstown."

Fuck. He needed parent friends in Fairwick Falls.

"I just don't know who to trust, and my sister is doing her whole bakery thing, you know?" Luca said, finally walking over to Pearl's Airstream trailer that was getting its coat of pitch-black paint this week. It was a gift from him and Reed to get her bakery kicked off.

"Babysitters are hard to come by. You can't just trust anybody with your kids," Ritchie said, stating the obvious.

"Can Olivia be my babysitter?" AB piped up behind Luca, playing with wrenches at the table.

Damn, he hadn't seen her come in.

"Finish your homework?" Luca said. Distraction was usually the best option for AB.

"'Livia is fun and we dance. She can help me be a better ballerina."

He couldn't imagine a worse idea than integrating the most beautiful woman he'd ever seen further into their lives.

His thoughts had drifted late last night to Olivia. Her thighs, her round ass, perky breasts in her ballet leotard.

Seeing her more often would be a disaster.

Just have to hold it together until December when she's gone and I can finally breathe normally.

Luca sloped a hand down AB's pigtail. "We need somebody more permanent. Ms. Olivia will leave soon."

"No," AB said, getting whiny.

Luca looked at the clock. It was 6:30. Normally, he'd avoid

having AB here because it was a distraction to his guys, but they were doing overtime catching up after Cam had fucked around all summer and pissed off half his clients.

"Go finish your homework, and then we'll go home and hang out."

"No," AB said, stamping her foot. "I want to hang out with Ms. Olivia."

Luca had imagined a babysitter who was elderly and not so alluring. Like Beulah, his ancient neighbor, who had the temperament of a twenty-one-year-old chihuahua—snarling, a little smelly, but probably harmless.

"How about Beulah?"

"Ew." AB recoiled. "Her breath smells like that bottle in the cabinet."

"What bottle? Luca said, eyes connecting with Ritchie's.

"The brown one you said I can't have because it's for grownups."

Ritchie caught Luca's eye and shook his head back and forth.

No shit, Luca mouthed to him over AB's head.

Damn. Noted. Not Beulah.

~

OLIVIA

RUUUUUHHH-RAWR-RUUUUUUUH-RAWR-RUUUUH—

"Someone stole my engine and replaced it with a cat in heat. That's the only logical explanation," Olivia muttered.

She gripped her key tighter, as if that would do anything. As if the engine not turning over was her fault for not pressing the key tightly enough.

Ruuu-ruuhhh-rawr-ruuuu-ruuuh-rawr—

Ruuuuuuuur-raaaaawr-ruuuuu—

Olivia gave up, sitting there in the quiet afternoon. She'd been dreading going to look for part-time jobs anyway.

Who would hire a ballet dancer with little to no marketable skills that needed to take time off each week at random times to teach a handful of classes?

She'd need to save thousands for her safety deposit and first month's rent once she moved to a new city. Her checking account laughed at the thought.

If only Pop still owned the restaurant, she could have begged a waitressing job there, but some anonymous big company owned it now.

She refused to ask her mother for help. No one knew how dire her finances were, and her mom worried about her enough as it was. Her mom was so focused on her being a success. She couldn't let her know just how much *not* a success she'd been.

Olivia revved the coughing engine again. "Come on, Baby," she muttered through the embarrassing engine noises that now sounded like "*Let me diii-iii-iiie.*"

Maybe that last road trip wore her out.

A screen door slammed next door, and the friendly, neighborhood, tattooed Mack truck of hotness slowly ambled down the stairs.

Over black joggers and a tight black T-shirt, he wore a bright cosmic-cloud-and-rainbow-themed unicorn apron.

Olivia swallowed a smile because he seemed completely unbothered by walking around in a cartoon full-body apron. *Why is that so fucking hot?*

Olivia's chest tightened, both hoping and dreading that he would come over. She loved running into him but hated it all the same. Her body didn't know what to do with itself. She couldn't pounce on him, but she also couldn't take off running. That would be crazy.

Also, how could I look at his biceps that way?

She'd finally come to the honest realization that she had a big fucking crush on the single dad next door.

Like, certified seventh-grade, giggling when she thought about him, oh-my-god-he's-looking-at-me, don't-look-at-his-name-in-my-notebook crush.

As she spied the vein running down the curve of his bicep, she decided—fuck it—she would revel in this crush.

I'll find a notebook to write his name in a goddamn heart.

"Having trouble?" Luca's hands were in his pockets, but his eyes were kind and full of concern.

Yessss, he's in squish mode.

She got out of the car. She felt so awkward, like her tongue was practically lolling out of her mouth. "Uh, she's just temperamental."

"Mind if I take a look under your hood—under *the* hood?" he said, correcting himself quickly, squinting his eyes in embarrassment. "I'm, uh, pretty good with cars."

Of fucking course you are, hot dad next door.

What a slutty thing for a man to be—competent *and* helpful. Her pussy pulsed unexpectedly at the thought.

Jesus, get a grip. He cannot possibly be single.

"Want me to hold your unicorn apron?" she said as he reached for the hood of the car.

His gaze shot down as he realized what he was wearing.

He laughed, untying the back of the apron quickly. "Thanks," he said dryly. His eyes danced as he handed it to her, and she could feel some vital organ melt at the sight. "Can't get this dirty. I'll never hear the end of it from Annabelle."

"Birthday present?"

"Christmas," he said with a smile. "Everything has been unicorns, but ballet is giving them a run for their tiny, cloven-hooved money." He'd run his fingers along the edge of her hood, triggered the old catch and popped it open expertly, all while chatting with her.

Look, she was a feminist, okay? She thought gender norms were stupid, and anybody could do anything, but there was something about the rippling muscles as he lifted her car's hood and then looked over the engine with an expert eye that made her knees a little weak and her insides go liquid.

Straight into her panties.

Luca's dark eyebrows jumped to the top of his messy hair as he scanned her engine.

She gulped, trying to remember how to flirt. "Give it to me straight, doc."

"Not good," he said, his eyes flashing to hers with concern —no flirtation. "When's the last time you had this serviced?"

Ruh roh. "Uh…about eleven years ago? When I bought her? Though I didn't drive her much in Salt Lake."

He nodded, unscrewing a cap and peeking under complicated tubes. "What made you come to Fairwick Falls?"

His arms rippled as he turned some sort of cap on her engine.

Why was it the triceps that always got to her?

She wanted to bite them, just a little. Just to feel the pressure against her teeth and claim it as hers.

There was something about this man that turned her into a lusty cavewoman.

"Olivia?" His brows knitted together with concern.

Whoops! "Grew up here. I'm just here between gigs. Auditions for ballet companies are in January, so I have some time to kill." She shrugged. "Normally this time of year, I would be knee-deep in rat costumes working on *The Nutcracker.*"

He smiled. "I know that one."

"Yeah, you're a bunhead?"

"Bunhead…?" he said slowly with confusion. His dark

eyebrows left no feeling unspoken as they moved across his face. "Like…an ass man?"

She burst out laughing at how fucking adorable he was.

His cheeks went crimson and a wave of guilt washed over her.

"No, no, it's, um." She swallowed, not wanting to embarrass him. "It's a word for a ballet dancer. Because of the"—she pointed at her head—"you know, the buns? We wear. On our heads, not our asses."

His entire face went red, and he ducked under the hood again.

Great. Now he's embarrassed and *might think I'm a snob.*

"This needs a lot of work to get it back up and running. I'm happy to do what I can, but—"

She waved him away, feeling bad. "Oh, no. I can't pay you or anything—"

He gently held up a bear paw-sized hand to stop her. "No cost. Let me see if I have some extra stuff in the garage. I can at least fill up your oil and see if you can get the engine to turn over."

"Miss 'Livia!" a tiny voice called out before the screen door slammed. Annabelle was already two steps down, running in that little kid, tummy-first way. "Wanna be my babysitter?"

Olivia's eyes shot to Luca, who hung his head in frustration.

"Annabelle, we—" he grumbled.

"My dad was going to ask you—"

"Annabelle," he said, more firmly.

"Oh, um…." Olivia barely had time for her own practice right now.

"Please," Annabelle said, tugging at Olivia's hand. "I'll be *so* good. We can play Barbies, and dance all the time."

Luca crouched down in front of AB. "Hey. This is a grown-up discussion, and when you're eighteen, you can contribute—"

AB interrupted. "I won't *need* a babysitter then—"

"Until then"—Luca looked her in the eye with a serious face, but his voice was gentle—"I need you to listen to what I'm saying."

He looked so stern, so caring, so...*perfect* in his tender love for his daughter that Olivia's mouth did the unthinkable.

"Sure," she said, the word tumbling out of her mouth.

Luca stood up.

She was too close to him, she knew, but all of a sudden she had a sort of woozy feeling that made her lightheaded.

Like she'd made a tectonic shift in her future.

Could barely breathe when her eyes connected with his.

Some sort of cave woman-like instinct took over when her body was near his. *My face would fit perfectly between his pecs and shoulder.* Like a hollow little dip made just for her.

"Oh my gosh, we're gonna dance so much," AB squealed, yanking Olivia's hand and bringing her back to reality.

Olivia laughed, coming out of the Luca Lust haze.

This could work, she realized, thinking about the possibilities. A flexible schedule, a kid she already liked. A one-minute commute next door.

"Do you"—he cleared his throat—"have childcare experience?"

Oh, now, this is awkward.

She pushed her hair behind her ears and stood straighter. "I babysat a lot in Salt Lake for extra cash. I could find some references."

"We can talk about it more later. I don't want to pressure you or anything," Luca said, catching his lip between his teeth.

She wanted to bite that lip too. What would he taste like? Spicy and with a hint of sweet? Like the cologne he wore?

Oh, this is a very, very bad idea.

"*Please.* We can look at baby bunnies! There are some born last month in the backyard." She tugged at Olivia's hand, and Olivia spun her in a circle that made AB giggle.

Annabelle was a really fun kid. Most of the kids she'd babysat for in Salt Lake had been, frankly, little assholes. Rich kids with snowboards, private tutors, and little concern for her or the small joys in life, like baby bunnies.

As she twirled AB around and around, her giggles floating up between the two of them, Olivia decided that maybe something easy and fun and full of laughter could be exactly what she needed right now.

"*Come on,*" AB said, pulling at her arm.

"They're pretty cute," Luca said with a laugh. "I'll fill up your oil and water, and we can talk later."

She let herself be pulled by AB back around the side of the house to the yard, her eyes never leaving Luca's as she wondered what the hell she might be getting herself into.

Chapter Seven

LUCA

With his heart hammering in his throat, Luca walked to the small cottage next door the next night.

Probably a giant mistake asking her to be my part-time nanny.

But he had a good feeling about her. AB loved her, too, which mattered a whole fucking lot to him.

A light bulb was in his hand to replace the burnt-out bulb above Olivia's front door.

He'd noticed it the night before with a scowl. *It's not safe to just fumble for your keys in the dark.*

Fairwick Falls was small, but bad things still happened in small towns. It had made his skin crawl to think about her not being safe. He'd barely been able to sleep.

He unscrewed the light bulb in the little lantern above Georgia's front door. His guts still churned from nerves as he slowly turned the light bulb in.

It's fine if she says no. It's fine if she says yes. You'll make sure you barely see her.

Even though his body came to life when she was around. The world seemed brighter, happier. Full of possibilities.

It'll probably go away. That wanting her that tears you up so badly you can't even think.

The fresh light bulb flooded the front steps of the cottage with a warm glow.

Gulping with nerves, he knocked on the door firmly.

The curtains on the front door window moved, and wide, pretty blue eyes stared back at him.

He was happy to hear a lock disengage before the door opened.

As the door swung open, every thought in Luca's brain gushed out of his ears.

Holy fuck.

Olivia wore a purple sports bra, clinging yoga pants...and nothing else. Her tits—*stop staring*—were pushed up and a small line of cleavage peeked out from the top of the curved, low neckline. His breath caught as her nipples pebbled, pointing against the soft material. A sheen of sweat made her chest, arms, and long, toned abs glow.

Want to lick it off.

Fuck.

The curves of her hips flared out from her waist. They had those hip dips that looked made for his hands to grab. To worship. Her thighs were meaty, muscular.

Perfect.

...Fuck!

He forced his eyes to her gorgeous face, and that didn't help the war he was losing against his cock. Her long hair was in a thick ponytail, with cute flyaways from the glow of sweat on her face.

He scooped up the brain cells that had melted out of his eye sockets and shoved them back in. "Hi...ya."

Should've scooped some more in, idiot.

"You fixed my light bulb?" she asked, peering outside the front door.

"Uh, it was out," he said stupidly.

Of course, she fucking knew it was out.

"It's not safe to go in and out in the dark," he added, again stupidly.

She bit her lower lip, looking like she was trying not to smile. "I could have gotten it. You didn't have to."

He spied a long piece of wood she was holding behind her back. "Is that...a baseball bat?" he said, quirking a brow.

"Oh, um..." She looked embarrassed and tucked a strand of swooping hair behind her ear.

His fingers itched to touch what looked like the softest, silkiest strands he'd ever seen.

"There was a strange man on my porch," she laughed. "And it was dark, which I've heard is very unsafe." A twinkle in her eye made the tightness in his chest relax.

He laughed. He realized he did that a lot with her. *Way more than usual.*

"Sorry for scaring you." He handed her the dead light bulb.

Their fingers brushed as she grabbed it. He gulped, his skin coming alive at the hint of contact.

God, this is such a bad idea.

He stared at her hands holding the bulb. Long fingers held it elegantly. Pretty, light pink long nails curved against the delicate glass.

Everything this woman did was so fucking...*elegant*. Too good for him.

She probably has some fancy-ass boyfriend somewhere.

"Did you...need something else?" she asked, looking confused.

Fuck. He'd been lost in thought. "Listen, I'm sorry if AB put you in a bad position. If you aren't really interested in babysitting—"

"No, no," she said suddenly. "Want to come in and talk about it?"

He looked over at his house. His Wi-Fi could probably extend from here, and he should still be able to hear AB in the app on his phone.

"Oh, we could also do this at your house if AB is, you know, asleep," she said suddenly, picking up on an unspoken cue.

"She's asleep. Baby monitor app." He held up his phone. "Sure, let's talk."

This woman was hot with a capital H. Round, firm ass. Strong, muscular legs. Those ab ridges that were usually airbrushed onto people. They moved and twisted as she laid down the baseball bat. She shrugged with long, elegant arms to say, *No weapons now.*

He ducked inside the low door of the little cottage. He'd been here a few times when Georgia had needed help. Though he was pretty sure she just liked to look at his butt as he'd grab something off a high shelf.

Unlike when Georgia lived here, everything in the living room was neat and put away. Candles burned, low jazz played. *Does she just live like this?*

Every surface was cleared, and it smelled good. It smelled like her.

Cinnamon.

Fucking hell, that's what it is.

It had haunted him not knowing what the core scent of her was. It wrapped around her when she moved, and sometimes he'd been lucky enough to catch it.

He scratched his head, feeling deeply uncomfortable. He'd never had a personal employee like this.

He could be a hard-ass to his guys at the shop, but this

woman looked like a fairytale princess come to life. Yet he would be entrusting her with the most important thing to him in the entire world. His shop could blow up, and he wouldn't give two shits.

But if anything happened to his Annabelle, he'd be beside himself.

He decided to be Boss Luca. The tough guy who didn't take shit from anybody. "I asked around. Called…"

All thoughts left his head as he saw a sex swing on the closet door beside Olivia. It was hooked from the top of the door, with bands hanging down it for limbs to go in.

His brain scrambled in static for a solid five seconds.

"Something wrong with my stretching bands?" Olivia said following his gaze, lifting them up.

Right. She was a dancer, they needed to stretch. *Stop being a creep.*

"Oh, uh no." Luca shook the mental images out of his head. "Uh, sorry. I…I called the references you left on my door, and they had great things to say. Asked around town. People love you."

It was easy to see why. She was sweet and kind, that much was obvious from his interactions.

"But Annabelle's my whole world, and I need you to take her safety really seriously."

"Of course," Olivia said, her face earnest. "I would never want anything to happen to her. Is there something I need to know? Or just general kid safety stuff?"

He *hated* thinking about this. Even though he thought about it almost every fucking day. "AB has a deathly allergy to wheat. We—" His voice caught and he swallowed past the lump of emotion. "…Uh, we almost lost her one time. When she was a toddler. It was pretty scary until we figured out the allergy."

"Oh no. Oh, Luca, I'm so sorry."

Hearing her say his name mesmerized him. Made him feel lightheaded, needy.

Olivia's eyes were dewy with emotion, and she rubbed a hand on his arm in sympathy. "That must have been terrifying. AB is the sweetest kid, and I can't imagine seeing her like that."

The warmth from her hand on his fucking *elbow* radiated to his heart like a heated emotional blanket.

It felt so nice to be with someone who just made him feel safe.

Like she took their shit seriously.

Like she cared.

He nodded, underplaying the torture at being so far gone for her already. "Yeah, so anything that doesn't come from our kitchen, I'm skeptical of. Have you ever used an EpiPen?"

"Shrimp allergy," Olivia said, raising her hand with a self-effacing, lopsided smile. A dimple popped into her cheek and his heart stopped.

God fucking damnit. She's cute *on top of everything else?* He tried not to laugh at his own torturous misfortune.

She just kept redefining *perfect* with every minute.

Olivia stretched her quads with a bright smile. "So, unfortunately, yes. I have personal experience that it is no-percent fun. I will happily carry an extra EpiPen if she needs it in a kid dosage size. I'll assume all other snacks are a no-go unless cleared with you."

A small knot of concern in Luca's chest unwound. *I didn't even know it was there.*

"Yeah," he said, trying to keep up with her. "Sounds good."

"Is there anybody else on the approved contacts list she can interact with?"

He hadn't thought about that. It was a good idea.

"Pearl, I'm guessing," she continued helpfully. "And AB's mom? Or any significant others I should be aware of? Girlfriends, boyfriends?" Olivia asked, an innocent expression in place.

Is she seeing if I'm available?

Don't be gross; she's just being thorough.

"AB's mom died several years ago. Car accident when AB was a baby," he said with a sad smile.

Her pretty face instantly looked sad. "Oh, I'm so sorry."

"Thanks," he said, clearing his throat. *Better to not linger on it right now.*

He scratched his eyebrow, embarrassed to talk about so much heavy stuff with a woman who seemed like light personified. "And I don't...uh, date. Trying to keep all my focus on Annabelle until she's, you know." He flicked his fingers as he stared at them. "Outta the nest."

He decided to skip the real reason.

Because it almost destroyed me to lose someone I loved.

Because Pearl had to step in to take care of AB and I hate myself for it still.

Pivot this back away from my personal life. "Is twenty-five bucks an hour fair?" he asked, Boss Mode re-activated.

He'd done a little research, but he didn't want to be cheap.

"I actually feel really bad about taking money for this," she said, avoiding his eyes. "People used to babysit me all the time. My mom was a single parent, too. Plus, I'm your neighbor."

No. He needed to compartmentalize. "I'd feel better if you were getting paid. Keeping this, you know...professional."

The word had landed like an unspoken question between them.

Her freckled cheeks blushed prettily.

Whatever this was between them, it couldn't only be in *his* head, right?

Hell, maybe it was. Maybe he was imagining what he wanted to see.

He continued, "I let AB know this would just be temporary. I don't want her getting too attached, you know? She loves real hard."

"She get that from you?" Olivia said, smiling softly.

"Maybe," he said with a laugh.

Definitely.

She pulled a sweatshirt over her sports bra—*thank god*—but unfortunately it did that incredibly sexy thing where it sloped down, exposing one shoulder.

Goddamnit. Can't she just do something to make me hate her?

She leaned against the back of her couch. "Can you give me a rundown?? My schedule is pretty flexible, except for the handful of classes I have to teach at The Barre."

Yes. Logistics will calm my cock down. "Pickup and drop-off for all her activities and school. I'll try to pack her lunch ahead of time so you don't have to do that."

"Oh, I'm happy to. *If* I get to wear the unicorn apron." She gave him a mischievous smile.

He burst out laughing. "Sorry, that's a hard no. Can't risk anything happening to it. But I'll buy you your own. Purple looks good on you anyway." He let the flirty sentence escape his lips as he pointed to her all-purple outfit.

A sparkle danced in her eyes as she licked her cupid's bow lips, rubbing them together with a smile.

He almost moaned at the sight of it.

Back on track, dummy. Payment, car, number. The three things you came for.

"The one sticking point." He held up his keys. "You'll need to drive my SUV until I can service your car."

"Oh, that's not necessary. I'd feel so bad taking your car." She looked worried, as if she was putting him out. Not saving his sanity by hanging out with her number one fan.

Maybe number two fan.

He was starting to think he might beat AB for first place.

"It very much is necessary. That's a death trap that you've been driving. I have a work truck I can drive in the meantime. I'll service your car sometime and get you a booster seat so AB can ride in it. There's a house key on here too," he said, setting the keys on the entryway table.

Don't need to get half-hard again from brushing her fingers.

Last one. Don't be awkward. It's totally normal to need your babysitter's number.

"Can I, uh, have your number?" he said, the ask caught in his throat. "For, you know, logistics."

The longing must have been obvious on his stupid fucking face because a blush tinted her cheeks.

"Yeah," she said, avoiding his eyes.

He handed his phone over. "School's at 7:30, and be warned, she's a monster in the morning."

"Same!" She laughed, snorting hard and long, and slapped a hand over her nose. "Oh my god, so embarrassing," she muttered with closed eyes.

His breath caught at how adorable she was. It was ludicrous to think she'd be embarrassed by anything she did.

"I think it's, um"—he cleared his throat, avoiding looking at her—"it's cute. It's not embarrassing."

"Yeah?" The hope in her eyes nearly broke him in half.

He nodded in response, biting the inside of his cheek to deal with his feelings.

How had someone not told her yet that she was perfect? That everything she did—how she moved, smiled, spoke, fucking *blinked*—was exactly right.

Right for me.

They stared at each other in that hungry silence. His stomach ached from the fucking *yearning* for her coursing through his bloodstream.

"I should go," he said suddenly, realizing he needed to get the *fuck* out of here.

"If you could text me a list of approved recipes and ingredients that AB likes, that would be really helpful," she said, opening the door for him.

He loved that she was taking this seriously.

"Yeah, I'll do that. Tonight." He hovered in the doorway, betraying his own voice of reason telling him to leave.

She leaned against the open door. His eyes feasted one last time. His hands itched to frame the curve of her hips hugged by her yoga pants.

"Good luck getting home," she said with a mischievous smile. "I've heard when it's dark out, it's not very safe."

He laughed with surprise. *Of course she's funny. The universe must fucking hate me.*

"Yeah," he said stupidly in response.

He stepped back but didn't turn his back on her. *Don't want to stop seeing her.*

He didn't talk much as a rule, but everything seemed to come out dumber when she was near.

"I'll see you on Monday morning," she said with a wave.

He nodded, deciding to keep his mouth shut.

He jogged down the steps, noticing the last one was wobbly.

I'll fix it next time.

He looked over his shoulder as he walked to his house, wanting one more glimpse. She watched him from her front window. Glowing in the candlelight, hair framing her pretty face.

A fucking movie star, that's what she looks like.

Perfect, perfect, perfect.

She waved as she sipped from a mug of something warm,

her long elegant fingers peeking out of the oversized sweatshirt that still exposed one pretty shoulder.

He waved back and growled out a miserable, tortured groan in the night air.

The next time AB made him watch *The Sound of Music*, he was going to feel *way* sorrier for Captain von Trapp.

REED

How's Project Raven coming along?

I convinced Pearl to sign up for the fall festival as a vendor, so we'll need to have it ready in time for that.

LUCA

The what?

Oh. The airstream. Fine.

You and your code names

REED

She might see my texts! It has to be perfect AND a surprise.

Pearl gets this dewy, misty look in her eyes when she's surprised and it's the cutest thing I've ever seen.

But also somehow she gets cuter every day.

LUCA

Baaaaaaarf.

But you know, thanks for seeing that she's great. Pearl needs more of that in her life.

How did you know she was…you know. Your person.

REED

You asking as a big brother or the guy who had his brain knocked out by two toe shoes and a tutu the other day?

LUCA

REED

Toe shoes, got it.

LUCA

She moved in next door and I asked her to be AB's nanny. So I can get things done and not bother you guys.

REED

Hahahahahahahahahaha

Hahahahahahhahahaha

Haaaaaaaaaaaa

hahaha

LUCA

Alright, fucker, I get it.

It's fine. We'll hardly see each other. Probably.

AB just loves her and her references and background checked out. I don't know anyone else in the area.

Called your sisters who grew up with her and they said she was great too.

REED

Luca, I say this with all the love in my heart for my best friend

Who I would take a bullet for

Who I already think of as my family.

This

Is the dumbest idea

You've ever had.

Including when we tried to fly from the treehouse using wings we made from cardboard.

LUCA

Trust me

I am fully aware.

Chapter Eight

LUCA

A tinkling pulled at the edge of Luca's consciousness.

What is that sound?

It sounded like noise in a diner, the clinking of cutlery. He sat bolt upright when he saw the morning sun streaming in through his curtains.

He grabbed for his phone and a pair of pants. *Shit, shit, shit.*

"Fuck," he muttered. He'd fallen asleep at 3:00 AM last night, putting in extra time in his home garage on a special part for Pearl's Airstream.

It was already seven in the morning. *We'll be late again,* he thought groggily.

He tugged on his pants as he walked, stumbling to get them on. He pushed into Annabelle's room. No Annabelle.

Her covers were pulled back, and panic shocked through him, finally waking him up.

It was then he noticed the smell coming from the kitchen.

Right. Shit. Olivia was here. He walked slowly down the steps, wanting to observe how it was going without AB seeing him. He crouched on the stairs, peering into the kitchen through the living room.

The scent wafting to him smelled great, but the scene in front of him?

It looked even better.

Olivia was french-braiding Annabelle's hair, a heaping stack of pancakes on a plate beside them. His gluten-free pancake mix box sat open on the counter.

Annabelle was giggling with her feet flopping back and forth on a stool, munching on a plain pancake she held in both hands. Gentle, quiet, upbeat music floated through their soft conversation.

His heart thudded hard as Olivia smiled down at Annabelle while she fixed her hair. Annabelle beamed at her. Olivia talked with her like an equal, took her questions seriously and with kindness.

God, he loved that.

Olivia was dressed in a casual t-shirt and jeans, her long hair swooping down like a curtain as she bent over to gather sections of hair. She looked like she belonged in his house.

He wanted to keep seeing her right there every morning.

He slowly walked down the stairs, needing to be closer to them.

"Daddy," Annabelle said with a bright smile, "see how cool my hair is?"

He nodded, padding across the living room floor. "It's very cool," he said, voice low and gravelly.

Olivia stopped and stared, frozen, as he walked toward her, her eyes caught on his chest.

Ah, shit. Didn't think to put on a shirt.

He grabbed a flannel shirt from the back of a chair and pulled it on so he didn't make her feel uncomfortable. "Smells good," he said quietly to Olivia.

"Um." She shook her head and focused back on Annabelle's

hair, snapping the end of her braid in a barrette. "There's a stack of pancakes for you."

She patted AB's shoulders. "All done. Go get changed, and I'll meet you down here with your lunch."

AB immediately ran upstairs.

Wish she listened to me that well.

His heart was still thundering from the confusion of all of it.

"AB heard me come in and crept down to the kitchen. Love"—she spun around in a complete circle as she spoke, full of energy—"those unicorn footy pajamas of hers, by the way."

There needs to be a stronger term than "morning person" for this sunbeam dancing in my kitchen.

Her bright eyes sparkled with humor as she grabbed a large container from his cabinets. "Think they make them in adult sizes?"

Stepping in front of him, she leaned across the wide kitchen island. His eyes landed on her ass nearly in front of his face. His jaw ticked, instantly picturing *exactly* what else they could do in that position.

Don't be gross. He slammed his eyes closed, covering them with his hand for good measure.

She rifled through the refrigerator and pulled out cheese sticks, vegetables, and grilled chicken tenders.

His nerves kicked in at her possibly forgetting how he liked the lunch fixed. "AB likes the cucumber—"

"Cut into shapes," she finished for him with a confident smile. "I remember from your note."

"And I like to make sure that she has something fun in it, not just vegetables and protein, you know?"

"Love that," she said as she gathered things around the kitchen with a singular focus.

"And don't forget something to drink," he said, trying to be helpful.

"So... tequila shots?" She smirked over her shoulder as she pulled out a small water bottle with a *ta-da* motion.

He sat on a stool, wiping a hand across his beard.

He was anxious about this, and he didn't like that about himself. He felt outmaneuvered and not in control.

"I might need to turn the AC on if you keep steaming in the corner like that," she said, cutting a carrot into bite-size bits and putting them in a little container with the star-shaped cucumber slices.

"Not steaming." He sighed. He'd fucked this up already. He wasn't *mad*, he just needed to make sure it was done exactly right.

"Tell that to your face scowling at me." She huffed out a laugh.

I'm scowling? "This is, uh...hard for me. Just a little stressed."

"Look." She finally stopped moving in her sprint around his kitchen and cocked a hip, leaning against his island. "I get it. I don't like giving up control either."

Her knowing smile gave him permission to just...be.

The quiet kindness of her overwhelmed him.

"She's my whole world," he said finally. It had come out unexpectedly rough, more emotion caught in it than he'd realized.

"I know she is," she said quietly, touching his arm briefly with kindness. "She'd be mine, too, if I had such a fun, cool kid in my life. That's why I made pancakes today." She was back in motion, clicking the Tupperware closed and putting it in the lunch box. She buzzed around the kitchen in a way that made her look like she was at home.

He huffed out a laugh to himself. *If only.*

She shrugged as she chopped chicken tenders. "I wanted

her to be excited about the change. Plus, I'm great at getting feedback, so just let me know what I need to change to be better."

Better?

The idea was, as AB would say, bananapants.

Have you met you?

There literally couldn't be anything better than you right here being yourself.

But he couldn't say that, could he? "I'm sorry if I come off harsh. I don't mean to."

"I've been cursed at in seven languages and told I was a stupid, fat cow in three. You don't scare me," she said with a ghost of a smile, grabbing ranch from the fridge.

Horrified anger exploded in him like an atomic bomb. "*What?*" he yelled in a sharp, hateful voice, startling her as she opened the ranch bottle. Splatters of ranch squirted into the air, landing on the counter and floor.

"Jesus, sorry." He was already up, wanting to fix it.

She burst out laughing as she grabbed a paper towel.

"I'll get it, don't worry about it," he said, grabbing the roll and wiping the mess. "Why would somebody say that?"

And can they fight, and would anyone miss them if I killed them?

"It's fine," she laughed, waving him off as she scraped ranch into a small sauce container from the counter. "It's part of the ballet gig. But my point is, tell me, okay? I want to make sure you can trust me, and I know that's earned."

She zipped the unicorn lunch box closed—*how did she do that so quickly?*—with a resolute nod. "I'll pick AB up from school today, and then we'll come here or go to the playground at the Falls Park. Is that okay?"

This woman is practically Mary fucking Poppins.

She danced circles around him, making an amazing breakfast, did something to Annabelle's hair he barely understood, and packed a lunch all while he was just waking up.

Despite my piss-poor attitude too.

"Uh, yeah," he said, trying to keep up.

He appreciated that she seemed to *get* him, that she wasn't annoyed by his overprotectiveness like Pearl had been. "Can I have the keys to your car? I'll take it into the shop and start to service it. Or, I can take it wherever you want."

She tossed him her keys. "I trust you with Baby. Do whatever."

"You don't know me," he said quietly, amazed at her.

"Hmm." She sipped a mug with a knowing look on her face. "I also asked around about *you*." She pointed a finger into his bicep as she walked past, and he had to bite his lip at the touch.

She tidied up the counter where she'd made pancakes. "Georgia said you were, and I quote, 'a hunk of good-ass man.' Now, did she mean your ass is good? *Or* that you're a good person? Or both? We'll never know, because I definitely wasn't asking follow-up questions. Pop said you *egregiously* overtipped Margie, who waited tables at his diner—"

"—She was like, seventy! She should be relaxing, not hefting twenty pounds of plates every morning," he interrupted.

"—And I've known Nash Donnelly my entire life. If he trusts you with his precious BMWs, you obviously know your way around a car." He'd done some body work for Nash and now considered the guy a friend with how much he'd hooked him up with all of his rich buddies.

She turned around, looking pleased with herself. "Do whatever you must to Baby."

His lips twitched. It was pretty fucking cute she'd named her car.

AB ran into the room with her backpack, and he watched

Olivia manage the chaos of her like a champ. He gave AB a rib-crushing hug and kiss goodbye.

He saw them off as Olivia drove away in his car. Was he absolutely fucking nuts to trust his car and his daughter to a practical stranger?

Maybe I should get to know her.

What her hobbies are, why she dances, what she does to unwind.

Yeah, that's it, you idiot. Fall in love with her a little more.

He shook his head, knowing he needed to actually focus on work now. The faster he got all his business back on track, the faster he could take back control. He wouldn't have to depend on Olivia or anybody else to make his life run the way it needed to.

Thirty minutes later, he jogged to his truck for his first appointment. The shop was closed on Mondays, so he'd tour the rental options for his shop in Fairwick Falls he'd bookmarked last night.

He felt unusually light and relaxed, not having to deal with the chaos of drop-off.

As he hopped in his truck, texts pinged from Olivia. A selfie loaded of her and AB making silly faces inside his SUV before drop-off.

OLIVIA

We changed your radio presets to pop stations. Hope that's fine! 😄

The eagle has landed in first grade.

No drama to report. 🫡

His mouth quirked into a smile.

LUCA

Thx

OLIVIA

Sir, yes, sir.

His insides warmed. He shouldn't think about her calling him *sir*.

Luca spent the day in a fugue state, touring locations, squeezing in more work at his shop in Elliotsville. He'd worked straight through lunch and had lost track of time until three o'clock.

Texts popped up from Olivia using the special ringtone he'd given her. So he'd gone through the trouble of figuring out the perfect twinkle sound that reminded him of her laugh. *What of it?*

OLIVIA

We've decided that playgrounds are for babies, and we're going home to dance instead.

LUCA

K

OLIVIA

...Is that not okay?

He frowned at his phone, confused.

LUCA

I said K?

OLIVIA

That's what somebody says if they hate the other person.

Well that was news to him.

LUCA

What should I say instead?

A photo of AB making a goofy face from Olivia filled his screen.

OLIVIA

You know what? K is just fine.

As long as it means you don't hate me.

I could never hate you, he typed out, but then erased it.
Too real. Too much.
K is what he sent back instead.
Better to keep her at arm's length.
Don't let yourself fall even further.

THAT NIGHT, Luca finally got Annabelle to sleep after reading her ballerina bunnies book two times in a row.

He checked his phone as he closed her door.

OLIVIA

Hi there! There's a permission slip on the counter for you to sign for a Girl Scout lock-in.

Also, I will be over at 6:30 again tomorrow.

Was that okay?

Please let me know if it wasn't.

Luca lingered over every message, savoring it.

Here in his private space, just by himself, he let himself enjoy every bit of Olivia that he got.

She was thoughtful, remembered small details, and open and warm with him.

Some people were intimidated by his tattoos and his size. He sort of liked it that way. Made him feel like no one would fuck with him.

But she saw right past it to his heart, it felt like.

More texts came in like waves lapping at the shore. He savored each one.

OLIVIA

> I can let you know when I'm heading over or when I'm about to come in, if you prefer.

> Also, we'll do leftover pancakes tomorrow morning.

> And maybe some scrambled eggs.

> Hope you have a good night.

K, he typed.

Wait, don't be an asshole. She's being so nice, and I was kind of a jerk this morning.

At least texting allowed him to be more articulate and not revert to a caveman that wanted to stare at her perfectly sized tits or get lost in her dimples.

He thought for a second about how to respond.

She deserved to be treated with the most kindness in the world. The most consideration.

He drafted a message and read it three times to make sure he didn't misspell anything or sound stupid.

LUCA

> I'm sorry if I made you feel bad this morning. I apologize.

Still needs more, he thought, looking at the wall of texts she'd sent him. *Don't want her to think I hate her.*

You did a good job, he typed. Then rolled his eyes.

He deleted the draft, groaning. *You did a good job* was

what you told a ten-year-old after they mangled their first chore. Not the stunning woman you entrusted your child to, who had actually been far better than he'd thought to hope for.

He groaned as he walked downstairs. He needed a drink for this.

He eyed his phone on the counter while he poured a drink, trying to think of the right thing to say.

After a swig of whiskey, he just went for it.

LUCA

AB had a great day thanks to you.

So did I.

He sent it.

Wait, no. Fuck. Is that stupid? It's probably stupid.

He was probably bothering her. But also, she'd asked him a question he'd forgotten to answer like an idiot.

It's fine for you to come in any time tomorrow.
Have a good night.

He sent the message quickly, so he would stop bothering her. He could see her lights were on next door, but he didn't want to hound her after hours.

OLIVIA

Is it my birthday????

I'm getting more than one-letter responses.

He huffed out a laugh into his glass.

You had a good day?

Tell me more.

Luca stared at his phone, as if it was his enemy, and slowly sipped his whiskey as he looked at the message.

He leaned against the counter, weighing his options.

She's probably just being nice.

She seems like a person who would go out of her way to be nice.

But then...she asked for more?

Do I tell her that when I grabbed a cord from the SUV, my evening was better because the car smelled like her?

Or that AB couldn't stop talking about how much fun they'd had after school all through dinner?

And bath time.

And bedtime.

Olivia had shown AB videos of her ballet performances, and now AB was using words like fouetté and pirouette. Fucking adorable *and* educational.

No.

Maybe it's a bad idea to answer.

Gotta put some distance between her and me so my heart doesn't get smashed like it's caught in a hydraulic press.

OLIVIA

Orrrrr

You can just stare at my typing.

Leave me on read.

It's fineeee! My feelings aren't hurt.

I'll see you in the morning!

"Aaaagh." He scrambled for his phone, sloshing his whiskey over the screen in surprise.

He was being rude again.

Thoughts poured out of his fingers as fast as he could type them.

LUCA

Sorry, I was thinking. You made the day better by being you

I could actually focus on work and wasn't stressed about being late

Half the time, I'd forget my work or the lunch box or her backpack

Hell, one time I forgot my underwear and my balls hurt so bad by the end of the day

I felt like I could just do the things I needed to get done today

So, thank you

He watched her read all of his texts, her little status bubble plopping down through each message.

He watched his screen for five *full* minutes waiting for her response, but it was silent.

Goddamn it, I fucked something up. Biting his nail, he reread his messages. *Where did I go wrong?*

Ah, found it.

LUCA

Sorry for mentioning balls

He grimaced as he downed the rest of his whiskey.

OLIVIA

Hahahahahahaha

A laugh rumbled out of him as sunlight poured into his veins at having made her laugh.

Are you fucking with me?

Maaaaaybe.

I will see you in the morning.

Good night, Olivia.

Yes, you will!

Look to your left!

He looked out his kitchen window across from Georgia's dining room window. She waved, giving him a bright smile. She was stunning in her purple flannel pajama pants and a clinging V-neck, long-sleeve shirt. Her hair was over her shoulder in a thick, long braid.

Good night, Luca.

He waved back, trying to seem unattached and not completely lovesick over the mere sight of her.

A glimpse of what she was like when it was just her.

Stunning. Sexy. Adorable. Funny.

All those things, but definitely not mine.

She turned out her light and walked out of sight.

A sigh escaped him as he realized this was just the first day in a *long* string of days.

Can I take another three months of this torture?

Chapter Nine

OLIVIA

"So we have to pick fruit?" Annabelle asked, looking skeptical.

Olivia laughed as they walked through the straw-filled parking lot of Engelbert's Apple Orchard at the edge of Fairwick Falls.

"We only have to pick apples if you want to. I loved doing this when I was a kid. We would pick apples and take silly pictures. Then we would bring a jug of apple cider home, heat it up, and cozy up on the couch."

"Yeah, let's do that," AB said with an excited smile.

The sun was already golden in the afternoon as a few families walked into the pretty orchard. She squeezed AB's hand firmly, as AB had a tendency to run. It had been a solid week of nannying thus far, with cozy mornings full of pancakes and muffins and afternoons spent doing homework and making up silly games.

Annabelle needed to write about fall for her assignment (one whole sentence!), and Olivia had asked Luca if he was okay if they went to one of Olivia's favorite hometown spots.

Olivia paid the entrance fee and grabbed a small wicker basket.

"Catch me, 'Livia!" AB said.

"*Annabelle*," she said, running after her, though luckily she easily caught up with AB as they dissolved into laughter, chasing each other around the apple trees.

They walked through each row around the small orchard, picking only one apple from each tree. AB had been very concerned they'd make a tree sad if they left any of them out.

She liked her thinking, so they visited every tree so no one would get too lonely *or* too empty.

They paid for their basket of small apples and sat at a picnic table. Olivia got out a notebook. "Let's think about what you want to write," she said, handing AB a pencil.

The joy went out of AB's eyes. "The lines are too little," Annabelle whined. She grabbed the pencil with her whole fist, looking annoyed.

"Just do your best," Olivia said, crunching on a fresh-picked apple warm from the sun.

"I," AB said slowly, drawing a wobbly letter *i*. "Luv..."

"Love is spelled L-O-V-E."

AB sighed and erased it hard, so hard that the paper started to pull.

"V...E... How do you spell apples?" AB said with a quizzical look up at Olivia.

"How do you think?"

AB sighed in existential dread. "That's a really hard word, 'Livia," AB said, thunking her head down on the notebook.

Olivia swallowed a laugh. "You know what? It is. That's fair. How about this? *Ah.* What does that sound like?"

"A?"

"Great. And then a *p*. And a *p*."

Annabelle drew both *p*'s backwards, looking like *q*'s.

Olivia watched closely. "L-E-S. Good job, that's a great first draft."

"What's a draft?" Annabelle asked.

"Like when we practice in dance. We'll go home and you can write it on *your* piece of paper. We can work on it together."

Olivia's eyes caught on the backwards letters that looked so much like what she'd written on her own homework as a kid.

"Can you write your name?" Olivia asked, innocently enough.

Annabelle wrote out her full name, but her *b* was backwards. And her *e*'s were out of order in her name.

Olivia's intuition tingled.

She'd done the exact same thing as a kid. Gotten her letters too close together or mangled, usually backwards.

For some kids, it was just part of how they learned. For her, it had been ongoing. Unfortunately, the Fairwick Falls Elementary School hadn't had enough training, and no one had figured out until she was in high school that she was dyslexic.

She'd struggled over every assignment in school, getting Bs and Cs at best. Olivia had been the odd one out in her family. While her brother, mom, and dad all were incredibly book smart, she'd only excelled at dancing.

It was why it was so important that she actually be *good* at it.

It's the only thing I have going for me.

"Come on," she said with a resigned sigh, hoping she was wrong. "Let's get a quart of cider before we go."

"Daddy," AB yelled. Olivia turned to see Luca walking toward them.

Luca waved to Olivia as AB ran toward him through a small archway of apple trees bathed in golden light. The setting sun was hitting just right, casting an orange glow against their skin. He walked—no, *swaggered* in that lazy, sexy way of his. Each muscle moved within his long-sleeve shirt as he walked, and her eyes traced the movement hungrily

He caught Annabelle with a bright—*holy hell he was so handsome*—smile and tossed her into the air, making her laugh.

Olivia's heart wrenched at the sight of the pure love they had for one another. Luca was an amazing dad. He loved Annabelle with his whole heart, and it was obvious that everything he did, he did for her.

Emotion caught in her throat as she thought about the last time she'd talked to her dad. It was a short message on his birthday.

He'd been on a yacht somewhere and told her he'd call her back after speaking to a business partner. Which he'd never done.

She felt a guttural, primal pull toward the two of them as Luca walked with Annabelle upside down over his shoulder giggling, a bright smile on his face.

"Funny seeing you here," he said with a happy smile. It warmed her down to her toes, that rare moment of joy on his face.

"Come here for all your apple cider needs?" Olivia asked, grinning flirtatiously.

He slid AB from his shoulder and swung her down, a mess of giggles and swinging pigtails until she landed on her feet.

"I missed the apple picking?" Luca said with disappointment as he looked at the to-go basket Olivia had bought. His bottom lip pushed out just a little.

So. Fucking. Cute. And he doesn't even know it.

She wanted to toss the basket over her shoulder so they could do it all over again.

"I can let you guys do your thing if you want to go again together." Olivia started packing up her things into her purse.

"You're going to leave? We don't get cider?" AB said, looking hurt, as she leaned against Olivia's arm.

Olivia smiled as she picked a leaf out of AB's hair. "I don't want to interrupt your time with your dad."

Luca offered a hand to steady Olivia as she climbed out of the picnic table. Completely unnecessary, as she regularly spun on one toe, but she took it anyway.

"Come on, my treat," he said with a smile.

AB whooped and Olivia concentrated on the feeling of his hand against hers, lingering on it, and finally dropped it once she was standing.

"'Livia used to come here as a kid." AB said, swinging her dad's hand.

"Yeah?" he said, arching an eyebrow at Olivia.

They started walking to the cider stand as yellow leaves tumbled by. She nodded. "How about you?"

"Not a lot of apple picking in my childhood," he said with a quiet smile.

AB weaseled her way in between them to grab both of their hands.

Olivia swung her and AB's arms. "My favorite cider was technically from this place in Massachusetts. But a couple years ago, they got involved with a mafia smuggling ring, apparently?"

Luca laughed in surprise. "A *smuggling* ring for apple cider? That's nuts."

Olivia laughed with him. "Right? It was a *whole* thing with the FBI. It was wild. So now." She shrugged. "I just try to buy local."

They looked through the jugs of flavored apple cider. Luca picked one and looked at the back of it for the ingredients.

She didn't want him to think she wouldn't have checked. "They don't use any emulsifiers like wheat, but I would double-check, obviously, and send you the ingredients if we had bought anything. I know it's in the craziest things."

"I know," he said quietly, glancing at her as he finished reading the ingredients. His eyes held hers with a kindness and warmth that took her breath away. "I trust you."

She might as well have been a literal fucking peacock for how much she wanted to preen at that.

"I'm gonna go play," AB said as she ran to a small playground where the photo-op cutouts were.

"Stay where I can see you," Luca said, at the same time Olivia called, "Stay close."

"Sorry," Olivia said, closing her eyes and grimacing.

Don't step on the parent's toes, dummy. Number one rule of childcare.

"No, it's fine," Luca said, his tender stare warming every vein in her body.

His lips tended to twitch when he looked at her, as if he was fighting off a smile.

She *loved* it.

Luca's eyes followed AB like a hawk to the playground. "She probably needs to hear it twice. She's a little stubborn."

"*No*," Olivia said with sarcastic dismay.

He laughed and grabbed a second jug of the same original flavor. "She gets that from both her mom and me, I'm afraid."

"You don't talk about her a lot." Olivia didn't want to pry, but she was curious about the woman who created such a cool kid, and who Luca obviously had loved so much.

He shrugged. "It usually makes people feel uncomfortable." They watched as AB went down slides and climbed on the equipment.

"You can talk to me anytime you want," she said, with an encouraging smile. "Talking about my grandparents with my mom helped her a lot when they passed, I think."

Luca stared at AB and quickly nodded at Olivia. "Marcy was special. We were friends as kids in school. After high school, we sort of fell into dating. She was a tattoo artist," he said, holding up his arm. A small tattoo that said 'For Our Future' ran along the inside of his bicep.

Olivia nodded, understanding why he was probably covered in ink then. "I see you took advantage of the friends and family discount," she said with a smile.

He laughed. "Perks of being engaged to a great artist." They wandered over to the playground fence and leaned on it.

"You were never married?"

"When we got pregnant, I wanted to do the right thing. I loved her, and she loved me. It had been a slow slide from childhood. I wanted to start life off the right way with her. We were saving for a wedding and..." He shook his head, trailing off. "Then a drunk driver changed it all."

"That must have been hard."

He nodded. "She loved AB so much. Was so excited to do mom stuff. She loved Annabelle so completely *in* every moment. She was so present and she never missed a moment when she was alive. Unlike me."

Oliva shook her head with a frown. "Luca, you're doing amazing. *Anyone* can see you're a great dad. You've uprooted your whole life to make sure she gets what she needs."

Luca sighed, looking hopeful, like maybe she'd relieved some of the unnecessary pressure he put on himself. "That's why I have to get everything settled with the shop. In case something happens to me, I want to make sure AB is taken care of, and we get to have as many good memories as soon as possible. I want her to love her childhood, love school."

They watched as AB went down slides and climbed on the equipment.

I should tell him about the spelling thing.

But would that be overstepping?

But if she could save just one kid from her same fate in school...

"We were working on homework," Olivia said tentatively.

No, keep your mouth shut. You don't even know what you're talking about.

"Did she do okay?" Luca said, walking up to the register with the jugs of cider.

Olivia reached for her wallet. "Let me—"

He waved her away. "My treat. What about her homework?"

Olivia sighed. "AB wrote some letters backwards. *P*'s and *b*'s. She also mixed up the order of some letters."

"Isn't that normal for kids?" He shrugged, handing her the jug he'd bought her.

She smiled as she took the cool plastic and held it against her. "It can be. I'm not an expert or anything, but I, um... I did the same thing for a long time, and it was missed. I'm dyslexic. I hated reading and hated school. I didn't figure it out until it was too late."

His brows furrowed as he looked at AB on the playground. "AB might be dyslexic?"

"Maybe talk to her teacher. It may not hurt to keep an eye on it. "

"Was college better for you?" he said as they wandered to the fence on the playground.

There were piles of early leaves that had fallen, and Olivia enjoyed the crunch of a few as she walked through.

"No college." She shrugged. "School was so painful, I couldn't wait to not be in a classroom. I finished out high school and my apprenticeship in ballet school. Then, went straight to dancing professionally."

He nodded, looking impressed her. "At eighteen? Impressive."

Ah, there was that dopamine rush she craved.

"Seventeen, technically"—she shrugged and flipped her hair—"but who's counting?" She smiled at herself.

"Thanks," he said suddenly, stopping. "For this"—he gestured to the orchard surrounding them—"and for letting me know about the school thing."

"Just don't want her to have the experience I had, you know?" She shrugged. "She's too sweet of a kid."

He stared down at her with such warmth that goosebumps ran down her arms, like she'd been dipped in a hot bath. The cologne he wore drifted toward her on the breeze, and she forced herself to look him in the eye.

A heat grew there, and she was doing everything in her power not to stare at his lips.

AB ran to them, kicking up wood chips as she went.

"Are we gonna drink cider now?" She slammed into Olivia's legs, and Olivia wrapped an arm around her, hugging her.

She crouched to meet AB at eye level. "I can't, sweetie. I have to go back to work. I have a Zoom with a coach who gets to tell me *all* the ways I'm wrong in an hour."

"Sounds like fun?" Luca said, grimacing.

"It'll be good for me," Olivia said with a resigned sigh. She was eager to get better, but the process would be a little painful. "Hey, kiddo, I'll see you tomorrow morning, bright and early."

AB cheesed up at her with hope in her eyes. "Can I have four pigtails tomorrow?"

"Annabelle," Luca said with a sigh. "Olivia is not your personal hair stylist."

"How about," Olivia said, "if we both wear pigtails, then there will be four." She gave Annabelle a challenging look.

"Deal." AB nodded.

They high-fived, low-fived, and twirled like a ballerina for their signature handshake.

She looked up to catch Luca's eyes. He looked confused, gulped without saying anything, as if trying to figure something out.

Had she done something wrong?

He waved silently to her and she mirrored him.

Olivia walked to the car and was already missing them as she heard AB giggle with her dad.

She'd only seen them a little over a week. But she'd been feeling even more lonely than usual when she was alone these days.

She'd forgotten what it felt like to be surrounded by people who genuinely cared about you and who made you happy. She'd never really found a home in all the years she'd been away.

The afternoon sun turned into an evening orange, painting each leaf she walked through the apple orchard. She grazed a steady tree trunk with her hand, savoring the grounded feeling of being here..

If only I could find a home like my hometown.

Chapter Ten

LUCA

Luca fought with an unruly screw. "Why can't things just do what they're fucking supposed to do?" he muttered, growling at it. He was behind schedule at the shop and had barely even started the work of moving it to Fair-wick Falls.

He'd stayed up late last night to find more rental space options, and he'd come in early to finish this fucking Airstream for Pearl. The Airstream now had a roll-top window for orders, a warming station for her baked goods, a sink—everything that a mobile farmer's market stand could need.

"Knock, knock," a bright voice said.

"Hey," Luca called to Reed, who ambled through the doorway like he didn't have a care in the world.

"Brought some final touches." Reed held up a menu sign and a few other items to outfit the Airstream. "I can install the digital register thing today."

"Already done," Luca said, in too sharp a voice as he finally got the fucking screw in.

Luca moved on to put one more coat of polish on the wood countertop. It took fucking forever to set in, but it would have to be good enough for now. He searched the shop for the rags and bucket of water. The last thing he needed was for this place to go up in flames if the rags self-ignited from oxidation.

His best friend leaned through the customer window on his forearms, sporting a friendly smile that for some reason irritated the shit out of him right now. "It's been a minute since we've seen you. We miss you, Pearl and I."

"You saw me last week for dinner." Luca huffed. "I'm doing every fucking thing here, and I don't have extra time when I'm trying to keep five people employed."

Silence greeted him in response.

He was being an asshole. He knew this.

"I know *you* know you're being an asshole," Reed said, reading his mind.

"Yeah, so?" Luca said, wanting to enjoy his bad mood with somebody who would tolerate him.

Reed peered around the window inside the Airstream. "Maybe somebody else could do some of this work? Like me?"

"Don't touch that," Luca said as Reed picked up a rag and then dropped it.

"I know you have a lot of work to move all of this to Fairwick Falls. You have a team, right? Maybe you should...use them?"

Luca sighed, rubbing in an even layer of oil on the raw wood counter.

"Leaning on loved ones is what they're there for, Luca. You need to be able to rest sometimes, you know? You do a lot for everybody else."

Luca shook his head. "No, I don't. Not enough."

Pearl had dropped everything when he'd needed her. For fucking *years*. Reed had been his constant sounding board of support since he was twelve. His team had covered his ass when all hell broke loose over the summer when he wasn't here.

He was in everyone's debt, and he hated it.

Reed followed him, not letting him escape. "I'm going to remind you that you are in a formerly totaled Airstream that you remade into an on-the-go bakery for your sister, just because it would make her happy."

Luca swallowed a smile. "What did you need again?"

"Hey," Reed said calmly. "Can you take thirty seconds?"

Tension coiled up in Luca's shoulders. "Not really," he said, tossing the rag in the bucket of water.

"Listen, asshole," Reed said with a laugh. "I know you're bigger than me, but I can still fight."

That made Luca break into a laugh. "Yeah," he said, stepping out of the Airstream and stretching his back. "I remember. Still have that scar." Luca pointed to his eyebrow.

Luca had taught Reed how to fight so he didn't get his ass handed to him in high school, and Reed had clocked him when he wasn't expecting it.

"Alright, thirty seconds. Go," Luca said, gulping down a glass of water.

Reed stared at him. It was a long, serious look.

Oh, fuck. This is bad.

Have I done something? Missed something important?

Is Pearl okay?

Is Reed okay?

Who's dying?

Reed gulped and stood up straighter. There was a challenge and a tinge of fear in his eyes. "I'm going to marry Pearl."

Luca noticed it wasn't a question.

"No shit," Luca said, not believing it.

"Yes, shit," Reed said with a laugh.

"You, the sweetest man I know, are going to marry my black-cloud, death metal-flavored, acid-rain-upon-her-enemies sister," Luca said, saying it out loud one more time just so he could believe it. "For forever," he added.

Reed pressed at his chest with his knuckles, as if staving off a heart attack. "Going to attempt to, yes."

Pearl and Reed had started dating when Luca and AB were in Florida. No one had been more flabbergasted than he had been at seeing them tangled up on the couch when he'd gotten home early. He'd thought, honestly, that he'd been hallucinating from the fifteen-hour drive back from Florida.

A bright spark of warmth slapped Luca across the face. "Come here." He pulled Reed in for a hug, lifting him off the ground with a groan, making him laugh.

Reed adjusted his glasses when Luca set him down. "So you're okay? I mean, she'd be really pissed if I did the whole asking-for-your-blessing thing."

"Oh, she'd murder you." Luca laughed. "Both of us."

"But you're okay with this?"

"Man." He grabbed Reed by the shoulders. "Best news I've heard all week."

"You're gonna make me cry." Reed slapped Luca's face playfully, and Luca pushed him away with a laugh.

They'd been friends since sixth grade when they were both giant nerds and Reed had moved to the nice house down the block with an extensive comic book collection that Luca had coveted. Luca had always been tall and chubby for his age, and being the poor kid in class meant he'd been as much of a bully target as the new tiny nerd.

They'd formed an alliance. Luca would protect him on the playground, and Reed would give him free rein of all the comic books in his treehouse next door and the snacks in his mom's kitchen.

He'd never have guessed letting Pearl up into their treehouse club would have such lifelong consequences.

"I'm very happy, for the record," Luca said, picking up a wrench because he needed to do something with all these feelings.

I'm aching for something like that myself.

"I should go. I just wanted to make sure we were good," Reed said. "But um, keep this quiet. I need to figure out how to make all of her little black-hearted dreams come true."

Luca nodded, a lump in his throat at the happiness of it all. Pearl, his spikey sister with a soft, squishy heart—who fiercely protected every underdog she'd ever met—deserved every happiness in this lifetime.

Reed started out the door but Luca turned suddenly and pulled him into another squeezing, hard hug.

"Can't propose...if you liquify...my *spleen*," Reed muttered through a strangled breath with a laugh.

Luca finally released him and pushed him out the door with a smile, hiding his face so Reed wouldn't see the emotion there.

The door clicked closed.

It was hard for him to process emotions and thoughts when other people were around. Too much to manage.

Too much for somebody to see him deal with his own feelings. Even the guy who was his best friend in the whole world.

He gulped down the complicated feelings of sadness and joy in the weird confetti cannon that thumped through his chest.

It was fast, he realized. Pearl and Reed. They'd only been together a couple months.

But... He thought back to the pretty neighbor next door. *Sometimes when you know, you just fucking know.*

Even if it's doomed from the start.

Happy tears pooled in his eyes, and he brushed them away with the back of his wrist.

He rolled Reed's words around in his head. *Leaning on others?*

He snorted at the idea.

He carried a heavy load: boss, dad, employer.

Who could possibly be strong enough for me to lean on?

***

OLIVIA

"AND LEFT STEP. No—Harper, your other left—and step, and hop, and step. Front. Turn. Side. Step, step."

The girls held hands as they wobbled their torsos, like falling leaves.

"And now—spin!"

The girls were *supposed* to grab hands and form a circle, but instead, two had started to skip in a circle already. Annabelle grabbed two little girls' hands and pulled them along flailing behind her, dragging them on the ground. They started crying.

"Okay. Okay." Olivia paused the music. "Let's—" she ran her hand up and tightened her ponytail. "Let's take five."

Olivia had drafted the most basic choreography she could think of for their Fall Festival number, but it was still a disaster.

Olivia crouched down to a little girl who'd toppled over. "You okay, Sophie?" Sophie nodded, looking used to getting dragged around. "Annabelle, can you be more gentle next time?"

AB looked exasperated. "I was taking them in the circle! Sorry, Sophie," AB said, pulling her friend up. And just like that, the girls were back to giggling and laughing. A familiar laugh floated into the room, and Olivia glanced up to see a godsend.

"Ms. Georgia!" three little girls screamed as they ran over. Georgia had been their teacher last year.

Thank god. She ignored the confused, concerned looks from

the parents, and she pulled Georgia away from the girls into a separate corner.

"This is not going well," Olivia said, turning her back so the parents couldn't watch her face. "It's a trainwreck. What's your secret to getting them to learn the choreo?"

"Sweetie." Georgia set down the large box she'd been holding, her metal bangles clanking as if she'd set a ball and chain down. She tossed her giant scarf over her shoulder and gently held Olivia's hands. "The secret is: it's not that serious," she whispered through a laugh. She squeezed Olivia's hands. "This is supposed to be *fun* for them, dear. And for you."

Olivia gasped. This was *ballet* they were talking about. "Georgia!" she whispered back, at her wits' end. "Of course it's serious. Their parents paid for ballet lessons. They expect them to do, ya know, *ballet* by the end of it."

"It's *not that serious*," Georgia said slowly with a knowing smile. "Just have fun. This *whole* thing is supposed to be *fun*. See?" She pointed over to the girls.

AB was being a goofball in the mirror to make the other girls laugh.

"Honey, you are one of my only students in forty years that danced beyond middle school. None of these girls will dance past that point, and you know what? It doesn't matter." She squeezed Olivia's shoulder as they watched the girls be silly. "Parents want them to move their body, make friends, and get confident. You are building life skills with every class. And," she said, pointing a red manicured finger in Olivia's face, "*that* is more important than any recital. Remember: it's the journey that needs to make you happy, dear. Not the performance."

Georgia picked up the box. "Plus, they'll look so adorable in whatever costumes you design, no one will notice it's a disaster." She handed the box to Olivia with a smile. "Here are a few leftovers from last year in case it's helpful. The committee insists that it matches whatever the theme is."

"Theme?" It had been decades since she'd been to the fall festival. "Isn't the theme...fall? Every year?"

But Georgia had already left the room and was chatting with the man that had starred in Olivia's sexy dreams the last six nights. *And five vibrator sessions.*

Luca's shy smile and wave were interrupted by Georgia pinching his cheeks.

It made her more nervous, for some reason, that he was here.

She didn't have a lot going for her. No fancy career, no pile of money, no real skills.

She was good at *one* thing, and she really, really wanted to be good at it in front of Luca.

"Okay." She clapped her hands. "I need your help. Come here," she said, squatting down, and the girls came running. "Who can tell me what a fall leaf looks like?"

They all raised their hands, excited to help. "Yes, Sophie?"

"It looks like our hands!" Sophie said, raising her hand high with fingers spread.

AB yelled out, "And it's crunchy sometimes."

Harper was so excited she stood up to answer. "Leaves at my house fall in our yard! Like, a whole bunch at a time."

Olivia liked seeing the light in all of their eyes again.

"Okay, let's pretend to be leaves. We're going to free dance, and you do whatever a leaf does."

Olivia started the first Autumn movement of Vivaldi's *The Four Seasons* concerto.

The girls instantly started skipping around the room to bouncy, cheerful violins. Sophie ran like a plane around the room.

"What kind of leaf are you being?" Olivia asked.

"I'm the winds," Sophie yelled between her "*neeerooom*" airplane sounds.

AB walked like Godzilla, slowly slamming each foot down hard. "I'm crunching! I'm crunching the leaves!"

Olivia belly-laughed at all the interpretations, even star-jumping with the girls like leaves falling. She caught the eye of Luca in the mirror who tipped his head as if to say, *Nicely done.*

Olivia mentally grabbed a move from each girl's interpretation to put in the choreography. The girls were so excited to have helped, and the spark was back in their eyes.

She hadn't realized how much originality had been beaten out of her by ballet instructors. She'd spent her middle and high school years at ballet-focused intensive training. Technical proficiency had been the most important part of her education rather than enjoying it.

As class wrapped, she gave each of the girls a high five as they walked out of the studio. AB, per usual, was last and hung onto Olivia's hand. "Can I have pigtails tomorrow?"

"Sure can," Olivia said, smiling as she smoothed hair from AB's forehead.

AB jumped up and down as Luca ambled over. "Dad, did you see?"

"I saw. You spun like a perfect leaf." He slid her tiny unicorn backpack onto his shoulder. "I think you both worked very hard and deserve some ice cream."

"Yes!" AB pumped her fist up and down.

"Think they'd add a shot of bourbon?" Olivia laughed, tugging on her ponytail that had bounced loose during star/leaf jumps.

"Oh, I want one of those," AB said, tugging on her dad's hand.

"No bourbon for either of you, I'm afraid. Just milkshakes at the diner. Hey, goob, why don't you go toss on your jeans over your tights? It's getting cold out there." AB ran over to the bench and dug out her pants to toss over her tights.

Olivia needed to record a new session for her coach and work on her form and work out.

I can't dance after dairy for two hours or I'll be sick.

"I missed you this morning. I mean"—she squeezed her eyes shut—"not that *I* missed you, but you weren't..." She gulped. "I mean, I've barely seen you the last few days."

"Right," he said. "I, um, was busy dealing with a client call and... couldn't step away. I, um." He stopped himself. "Yeah." He shrugged awkwardly.

They both stopped, waiting for the other to speak.

"I—" they both started, and burst out laughing.

A snort ripped through Olivia's laugh. *Crap.* Her hog laugh, her worst ex-boyfriend had called it.

Though Luca had said it was cute. She blushed remembering the life altering moment when he'd mentioned it and she'd blushed like a tomato.

She grimaced. "Oh, god, I'm so awkward. Just go enjoy your ice cream." She waved him away.

"You're not coming?" AB's face fell into a sad pout. "You don't want bourbon with us?" Luca reminded her that Olivia had work to do.

Georgia's words rang through her head though.

This is supposed to be fun. This whole thing *is supposed to be* fun.

She bit her lip, weighing her choices.

I could work out this evening and come in early for practice tomorrow instead.

Luca and AB started toward the door. She'd been responsible and austere for most of her life, eating only exactly what she should, working out almost every day, putting discipline above all else to be a dancer.

And it had gotten her nowhere.

Plus, how often did a hot guy in your hometown ask to buy you ice cream at your favorite diner?

Fuck it. She tossed off her ballet slippers and tugged on street shoes.

"Wait up!" she called as she pushed open the door.

Luca spun around with a blinding smile. It hit her in the stomach like that first time she'd seen him.

"Only an idiot would say no to Pop's with her two favorite neighbors," Olivia said as AB grabbed her hand, and they walked down the street through the falling maple leaves as the sun set behind them.

* * *

LUCA

How did your practice go?

OLIVIA

I am curled in a ball, now melded with my couch, courtesy of that milkshake.

LUCA

I thought it was just me.

I tried to convince AB that she was full because I knew she wouldn't feel good afterwards.

OLIVIA

I'm SO CLOSE to telling my 83-year-old stepfather to go back into business just so I can have a decent milkshake and erase all memories of this one

LUCA

Sorry for ruining your evening plans.

OLIVIA

I promise you I had 4000% more fun with you guys eating disgusting milkshakes than I did torturing myself in the studio.

Is AB okay?

LUCA

Meh. We both had some Pepto-Bismol and things seemed to be a little bit better after that.

I can get AB to school if you need to work in the studio to make up for lost time.

OLIVIA

No, that's very sweet of you. But I'll figure something out.

LUCA

Just let me know if we are in your way.

I don't want to take up too much of your time.

OLIVIA

I like it when you take up my time. 😊

LUCA

AB likes it when you're around, too.

OLIVIA

Only AB?

LUCA

I'd obviously have you anytime.

Have you here I mean.

At the house.

I didn't mean anything…weird.

OLIVIA

No, no! I get it

LUCA

Sorry, I'm sort of new at this friends-but-work thing.

OLIVIA

But you seem so natural at it? 

LUCA

Oh, god, wait, no, that was inappropriate, too.

Oh, god, I'm so sorry.

Fuck.

OLIVIA

Gasp. I am scandalized!!

Hahahahaha

LUCA

Sorry, maybe we should just keep things professional. Need-to-know only.

Sorry for bothering you.

OLIVIA

Noooo

I was teasing. You're never a bother.

Text any time.

Good night.

I will see you in the morning.

…If I'm not dead from milkshake poisoning. 

LUCA

Good night, Olivia.

OLIVIA

"No, *lift*," a French voice called from Olivia's phone, cradled on a tripod in The Barre dance studio.

A video screen of her ballet coach, Natalia, filled her phone screen.

The woman pulled her head as if it was on a puppet string. "Do you see how your head is *ah*? It needs to be like this: Ah." The dance teacher angled her head, as if listening for a call from far away.

Her coach used the universal dance language of grunts and guttural sounds to indicate fine movements that no one had a name for. "Again."

Olivia wiped the sweat from her brow and took 10 steps back, her toe shoes clopping on the hardwood. *Should have broken these in more.*

"And five, six…"

Olivia tightened her core, prepping for the run into her grand jeté.

Natalia coached along with Olivia's movements.

Four steps to leap into a grand jeté, land. Pull up into an arabesque. Find my spot, spin hard for two, three, four times.

"And up!" her coach called.

Olivia stopped on a dime from her pirouettes, pressed her chest forward, with her head angled, like Natalia had coached.

Two more quick pirouettes, and curve the thighs in, land in second position.

Olivia stayed still for the end of the combo, controlling her breath, knitting her abs around her rib cage to stay still.

"Eh, a little better."

At least her disappointment sounds nice in the French accent.

Olivia broke her pose and nodded, catching her breath. Their session was almost over.

Natalia's severe face nearly smiled at her. "Record the entire thing, send to me, and I will send you more thorough notes. It will be less terrible soon, I promise."

To say the ballet world was not warm and fuzzy was an understatement.

Olivia nodded her head and smiled at the video. *Be easy to work with, be grateful, don't be a bother.* "Thank you so much. I appreciate all the feedback."

Olivia said her goodbyes and curled into a ball on the tumbling mats, catching her breath.

Stepping into the ballet world from Fairwick Falls felt like plunging into ice water from a hot tub.

The harshest words in Fairwick Falls were head pats compared to the daily constructive criticism she'd endured for fifteen years. She'd been compared to everything from a grace-less cow to a dog shitting itself while trying to dance.

Olivia rolled her forehead on her knees. *But with no other life skills, what else would I do?*

She stood up and put her hands on her back, stretching, all the while her inner critique pecked at her like a deranged woodpecker.

"*And you can try all of that, and it still won't matter,*" Inner

Critique said, her voice sounding like Olivia's but dripping with disdain. "*You still may not make it. Because let's be honest, no one wants you. They never wanted you. It was probably a mistake that you lasted this long.*"

She inhaled a breath, scraping from the bottom of her toes to find some energy and inspiration to record the next full take.

It's okay, she told herself with hope. *Just push through. Do a couple more takes of the audition routine across the floor.*

The highly technical Gregorovich variation of the Sugar Plum Fairy solo was sewed into her bones and muscles. She'd understudied it for eight years but had never *once* performed it.

She ignored the laughing, contemptuous huff of Inner Critique. "*Not like this time will be any better than the last thousand times you practiced it,*" she hissed.

She'd always been praised for her technical execution in dancing, but all her notes highlighted her lack of musicality. That mysterious "other" quality that made dancers stand out.

Swiping through her music to cue it up, "Under the Sea" caught her eye.

What if I did it like the kids, just this one time. For...fun?

She made herself laugh at the idea of channeling that chaos-fueled energy into the hyper technical Sugar Plum solo.

"Fuck it. Let's just try it," she said with a smile, cuing up a famous Nutcracker song and letting herself have fun with it.

Just this one time.

~

LUCA

Luca gulped, trying to focus on the fourth potential shop space in Fairwick Falls. The woman in front of him looked like a wolf hunting its first meal in two weeks.

He sidestepped her and took a few more photos of the empty garage space. This had been a mechanic shop before the owner retired. Now a large real estate firm owned and leased it.

"So, like..." The building agent—Audry? Amber?—twirled her keys loudly. "You lift heavy things a lot? Your arms are, like, so big." She laughed as if he'd said something funny.

"Uh." He scratched the back of his head, uncomfortable. "Yeah. Comes from dealing with cars, I guess. You said we could move in any time?"

"Yeah, I don't really know." She laughed. "But I know they want to get somebody in the space. I could get you a really good deal."

"Yeah?" he said with a smile over his shoulder. He loved a deal. It had been years since he'd bought anything full price—other than when AB wanted something special.

This was the biggest spot he'd looked at, only one big enough to house all the work he'd need to do. It had a lot out back and would be easy for customers to find. He could already see it: where the first bay would go, what he'd have to change, how the workflow would move from intake to finish. He'd need a place for the air compressors and the paints.

Best of all, it was a three-minute drive to Fairwick Falls Elementary and a blessed seven minutes from his house.

"You could take me out as a thank-you," Audry/Amber said.

"Uh..." He gulped. "I'm flattered, but I don't date."

She winked. "You have my number if that changes. Want me to put you down for a twelve-month lease?"

"Yeah," he said, a small weight lifting from his chest. He'd move the shop here and finally have more peace in his life.

In a stroke of luck, his sister walked out of the credit union next door, so Luca said goodbye to the agent a little too fast.

Pearl stood outside the Fairwick Falls Credit Union talking with Nash.

"A *baby goat*-shaped cake? For Lily's birthday?" Pearl scratched her head in confusion.

"Wearing a Hawaiian shirt, if possible," Nash said, looking determined.

Nash chuckled and waved a hand at Luca. "I know my wife, trust me on that Pearl."

Pearl hit Luca's arm, smirking, as he met them between the buildings. "Look at us! Titans of fucking industry."

"Hey, man." Luca shook Nash's hand.

Luca had busted his ass to make the best farmer's market van for Nash's wife Lily and her flower shop, and that investment of time had yielded endless luxury cars in need of ding and scratch repair.

Luca jerked his head to the building next door. "Think I found a space for our shop next door," he said with pride.

"Hey, man, that's amazing." Nash patted Luca's back.

"Thanks again for all the referrals. It's been a big help as we save up to move the shop here."

"My pleasure. My branch manager in Cooperstown said you fixed his teenager's fender bender nearly instantly."

He respected the hell out of Nash. From everything he'd heard, people loved working for him, and he'd built a credit union practically overnight so the town could avoid predatory fees from the only bank in town. They'd opened two more locations in the last year.

"How do you do it all?" Luca said, amazed. "I have one place I'm trying to move and I'm about to lose my fuckin' mind."

Nash shrugged, shoving his hand with the expensive watch into his equally expensive khakis. "I have a great team. Can you imagine me trying to do all this by myself?" He laughed as if it would be ridiculous.

Luca gulped and tried to match his laugh. Pearl cocked an

eyebrow at him that he ignored. *So I have trouble delegating. Sue me.*

Nash continued. "I took all the people I trusted most—people who'd been with me for a long time—and let them do their thing. When I find people I can trust, I get out of their way." His phone dinged. "Speaking of which, I'm late for a meeting."

"Wait, I need to give you a quote for your cake," Pearl said, typing on her phone.

"Just text me. See you at family game night?" Nash said, walking backwards as he talked to Pearl.

"No snacks this time! Reed can't stand the sound of people eating pretzels," Pearl called.

"Cocktails and milkshakes only, got it!" Nash said, jogging to his BMW.

With a thundering realization, Luca realized that Pearl and Nash would be in-laws when Reed popped the question.

Reed and Nash's wife Lily were half-siblings, and he couldn't imagine two people more unalike than Pearl Bishop and fancy-pants Nash Donnelly.

"Word to the wise," Luca said, his stomach turning. "Skip the diner and make the milkshakes at home."

Pearl snorted. "Don't have to tell me. My BLT last week was missing the B and the T, and the L tasted like A-S-S."

Luca's phone dinged.

OLIVIA

AB insisted we stab some pumpkins.

Her words, not mine.

Is that okay? I wasn't sure where you stood on Halloween.

A photo of AB clutching a pumpkin nearly the size of her filled his screen.

Luca gave the message a thumbs-up.

Gonna need a liiiiiittle more context, buddy.

LUCA

Halloween: thumbs up.

Stabbing: thumbs down

Oh, god, I would never give her anything sharp.

She's making the design. I will do the stabbing.

Another selfie of them holding paper drawings of jack-o'-lantern faces over their faces popped into her phone.

"Oh my *god*," Pearl said in horror. "Your face is a disgusting puddle of lovesick right now."

"Shut up," he said without any heat, elbowing her.

She looked at his phone as if it was radioactive waste.

"Aw—wait," she whined, now missing out on the fun. "You guys are doing pumpkins without me?" Pearl said with a pout that looked exactly like AB's. "You *know* I love stabbing things."

"We can stab pumpkins anytime you want."

"AB looks really happy," Pearl said quietly. "And, um"—she hip-bumped him—"so do you."

"I don't know what you're talking about," he said, trying to make his face stop smiling.

"You know *exactly* what I'm talking about. Your face. Look at it." She pointed to the credit union's glass door.

A dopey-ass grin was indeed on his face.

He shoved his phone into his pocket. "She's my nanny. Shut up."

Pearl tried to contain a burst of laughter. "I don't know..."

she teased. "I know from personal experience that banging the boss is pretty *hoooot.*"

"*Bleurgh.*" He grimaced, knowing she was talking about Reed, who she'd worked for over the summer in the bookstore.

He shook his head. "I don't date. You know that."

"Luca, it's been years."

"You know the rules—"

"That you made up!" Pearl pushed his shoulder.

"For a good reason. I don't want you to step in again if shit goes sideways."

She'd let him mourn Marcy's unexpected passing for weeks, taking on every single thing in his life. She'd kept a toddler AB alive and happy while he alternated between despair and sleep. He'd stopped eating, smiling. Even looking at AB had been painful because she'd looked so much like Marcy.

In the fourth week, Pearl had tossed a literal bucket of ice water onto his face as he slept on the floor and told him to get his shit together.

She poked him with each word. "That's what we do. You and me against the world, right?" Her smile broke his heart because it reminded him of exactly what she'd looked like when she was AB's age.

Pearl was younger than him by a year and a half, and they'd been thick as thieves growing up.

He'd always been the protector.

And he'd had to protect her a lot, unfortunately.

His phone buzzed again. He hoped it was another update from Olivia.

UNKNOWN

ned 2 talk 2 u. need help this month

"Fuck," he muttered.

He knew exactly who that unknown number was.

"Everything okay?" Pearl asked, trying to look at his phone.

He hid it from her and stuck his phone back in his pocket. "Just a work thing."

Pearl would lose her absolute shit if she knew he still talked to their mom. She'd gone no-contact as soon as she'd hit eighteen.

Luca couldn't abandon his mom. Like she'd told him a million times growing up, she didn't have anyone else. She had to depend on *him*.

She'd depended on him when he was eight, watching Pearl so she could go out drinking. She'd depended on him to take care of the house at around the same age. He'd even learned how to call the light and water companies when he was in high school so they wouldn't get their stuff turned off.

For some reason, he felt a responsibility to make sure that his mom was okay, even though she'd never returned the favor.

"Look, I gotta go."

"Ooo, was it a dirty text?" Pearl teased, trying to get a rise out of him.

"Go away," he said, walking away from her with a laugh.

"I'm happy to babysit anytime so you and your nanny can get freaky."

"Pearl!" he yelled.

She burst out cackling as she walked to Bookish.

He let out a long, heavy sigh as he sat in his truck. He checked that Pearl was walking around the corner before he responded.

LUCA

How much?

He didn't even bother to ask who it was.

UNKNOWN
this is mom BTW

2k

He sighed.

I can do 1k.

i'll ask Pearlie for the other then

Fuck. He slammed his hand against the steering wheel. She always did this.

But the thought of his mother homeless—or worse—was unbearable. It wasn't like her childhood had been great either. She'd had it worse than him.

There had been a handful of bright spots in his childhood, he remembered. When she was between boyfriends, sometimes they'd even almost had fun. In the end, though, she always chose the boyfriends over them.

He'd made the mistake of getting attached once—a nice guy who'd stuck around for a year. Luca had fooled himself into thinking they could be like those other families. The ones who went to the zoo and the park and had birthday parties.

Spoiler: that never happened, and they always ended up in yelling fights at the trailer. He'd console his sobbing mom as she asked him never to leave her.

He sighed, hating himself.

LUCA

I'll send it.

UNKNOWN
you're the best son

how's ur kiddo?

That was always how it was with her: she'd ask for what she needed first, and then she'd pretend to be interested for a little while.

He wouldn't fall for it this time.

He tossed his phone to the other side of the cab, just so he wasn't tempted to answer. He wouldn't pretend that she gave a shit about him or AB.

Annabelle hadn't seen her since she was a baby, and that was by design.

He'd leave the stench of that smoke-stained, boozy trailer behind so that Annabelle would never know what kind of life he'd come from.

Chapter Twelve

LUCA

Grimacing at the clock on his dash—shit, he was *so* late—Luca hurriedly parked on the dark street in front of his house.

The Bishop Body Shop team had spent all evening packing up important and expensive chemicals to start the transfer of his shop to Fairwick Falls. It was almost 10:00 PM. Olivia had been fine staying late with AB, but he didn't like making a habit of it.

He jogged up the front walk.

Warm, yellow lights glowed from his living room. The curtains were open, giving him a picture-perfect view of Olivia curled up on the couch.

She looked like a timeless marble sculpture, and the beauty of it made him stop in his tracks in the dark.

Her long hair framed her face like rivers of sunset rays. The elegance of her legs tucked under her and her arm posed on his couch in thought looked like an old painting you'd see in a museum.

This is probably creepy.

But he wanted a moment to just really look at her. He normally had to do everything he could to avoid staring at her.

She wore his flannel shirt that he kept in the kitchen. It was oversized on her, and something primal in him thrummed at the sight.

New fantasy unlocked.

He slowly walked closer to the front porch, savoring the last bits of the view. To his horror, he realized she was sobbing. Her hand was over her mouth muffling her cries as she curled into a ball. The cascade of her hair curtained around her knees.

An initial jolt of panic made him think about AB. *No, she would have called if there was a problem.*

He recognized this kind of crying—the overwhelmed weight of the world on your shoulders, the nothing's-gone-right, hopeless feeling.

She wiped at her eyes with the flannel sleeve.

My god.

She was beautiful, even when she cried, her bottom lip pushed out, tracks of tears running down her cheeks. He wanted to pull her in and hold her forever as he took the steps two at a time.

He tried the front door handle and was pleased to see it was locked.

Good. He wanted both of them safe.

He unlocked the front door, his eyes immediately went to the couch but not finding her there.

Rattling coming from the kitchen told him that she'd moved there.

"Hi," she called with a forced, cheerful voice. Tears echoed in it.

"Hey," he said quietly, knowing AB would be asleep, and toed off his work shoes. He quietly joined her in the kitchen.

"AB did great for bedtime. Especially brushing her teeth, we went the full two minutes." She stuffed her things in her bag, not looking at him.

"Hey, you okay?" His body ached to be near her. *Just a little closer. Just to make sure she's okay.*

"Oh." She laughed as if he was being silly. "Yeah, just, um. Just read a sad book," she said quickly.

She's lying and she doesn't trust me enough to talk about it.

He could feel his heart breaking at being boxed out. He wanted to fix it. That was how he showed people he cared.

"If this is too much, if something happened with AB, we can talk about it. We can pull your hours back."

He didn't want to lose her.

Couldn't lose her. In any sense of the word.

"No, the hours are fine. It's just been a lot, you know?" Her voice cracked on the last word. "Oh, I should get my bands." She walked into the living room, looking embarrassed.

Shit. Shit fucking shit. It *was* too much.

"We can adjust your hours. I'm sorry for staying too late."

"No, no. I meant my life," she said, her voice breaking again. "This"—she gestured around her at the living room—"is the best part of it. Everything else is fucked."

He bent down to catch her eye, feeling a bit of relief that he wasn't the problem.

Still want to fix it, though. "Hey."

She stopped in front of him as she wiped away a tear, looking everywhere but at him.

"Anything I can do?" His heart was in his throat, feeling the pain she felt.

Her lip wobbled as a tear spilled down her cheek. "No." Her voice was a pained whisper through the tears.

He *needed* to make her feel better on a cellular level.

He hated the idea of her crying alone in her house next door.

If she was going to be miserable, he wanted her here, where he could take care of her and maybe make it all better. "Want to talk about it?"

"I just, it's all worthless, you know?" She sniffled as she wrung her stretching bands in her hands. "I got notes back from my coach again today. For my auditions." She shoved her long hair behind her ears. "And, I didn't do *anything* right. It was worse than my last critique tape. I was trying to have joy in dancing, like the kids have. You should see, they have so much more fun than I've ever had." She wiped her eyes.

He was literally fighting not to wipe the tears away himself.

Her voice came out a strangled whisper against the tears. "I can't take any more rejection. It's just so embarrassing." A loud, deep sob escaped her mouth.

Fuck it.

He couldn't take it anymore. He pulled her against his chest, wrapping his arms tight around her, and she melted into him.

It felt like liberation, her leaning against his chest.

A stroke of luck.

The warmth of the sun against his face.

All the good things in his life wrapped into one, to finally have her safe in his arms.

As he held her tight, she sobbed hard against him. Sobs that sounded like the full weight of someone's life.

"I'm sorry." She hiccuped into his chest but didn't make any move to leave.

He hugged her tighter. That cinnamon scent engulfed him, and he let himself dissolve and simmer into it. He nuzzled his chin against her head, tucking her in closer, wanting to protect her from whatever demons roared in her brain.

He let her cry, stroking her hair. The silky strands of it felt like poured sunlight. He lost count of the minutes she stood there crying, tucked into his chest.

Suddenly, her arms wrapped around his waist, and he knew —this was it.

This felt too fucking right. That stupid thought he'd had weeks ago in the bookstore?

He'd been right.

And it was breaking his heart that he'd have to let her go.

Even as he was trying to memorize every strand on her head, the feel of her hair against his cheek, how perfectly she fit into his chest, pieces of his heart were hitting concrete and shattering.

"I don't even know if I like dancing anymore. I only have a few years left in my career." She sobbed against him. "But I can't *do* anything else. Not full-time, not as something that'll support me until I'm seventy, surrounded by my grandkids. Fifteen years of professional pirouettes isn't a transferable skill." She hiccuped.

Stay with me, he thought. *Forever. I'll work every hour of every day. If you just stay with me.*

"I'll—" He stopped himself. "*Take care of you*" was the rest of that sentence, but that was fucking ridiculous to say out loud to his nanny. "Anybody would be lucky to have you," he said quietly, moving a hand down her back.

Her cries quieted, and her arms dropped after a small squeeze around his waist. That was his cue, and he made himself pull away from her but didn't step back.

She wiped at her eyes and nose with a self-conscious laugh. "This is so embarrassing."

"Hey." He pulled out a handkerchief from his back pocket and tilted her chin up to him. "Don't be embarrassed. I like..."— *taking care of you*—"being here,"

Her sparkling eyes had twin looks of surprise and then amusement, as he wiped mascara from underneath her eyes.

"Is that"—she hiccuped—"a hanky?"

He just smiled in response and gently dabbed underneath her eyes, trying to get most of it.

"Good thing you wear black shirts, I guess," she said with a watery laugh as she held her face up to him.

"It's my mascara absorption machine," he said quietly. A bright burst of her unexpected laughter made him float from joy.

This woman. Pure light that warms me through.

Mascara now off, he stopped wiping. His thumb lingered, tracing the curve of her cheek.

No one would ever believe that this curve made him realize she was his. He'd only had to look at her profile in that bookstore to realize that she was it.

She was the one.

Her breath caught as his fingers stilled on her cheek, lips parting.

Every instinct urged him to kiss those parted lips. Soothe away her worries with his tongue against hers. *Against any part of her, really.* He'd come into his hand more times than he wanted to count in the last two weeks, picturing only her.

He got a handle on the beast inside of him. He'd never cross that line. She was an employee for god's sake.

Don't go, not yet.

"I think this calls for a drink," he offered, stepping back.

"Better make mine tea," she said. He handed her the handkerchief, and she wiped her eyes and nose. "I have an early day tomorrow and alcohol makes my joints achy."

He pulled out two decaf ginger tea bags and two mugs.

"So?" She took a long, shuddering breath. "How was *your* day?"

"Meh." He made a dismissive sound as he ran hot water from their water dispenser in the corner.

She stretched, bending over the kitchen island. A vision of

exactly what he wanted to do to her in that position clutched his cock.

Fucking focus.

"Oh, come on," she egged him on, now more cheerful. "You have to tell me. I cried in front of you."

"Need leverage?" he said over his shoulder with a smile.

"Exactly!" Her smile was impish as she took the mug of ginger tea from him.

They walked back to the living room couch and sat side by side.

"Well, one guy came in hungover. One guy came in late. I'm behind on everything, and I've barely even started the work of moving the office to Fairwick Falls, which was what I was supposed to do now that you're here."

"So you had a great day, just like mine?"

He chuckled into the ginger tea that his sister had gotten him hooked on.

She rubbed at her calf as she talked. "Can't you, like, reprimand them? Because you're their boss? One late day and you'd be fired at my old job."

"You hurt yourself?" He pointed to her calf.

"Just an old injury. I pull it sometimes when I overwork muscles."

She needed to be in top physical condition. He knew that. *She's a fucking ballerina for chrissakes.* Even he knew she was essentially an athlete.

"Here." He set his mug to the side and offered out his hands. She had on long bright yoga pants and fuzzy socks.

"You don't have to." She looked embarrassed.

"Marcy had something similar, but it was worse when she was pregnant with Annabelle. Please?" he asked, feeling like an absolute fucking fool for begging his nanny to let him massage her calves.

"You know what? Normally, I would say no, but it hurts like a motherfucker. So, do your worst." She placed her legs in his lap as she twisted around, curling up against the couch with his mug in her hands.

She looked like she belonged there, cuddled into the old flannel couch, wearing his shirt and drinking from his favorite mugs.

His hands traced her shapely calves. *This is a bad idea, but I'm gonna do it anyway.* "Right here?" he said, feeling a knot in the base of her calf.

"Oof," she said, her eyes closing, her bottom lip caught between her teeth. "Yep."

His fingers dug gently in, and she bit back a moan as he kneaded into the knot.

She spoke through pursed lips, her eyes still closed. "Please, just ignore any sound I might make. I apologize in advance."

He really hoped she'd make as *many* sounds as she could. He chuckled, not knowing how to say the truth of it without making her feel uncomfortable.

"So?" she said as he glided up the other calf, taking her muscular leg in his hands and tracing the curve of it. "You have a lot to do?"

"Hmm." He shook his head to remember what they'd been talking about. "No more than anybody else, I'm sure. But, it's fine, I'll figure it out. I'm almost done with Pearl's surprise gift thing."

He kneaded into her calf and glanced up, seeing her face tucked against the couch, a peaceful look on her face.

"You asleep?" he said gently, half hoping she was so he could tuck her in, put a blanket over her and have her sleep here where he could take care of her.

She cuddled into the couch. "Just resting my eyes. Just keep talking." She waved an elegant hand at him to continue.

"I need to finalize the floor plan where we'll move. The new place will be by the credit union."

She'd tucked his shirt around her tighter.

"You can turn the thermostat up when you're here, you know," he said.

"Hm?" That caught her attention, and she lifted her head up in confusion. Her pretty hair had gotten mussed as she cuddled into the couch.

She looked cozy. In a different lifetime, in a different circumstance, he would have picked her up, taken her upstairs, tossed her in his bed, tucked her in under weighted blankets, and in the morning, had his way with her.

He nodded to her. "You were cold?"

She looked even more confused. "Um. Not particularly."

"I assume that's why you have my shirt on?"

She looked down at the oversized flannel shirt and smacked herself in the face.

"Yes," she said quickly. "I was cold. I'm so sorry." She started to take it off.

"No, no. Keep it." He kneaded another knot on her calf, and she moaned, low and needy.

She slapped a hand over her mouth in surprise.

"Looks good on you," he said, his voice rough.

He was keeping a thin leash on his lust right now, but seeing her in his shirt, moaning like that underneath his fingers?

His cock was throbbing. He couldn't take much more of this.

Even as a kid, he hadn't liked to play with fire, so he reached for his mug with both hands.

"I should probably go," she said, leaning her head against the couch and not moving. "I have to be back in"—she peered at the clock—"seven and a half hours?"

She slowly tucked her legs back underneath her, and he hunched over to hide his hard dick. *Think about this ginger tea, and how it is so very unsexy.*

"You feel okay, though?" he said, his treacherous eyes still gobbling up the beauty of her.

She sighed, giving him a smile. "Yeah. Just needed to cry, I think. Thanks for, you know, not weirding out? Anytime I'd cry, my brother would freak out. He'd freeze like a deer in headlights."

Luca laughed. "Pretty much the only constant in my life has been women who feel very comfortable wearing their emotions on their sleeves. I don't scare that easy." He couldn't tear his eyes away from the curve of her lips.

He gulped down the rest of his tea, trying to think of other things as she stood.

Her scent had rubbed into his shirt, and even though she was already across the room, it felt like she was right next to him.

"I think I'm gonna just leave a bunch of stuff here, since I'll be back in the morning," she said, gathering her things and tossing on sandals.

Wouldn't it be nice if she moved in?

He liked seeing her things mixed with his.

"Leave whatever you like," he said, trying to find a middle ground of what he wanted and what wouldn't make it sound like he'd lost his mind.

"I hope your day is better tomorrow," she said with a bright smile, all her sobs and overwhelm now completely gone.

He opened the back door for her as she walked out, not meeting her gaze. "You too."

She walked down his bright back porch steps and crossed through their yards to her dark back door.

It was even darker than her front door had been. *Why didn't Georgia check her lightbulbs, geez.*

He clicked on a small flashlight he kept on his keychain, spotlighting her way. . "We have possums and raccoons here."

"I'm bigger," she yelled, smiling.

"Barely," he mumbled. "Need help with this light too? " he called.

"I'll get it tomorrow," she called back, putting her keys in the back door.

He made a mental note to change this one too.

As he walked through the house turning off lights, her fall, cinnamon nutmeg scent on his shirt followed him.

Reminded him of what he could have if he made a better living and they were in a different lifetime.

One where she wanted to stay in her hometown, where he could take risks.

Cinnamon warmth swirling around him like her laugh as he moved.

Surrounding him like her arms had.

Invading his good sense until having her was all he could think about.

Goddamnit.

He yanked off his shirt, and tossed it on the ground. His chest heaved up and down, unable to take the torture anymore.

Need to catch my breath without her scent all around me.

He needed to get a handle on this. They had three more months to go. He needed some self-restraint. Because he would *not* let himself or AB get more attached than they already were.

He stared at the dark t-shirt on the living room floor as he walked toward the staircase.

His chest rose and fell with the memory of her underneath his hands, the soft moans, the press of her into his palms as he held her. *Those fucking calves for Christ's sake.* He'd worship any square inch of skin on her body that she'd let him.

Rolling his lips together, he fought the urge to let his obsession deepen, root further into every nerve ending.

But with a damning disappointment in himself, he stalked to grab the shirt from the floor and inhaled it like a lifeline as he ran up the steps to his bedroom.

Chapter Thirteen

OLIVIA

Olivia swung open the door to the diner. It was warm and cheery, covered in soccer team photos from years past that Pop had sponsored. He'd even been the coach when Wells, her older brother, had been the right age.

The new management had kept the old name and left most things untouched, though the flowers that Pop had kept on every table were gone.

Familiar faces waved to her as she walked through. She spotted Lily near the back, talking to Pearl and a woman Olivia recognized from the last Fairwick Falls Christmas party.

Part of her desperately wanted to impress Pearl. She was cool and aloof in that give-no-fucks kind of way.

The fact that I have an all-consuming crush on her brother is unrelated, obviously.

She'd had to change the batteries in her vibrator this morning because she'd worn them out last night.

She clenched her core thinking about the night before. *Those fucking enormous hands on my legs nearly made me come on the spot.*

"Oh, hi, bestie," Lily said, dragging Olivia out of her naughty memories.

"Hey you. Hey Pearl." Olivia waved.

Pearl glared through narrowed, judging eyes. "Hey," she said flatly.

That's fine. I'm no stranger to winning people over. I'll keep working on it.

The tall woman across from Pearl with peachy-pink hair stuck out her hand. "Allison, I work at Bloom with Lily."

"Oh, I *remember* you from the Christmas party," Olivia said, taking her hand and laughing. "I've already decided we're going to be best friends."

"I'm still *so* embarrassed." Allison grimaced. She looked like an actual sweetheart in her pink plaid dress.

"That you shoved a cake in my brother's face? Honestly, it was the best thing to happen to me last year," Olivia said with a bright laugh. Allison had had some very strong, very negative feelings about Wells, Olivia's brother, but he'd been tight-lipped about the reason why.

Allison smiled gratefully. "I'd ask for you to both join us, but we just finished up."

"Hey," Pearl said so sharply at Olivia that she jumped. "There's a ladies' night at the Thirsty Beaver. Next week. We're going." Pearl stood up.

"Oh...kay?" Olivia responded.

"What Pearl is *trying* to say is, you should come, too. It'll be fun!" Allison said with a smile. "Lily will be there, and we can probably drag Rose and Violet away as well."

Eeep! Friends!

"Count me in," Olivia said, smiling brightly.

Pearl gave her a ghost of a smile as she left.

She joined Lily in a big booth.

"I desperately want Pearl to be my friend," Olivia said, thunking her head against the back of the booth.

"Would it have something to do with the very tall, very handsome neighbor you see every day?"

She kicked Lily underneath the table with a glare. "Yes."

"Hey, guys." Jessica, one of the long-time diner waitresses, stopped at their table, looking frazzled.

"Hey Jess, I'll get the apple-pie pancakes."

"No," Jessica said as she delivered drinks to the booth next to theirs.

"What do you mean no?" Olivia turned to Lily, who shrugged.

Jessica shook her head, disgusted. "We fired the kitchen staff last week, and the new staff is *worse*. Can't order anything too complicated. Single ingredients only."

Lily looked hopeful. "Can they do a vegan chef's salad?"

"What do *you* think?" Jessica arched an eyebrow.

"Ugh, fine. Fries," Lily said, handing her the menu.

Olivia handed in her menu. "Cheese on mine please."

"No promises," Jessica said with a battle-worn grimace and stalked off.

Olivia grabbed the small coffee pot that was always on each diner table. She poured both of them a cup of coffee.

"So," Lily said happily, "catch me up, bestie. Ugh! Can you believe I get to say things like that to you in *person*? So exciting."

Olivia dug through her huge bag and pulled out a stack of old photos. "My mom found these of us as a kid."

"Oh my *gosh*," Lily squealed as she laid out the photos. It was the two of them playing dress-up as kids, with terrible makeup and crazy clothes. "I *loved* playing Fashionistas with you."

Olivia was surprised. "What did you call it?"

"That's what we called it. Remember? We were fashionistas. We made our own outfits, and we had fashion shows...?"

"Oh," Olivia said, looking at the photos again. "I thought—I don't know—it was just the photos the one time."

"No, we would do it every weekend!"

Olivia took a sip of coffee but then spit it right back into her cup as bitter, burger-flavored liquid filled her mouth. "Is this coffee... greasy?" she said in horror, smacking at her tongue.

"Don't tell Pop," Lily said, eyeing her untouched cup like it carried a disease. "It's really bad now."

"It might kill him," Olivia said. "Maybe literally. The man's eaten hamburgers and fries for eighty years." She took a napkin and wiped the taste off her tongue.

She'd thought the milkshake incident had been a one-time thing.

"I'd have suggested going to Fox and Forrest, but there's never an empty seat since this dumb company ruined the diner." Lily scooted her cup of coffee further away like it might bite her. "So, tell me more about your neighbors."

Olivia could sense an impending Lily inquisition. *Better distract her.* "What's it like being the unofficial first lady of Fairwick Falls?"

"I will not allow your misdirection, thank you *so* much."

Olivia rolled her eyes.

"This is for me to catch up with *you*, about *your* life and what *you're* doing, Miss I'm-just-taking-a-few-months-off." Lily arched a well-manicured eyebrow at her.

Olivia twisted a ketchup packet on the table, avoiding her gaze. "Maybe..." She sighed. *Time to fess up.* "Maybe I didn't get renewed with the Salt Lake City Ballet."

"What? *No*," Lily said in surprise.

"See, that's why I don't want to tell people. I'm disappointing them."

Lily squeezed her hand. "No, I'm sad for you."

"I don't like being pitied either," Olivia said, taking a sip of coffee and then—*Ugh, fuck!*—spitting it back out again. "I just like having the reputation of the one who made it. You know? I was really good at that one thing, and now I'm not good at it anymore."

"If I had ever had that reputation, I'm sure I wouldn't want to lose it." Lily squeezed her hand, and one tiny drop of shame evaporated.

It felt so good to feel seen.

"I mean, imagine how exciting *your* life is right now," Olivia said, gesturing at her friend. "Great husband, interesting job, lots of fun things in your future. That's what I felt like at eighteen. I had so much promise. Everybody talked about how *big* my career was going to be." She bit her lip, feeling disgusted.

"Your career *was* big. *Is* big," Lily said, correcting herself. "You've been all over the world!"

"I've been mostly in the U.S., and Argentina one time," Olivia corrected. "I'm terrified about my auditions in January. I'll be so old."

"You are the same age as me," Lily said with a deadpan look.

"Which is perfectly fine in real life, but in ballet, it comes with compression socks and an AARP card."

"Yikes," Lily said. "Do you want to keep dancing?"

Olivia shrugged. "That's the only thing I've ever been good at. Though"—she laughed at herself—"maybe I'm not even that, you know?"

"That's not what I asked," Lily said, giving her a pointed look. "You've just seemed down the last few years. You were practically *mopey* last Christmas at Pop's retirement party. Maybe it's time for something new. Never in one million years did I expect to end up in my hometown and marry the boy I'd crushed on when I was six. But—" She wiggled her eyebrows, taking a sip of coffee and then grimacing. "Shit, horrid," she whispered.

"Like if burgers were made with battery acid," Olivia said.

Lily nodded with grimace and shoved the cup to the end of the table. "Anyway, it's all worked out. I get big O's on the regular and big happy feelings when I launch new flower shops with my sisters."

Jessica appeared, putting two plates of fries on their table. Olivia's had a hunk of cold cheddar cheese on the side.

Jessica sighed, shaking her head as she walked away. "Best I could do."

They burst out laughing. Lily shoved fries in her mouth. "These are passable. How's your hunk of cheddar?"

Olivia poked at it, and it wobbled for some reason. "Pass."

Lily's phone buzzed repeatedly on the table. "Ah, shit on a stick. Rose is in a tizzy. We're working on this new big location pitch, and she's freaking out. Can we reschedule?"

"Maybe at a place where we can actually eat real food?" Olivia said with a smile, biting a fry.

"Done. I have to run." Lily tossed some fries in a napkin and threw twenty dollars on the table. "Pray for me that Rose got some hot action this morning and won't be on a tirade today. Love you, bye!" Lily ran around the back of the booth and kissed Olivia on the top of her head on her way out.

Olivia broke off a chunk of the wobbly cheese and paired it with a fry.

As she contemplated giving up on this very sad lunch, a familiar face and six-five frame appeared unexpectedly.

Wells, her older brother, walked quickly from the kitchen galley, ducking down behind the back of the booths as he made his way toward Olivia.

Wells lived in Philly over five hours away and worked nonstop as a divorce attorney. She loved seeing him, but it was rare to run into him without months of planning given his job.

"Wellesley Ethan Maroo, *what* are you doing here?" Olivia said, shocked. Befuddled, even.

Wells shushed her and ducked into her booth in the back of the restaurant. He wore a suit and expensive tie, and the roundness of his tummy pressed against the edge of the table as he attempted to make himself smaller.

"Don't say my name out loud. Don't want people to know I'm here," Wells whispered in a panic.

"Tell that to your not-see-through linebacker body, weirdo. Why the hell were you in the kitchen? Are you responsible for this chunk of cheddar not being on my fries?" She tossed a fry at him.

"Well." He grimaced, slinking further into the booth. "Sort of."

She squinted, knowing him well enough to know some game was afoot. "What does a divorce attorney have to do with shitty cheese fries?"

"You have to keep this a secret." He leaned over the table to her, his face as serious as a heart attack.

Her hair tingled on the back of her neck. "Wells, what did you do?"

Wells regularly took matters into his own well-meaning hands, and Olivia had spent her life watching the chaos he left in his wake. It always turned out better in the end, but people usually lost their shit along the way.

"I, um." He looked over his shoulder. "I bought the diner."

"*What?*" she yelled. He covered her mouth. She did the age-old younger sibling trick: licking his palm.

"Eeeugh," he groaned, yanking his hand away. "What are you, ten?"

"Does Pop know?"

He wiped his hand on a napkin in disgust. "Of course not."

"*That's* why Mom said you've been popping into town more and more."

Wells sighed, adjusting his cuffs. "I just wanted Pop to have a good retirement. Nobody was going to buy a small restaurant in Fairwick Falls that had an outdated kitchen, outdated electrical, outdated everything. The only thing good about it was the food that the *owner* cooked."

He grabbed a fry and took a bite of a rubbery piece and then spit it back out into a napkin. "This is the second staff I've gone through. I'm going to have to fire this team and bring in a *third* one."

"Wells, you are running this place into the ground," Olivia whispered, now panicked. "What if Pop finds out? Oh god, what if *Mom* finds out. She will *lawyer* at you until your ears bleed."

The desperation in his eyes magnified. "They won't because it's all a secret, and you can keep your mouth shut. Hey, you're looking for a job, right? Can *you* cook...?"

Olivia leveled a gaze at him.

Wells shook his head. "Right, obviously not. Oh, fuck." He collapsed back down in the booth.

Olivia turned, seeing if someone had come in. "Is it Pop?"

"Nope."

Allison, Pearl's friend, was talking with someone outside the diner window behind them.

"Is she coming in?" he asked, trying to peer over the booth.

"No," she said slowly, remembering the whole cake-in-Wells's-face incident from Pop's Christmas party. "Look, you're usually all over the place, but you're acting crazy. What's the deal?"

"None of your business," he responded from under the table.

"Oh wait, never mind. She *is* walking in, holding a single piece of cake."

A middle finger rose above the table at her.

"Wells!"

"Okay, I honked at her this morning—"

"Jesus." Olivia wiped a hand down her face.

"It was a petty attempt at payback. She was crossing the street. I was at a stop sign, and she spilled her latte all over her shirt in surprise. She was about to climb onto my hood if I hadn't three-point turned out of there."

Olivia munched on another cold fry, wanting the dirt on her brother. "Why does a random woman who moved to Fairwick Falls hate you so much? And why don't you like her?"

His eyes narrowed. "Oh, it's moved beyond don't like. Someone—I'm assuming her—signed me up for every cat facts-style text messaging system she could find. It started after the cake fiasco, so I assume it was her."

He held up his phone and three new text messages came through.

Endangered llamas in Peru need your help. Scan your passport to get started!

Click here for hot new CAT FACTS in your area

Doctors hate this one weird trick—try vinegar bombs today!!

"I can't block them fast enough. Can you run interference so I can get to my car?" He pointed to the street.

Olivia's cheeks were practically aching from smiling. "She's a genius. Never in a million years would I have thought to spam you as a hobby."

"I'd hope my sister doesn't hate me."

"Fine," Olivia sighed and rifled through her purse for her sunglasses.

"Hey," Wells said, stopping her, crouched down so that no one would see him. "You look... better."

"Than *what*?" Olivia said with a bemused smile.

"Than the last time I saw you." He'd stopped in Salt Lake City a few months ago, right before she'd gotten the news that her contract wouldn't be renewed. She'd assumed he'd wanted to see her dance, but maybe?

Maybe he'd been checking on me.

"How am I different?" she said, surprised.

"You look... happier. Just keep doing whatever you're doing, freckles." He looked almost like he'd been worried about her.

Her heart melted for her chaos, golden-boy older brother who had always kept one eye out for her.

"Now go," he said, shooing her. "Just walk her *away* from my car before she keys it. The next county is preferable. Bye. *Anddon'ttellMom*," he added quickly at the end.

"Love you, too, weirdo," she said, sticking her tongue out.

She'd left Pop's sooner than she'd anticipated, still starving, but somehow her heart felt completely full.

Chapter Fourteen

LUCA

Luca slowly bent down in his home garage.

He positioned the final, important piece of Pearl's Airstream: a custom roll-down window with her logo on it.

Whenever possible, he tried to do after-hours work in his garage so he'd be closer to Annabelle.

She couldn't be in here because of the fumes though, so Olivia was watching her this evening.

The back window of his garage looked out onto his backyard. Toys were scattered around, a swing set swung in the fall breeze, and yellow leaves fell gently from the trees in the setting sun.

AB and Olivia were outside playing with her bubble wands as they both shrieked, trying to catch one another.

Luca's heart wrenched at the sight: AB in her flannel shirt and overalls and Olivia with her pretty hair flying as she ran laughing through the crunching leaves of the yard.

He tried to take a mental snapshot, to keep with him always.

The perfect fall he'd had with the perfect person in his life and the best kid anyone could ask for.

Everything about his life with AB felt precious right now. He wanted to remember every moment even after she was grown up. He assumed he'd only have the one kid, so this was his one shot.

No mistakes. Everything had to be perfect.

Speaking of one shot to get everything perfect...

He pulled his respirator down and grabbed the thin metal sheet that had Pearl's logo on it.

He'd bond it to the original, larger piece of metal that had come with the Airstream. There was exactly one chance to get it right.

The bonding agent he used was time-sensitive, and he'd asked Olivia to not come in for the last hour; otherwise, it would completely derail him.

He had approximately fifteen minutes once the bonding agent started mixing. One distraction and he'd have to strip it all off, toss everything, reorder a new sign, and it would be a whole fucking thing.

Now or never, he thought as he started the mixing gun.

He got one bead of bonding agent along the short side of the rectangle, and then a long side.

Over the sound of his machinery, he heard shrieks of laughter. He needed to move a little quicker, but he allowed himself a lingering look to be sure AB was okay.

They'd both fallen in the leaf piles in the back yard, and he breathed a sigh of relief.

He lined the other short side with a thin bead of bonding agent. Carefully, slowly, not too much or too little.

He rolled his shoulders. *One last side to go.*

He placed the mixing gun and started it.

Something caught his attention from the corner of his eye

as he started. A person had entered his backyard. They'd gone around the house and back in through the fence.

Luca squinted in the distance.

Oh, fuck.

His mother.

He watched as Olivia called AB to her from across the yard and pulled AB behind her.

Annabelle didn't know his mom, and he wanted to keep it that way. He'd never trust her to keep her safe.

Fuck, fuck, fuck. He finished the last bead of the bonding agent as quickly as he could. He should make a large X across the metal to better bond it together, but—fuck it.

He quickly grabbed the thin metal before the bonding agent dried and saw his mom crouched down with open arms in the yard, beckoning AB to her.

Annabelle peeked out from behind Olivia, who put a hand out as if to say, *Stop right there* to his mom.

She and Annabelle walked backwards toward the garage as Luca slid on the top piece, working as quickly as possible, his hands shaking.

She'd never had the balls to come to the house before.

He clamped the piece of metal together lightning fast. All in, the process had taken probably fifteen seconds, but it had felt like an eternity.

The door to the garage opened as he turned around and threw off his mask and eye protection.

"Luca," Olivia called, her voice sounding nervous.

"I got it," he said, brushing past her.

Olivia said, "I'm taking AB inside," right as Luca said, "Get Annabelle inside."

Luca jogged up to his mom but caught sight of Olivia hauling Annabelle up into her arms and walking with her to the back door. She held AB on the far side, shielding AB with her body and chattering to her.

The gratitude he had for Olivia in that moment practically choked him.

"What are you doing here?" Luca said to his mom.

His mother looked thinner than the last time he'd seen her, but meaner, too, as she glared at him.

Didn't think that was possible.

She hefted the huge purse on her shoulder in annoyance. "Just trying to spend time with my grandbaby."

"Did you take a photo of her?" he said. His mom had her phone out on camera mode.

"A grandmother wants photos sometimes. I was gonna see if she wanted to get some ice cream."

"Mom," he sighed. "You *know* why I don't want you here."

Because he'd trusted her *one* time—one fucking time—with Annabelle when she was a baby. He'd come back after eight hours to a cold, dirty diaper on Annabelle who was crying from hunger, his mom passed out in the recliner from alcohol or who-knew-what and a lit cigarette burning beside a piece of paper.

That had been her one and only chance.

"That was years ago," she said, wobbling on her feet. She had the hungry look of someone who lived on menthols and small bottles from the liquor store. He could smell it on her breath.

"Did you drive here?"

"My boyfriend is out in the car."

Protective anger made him grit his teeth as he tried to keep it at bay. *A strange man near my kid?*

Fuck.

No.

He raged. "Never come into my backyard uninvited. Never talk to Annabelle ever again without me present."

"That uppity bitch wouldn't let me talk to her anyway," she said with a hacking laugh, taking a pull from a lit cigarette and blowing out smoke. "You just think you're better than me, right?"

I know I'm better than you, he thought. *I worked my whole fucking life to make sure.*

"What do you want?" he said finally, crossing his arms.

She tapped the end of her cigarette, sizing him up.

"I just need a little more," she said, taking a long drag of her cigarette as if life had handed her all the lemons in the grocery store. "So I can get little Annie somethin' for her birthday."

"Her birthday was months ago."

"Oh, shoot," his mom said. "Right. What was the date again?"

The hair lifted on the back of his neck. "How much?"

"Oh, five hundred will be fine. I wanted to get her something special. Now, tell me the date so I don't forget next year."

He snorted. This woman had never bought him a birthday present. There was a fat fucking chance in hell that she was going to buy his kid one.

He didn't know what kind of information you needed to open things like checking accounts or credit on behalf of a kid, but he wasn't going to risk it. The less information this woman knew about his daughter, the better.

He kept her at arm's length, made sure she wasn't starving and on the street, but that was all she got. "Why do you want her birthday, Mom?"

"I'll just go ask her if you won't tell me," she said, turning around, hefting the giant, cracking leather purse on her shoulder.

"Hey!" he yelled.

"Don't you yell at me. I am your mother," she screamed.

God. This was his worst nightmare, the yelling from his childhood that echoed every day in the trailer. He'd pull Pearl into the yard and then make up games to keep her distracted. To this day, Pearl thought he'd liked tag as a kid, but he just did whatever he could to get her away from the trailer as fast as possible.

One of the nice older ladies would take them in and make sure they had juice and cookies every few days, nice doilies covering every surface in her well-kept trailer.

"Here." He pulled his wallet and took all the cash he had. "Eighty dollars. That's it. Never come to my house again. Never speak to Annabelle again. And if I find out you have, that'll be the last you get from me."

"Shit," she said, yanking the money from him. "Can't hardly get her anything with this, but I'll try, I guess."

"Yeah," he sighed, wiping a hand down his face. "You can try."

He watched as she tossed down her cigarette butt and ground it into his yard. He rolled his eyes.

He picked up the cigarette. His house would *not* look trashy.

"Tell Annie I love her," she called as she wobble-walked through the small gate.

He walked her all the way to the front of the house until she drove away.

Annabelle. His heart pounded again and again as he broke into a jog up his front steps. He tugged on the doorknob and found the front door locked.

Fucking *hell*, he adored Olivia for that.

Once inside, loud music boomed from the second floor. He locked the back door on his way past it.

The stairs were a blur under him as he ran up, needing to see AB.

Upbeat, classical music blared over hip hop beats from her room. Annabelle and Olivia were dancing like maniacs with the stereo turned all the way up. Annabelle was beaming with a sheen of sweat over her little red face. Twenty pounds of stress floated off of him at how unbothered she was.

"Come dance, Daddy!"

Olivia was twirling beside Annabelle, and she inserted a few headbangs between ballet moves. "I was craving a dance party!" Olivia yelled over the music.

He held her gaze as he let his arms be yanked back and forth by Annabelle dancing beside him. "Thank you," he mouthed.

She nodded with understanding as they danced. A laugh escaped him as Annabelle did an awkward cartwheel across the carpeted room.

He turned the stereo down to a reasonable level. "Hey, AB, I need to talk to Olivia downstairs about something."

"Can you get started on your homework?" Olivia asked her.

She danced over to where her crayons were on the floor. "I'm going to draw a ballerina."

Olivia wiggled with happiness. "Ooh, can she have reddish-blonde hair?"

Annabelle thought hard, then shrugged seriously in a way that reminded him too much of himself. "Best I can do is orange."

He actually laughed out loud. Goddamnit, he loved his little girl so much.

They walked downstairs. Olivia twisted her long hair up into a topknot.

"Oof." She took off her sweatshirt, revealing a tank top underneath it. "It's been a minute since I've done that much cardio in sweats."

He tried to shake off the haze of his past as he walked through the living room, that trashy feeling of neighbors looking at you. Airing out your dirty laundry in front of everybody.

He turned on the oven fan for some noise coverage and walked to the laundry room.

He wiped a hand down his face. "Thank you."

Olivia's quiet, understanding smile radiated like the hope of a sunrise at him. "Of course."

He leaned back on the washer. "We never even talked about my mom. I mean, a coked-out-looking lady came into the backyard, and you handled it like a fucking champ."

I thought I loved her yesterday. How could that miserable amount compare with the aching ton of it that's pressing onto my chest now?

God, I'm in fucking love with her, and I barely even know this woman.

She'd ruin me if I ever let myself get too close.

And then he thought back to AB's bedroom, their yelling in the yard having been drowned out.

She didn't hear it.

AB didn't hear the yelling.

This angel of a woman had made everything okay.

"Are you okay?" Olivia asked, her expression laced with concern.

"Yeah," he said, tossing away the comment. His feelings weren't really important. "Thanks—"

"Hey." She caught his eyes and stood closer to him so he couldn't escape her gaze. Her blue eyes had turned a stormy sapphire. "Are you"—she poked a finger into his chest, emphasizing who she was addressing—"okay?"

No.

That simple admission escaped his subconscious. *But that would be enough.*

He tried to look anywhere else but at her, and she wouldn't let him.

He wasn't used to this, to someone not letting him evade. All five-foot-four of her stared up at him with a mixture of sternness and care.

He cleared his throat as emotion clutched at it. He blinked it away, looking everywhere but at the red-headed work of art in front of him.

"AB's never been in a house with yelling," he said, coughing to cover the emotion, blinking his eyes rapidly. "I never want her to think I'm—"

He shrugged, trying to hide a quiver in his lip. He paced in the laundry room to the other side. He stared out at the back-yard. "Thank you for playing music to cover it up. I never want her to think we're trashy, you know?"

He turned to thank her—

"Jesus," he said, starting.

Olivia was two inches behind him—arms crossed, head tilted. She'd boxed him into the corner beside the dryer and the window.

Her brows drew together. "You did not answer my question. How are *you*?" She shook his elbow.

Christ, this was new for him.

"I'm—" He struggled with the next word.

What could he even share?

What was even going *on* in his head?

"A feeling usually comes next," Olivia said, quirking a smile.

He nodded, trying to do this her way. "Yeah. Mad? I think? At my mom." He felt lighter as the words evaporated from his mouth.

"And I'm... overwhelmed," he said, blowing out a sigh. "At how much I appreciate you for protecting Annabelle. She's not a nice lady, my mom."

The two feelings seemed to satisfy her.

"Hey. I've got you, okay?" she said, rubbing a hand up and down his arm. "And AB."

He stared at her hand rubbing against the fabric of his shirt.

When was the last time somebody had tried to take care of him?

He felt safe with Olivia, which he realized he did *not* like.

The harder you love, the harder you grieve. He knew that.

She pulled him down hard into a hug, leaning on her tiptoes and wrapping her arms around his neck.

He was surprised but let his arms wrap tight around her, then squeezed her closer as he savored this new feeling of being cared for.

She pulled back with furrowed brows. "Did you eat lunch?"

He'd been working in the garage since they'd both gotten home at 3:30. It was almost six o'clock now. "Um..." He scratched the back of his head. "No?"

"All right, well, dinner"—she clapped her hands with a bright smile—"is going to be the Olivia Special."

A grin curled onto his face. "Protein smoothies for everybody?"

"Hey." She spun in a full circle for effect, pointing a finger at him. "I am an excellent peanut butter and jelly maker."

"Don't you need to go do your practice thing?" It felt uncomfortable, even scary, to have someone take care of him.

What if they didn't do a good job?

Worse: what if they did, and you'd grow to depend on them and *then* they'd leave you?

"Eh, I can work out after dinner."

His eyes traveled the length of her taut frame and muscular arms. She looked like she worked out nonstop. But when your body was your job, he understood the need to be on top of things.

"I'm even going to add my special ingredient," she said with a mischievous smile.

"Love?" he asked, smirking.

"Lack of crusts. It's the way *Annabelle* and I prefer them," she said, comically sassy with her nose in the air as she walked to the kitchen. "Be nice," she called, "or I won't cut your cucumbers into stars."

He laughed to himself, resting his forehead on the wall, at just how fucked he was going to be when she left.

OLIVIA

"Uh, sweetie, the egg shells go *outside* the batter."

AB stared into the large batter bowl with a scowl. "Well, shit."

AB's deadpan delivery followed by her mangled attempt to grab the shells out of the bowl had Olivia nearly peeing herself trying to contain her laughter. "Let's ask your dad if you're allowed to say that word."

"I can," AB said urgently. "I can say it one time a week at home. 'Cause I'm six now. I got the C-word last year."

Olivia stared with wide eyes. "*Which* C-word?"

"The poop one!" AB said, giggling.

Olivia decided to distract her, hoping she wouldn't ask about *other* C-words. "Let's try the egg again."

Nothing said fall to Olivia like pumpkin muffins, so she'd found a Luca-approved wheat-free recipe to make for their Friday afternoon activity. AB stood on a step stool in her tiny unicorn apron. Luca had finally delivered on his promise to find her a purple one, so Olivia wore a matching one beside her.

AB successfully cracked the second egg into the batter bowl.

"Great job. Let's slop the pumpkin in now."

AB grabbed the open can from Olivia with confusion. "How do you slop?"

"Two hands, and shake it!" Olivia said with a smile, leaning on the counter. "Slopping is an important part of the recipe."

AB's face lit up, and she shook the pumpkin can upside down from her stool. It plopped out all at once, a cloud of dust landing on Olivia's face.

Nutmeg-y sweet dust lined her nostrils and she laughed, coughing from it.

"You look like a ghost." AB laughed. "It's on your nose."

"Here, we can match." She lightly sprinkled flour onto AB's nose as she belly-laughed.

Luca walked in at that moment with armfuls of grocery bags. His arms flexed from the effort, the clinging long-sleeve Henley following every dip and muscle of his frame. He'd pushed the sleeves up to his elbows where his forearms flexed against the grocery bag straps.

She licked her lips at how cuddly, how *hot* every part of him looked.

His smile was warm as his eyes connected with hers, looking delighted at something.

"Psst. Go try it out," Olivia said, nudging AB.

"Hey, Dad," AB said too loudly. "Can I help you?"

Luca stopped short and looked at Olivia in surprise.

She shrugged as if to say, *I don't know either*. They'd been talking about being helpers to people who they loved, like her dad or Pearl.

"Hey, kid. Can you get the bag that I left on the porch?" AB ran out to the porch.

"Is that your doing?" he said, looking skeptical.

"AB is a very sweet girl." She shrugged, a secretive smile on her lips. "Big plans tonight?"

"It's movie night," AB answered for him, slamming the door behind her. "Wanna watch with me? We're gonna eat candy."

"Oh," Olivia said, not wanting to intrude. "That's okay. Thank you, though."

"You don't like watching movies with me?" AB looked genuinely hurt.

Oh, her heart.

"Oh, no, sweetie." Olivia leaned down. "We can watch movies any time. You and your dad don't get to spend a lot of time together, and I don't want to get in the middle of that."

AB looked around, as if thinking of a reason for her to stay. "But you said you liked *The Little Mermaid*."

A smile tugged on Olivia's lips. "I do. Is that one of your favorite movies?"

"Yeah," AB said unconvincingly as Luca slowly shook his head *noooo* behind her.

"Well, we can watch *your* favorite movie, okay? It's your movie night. Someday we'll watch my favorite movie on movie night," she said, accidentally committing herself to another one.

"Why don't you go get your pj's on, goob," Luca said as he put things away in the fridge.

"I can show you my new crow pjs AP got me," AB yelled as she ran up the stairs.

Luca said, "You should stay," as Olivia said, "Is that okay?"

"Oh." Luca nodded nervously. "Only if you want to. I'm sure you have plans." He hefted two heavy jugs of water and set them in the corner.

Olivia laughed hard as she mixed the batter, and a snort crept through. *Yeah, plans with my vibrator, pretending to be that five gallon jug of water in your hands.* "I can move things around my bustling social schedule," she said sarcastically. "Plus, I lost track of time, and these muffins need a while to bake. But only if you're sure."

She tossed the empty pumpkin can in the trash and licked pumpkin off of her finger.

Luca gulped as she met his eyes, looking lost in thought. "D-definitely." He shook his head to clear it. "You should stay."

Luca reached past her to put vitamins on a high shelf beside her. She tried to catch a whiff of his cologne. *You know, like a serial killer probably.* Something about this man's scent flipped the on switch on a cave-woman mode she didn't even know she had.

Add in the rolled-up sleeves and she was practically in heat.

He stopped beside her, watching her scoop batter into a muffin pan. "How's the apron working out?"

She twirled, showing it off, spatula in hand. "Fabulously. Doesn't it look great?" She said it lightly, but her laugh faded as she met his heated gaze. He nodded.

"Perfect," he whispered, almost to himself.

There was an us-ness when he was close. That was what she called it in her head. A pretend time where they were a unit, a team.

"You have…" He brushed his own nose.

"Ah, yeah, the flour shot first."

"May I?"

She stuck her face toward him, her eyes looking everywhere but at him.

But then his rough fingers swiped her nose. Gently along the ridge and across her cheek.

She couldn't breathe and couldn't look away from the stubble in front of her face, wanted to rub her face against it.

Thank god she heard thundering little feet running down the stairs or who knows what she would have done next.

"Got it," he said finally and stepped back.

Thirty minutes later, AB sat between them on the couch. They all had heaping plates of pasta and junk food on their laps, watching *Frozen* for what was probably the ten-thousandth time if Luca silently mouthing the words as he watched was any indication.

She had trouble eating her pasta with all the butterflies in her stomach.

A group sing-along nearly broke the windows during "Let It Go," right as AB's sugar buzz kicked in. Luca had been game, wearing a blue tiara AB had insisted on as she and Olivia did their interpretive dances. They sipped from heated mugs of apple cider as AB belly-giggled at the silliest jokes.

AB insisted on stretching out on the edge of the couch, which meant Olivia had landed in the middle between them.

The house was chilly, and Luca had grabbed blankets that they'd spread over their legs as AB sat on the couch squirming in the way that kids did. Her eyelids started to droop, though, as the sugar crash swooped down, and she leaned her little body against Olivia. There was plenty of room for three people, but AB kept pressing her feet into the side of the couch arm and scooting Olivia closer to Luca, completely unknowingly.

Their arms brushed. "Sorry, I can move down to the ground," she whispered to Luca.

"No, it's fine," Luca said, his tiara still glinting in the light from the TV.

Olivia bit her lip as she watched the movie, feeling the heat along their arms and thighs that were smashed together.

She leaned over to whisper. "You're a really good dad."

His eyebrows knitted together in genuine surprise. "Really?"

She bit her lip to keep from laughing. "Not every dad would take the third-best tiara."

He realized it was still on his head and pulled it off quickly. "Shit, thanks." He laughed. "You an expert in good dads?"

She huffed out a hollow laugh and stared back at the TV screen, shaking her head. "When you don't have one, you are acutely aware of what you're missing."

"I'm sorry. You deserve to have a great dad," he said quietly. He moved his fingers so they brushed the backs of hers, comforting her.

She had to close her eyes at the yearning for him that hit her stomach.

AB was dozing in and out of sleep and pressed her legs harder against the couch, shoving her into Luca.

"Sorry." Olivia laughed.

"It's fine." He lifted his arm and wrapped it around the back of the couch.

Olivia had to close her eyes to steady herself as a wave of his cologne and scent washed over her.

She'd been a giant fucking liar the other night.

She hadn't been cold.

She'd taken his shirt and wrapped it around herself to smell his scent and huff it like a safety blanket. She wished she could live in this moment forever, with the feeling of being wanted, being part of two special people's lives.

She was tucked into his side, practically on his lap.

Armageddon could have been happening outside and nothing would have distracted her from how much she was trying *not* to turn and cuddle against his chest.

As she shifted on the couch to cross her legs, he got up suddenly. "I'll do the dishes. Can I get you anything?"

"Oh, let me help."

"It's fine," he said, pointing to AB, who was nodding off on her shoulder. "Do you mind staying there?"

"Have a man cook me dinner and *then* do the dishes? Not at all," she said with a smile.

An unexpected flash of white teeth as he laughed had her stomach somersaulting. She followed him with her gaze as he walked through the arched doorway, moving to the side a little so his shoulders wouldn't brush the walls on his way through.

She sucked in a deep breath, trying to blow it out slowly, focusing on the movie.

You cannot be attracted to this child's father while she is leaning on your shoulder snoring adorably.

AB's mouth was starting to fall open. She was a cute little kid, and Olivia realized she'd rarely ever seen her still. AB had her father's upturned nose, his eyebrows that tended to furrow. She looked so much younger when she was asleep. Olivia tucked the blanket tighter around her.

The movie continued, and Olivia felt her eyelids grow heavy as well, hearing the comforting *clink* of silverware in the sink and the sound of pans being scraped.

She decided to enjoy the moment and let her eyes close, her head resting against the back of the couch, sinking into the warm comfort that was a belly full of pasta, a familiar movie in a dark room, and the sound of somebody taking care of her.

Suddenly, something pulled at her side, and she jolted instinctively, clutching at AB's shoulder. Luca was gently pulling AB up to take her to bed.

"Sorry," she said, blinking awake.

The menu screen of the DVD blinked back at her. They must have been out for a little while. She rubbed a hand over her tired eyes.

"It's fine," he whispered. AB grumbled in her sleep as he bundled her, blanket and all, up against his shoulder.

Now she realized why Luca had the forethought to have AB go get into her pajamas at the start of the movie.

He quietly carried AB up the stairs. Olivia let her eyes close as she suffered another wave of crush-induced whole-body goosebumps of lust.

Good dads were so...

Fucking...

Hot.

She stretched and realized she should probably leave. Luca softly came down the stairs as she turned off the TV.

"How long was I out?" She yawned.

"From the seventh song onward. AB had a great time. You made her week."

"Ugh, how is your couch so comfortable? I don't want to leave." She leaned over to the pillow Luca had used under his neck and huffed it.

Yes, more. Into my veins, cedar-scented dopamine.

He walked in with two glasses from the kitchen and a bottle of whiskey. He looked at her with the raised bottle and arched an eyebrow in question.

"I sat through *Frozen*. What do *you* think?"

A smile grew on his face as he gave her a healthy pour.

The spice of the whiskey warmed her tongue. Alone time with Luca.

And whiskey.

What could go wrong?

She realized just how little she knew about him. "What made you move to Fairwick Falls?"

"Why do I do anything?" he said with a sly smile, tipping his glass.

They both answered "Annabelle" at the same time.

"The Elliotsville school wouldn't accommodate her food allergy, so we had to look for a place that would. I knew she'd be an only child and I wanted her to have friends at school. Enter the only town I've ever known to have monthly festivals."

"My mother is a menace." She laughed into her cup. "She's responsible for half of them. Barbershop Quartet Fest, Hot to Turkey Trot Fest, not to mention the Valentine's Day date auction for the food bank that has really gotten out of hand. There was a fistfight last time."

"I *know*. They were fighting over me," he said uncomfortably, adjusting his shirt.

She cackled into her whiskey. "No way." She was shocked. "Did you really pick up Margie and Beulah at the same time to pull them apart?"

He smiled into his cup as he sipped. "A gentleman never fistfights and tells. I like your mom a lot."

Oh god, he's perfect. Please say something terrible or reveal a mansplain-y personality flaw so I don't upend my life for you.

"And Pop too," he added. "He was always so careful with AB's allergy. His diner was the only place I trusted. What about your dad?"

"My parents divorced when I was little, and then I didn't really see my dad until I went to live with him in Philadelphia as a teenager."

Luca took a melancholy sip from his glass. "You wanted to leave all of this small-town life behind?"

"No"—she shrugged—"I wanted to be a professional dancer...anywhere. And at sixteen, I started my internship. So. That was the best place to do it."

"Did you miss out on all the teenage stuff?" he asked.

She shrugged. "I went to a few homecoming dances. I had my fill of it by my sophomore year. I was ready to go to the big city and be a big success. Joke's on me." She laughed, flouncing her hands out as if to indicate she knew how ridiculous that was.

She took a big sip of the whiskey and stared at a spot on the carpet, realizing something. "It's more that I missed out on my college years. Figuring out who I am. I had to decide when I was AB's age whether I wanted to go after being a professional. So...I don't know. I never considered what if that wasn't what I wanted forever."

He shifted on the couch. "Maybe that's what this time is for, you know? If you don't love the dancing part."

She lolled her head back and forth in indecision. "I don't *hate* it."

"Olivia...What do your friends call you?"

"Olivia...?" she said slowly. "I've always liked Liv, though."

"Okay, then, Liv." He shifted in his seat and looked right at her, his head resting on the back of the couch inches from hers.

A little sparkling burst in her chest, and she swallowed a smile. "Yes?"

"You were crying in my arms the other night. That didn't seem super happy."

"No," Olivia sighed out. "But admitting defeat means *I'm* defeated."

"What do you really want?" He had the audacity to ask her that, looking kissable and handsome in a dark, cozy room.

You. On a silver platter.

Naked.

In a king-size bed.

"Are *you* happy?" she asked him instead.

He bit his lip, considering her question. "I've been happier in the last month." He clinked his glass to hers and leaned back on the couch, propping his feet up.

She leaned back against the couch and propped her feet up to match him. They sat side by side, slouched down into the couch. "Because you're moving your shop?"

"...Yeah," he said finally.

She set her mostly full glass on the coffee table to avoid any achy practice tomorrow.

She settled back into the couch, letting herself enjoy the scent of him, the heat of him running along one side of her body. How it kept building into a thumping ache between her legs.

He fiddled with the plastic tiara in his lap; it looked comically tiny in his big hands. Luca was a big guy, and his hands looked like they could destroy her in the best way possible.

"You have nice hands," she said as she clinked her plastic tiara to his.

"Yeah?" He turned his hand over. "Even with all the tattoos and the shop scars?"

She took his hand in both of hers, examining it, turning it forward and back.

Tattoos ran along his wrists and hands. Each knuckle had a letter of Annabelle on it, with a heart on his last pinky.

"Especially with the tattoos and scars," she said, tracing healed, jagged cuts around his thumb on the side of his hand, probably from work.

There was strength in them, roughness. A raw honesty that didn't bullshit around.

She'd seen how capable and kind they could be. How gentle he was with AB, how helpful he was to everyone else.

These were hands that worked for everything they'd earned. Hands that showed up, day after day, protecting, caring, and loving.

She slowly kissed the palm of his hand, overcome with affection.

She froze as her lips landed on the heat of his palm.

Fuuuucking shit.

I just kissed him.

His eyes were wide with shock as he stared at her.

Oh, fuck.

He said he wanted to keep things professional and I just kissed the palm of his hand like we've been married for ten years.

She dropped his hand and scooted away. "I'm—I'm so sorry. I don't know why I did that." She leapt to her feet. "I should go."

"Olivia," he whispered after her.

She grabbed her keys and tossed her shoes and coat on. She'd get anything else she needed on Monday.

He followed her into the kitchen. "Olivia, it's not a big deal."

"I'll see you Monday morning, okay?" She rushed to the back door.

"Liv," he called after her.

"Sorry again," she called as she shut the door behind her.

The cold night air smacked her in the face, and she stilled on his back porch.

Hundreds of stars in the sky sparkled back.

She felt insignificant and small and lonely.

Wait, *was* she sorry?

Mortified at coming onto the guy who pays me each week. At kissing someone who is quickly becoming one of my favorite people who might not like me back.

But *was* she sorry?

Of finally being honest with herself and him?

Letting her body do what it had craved for weeks?

The door slowly opened behind her.

Maybe he's upset? She needed to make things right. *No mistakes is the bare minimum.* "I understand if you don't want me to babysit anymore. Sorry, that was—"

"Stop," he said gently, shutting the door behind him.

He stood close to her. Even then, she felt her body want to angle into his—like they were made to be together.

"Are you?" He said it slowly, cautiously. "Actually sorry?"

His tone was disbelieving.

As if waiting for her to admit something.

She finally met his gaze.

His eyes were full of care and agony. *Please put me out of this misery* was written across his face.

And she had to agree.

She took in his handsome, sculpted features, his kind eyes, the lips she'd tried not to stare at, and his scent that reached into her soul and soothed it.

She was so tired of being unhappy.

This man made her *so* happy.

"No." She sucked in a breath as she stared at his mouth. "No, I don't think I'm sorry at all."

Chapter Sixteen

LUCA

T*hank.*

Fucking.

Christ.

He exhaled out a disbelieving laugh that she matched. "I can't *take* this anymore."

The exhausted 'what the hell is happening?' shaking of their heads was almost in sync.

Mirth danced in her eyes. "Worst game of chicken, ever."

It was all just tumbling out of him now. He couldn't keep it in. "I can't wait to see you every morning. You're gorgeous, and kind, and"—he wiped a hand down his face at his inability to stop talking—"*fuck*, you're so hot. Your hair looks like the best part of a sunset. Like, I've tried to look up the color but it doesn't exist? How is that possible?"

She laughed at their shared frustration.

He tugged at the ends of his hair with both hands in frustration. "I get up early just so I can catch a whiff of—what on *god's* earth do you wear? *What is that scent?*"

She laughed in disbelief, her hand muffling her mouth. "I'll tell you mine if you tell me yours."

A wave of overwhelming happiness made him dizzy. He put his hands on his knees, just trying to reel in all the feelings, and he shook his head. "So it's not...just me?"

She rubbed her hand on her breastbone. Her long lashes fluttered as if she was catching her breath. She bit her lip and shook her head. "*So* not just you. I thought someone punched me in my soul when I saw you the first time."

He held his attraction on a short leash.

It pulled and thrashed against his control.

He wiped his lip, trying to stop his body from doing the one thing it wanted. His head spun. "What *is* this between us? Did one of us piss off a witch?"

"I don't know." She shook her head with a grimace. "But it's a motherfucker."

"Yeah," he said with a hollow laugh, knowing they'd both do the responsible, adult thing. "It would be a disaster. We can't...you know. It has to stop here."

"I mean, I'm leaving. I *must* leave," she said, jutting her hand like a plane taking off for emphasis. "We can't. The Hindenburg would look like a fender bender in comparison, it would be such a disaster. I mean if it feels like this now..."

He groaned in agreement.

She lingered near him though, and his breath kept catching with the effort it took to be responsible.

"I don't want AB to get attached," he said quietly, even as his fingers slyly brushed the edge of her coat.

He didn't want to get attached.

More attached, you asshole. Her leaving would be like losing a semi-vital organ at this point.

"Plus, I'm paying you. So this"—he gestured between them —"would be a pretty terrible idea." He tightened her coat around her.

She bit her lip as she stared at his mouth, slowly nodding.

"Those are all really good reasons. This is just...chemistry." She waved it away.

It's my undying devotion of who you are as a person.

"It'll pass." She shrugged, not looking at him.

When I die, probably.

But he nodded like he agreed. *Be an adult. Protect yourself and AB.*

It was still dark around her back door. "Let's get you inside. I'll walk you home."

She smirked, rolling her eyes as they walked to the back steps.

It was a pretty flimsy reason to spend more time with her, to be fair.

He slyly grabbed the light bulb he'd set out on his back porch and turned on the monitor app on his phone in case AB needed him.

"Still haven't gotten to that light bulb?" he asked.

"I've been a little busy," she said, acting scathed. "I don't know if you've heard of this movie called *Frozen*? I just watched it with my favorite people."

He chuckled and caught her scent as he walked beside her.

When she got to her back door, she stood in that lingering way women did on dates.

Keys? Fiddled with.

Dewy eyes and plush lips? Check and check.

Looking at her pretty face, he slowly reached up to unscrew the dead light bulb. He was pleased at her waterfall of laughter as he reached up with a fresh one. The new bulb cast a warm glow with his final twist.

"Pretty smooth, Bishop."

Her smile was sultry and warm, and he finally understood why men went to war over beautiful women.

He'd do anything for her at that moment.

His fingers itched to touch her again. Instead, he perused the freckles on her face, the faint smile line of her cheek. "I just want to keep you safe. That's all," he said quietly.

Never taking her eyes from his, she reached up to stand on her tiptoes. She placed a hand on his chest for balance, and he clutched it against him, enveloping her hand with his.

She was *just* tall enough to reach the light bulb.

She slowly unscrewed it until darkness flooded around them again.

His heart hammered in his chest as she leaned toward him, inches from his mouth.

"Thanks for walking me home."

He licked his lips. *She'd taste so good.*

"Any time," he whispered, his thumb stroking her fingers.

Hammering, hammering, hammering.

His heart beat faster against her hand.

He brushed her cheek gently, his thumb swiping the apple of its perfection. Her breath stuttered.

"Eyelash," he said.

She leaned into his hand shamelessly, closing her eyes. Christ, he could die happy now, being the person she'd nuzzle into.

"Was there..." Her breathless voice hitched as he stroked the soft roundness of her cheek again as it pressed into his palm. "W...was there really an eyelash there?"

"No," he quietly admitted. *Just needed to touch you.*

His forehead met hers, and a primal need to taste her gripped his body.

"We should stop," he whispered against her cheek.

"Definitely," she said, not moving a muscle.

His breaths came in needy pulls. The ends of their noses brushed.

Again.

And slowly, again.

His eyes closed as he lingered there. Her skin felt like velvet against him. He never wanted to stop touching her, being beside her.

He gulped down the whiskey-laced wine of her breath, inhaling as close as he could, restraining his lips and tongue from tasting it for themselves.

This is agony.

Pure, needy, mewling agony.

The ache of wanting her was un-fucking-bearable.

"Please, Liv." He puffed the plea against her cheek, his nose nuzzling hers.

The bow of her top lip brushed his chin in exquisite, slow agony as her heavy breaths came out hot against him, the heat of it flushing his skin, taunting him.

Just once. Just one kiss. So I don't die from this. He was so close his lips brushed her cheek as he spoke. "Please. Can I kiss—"

Soft lips pressed against his.

The dam he'd built to contain his need exploded into dust clouds of sapphire and sunset.

His hands were in her silky hair, cradling her head as he kissed her deeper, harder, pulling her into him.

There you are. Mine.

She tasted as eternal as the sky and the moon and the crisp autumn wind around them.

Stars in their brittle constellations ached for the permanence of the devotion running in his veins for this woman.

She'd always been his.

She'd always *be* his.

Her tongue traced his lip and a moan—*was that him?*—groaned out, low and needy. He slid his arm around her waist, pressing her closer. Her arms wound around him, pulling him closer, and his cock throbbed, wanting her. Wanting more.

Showers of pleasure cascaded down his spine as her nails raked up into his hair.

Their kisses grew sloppy and claiming.

Pure lust-drenched hunger took over as he gasped against her lips.

He feasted on her mouth.

Tasting, biting, needing.

Gulping each mouthful of her scent to store it away for the rest of his life.

Her teeth raked against his lip, and he pulled her up with one arm around her waist so she was at eye level with him. His other hand braced her jaw so that he could worship her properly, dragging each long kiss out of her, tasting that scent that made his cock pulse.

Her feet dangled off the ground, and his hand slid down to her ass, gripping it. Claiming it.

An unslakable need was finally met at feeling her in his hands.

Her soft, warm tongue met his, and a lightning strike of need thumped in his body.

Need her, want her.

More.

She wrapped her legs around him. White-hot desire took over as the heat of her pussy in her thin yoga pants met his cock, which now felt like granite in his jeans.

He pressed her against the brick of the cottage, wanting the feeling of pressing against all her softness. Pressing against her heat.

But the cold brick against his hands was a splash of reality. *She lives here. Temporarily.*

But fuck, she felt so good against him, her breasts pressing into him, how perfectly she fit there.

Gotta stop.

He kissed her with his entire being, savoring this last taste. *Last one.*

He dragged his lips away, even as his tongue darted out to lick at her bottom lip.

Clouds of their breaths mingled together as they panted, staring at each other.

She was silent with wide, shocked eyes.

"That should be the last time, right?" he muttered, trying to gauge her reaction.

She nodded slowly, her eyes on his lips. "Obviously," she murmured as she pulled him down to her mouth.

He groaned in relief, cupping the back of her neck as he deepened the kiss. Tongues and lips and sighs mingled lazily, breathlessly.

Back home. Right here with her is home.

Each lick into her mouth made him think of licking her everywhere; each nip from her teeth made his cock jump.

She squeezed her legs tighter around him, and his hips ground against her in reflex. *Fuck, it would be so good with her.*

He ground against her again, and she gasped into his mouth. *Yes.*

What he'd give to hear her come. Scream his name.

The tease of the pressure on his cock made it even harder. *Fuck, I might come from kissing her.*

He squeezed her ass hard, imagining what it would be like to rock into her again and again and again.

She smiled and whispered against his lips, "Bunhead."

A laugh rumbled out of him as she kissed his jaw, his neck, and he cradled her head against him, kissing her temple slowly.

Her arms wrapped around him in a hug as her heart beat against his. "*That* was the last one," she muttered into his neck.

They teetered on a ridiculous ledge.

He set her down but kept his hands on her waist, not

wanting to break contact yet. She pressed her face into his chest.

"Uggggh. Just as I found my happy place," she said, voice muffled by his shirt. "It has to go away."

He ran his fingers up from the base of her neck, over her scalp, until he cradled her head. Tugging gently on the silk strands, he slowly pulled her head back, exposing her long, elegant neck.

"Fucking perfect," he growled.

He lowered his mouth to hers, savoring the feeling of her swollen, bee-stung lips with one long, slow kiss.

He poured all of himself, all the love he already had for her, into it, tracing his tongue along her cupid's bow lip, the weight of her safely in his hands.

"Last time, mean it," he whispered with disappointment as he pulled back.

No more. Think of your priorities.

She pressed her forehead against his chest. "Urgh," she groaned in frustration. She slowly pushed herself away, the effort looking painful.

They stared at one another in understanding, sharing their disappointment.

"I shouldn't do that again," he said.

Or I might throw my entire life away at a chance to make you happy. Be selfish like my mother.

She nodded, staring at the keys she'd pulled out of her pocket.

He twisted the light bulb back on, and its warm glow flooded the back porch. Her lips were red and her cheeks were flushed. Pink patches surrounded her lips where she'd rubbed against his scruff.

Gorgeous.

She fought to contain a smile as she rubbed her cheek.

"Even with beard burn?"

Fuck, he hadn't realized he'd said that out loud.

"Especially with it," he said, heated.

The goddamn caveman in him liked that he'd marked her, for a few minutes at least.

She unlocked her door, gave him a lingering wave as she closed it, and locked it.

His chest ached with missing her already as he stood alone on her back porch.

Luca was not a religious man, nor a spiritual one.

All the same, on his walk back to his house, he still raised both middle fingers into the air, aimed at whichever gods that had created this exquisite torture.

Chapter Seventeen

OLIVIA

As Olivia looked up to see her mother dancing on a table at the Thirsty Beaver dive bar, she realized she should've come home more often.

"Your mom is cool as fuck," Pearl yelled in her ear over the loud thumping music. Olivia had been nervous to join them at ladies' night, but she'd broken the ice with Lily when they first got there.

The dive bar at the edge of Fairwick Falls was packed shoulder to shoulder with all the women in town. In fact, the president of the credit union, Olivia's second-grade teacher, and her stepaunt were currently cheering her mom on as she danced on one of the sturdy tables.

"You'll hurt yourself," Olivia yelled up at her mom.

"Everyone's gotta die some time!" her mom yelled, swinging her sequin-covered wristlet in the air to the sound of whoops.

"Don't worry." Pearl patted Olivia's shoulder. "Tiny'll catch her." She pointed to a large man in a denim vest and a camo bandana who stood behind her mom. "Come on, I got shots!"

She was going to need about seven of them to stop thinking about the make-out session that had been running on a loop in her brain for the last twenty-four hours.

Luca's hands on her ass. Tugging her hair. Biting her lips. Feeling his biceps—*fuck me, was it everything I always thought it would be*—and wanting to bite them. He'd tossed her up and taken what he wanted. She'd been ravaged, plain and simple. She hadn't even waited to get her vibrator; she'd had to just come right there in the kitchen after he left.

Pearl lifted a tray of shots over the crowd as they wound their way through the packed bar, kicking up sawdust on the floor as they went. She came back to the table, scattered with glasses, where Allison sat knitting a pastel yarn. Olivia was incredibly curious about the woman who had her hotshot brother terrified.

"Some ladies' night." Pearl jerked her head at the back of the bar where Lily made out with her enormous husband.

"They are nauseatingly romantic," Allison said, shaking her head. She was their DD and stone-cold sober. Olivia didn't know how she could handle being here.

Olivia's tongue already felt a little heavy in her mouth from the two buttery nipple shots she'd had.

"I think it was that third nipple that made her cling on like that," Pearl said, twisting her head as she looked at Lily and Nash. Olivia burst out laughing and Pearl smiled with her.

"Who are all these shots for?" Olivia said, looking at the tray in horror.

"They're for us," Pearl said, lining them up on the small table.

"There's like twelve glasses here! You tryin' to kill me?"

"Half of them are maple syrup. You shoot one, and then you chase it with whiskey. Or vice versa, if you're a pussy," Pearl said with a snort.

"All right, well, I've got to impress you," Olivia said, trying to turn all her charm on. She desperately wanted Pearl to think she was cool.

Pearl rolled her eyes. "I'm already impressed. My brother likes you, and the coolest person I know, AB, thinks you've hung the fucking moon. I'm very jealous," she said, picking a shot glass, "but also impressed."

Olivia picked up a shot glass and yelled over the music to Allison. "Thanks for being DD!"

Allison cheersed her back with her sparkling water and lime. "No problem. I'm hoping no booze will make the latest round of sperm work."

"Let's get you pregnant!" Pearl yelled out. Allison covered her face, mortified, and laughed, her wavy, short hair shimmering in the neon lights.

"This is the last one I have money for for a while, so let's hope this one sticks!" She pointed with both fingers to her uterus.

"That sounds so nerve-racking," Olivia said, thinking about how nervous Allison must be.

"I'm sure you don't want to hear about my drama. Your life sounds so cool. You're a famous dancer. You're going to go live a big life in a big city after Christmas. I'm just trying to make a baby with 'provider' 785-A."

Olivia looked at Pearl in confusion. "Who's that?"

"A six-foot college grad who likes chemistry. That's all I know about him." Allison laughed in exasperation.

Olivia wanted to ask more but didn't want to offend her. Did Allison have a partner? Did they have struggles getting pregnant? It sounded scary to put all your hopes on a random sample every month.

Since none of that was her fucking business, all she did was squeeze Allison's arm affectionately and say, "All of my fingers and limbs are crossed for you. And I am not that fancy." Olivia's mood dropped. "I'm actually—"

"Come on—shots," Pearl interrupted, scooting glasses toward Olivia, trying to get her back in a festive mood.

Olivia looked at the six shots in front of her. "No way."

"I will tell you anything you want to know about my brother," Pearl said with a challenging glint in her eye.

Damn, now that's tempting.

"Okay, but you have to take some, too."

"If I get three questions about *you*." The steely glint in Pearl's eyes met Olivia's.

She raised a shot glass and clinked it to Pearl's. "What was Luca like as a teenager?" Olivia asked, taking the first shot of maple syrup and then chasing it with a burning whiskey. It tasted like her night with Luca, and she squeezed her thighs together.

"He was kind of a troublemaker. He started getting tattoos around sixteen because he could pass for older. School wasn't a big deal in our family, but he managed to graduate. He was a troublemaker, but not an asshole, you know? Got really into cars. And then at eighteen, started doing body work for his buddies' cars, and he's worked on that ever since."

The whiskey warmed Olivia's belly as she thought back to what he would have been like in school. A bad boy with a heart of gold. She sighed over it. "Your turn."

"Are you really leaving in four months for a fancy new job?" Pearl said, double-fisting the maple syrup and whiskey.

Olivia sighed. "I don't know." She shrugged, feeling sad all over. "I have to audition, and then I'll move anywhere that'll have me. I actually lost my job in Salt Lake this last spring."

The whiskey had settled into a gooey warmth in her limbs, making everything feel a little better.

"Oh, no," Allison said, leaning in with concern as her knitting needles click-clacked. "What happened?"

"I turned thirty-three. My fouettés can't fouet like they used to," Olivia said, tossing her head back and laughing at herself. "I thought I had more time before I'd have to retire. I'm going to give it one last shot. Unless AB needs a nanny for the next, I don't know, thirty years?"

Pearl pushed two shot glasses at her. "You."

Olivia thought through the whiskey haze. *He was a troublemaker in school...hmmm.* How could she know if Luca's white knight stuff was just an act? She'd fallen for plenty of 'white knights' who'd really just been regular dudes coated in bird shit. "What would Luca spend a million dollars on?"

Pearl waited until Olivia took the two shots. "Easy. Annabelle. He might make me get some new baking equipment and would probably buy some fancy book collection for Reed."

"Nothing for himself?" Olivia said. "New tat or unicorn apron?" Her insides warmed at how adorable he was.

"No," Pearl said, "not his deal. He kinda has to be *made* to spend money on himself, unless it's for work. He wants everybody else to be taken care of, which is annoying as fuck because he is a pretty amazing big brother. Sometimes I just wish I could figure out how to make him happy, you know?" Pearl's eyes went misty, and she angrily wiped the tears away.

Olivia filed that away in what she knew would be a foggy memory. Luca needed to learn to put himself first, though she kind of knew that already.

She scooted two shot glasses at Pearl.

Pearl arched an eyebrow. "How badly do you have the hots for my brother?"

Allison scream-cackled as Pearl took two shots simultaneously of syrup and whiskey, smiling as she gulped them down.

Olivia thunked her head on the table. "*So...fucking... baaaaaaad.*" They all cackled. "We kiiiind of kissed last night."

Pearl whooped, standing up and punching the air as Allison screamed "I told you," at Lily in the corner.

A cold glass was pushed into Olivia's hand. She skipped this syrup this time.

"Last one," Pearl said.

"Urgh, I'm going to hate you in the morning," Olivia said as she shot it back. "What's his dating history?" she said, wiping her mouth with the back of her hand.

Pearl shrugged. "Nada. I mean, obviously, he was in love with Marcy. And then, I don't know, he's kept it quiet to himself, not dating anyone I know of. I've tried to set him up with people."

Allison raised her hand with embarrassment as if to say *me*. "Talk about a blow to my confidence. I practically threw myself at him."

"You did not *throw* yourself at him," Pearl countered. "You asked if he wanted to grab a drink. And he said, 'No, thanks.'"

Allison looked flabbergasted. "That's throwing myself!"

"Oh, my gosh," Pearl yelled. "That's just, like, how dating is. She's been out of the game for a while," Pearl said, throwing a thumb at Allison.

Allison did some sort of complicated looping of her pastel yarn on her knitting needles as she talked. "I was married to an asshole for a long time, and then the last year, I've been trying to get out there, but..." She shrugged. "Dating in a small town is hard. Especially when you're a six-foot lady who feels so awkward trying to date anyone who's not taller."

Olivia nodded, understanding it deeply. "One of the reasons I was excited to leave Fairwick Falls. I grew up with the same thirty boys. Dated a third of them"—she cheersed her water—"in middle school and high school and decided: *No, thank you.*"

"Last one," she said, practically feeding Pearl the last shot.

"What's stopping you?" Pearl asked.

"From what?" Olivia tried to evade the question.

Pearl shook the shot glass to get the last drops into her mouth. "Any of it. All of it. Going for it with Luca. His face gets so fucking dopey when he looks at you. Or at pictures of you. Or talks about you." She made a *blech* face.

Olivia burst out laughing. "I think it's time to talk about Allison."

"Wrong!" Allison and Pearl said at the same time. They all burst out laughing, and Olivia spent the rest of the evening making two new girlfriends.

A short while later, they stumbled into Allison's car. Her first stop was Olivia's house, and Olivia was mortified to see that Luca was on the front porch fixing something on his front door handle with his toolbox.

"*Ooh, Lucaaaaa,*" Allison and Pearl teased.

"Shh, stop, guys. Oh my gosh, shut up," Olivia hissed as she attempted to get out of Allison's back seat.

She slowly, elegantly, tumbled ass over tea kettle onto the grassy sidewalk, clutching the car door as it swung open. The wheezing of her laughter went silent with how hard she was laughing.

"Gonna pee my pants," she gasped.

Pearl stumbled out of the front seat, crying with laughter. "You're so drunk," Pearl said, slurring her words. But she also misjudged the curb and tumbled next to Olivia as they laughed on the grass. That wheezing, high-pitched, can't-get-a-sound-out laughter. It felt so fucking good. Why didn't she go out drinking with new friends more often?

A large shadow stood over them. "You guys are a mess," Luca said with a laugh, pulling Olivia to her feet. She giggled as she stumbled against him.

"I beat Pearl in a drinking competition," Olivia said, hiccuping.

"Pffft," Pearl said as she stumbled getting up. Luca steadied her. "I'm drunk, not her. Wait." Pearl paused. "Backwards from that. That's what I meant."

Luca rolled his eyes as he opened the car door. He poured Pearl back into Allison's car. "You're a saint for dealing with these two."

Allison got out. "Olivia, want me to help you?"

Olivia waved her off. "Luca can help me," she said, patting his shoulder. "*He'sagentleman.* Text me when you get home!" Olivia said as she waved at the car.

Olivia walked across the grass and would have tumbled face first onto the sidewalk if Luca hadn't caught her around the waist.

"Thanks, the sidewalk is wavy." Olivia put her hand on her forehead.

Luca grabbed her elbow. She weaved to the door, and he caught her around the waist again right before she teetered into the bushes. "I take it Dave was running his two-dollar-shots special tonight?"

"Your sister is *so fun,*" she said, leaning on Luca's arm as they walked up the sidewalk. "Avoid the first step."

He scratched his ear. "Oh, I fixed it, actually."

She stopped and felt like she was about to cry, overwhelmed by her feelings for him. "You're so nice."

Such a handsome face.

Luca held out his hand and looked like he was trying not to smile. "Keys?"

"Pfft, I'll get it."

She tried for a full thirty seconds, missing and scraping the lock of the door before she gave up and handed them to him.

In a flash, he had the door open, and she stumbled inside, kicking off her shoes.

He stood in the doorway. "You guys have a good time?"

"Yes!" She turned around, dumping her keys and purse beside the staircase.

"Need some water or a bucket, maybe?" he said, grimacing at her.

She fought her coat to twist it off. "I hate outerwear."

"Here." He gently pulled it off and hung it on the coatrack.

She was tugging off high-heeled boots, and the next moment, they were off somehow. Luca had helped.

She was still registering how fast he'd done that as she saw him searching through the cupboard until he found a glass and ran some water from the faucet.

"Why does it feel weird you're here?" she said, staring at him as she sipped the water he'd handed her. She gasped in panic. "Annabelle!"

He held up his phone. "Monitor. It's fine, but I should go."

"You're so smart." She grabbed a banana that was on the counter. "I'm not that drunk; I'll be fine." She stumbled over to the stairs. "I just need some sleep, and then I'll wake up fresh as a daisy."

Her foot kept missing the bottom step.

"Step, why won't you stay still," she said, getting frustrated and hitting the wall. "Whatever, I'll just sleep on the couch."

Luca walked out of her downstairs bathroom, holding a bottle of aspirin and an extra glass of water.

"How are you so *fast*? Are you, like, a sex demon and this is where I find out?" she muttered as she lay down on the couch.

He grabbed a blanket from the basket beside the couch to drape over her.

The blanket was tucked carefully around her. She used all her energy to open one eye. "Are you tucking me in?"

He laughed. "No, I'm just making sure you won't freeze down here," he said, tucking her feet underneath the end of the blanket. He then lifted her up and put a pillow under her head.

"Liar." She grabbed his arm and pulled him down so he sat beside her on the couch.

"Can I get you anything else?" he said. His hands brushed the hair from her eyes.

Your face between my thighs.

She nuzzled against his hand, wanting more. His thumb traced the top of her cheek, and she sighed.

Want him.

With all of the savoir-faire of a drunken elephant, she grabbed the front of his shirt and pulled him down. She kissed against his lips, but he just smiled, not kissing her back, as he gently pulled away. "Liv, you're way too drunk."

"*Urgh*," she moaned, smashing her face against the couch cushion. *This is so embarrassing.*

"No need to be embarrassed, we've all been there. I've lost a drinking game to Pearl on occasion," he said, a smile in his voice.

"*Fuck*, that was supposed to be an inside thought."

Merriment danced in his eyes.

"Stay," she whispered.

"I can't."

She sighed against the hand that was the size of her face. "I like the way you smell. I lied the other day," she said, her eyes closed, cuddling against his hand.

"Hmm, what'd you lie about?" His fingers stroked the apple of her cheek.

"I wasn't cold," she said, pulling at his sleeve.

"Are you...taking my shirt? That I'm currently wearing?"

"Mm-hmm," she said, tugging at the flannel shirt with

closed eyes. "I wasn't cold. I just wanted to smell you. But that's weird, so I couldn't say it."

She sighed, cuddling up against the flannel shirt that smelled like a sexy house.

"That's what you are," she murmured. "A sexy house."

She felt a gentle kiss on the top of her head. And somewhere in the back of her mind, she heard him murmuring something about a key and locking the door. She heard the sound of the lock clicking and something being scooted underneath the door.

With a long, sleepy sigh, she smashed her face into the best smelling piece of fabric in the world and dreamed about having it wrapped around her forever.

ALLISON (NEW FRIEND)

I'm home! Are you feeling okay Olivia?

PEARL (AB CONTACT)

or is my brother smashing his face into yours right now?

BESTIE LIL

probably not all they're smashing.

hey-ooooo

PEARL (AB CONTACT)

GROSS

but also you know, do your thing girl.

ALLISON

She didn't answer. Should we be worried? Should I call her?

PEARL (AB CONTACT)

relax, mom. she's probably just passed out.

ALLISON (NEW FRIEND)

Hopefully not on her face!

BESTIE LIL

hopefully on HIS face!!

PEARL (AB CONTACT)

so we've learned tonight lily gets horny when she drinks

ALLISON (NEW FRIEND)

That was *quite* the show in the corner Lil.

BESTIE LIL

guys my husband is so hot 🥹

Did you know he's getting me a special cake for my birthday??

He won't tell me what it is but I think goats might be involved. I'll probably cry and then fall to my knees and then

OLIVIA

omgggggggggggg

shuuuutttt uppppppppppppppppp

I need to make phone sleep

Like quiet

But not off

PEARL (AB CONTACT)

hahahahahahhahahha oh damn. ballerina is a lightweight.

BESTIE LIL

She's *gone* gone. I'll ask her mom to bring The Hangover Cure to the fall festival planning tomorrow.

OLIVIA

see yu mrnings

ALLISON (NEW FRIEND):

See yu mrnings, guys

BESTIE LIL

See yu mrnings!

PEARL (AB CONTACT)

see yu mrnings weirdos

OLIVIA

Olivia's stomach roiled with the bad decisions of last night.

She smelled Pop's hangover breakfast burrito before she saw it.

Her mother strode up like a spring chicken, sparkly glasses shining in the morning light like a beacon. "Have a good time last night, hon?"

She peered over her sunglasses in the far too loud Fairwick Falls town hall.

"You are very loud," Olivia whispered, grabbing the aluminum-foil-wrapped burrito the size of a baby. The thought of cheese and potato and eggs made her stomach turn, but she knew she'd feel better after the first bite.

"I'm so glad you got out and had some fun. *Finally*," her mom added, sitting next to her and patting her head, fussing with her hair in that way moms did.

She loved it even if it embarrassed her.

Olivia picked at the burrito. "*You* were dancing on the table. I'm telling Pop on you."

"Already sent him photos, and it's his phone background now." Her mother beamed with an irritating cheeriness.

Pearl slowly walked in, wearing sunglasses, and plopped next to Olivia. She slid down in the folding chair like she'd liquified. "I will pay you a hundred thousand dollars for a bite of that burrito," she said with what sounded like a teeth-grinding hangover.

Olivia passed it to her. Allison and Lily sat down on either side of Pearl and her mother.

"Look at us," Allison said with a bright smile. "Hot Girl Group Chat in the flesh."

"Oh," Olivia realized. "Is *that* what HGGC stands for?" She'd seen the name but hadn't remembered from last night.

"It was your idea. All the way home, you just kept yelling, 'We're the hot girls!'"

Olivia squeezed Allison's hand. "You were a saint for putting up with me last night. The only currency I have to repay you with is this burrito." Hearing this, Pearl offered Allison a bite, still clinging to the burrito like a lifeline.

Allison squeezed her hand back. "I'm good. Don't want Pop's Cure to go to waste on me."

"Did you see Luca last night?" Lily said in a bright, teasing voice.

Oh god, not in front of my mother.

"You should have *seen* how swoony he was with her," Allison added, a twinkle in her eye.

If they only knew how much I embarrassed myself. Kissing him even though I could barely feel my lips? Stealing the shirt off his back like an eighteenth-century pickpocket street urchin?

Dreaming of him wrapped around me all. Night. Long.

"Speak of the hunky devil." Her mother nodded over her shoulder.

He sauntered toward them. *Did he even mean to saunter? Probably not. Probably just his natural sexy state.*

He held a tray of to-go coffees from Fox & Forrest. "Thought you all might need these. Got the good coffee after I dropped AB off at Girl Scouts."

"You've always been my favorite brother," Pearl said, grabbing a coffee and chugging it.

"Are you doing something with the festival?" Olivia asked, grabbing a coffee from his tray, barely able to look him in the eye. *Just don't think about how you threw yourself at him.*

"He's a sponsor!" her mom said proudly.

Luca started to say something, but a boom echoed from the front of the hall. A wooden gavel smacked against what had to be a brick of C-4.

Pearl passed the breakfast burrito back to Olivia, who took two bites.

Gerald, the mailman from Olivia's childhood, cleared his throat and smoothed his mustache. "We are so excited to have all the vendors here to kick off the informational session for the forty-ninth annual Fairwick Falls Fall of Fairwick Festivities Festival."

"Jesus Christ," Pearl said, loud enough to have three rows of people turning around. "What? That's a dumb-ass name."

Was it a weird name? Olivia had never really thought about it. It had been such a fixture of her childhood.

"All right, first up, we have to kick off the festivities—"

A woman who was Luca's neighbor raised her hand. "Should be the Festivities Festival," she croaked in a whining voice. "Get 'er right, Gerald, goddamnit."

"To kick us off with the *Festivities Festival*," Gerald said in a long-suffering sigh, "we have Ms. Georgia's ballet class led by Olivia Maroo."

Polite applause sounded like a thunderstorm in Olivia's

head as she waved and smiled from the back, slinking down even further.

"Are you ready?" Gerald asked, looking expectant.

Everyone turned to look at Olivia.

Nightmare fuel. "Yeeeeees...?" she said slowly.

"Great! Stage is all yours."

Cold panic sweat covered Olivia's body. She wasn't ready. In fact, she'd kind of stopped even trying to get the kids to do any semblance of a routine in the last few classes because it seemed impossible.

"What do you mean?" she said, hoping she was misunderstanding.

Pearl snorted with laughter.

Gerald scratched his head, embarrassed. "Miss Georgia gives us a preview of what the dance will be."

"And the costumes!" somebody piped up from behind him.

"*Oh, fuck,*" Olivia whispered. She was going to look like a fool in front of every person she knew in town. She slunk off her purse and sunglasses, grimacing against the bright light.

"Ms. Olivia Maroo," the man said, as everyone clapped politely. "Our world-famous hometown ballerina."

Oh, that makes this so much worse. As she stood on stage, four smiling faces in the back row were trying to swallow their laughter. She couldn't even *look* at Luca.

"So first, my first-grade class will come up. They..." She spoke slowly, trying to figure out what to do. "...will be wearing tutus."

"Aw," the crowd sighed.

Okay, point for tutus.

"Do you have a costume to show us?" June, her old second-grade teacher asked.

"Um, I am finishing... the touches. On the costumes." She blinked through a wave of nausea.

I have not started.

"Could you preview the dance? Georgia always gave us a preview," Margie in the front row called.

Olivia mentally sent her mother and Lily a message to start a fire so she could leave, but they weren't getting the hint. In fact, Pearl and Lily had tears of laughter running down their faces.

Oh, fuck it. How bad could making it up be?

"So, it uh... starts off with a kickball change and a grapevine," Olivia said, doing basic moves. "Then, uh, they do this." She moved her hand from side to side, wobbling like a children's character at an amusement park. "Their costumes will be leaves."

A man raised his hand. "The tutus will be on the leaves?"

"Uhhhh." *Crap.* "Yep. Giant leaves wearing tutus. And then guess what else happens," she said, realizing how she could fix all of this.

"And then they dance in a circle," somebody yelled.

"That's exactly right! How did you guess?" At this point, Lily had fallen off her chair, her great snorts of laughter coming from the back. "Then they... take real leaves from their baskets."

"Do they throw them out into the audience?" somebody else called.

"Oh, my gosh. That's exactly right," Olivia said, smiling and sweating out pure whiskey. "Then they dance in a circle like this." She skipped, holding her arm out as if running around in a circle with other girls. "And then"—*Don't throw up*—"they take a bow."

Beaming faces stared back at her, clapping politely.

Georgia was going to kill her for ruining her dance class.

She risked a glance at Luca, who looked at her like she'd hung the moon.

Still? Even after looking like an idiot?

"Oh, this is going to be wonderful," the man up front said. "We can't wait to see it."

Phew. She breathed out a sigh. She walked back to her seat, happy to be done.

She pulled out her chair to sit back down in it as her best friend, mother, and two new friends wiped their eyes.

"I'm glad you all are finding this hilarious," Olivia said, swallowing a smile. "I'm never going out with you again," she said to Pearl and Allison.

"But we have Bitch and Stitch next Saturday at my house," Allison whispered, looking at her with pleading, earnest eyes.

"I'm making my special cocktail," Pearl added. "Gin."

"No shots, and you got a deal," Olivia said, sitting back and sinking her teeth into the rest of her burrito.

It was going to be so hard to give this up. She hadn't had a real life in... maybe ever? Drinking too much with girlfriends, her mother taking care of her, the man she had a raging hard-on crush on bringing her coffee, and the stakes feeling so low that she could be her ridiculous self and it didn't matter.

She looked over her shoulder at Luca, who was standing in the back, leaning against a wall. He winked at her, giving her a mischievous smile. She couldn't wipe the dumbest smile off her face at how adorable he was.

She turned around, exhaled a long, cheek-puffed breath, and tried not to fantasize about him for the next twenty minutes. Lily and Allison spoke on stage about what Bloom would be doing, and Pearl represented her pop-up, Blackbird Bakery.

As the atom-bomb gavel was rapped to dismiss them, her eyes found Luca again. She excused herself from the Hot Girl Group Chat and beelined to him. She had to clear the air.

"Some performance earlier," he said as they wandered outside.

She curtsied. "Fueled by only the best coffee and flop sweat in the county." *C'mon, you can do this. Be a grown-up.* She finally looked him in the eyes. "Hey, I'm sorry about last night. I…"

"Drank a little too much?"

"Got hammered," she finished at the same time, laughing so hard she snorted, slapping a hand over her mouth instinctively. He chuckled with her.

"I just wanted to apologize. I didn't mean to, um… tempt us. By kissing you. Or coming onto you. Making you uncomfortable."

He laughed a *little* too loudly.

She smacked his arm. "You don't have to laugh like that. As if I'm being ridiculous."

"I mean, resisting you normally is…" He gulped, keeping his voice low as people filed out around them. "Hard. But I'm only tempted when you can enthusiastically consent. And, you know, walk a straight line. And walk up a flight of stairs. And take off your shoes—"

"Okay, okay, I get it." She rolled her eyes. "Thank you for being a gentleman, though."

He looked embarrassed by that comment, and she loved the little blush on the tops of his ears as they walked out in the late-morning sun.

She smirked. "Can't blame me, though, for wanting to relive the best—" *Eep.* She cut herself off.

He stopped in his tracks. "Best what?"

Her entire face lit on fire as she realized he was going to make her say it. She looked everywhere but at him. "Luca, come on."

He looked incredibly confused.

She fiddled with her hair as they walked outside. "That was the best kiss of… my entire life the other night."

He looked pleased with himself. "Entire life?"

"Oh, don't look so smug about it," she said, playfully pushing him. "Anyway, I'm sorry drunk Olivia got too greedy and wanted another one."

He nodded but stood taller. "For what it's worth, I think I agree with her."

There was a tender cruelty in knowing someone wanted you but you couldn't be together.

"Ah, there you are," her mother called. "Allison and I are going to the fabric shop in Elliotsville. Want to come along and figure out how to give leaves tutus?"

She probably should have gotten started on them weeks ago.

"I should go pick up AB anyway. See you tomorrow morning," Luca said, giving Olivia a wave.

She fell into easy step with her mom and Allison but looked back over her shoulder to see Luca staring at her before he hopped into his car.

She waved, and despite being the most hungover she'd ever been in her life, she decided she wouldn't mind if she were home for just a little bit longer.

LUCA

"You mother*fucker*. You did not do this." Pearl clutched the sides of her head in shock.

She stood in Luca's shop staring at the cute, all-black Airstream trailer with a Blackbird Bakery logo on the side.

Seeing Pearl's dumbfounded look at the surprise was all the thanks Luca needed.

Confusion melded into shock, which then melded into surprised anger on his little sister's face.

He smirked. *It's okay. She just does that to mask her feelings.*

"I did. Well, we did," Luca said, nodding at Reed beside him. "And Angie helped source it, Ritchie did welding, and Braden installed the sink." His team waved, embarrassed, standing along the side of the shop. Pearl used to be a regular there when she took care of AB. They'd been happy to do overtime to get it finished.

Pearl blinked quickly, trying not to cry. "This is for me?" she asked quietly, still confused.

"That's your logo, ain't it?" Angie said with a gruff laugh.

"Thought we could haul it to the fall festival in a few weeks so you can stay warm," Luca said, crossing his arms to stave off the emotions trying to leak out of his eyes.

Reed gave Pearl a tissue. "You can put it outside of bookstore whenever you want, or we can keep it in the parking lot until we can get your store open."

"My own space," she whispered gently, stroking the glossy side of the Airstream trailer.

She peeked in before walking through it, open-mouthed, and gasped. "A register," she said, hitting Reed's chest in excitement.

"All set up and ready to go," he said, fixing his glasses as he beamed at Luca.

Luca thought his heart might burst from his chest in happiness. He had never in his whole life seen Pearl this speechless or happy. And to help Reed give her something like that?

He got a little choked up thinking about it.

People in his family weren't able to do things like this. Big, grand, expensive gifts. He'd certainly never gotten anything big, but he was proud to give it to someone who had helped him so much and never asked for anything in return.

Pearl barreled from the back of the Airstream into him, throwing her arms around him.

"I'm so mad at you," she murmured into his chest as he squeezed her back, pulling her off her feet.

"Pfft. For being an amazing brother?"

"For making me cry in *public*." She punched his side playfully. She squeezed him tighter. "Love you, buttface."

He rubbed a hand on her back. "Love you too, little monster."

Pearl pushed off of him. "And you," she said, pointing a finger at Reed.

"Hey, I tried to convince him to do this in the dead of night where no one would see and just mail you the keys—"

But she yanked Reed down to her mouth, and Reed's arms wrapped around her tight, squeezing her possessively.

And that's my cue, blech.

Luca busied himself with the drinks to avoid watching his sister make out with his best friend. Reed had brought some sodas and beers for the big reveal.

Luca went to go join his team. This would be one of the last things they did at the shop before everything was moved to Fairwick Falls. Felt like a good going-away party for all the work they'd done here.

The side door opened, and his favorite tornado ran through, followed by the woman he thought about every eight minutes.

Olivia took his breath away as she sauntered through in a sage-green off-the-shoulder sweater and figure-hugging jeans that looked expensive. *So fucking elegant.*

A good reminder, like most times he saw her, that she was too good for him. Too good for living a small life here when she wanted to go capture her dreams.

"AP, AP, AP!" Annabelle yelled, running in.

"AB, AB, AB!" Pearl parroted back.

Annabelle jumped up and down. "I knew the surprise, and kept it secret the *whole* time."

Luca snorted. He'd finally told Annabelle about it that morning and swore her to secrecy, but he wasn't going to tell Pearl that. *Let her have her wins.*

"This is so cool, Pearl," Olivia said, peeking in the trailer's door.

"If it isn't Barfly Ballerina," Pearl said with a warm smile back at Olivia. "Cool jeans."

Olivia twirled, looking down at them. "Thanks, they were on sale in the wrong size, but I tailored them so they'd have that trouser look."

"What's a barfly?" AB asked Pearl.

Pearl bent down to AB's level. "You see sweetie, sometimes tiny ballet dancers can't hold their liquor—"

Olivia burst out laughing. "AB and I got you a little something," Olivia said, interrupting her, smiling.

Pearl unwrapped a glass tip jar in the shape of a skull as they chatted, and Olivia grabbed her in a friendly hug.

Pearl looked both surprised and touched. He fucking loved seeing them be friends.

Olivia's eyes connected with his as they laughed, and she smiled shyly, giving him a little wave.

He'd kept his distance the last few days, limiting their overlap in the mornings and afternoons when he got home. She was like a decadent piece of cake he shouldn't have too often. Otherwise, it might bite him in the end.

Reed ambled over, looking pleased as Pearl and Olivia and Annabelle *oohed* and *aahed* over the newest location of Blackbird Bakery.

"Thought you were going to propose there for a minute," Luca said, smiling into his soda.

Reed tugged at his hair. "Still haven't figured out the exact right way to do it yet. It has to be perfect. Perfect setting, perfect timing, perfect words, maybe perfect book quote. I keep brainstorming different proposals—"

Annabelle tugged Pearl over to them.

"So," Luca interrupted Reed, "like I mentioned, Ritchie had a hard time retrofitting the refrigerator, but he did a great job utilizing the space."

"Thank you," Reed mouthed over Pearl's head as he wrapped his arms around her.

"Thanks, boss," Ritchie said with a backslap after grabbing a beer.

"I think the sink is the coolest part," Olivia gushed, a sparkle in her eye. "The way that the cutting board slides on top for extra counter space, plus the little temperature knobs *match* the exterior. It's the most adorable sink I've ever seen."

Braden, Luca's youngest guy on the team, raised his gangly hand with a proud smile. "That was me. I did that," he said, with a little squeak in his voice.

Olivia clapped as she talked. "That is *so* impressive. How did you do the sink cover that gives her more counter space?"

He watched Braden stand a little taller as he explained how he'd seen a DIY video on social media and adapted it.

"You are *very* clever," Olivia said with a bright genuine smile, and the kid's whole face went crimson.

Luca's heart fucking melted at how kind she was.

Olivia grabbed a soda from behind him. "You've told him that, right?" she said, taking a sip.

"Yeah?" He shrugged. *No.* "I mean, I didn't say it the way you said it."

"Did you say: 'Hi, kid who invented a cool thing for my sister. Thanks for being you, and I can probably trust you with more responsibility'? Think about it." She shrugged and grabbed two sodas, giving one to Annabelle as they walked over to Pearl.

"No sugar this late in the day," he called after her as AB was already sipping from it mischievously.

"That sounds like a you problem, bro," Pearl called, high-fiving AB.

He let his eyes linger on the sway of Olivia's hips. How her thick, long hair bounced as she walked. *Dancing beams of sunset.*

He considered Olivia as Angie walked past him to grab a beer.

"Hey," he said to Angie.

"What?" Angie paused. "Man, what did I mess up this time? I told you I'll call the van company tomorrow to make sure they actually want that bright-ass yellow that makes their vans look like fuckin' highlighters with wheels."

God, was this how he came off to his employees? Always reminding them of shit?

"Thank you," he said, realizing it came out a little rusty when he was at work for some reason.

Angie squinted her eyes at him. "You feelin' okay? Oh my christ." Her hands went into her hair in genuine despair. "Are you dyin'?"

"No! No." He shook his head, cutting her off. "I know this has been a lot...and I appreciate you. You've done a really good job managing the move to Fairwick Falls." He gulped, making a last-minute decision. "And I thought you should have a shop key until we finish up so you don't have to wait for me in the morning if I'm running late." He handed the key to her.

Her eyebrows shot up, and she held the key as if it might bite her.

"Plus, we're only here for another week. Think of it as a trial run. See how you like it," Luca added.

She tipped up her beer and took a sip as she eyed him suspiciously. "This is weird. But I like it," she said gruffly and turned away to talk to the other guys.

"I'm gonna head out," Olivia said, walking up to him. "Her bag and lunch box are in your truck."

Luca picked Annabelle up, squeezing her. Annabelle pouted, looking at the Airstream. "You don't want to play bakery with me?"

Olivia smiled. "I think Reed said he wanted to play," she said loudly.

"Excuse me, miss!" Reed said, getting Annabelle's attention with a wave. "Did you say you wanted fourteen slices of unicorn pie?"

"Yeah!" Annabelle pushed away from Luca's chest, hopping down.

"Oh god. Is that when pie is made *from* unicorns?" Olivia asked Luca as an aside, just for the two of them. A deep belly laugh burst out of him.

His entire team stopped talking and stared at him. He glared at them and turned his back, not wanting to deal with the questioning looks.

Olivia looked over her shoulder at AB playing with Reed and then turned to face him. Her pretty sapphire eyes danced with humor.

It was the only color he was ever tempted to wear. He'd looked for shirts online, but none quite matched the shade that stared back at him.

He decided to change the subject. "Big plans this evening? Heard it's karaoke at the Thirsty Beaver."

He swallowed a smile as she laughed. God, he loved making her laugh. It made him feel fucking invincible.

Olivia clutched her stomach. "I will not be visiting Dave's fine establishment anytime soon. My plan is to curl up with a good book and try out Georgia's wood fireplace. *And* I remembered to buy wood at the store. I am so excited! It's been ages since I lived anywhere with a fireplace. I will see you tomorrow morning," she said, saluting him and saying goodbye to Annabelle.

He physically made himself turn away from her just so he wouldn't watch her ass elegantly walk out of his shop.

Oh god.

He *was* a bun head.

～

Two hours later, Luca and AB wound their way home through their neighborhood streets. Orange leaves drifted in front of his windshield, and Halloween decorations started to glow in the evening light.

"Know what you want to be for trick-or-treating," Luca said to AB in the back.

She shrugged. "Probably a glue stick."

He squinted. "The school supply?"

"Yeah. The purple kind. Or a light bulb." She said it so off-handedly that his sides hurt from holding in his laugh.

"Those are very unique ideas. You're really creative, Annabelle." Her eyes lit up, which he could see in his rearview mirror. He should have been saying this stuff to people this whole time, he realized.

Two blocks from their house, he saw red and blue flashes off in the distance. It looked like it was coming from their street.

His heart dropped when he saw a fire truck in front of Olivia's house.

Olivia. A desperate clawing fear scraped at this throat.

"What happened?" AB asked from the back.

Luca's eyes searched the scene as he drove up. The house wasn't on fire, but her front door and all the windows were open. He couldn't breathe until he could see her.

Finally, he spotted her talking to a firefighter on the side-walk, looking unharmed.

He let out a whooshing breath and slammed his truck into park. "Stay right here, okay?" he told Annabelle in the extended cab. "I need to go check on Olivia."

Locking the doors and keeping the truck running, he jogged across the street as the firefighter walked back to his truck.

Luca gathered her in a hug, needing to hold her. "You okay?"

"Yeah. A neighbor called 911 when I opened the front door to clear it out. Something is wrong with the flue, I guess."

"Let me go get Annabelle. We'll figure it out."

She'd been so excited for her fire, and she did so much for them. *And I love her so much.*

A few minutes later, he and AB grabbed a snack, and they came over with his tools.

AB touched all the gems hanging from the lamps in the hallway. "Are we gonna roast marshmallows?"

Luca unpacked his toolbox. "Don't touch those. We're just here to help for a minute. Olivia isn't working right now."

"I, for one, am Team Marshmallows," Olivia said with a wink at AB. "I have some if your dad is okay with it. Oh." Her face fell. "No sticks though."

He shined a flashlight up the chimney. *Aha.* The same screw that held the flue in place that he'd helped Georgia with last year needed to be screwed in again. "There's a maple tree with young shoots in our front yard. I can cut some sticks from it."

"Please," AB asked sweetly.

"We don't want to interrupt your night though," he said, peering at Olivia from inside the mantel.

"I will take all the time I can get with you two," Olivia said, staring directly at him, looking so earnest it made him ache.

Thirty minutes later, they sat on the pretty Persian rug roasting marshmallows over the fire Olivia had expertly built. He made sure to tell her that and not be an ass like he'd apparently been for almost thirty years, withholding compliments as if people didn't want to hear nice shit about themselves. His ego still smarted from how obvious Olivia's words had been at his shop hours ago.

AB insisted that Olivia roast her marshmallows, and she "helped" by holding the end of the stick, telling Olivia which way to turn it. Her teacher had used the word "bossy" to describe her in kindergarten last year, and he'd had to physically restrain Pearl as she yelled "leadership material" at the older woman.

The scent of woodsmoke felt homey as he bit into a gooey marshmallow. They talked about AB's day, and his day. How the festival dance rehearsals were going.

The glow on AB and Olivia's faces as they talked animatedly in the orange firelight painted a picture that got all twisted in his heart.

Like it belonged there forever.

Like he'd think about it on his deathbed as the moment he was the happiest he'd ever been.

AB's face was a mess after eating two marshmallows, and he grabbed a damp cloth to clean her up so she didn't get sticky hands all over Olivia and Georgia's stuff.

She spied a ballet barre in the sunroom off of the kitchen.

"Can I practice my ballet here?" AB squealed, hopped up on sugar.

"Sure, kid," Olivia said, running a hand over AB's hair. She pumped a tiny fist in the air.

He sat on the couch facing the fire, keeping an ear out for any chaos that might ensue once AB started dancing.

Olivia sat beside him, knees tucked under her chin, a steaming mug in her hands. A cozy quiet settled into the jewel-toned living room. Logs crackled and hissed as the fire danced in front of them.

She'd kept her pretty sage sweater on but had changed into comfy leggings, and her thick hair called to his hands. It looked like burnished rose gold in the firelight.

Olivia tucked her sleeves over her hands and cuddled up, facing him. "Thanks for your help." Luca slid down the couch and fought the urge to loop his arm around her. She looked cold, all tucked up. "You need a blanket?"

"Oh, uh, I'm okay. You give off a lot of heat." She smiled, swallowing as she stared at his lips.

Their shoulders touched on the couch as he kept tracing the lines of her face with his eyes.

Nice to see you again, freckles. Smile lines along those cheeks, it's been too long. Ah, cheekbones. I've missed you too. The glow of the firelight looks gorgeous on you.

The cinnamon nutmeg scent of her wafted toward him, and he lost the battle with his hands.

He swept a strand of hair from her face, needing any excuse to touch her. She leaned into the touch, her breath hitching.

Stroking along her temple, his hand lingered. *That velvet of her.*

The wanting inside him ached as he held himself back.

"'Livia, come see me spin," AB called and they both startled. She blinked, shaking her head to wake herself up. "Coming!"

"Maybe we should limit our alone time," he offered, as she popped up from the couch. "Even if we start on opposite sides of the room..."

"We end up together," she said with a chagrined laugh. She nodded and went to AB.

Burying his face in his hands, he ached for the day when he could finally just be settled and not fight the urge to do everything he'd ever dreamed of to that woman.

Chapter Twenty

OLIVIA

Olivia mentally marked her audition choreography to cheerful classical music in her headphones as the scent of maple cinnamon cookies filled the air.

She'd wanted to do something special for AB's snack duty at Girl Scouts later. She didn't trust her kitchen to not be cross-contaminated with wheat, so she'd let herself into Luca's house after a hard workout at the dance studio.

She'd buckled down all morning, getting her head on straight to focus on her audition materials, and then had come straight to his house without even showering so the cookies would be ready in time.

It had been so hard to say good night to him last night and not kiss him.

Being here in his house, surrounded by all the things that reminded her of him, was the next best thing.

She wanted another taste of his mouth. His hands in her hair.

Feeling his arms wrap around her briefly last night after the fire scare had made everything feel okay again.

But he's right to make sure we keep our distance.

It would just make everything hurt worse if they got closer.

I only have one shot to join a new company after being let go, and I can't get lost in beefy muscles.

Beefy, beefy muscles.

And the scent of manly pine and cedar.

Imagining his huge-ass hands tugging on my hair.

Burying my face against his chest as he takes care of me. And, oh shit!

The oven timer had been going off, and she hadn't noticed it over the music pounding in her headphones. She grabbed a batch of slightly burnt cookies from the oven.

She forced her daydreaming back to her audition, mentally doing her choreo as she placed cookie dough on a new baking sheet. She pictured nailing each step with each measure of music, feeling so proud.

She'd been a little lax about her normal Pilates workout the last few weeks, so she'd pushed herself extra hard this morning. She'd then put in another grueling, sweaty two hours rehearsing her three audition pieces.

After I put these in the oven, I'll run back home and get ready, then come back, pack them up, go teach the Mommy and Me class, pick up AB, drop her off at Girl Scouts, and then Luca will pick her up. And at the end of the day, she'd finally start sewing the ten leaf costumes she'd designed. Though that would be fun, not work.

She scooted the cookie sheet into the oven, "Dance of the Sugar Plum Fairy" blaring in her ears. She spun, imagining herself pirouetting, lost in the Tchaikovsky of it all. Sweeping strings, tightening her core for the big leap, and—

"Holy fuck!" she screamed at the man behind her.

Her hand flew to her chest. "Luca!" She yanked off her headphones, gasping for air.

He looked equally surprised to see her. He stood frozen in

the back door, bare-chested and holding a paint-stained work shirt in his hand.

The beefy muscles she'd dreamed about were on full display. Dark ink wound across his muscular chest. A healthy layer of softness laid over his muscles that made him perfect for cuddling with and softened the definition of his muscles. Her pussy pulsed at how they gave way to a muscular thickness in his middle. Like he had abs that could pull a Chevy, but he'd never turn down a piece of pie. She liked that it dipped just a little over the band of his jeans.

Sturdy. Sexily sturdy. *Perfect for riding.*

"Hi?" he said slowly, meaning: *Why are you alone half-naked in my house in the middle of the day?*

She stood barefoot in a sports bra and yoga pants. *Whoops.* She'd been so hot from her workout and with the oven going that she hadn't bothered to put a sweatshirt on.

She busied herself cleaning up the counter, not meeting his eyes. "It's AB's turn for Girl Scout snacks. She asked if we could bring homemade cookies because everybody else did, and my kitchen has cross-contamination. I begged Pearl for the recipe AB loves most and..." She gestured to the mess in front of her. "You get the gist."

He looked rugged and roughed up from working that morning. His cheeks were pink from the cold, and he looked like he'd worked hard.

She liked it.

"Just came home to take a shower before a meeting later. Didn't mean to startle you," he said, cautiously.

"Sorry, I should've let you know I was here," she said, embarrassed.

"You're welcome here any time." His voice was rough as he stood at the end of the counter.

She finally met his eyes.

Tortured eyes full of wanting heated her from head to toe. A half smile tugged at his lips. "I like seeing you here," he added softly.

Oof. She felt that in her breastbone. That longing in his voice.

It feels like mine.

Her heart slammed against her ribs as she felt the crackling in the air between them.

His chest rose and fell harder the longer he looked at her. The pull between them was making her lightheaded, needy. That familiar ache between her thighs pulsed, and she stared at his mouth, biting her lip as she remembered what it tasted like.

He gulped and wiped his mouth. "Gonna grab some water, if I can reach past you."

Her cheeks lit on fire. *Right, fuck, he just wanted a water glass and I am standing right in front of it. He's not staring at* me.

A thick, muscular forearm passed her face to grab a glass from the cabinet as she swiped crumbs from the counter. The smell of him wrapped around her and turned the aching in her pussy to greedy need. She gulped every bit of the spice and musk of him down, grateful it was stronger with him shirtless. Hard nipples pressed against her sports bra in response.

Her cheeks heated in embarrassment as she realized how gross she was, inches from him. Her sports bra and yoga pants had been soaked through with sweat during practice. "Probably shouldn't stand too close. I'm gross and sweaty." She moved the cookies from the cooling rack onto a plate.

"Smells good," he said in a low, rough voice, still over her shoulder.

Goosebumps covered her arms at the nearness of him. She didn't want him to go.

"Maple cinnamon sugar," she whispered roughly as she

plated the last cookie. The last one crumbled in her shaking hands.

The raging heat coming off his chest radiated against her back like a warm sunbeam. She closed her eyes, digging for the strength to not press back into him.

"Not the cookies, Liv," he said between ragged breaths. A heavy, huge hand settled on her hip, and she sighed in relief. Fingers dug into her hip. "*You* smell good."

It had come out as a growl—possessive, low. He turned her to face him, and she was overwhelmed at the expanse of muscle in front of her.

At not burying her face into his chest and licking every inch.

"But I'm..." *Sweaty. I need a shower.*

"I know." His head tilted and an appraising look in his eyes, he stared hungrily, as if deciding where to take his first bite. "Didn't think it was possible to want you more than yesterday... but I do. Like this."

His eyes caught on her nipples, and he blinked before looking away.

Her pulse hammered in her ears. "You can look. I..." She sucked in a breath. "I...want you to look."

His jaw worked like he was holding himself back as he openly stared at the hard nipples poking against her sports bra. Staring at her breasts, he bit his bottom lip, then licked it.

Her clit pulsed at the brazen *want* on his face, at how his chest heaved and the hand on her hip dug in harder.

Which only made her nipples harder.

A thick outline pushed against his zipper as he studied every inch of her hips and thighs, breasts and abs.

She sighed, imagining it in her hands, her mouth.

Her pussy.

He drifted closer. His nose came close enough to brush her cheekbone.

They both gasped out a sigh at the contact. The featherlight touch spiraled need into her every *fuck-me* nerve ending.

His nose caressed a path along her jaw, brushing down her neck.

He kissed the spot where her shoulder met her neck, and a small flick of his tongue made him growl out a moan. She curved into him, wanting more.

His hand framed her jaw. "Turns out, I prefer you this way. Covered in sweat." They shared the same ragged breath back and forth, mouths an inch from each other. "Smelling like home —that I want to bend over and fuck."

She gasped as arousal flooded her thong.

Luca's nostrils flared. "Fuck it—"

Their open mouths met in gasping, clutching, messy kisses. He grabbed her ass and pressed her against him as she wrapped her arms around him.

More, more, more was the only thought that thrummed through her as she moved against him.

Closer.

Not enough. Grasping, desperate kisses deepened, and deepened more.

His tongue swiped against hers, and it reverberated into her core. She needed to touch him, feel every part of him.

She slid her hands to feel the hard cord of muscles around his back. She licked his chest, needing to press against him, taste him.

Need him closer, all around me.

He lifted her up to pull her closer, and she wrapped her legs around him.

Her pussy pulsed, grasping at nothing, begging for attention. Begging for anything he'd give her. *Tongue, finger, cock. Anything, please.*

He was carrying her somewhere. *The bed, hopefully?* She'd die if she couldn't keep doing whatever this was.

He sat on the couch, and loud electronic music from a toy made them both jump. He leaned up, taking her with him as he pulled the toy out from under him and tossed it across the room. A too-loud digital voice sang, "I'm a little tea pot." They both huffed out a laugh before they continued devouring each other.

His hand clutched the back of her neck, fingers threaded in her hair, holding her in place. *Want to stay right here forever.*

Warm, soft muscles flexed under her hands as she clutched at him. The only thing she needed from the next ten minutes was his tongue in her mouth, pulling needy, desperate kisses out of her.

His hand slid to her breast, palming it hard from the top, possessively. A firm thumb stroked against her nipple, up and down. Then harder, up and down again.

"Yes," she gasped.

He groaned into her skin.

He licked a path between her breasts. "Fuck, you taste so good, Liv."

She bit back a moan as she rolled her hips more slowly, enjoying the slippery feeling against her clit. Her panties were soaked through.

He whimpered as she rolled against his cock.

The warmth of his tongue was unraveling her. He licked between her breasts again and again, worshiping her as she ground against him.

He inhaled as he traced the curve of her cleavage. "I think about how good you smell in my dreams." He rubbed the scruff of his beard against her breast that was now spilling out of her bra. "I feel like an animal." He nipped against her skin. "But it's just you. You do this to me."

Huge fingers dug into her ass suddenly, rocking her clit against him hard. She moaned so loudly, she gasped and slammed her mouth shut, seeing if he'd judge her. If it gave him the ick like it had given her boyfriend years ago.

A cat-like smile pulled at his lips as he paused, panting up at her. "Why'd you stop?"

Shame crept up inside her. "You don't mind? I...I'm loud sometimes."

With molten eyes, he rolled her hips against his cock again and smiled as she moaned.

"Louder, Liv." He shoved her ass down and rocked her against him again.

"Yes," she screamed in short, needy bursts. The shields guarding her lust crumbled, and carnal, feral energy coursed through her. She finally didn't have to hold back.

"Perfect," he gritted out through a clenched jaw as they moved, grinding against each other. "I bet you can be louder though, can't you?"

She threw her head back, overwhelmed with how good he felt under her. How good her hands felt on his chest, in his hair.

He thrust up with each grind against her, and her moans turned into long, needy screams.

"That's it. Let go, Liv. Louder."

She gripped the couch on either side of him, riding him harder and harder as she screamed *yes* into his neck, feeling wet and sweaty and carnal.

And perfect.

"Fuck, I bet your panties are soaked." He groaned against her as he slammed her up and down. She wanted to show him what he did to her.

She pulled back. His eyes darted to her bright leggings against his jeans.

Biting his lip, his thumb stroked an outline of the dark, wet arousal that had seeped through. "Never…" He gasped. "Never seen anything hotter."

It was so hot that he wanted her just as she was. Not pristine and perfumed but the most feral, animal part of her.

She shoved her hand into her panties, and his eyes widened with fire. Slick wetness dripped from two fingers as she pulled them out.

As she was about to lick a finger to tease him, he grabbed her hand, letting out a growl. "Mine."

He brought her fingers to his lips with a tortured ragged inhale, eyes closed as if overwhelmed. Then he greedily licked and sucked every bit from her fingers, whimpering as he breathed through it.

New kink unlocked: a man who whimpers for it.

Grinding her teeth with need, she rocked against his hard cock. Pleasure pulsed through her with every stroke.

He angled her with both hands so just her clit touched his jeans. "Can you come like this?"

"Yes," she gasped as he moved her against him. She kissed him, tasting hints of herself on his tongue.

"Then use me," he ordered, yanking the front of her bra down so her tits spilled out. He licked her breast, and they both buckled when he sucked, his tongue swiping around and around the nipple in his mouth.

She grabbed the edge of the couch above his head with two hands.

The heated friction on her clit was too good as she moved and humped her clit against his cock, taking and taking and taking, not caring what she looked like. He sucked one nipple, then the other, moaning with each of her screams.

"Louder, Liv," he gasped. "Use me as hard as you want. Show me how you come. Please."

"Fuck," she gasped against his mouth, lost in how her inhibitions were gone, how she moved and craved as she fucked her clit against his cock.

"Doing so good, Liv. Just like that, take what you need." He panted, moving her against him.

Moans turned to screams of his name as she found it.

Just.

The.

Right.

Place.

"Gonna—" she gasped.

"That's it—"

"Luca—Luca—"

Too good.

"Loud as you want, Liv. Give it all to me." His hands on her ass made her fuck him harder and harder.

They thrust faster and faster—fucking mindlessly like animals against each other, finally giving in to grunts and screams and moans, lost in the consuming pleasure of fucking as fast as they could against each other in primal, dirty, needy sweat.

Until the pleasure was too much. Too high.

She screamed, "Fuck me," again and again and again in a high, needy, whining pitch as every muscle constricted in just the right spot, tighter and tighter, the *wanting* of it twisting her body.

Pleasure burst through her with a shattering, guttural scream of *yes* as he fucked up against her body that was frozen in ecstasy, prolonging it with each stroke. *Yes and yes and yes* ripped through her as he stroked her clit.

Moaning, biting her shoulder, he came with a shuddering, needy grunt, pulsing once, twice, then a final, longer time as she moved with him, wringing every last drop.

They stilled, and Olivia's heart hammered as she gasped for breath.

Heartbeats, gasps for air, and no thoughts.

I just...

That was...

Aftershocks of the orgasm shuddered through her.

His hands slid to her waist, hugging her tight against him as he sat up.

She wrapped her hands around his head, cuddling it as he kissed his bite marks.

She could *hear* her plans trying to fit themselves into a world where this could work.

I could just see him every few weeks. Or they could drive to me sometimes. Maybe I can limit my search to a six-hour radius from here.

He squeezed her tighter, enveloping her against his bare chest. A warm blanket of safety and oxytocin covered her as his big hands splayed on her thigh and head.

He angled her for a kiss. No embarrassment at having humped each other on a couch like teenagers. No pulling away.

"You." His jaw worked as his kiss-stung lips and lust-drunk eyes took her in. "You're perfect."

She snort-laughed against his lips at the thought of her being perfect right now.

"Don't you laugh adorably at me." He pulled at her bottom lip, and then he gently rolled her sports bra back up.

She smirked. "No, I get the appeal. A sweaty, poor, unemployed dancer who burns cookies dry-humping you is pretty perfect." She laughed at herself.

"Hey," he said sternly, all traces of joking now gone from his face. "That's the woman I—" He pulled back, gulped. "...That's the woman I have a crush on that you're talking about."

He shook his head slowly, his expression serious as he held

her. "Save your self-deprecation for other people, Olivia. I won't allow it in this house."

The world tilted off-kilter. Her brain slowly rewired itself into understanding that he was *serious*.

He's protecting me...from me?

After a lifetime of "corrections" at work and school, this aggressive positivity about herself was, uh...new.

I think I like it.

He bit his lip, his brows furrowing. "Okay?"

With a hesitant smile on her lips, she kissed him. They melted into each other, licking into a deeper kiss and letting out an exhale of need against each other.

The oven timer beeped, and she pulled away. "Okay, *sir*." She saluted him with a wink as she pushed off his lap. Hungry eyes went to the crotch of her bright yoga pants that were now dark with her arousal.

She pulled the not-burnt cookies out of the oven.

She noticed there wasn't any *not doing that again*s or *shouldn't*s about what had just happened coming from the couch.

Doesn't seem like the time for a "what are we" conversation. Just take the win.

Maybe we could be neighbors with benefits. Just get it out of our systems.

She moved the cookies to the cooling rack. *I know how you feel, molten hot cookies. I too was exploding from a hot-ass hunk of steel recently.*

"Your car is finally ready. It's outside and AB's booster seat is installed in the back." He placed her keys on the countertop.

He grabbed his shirt from the kitchen floor and kissed her slowly over her shoulder.

"What's the final total I owe you?" she asked.

He grabbed a hot cookie from the rack, not reacting to the heat. "Nothing. It's a perk of being AB's nanny."

Absolutely not. "Luca—"

He shrugged defensively. "I don't make the rules. AB negotiated your benefits package." He smiled as he chewed, his eyes dancing with warmth until he saw the oven clock. "Shit, need to hop in the shower. Client meeting's in twenty minutes."

She hugged him hard. "I have to run next door and take a shower too, but lock up. I can grab these after they cool."

"I'd invite you to join me," he said, placing another quick kiss on her lips. "But I don't think I'd make it to the meeting on time." He squeezed her hip and then walked to the stairs with a wink.

She watched until his feet disappeared upstairs to let out the That Was the Hottest Thing That's Happened in My Whole Fucking Life dance coursing through her body.

Happy vibrations twisted through her muscles and nerve endings, and she cracked her neck. It was like she'd gotten a chiropractor reset, massage, and her chakras blown wide open all at the same time.

She grabbed her car keys to Baby and considered what had happened on the couch as she started toward the back door.

She bit her bottom lip, remembering all the things he'd said. Everything he liked about her, like her sweaty scent and her taste. How he'd dreamed about her.

An incredibly naughty idea popped into her head.

I should at least leave him a thank-you present, right?

Grabbing a post-it note, she scribbled a heart and an O on it. Shimmying out of her yoga pants, she tugged off her panties, thoroughly wrecked from Luca having had his way with her. Tugging her pants back on, she walked to the bottom of the stairs.

And left her panties and the post-it where he wouldn't miss it.

* * *

> **OLIVIA**
> Good evening

LUCA
Liv

Are you trying to kill me

> **OLIVIA**
> I see you found my present

LUCA
I was 10 min late to my client meeting.

> **OLIVIA**
> Why??

LUCA
Because I had to...

Well you know.

> **OLIVIA**
> Hmmmm...I don't.
>
> Mind spelling it out for me?

LUCA
Troublemaker

Fine.

I stood on the stairs in my best business-owner clothes fucking my hand to how good you smell. Like an animal.

Lasted a grand total of 2 minutes.

Happy now?

OLIVIA

Very.

What'd you do with the other 8 minutes?

....

Come onnnn….don't leave me on read.

Tell me.

LUCA

Change my fucking clothes, Liv.

You made a mess of me and you weren't even there.

Chapter Twenty-one

LUCA

Luca wrapped AB in her unicorn towel as she chattered about her day. She still liked being carried to bed, and he probably could count on one hand the number of months he had left before she was way too cool for him. He bundled her up in the oversized towel and carried her to bed.

She'd been chattering about the festival nonstop. It was only a few weeks away. "Today we learned rell-a-vay for our dance routine. And then 'Livia and I—"

"Get your pj's on." He set her down, and she ran to pick out her pajamas. She was adamant that she should choose her own clothes now.

"When we got home we practiced our ballet moves and then played Ballet Princesses."

Luca picked up in AB's room as she wrestled herself into her pj's and tried not to think too much about Olivia. How sweet she was with AB, how sexy she'd been yesterday on his couch. How her eyes had sparkled when he'd come home. *Shit, now I'm thinking too much about her.*

"Our princesses did ballet, *but* we had to escape the bad

guys who wanted our magic ballet shoes. We scattered bad guy juice so they'd slip on it."

"Some smart princesses," he said, untucking her covers.

AB looked exasperated, hands on her hips. "Dad, all princesses need to be smart. They run countries, for crappin' out loud."

He swallowed a smile and almost lost his battle to keep from bursting out laughing. "Sounds like you had fun with Olivia."

"Can she live here?" AB said nonchalantly, climbing into bed.

Well, fuck.

I feel you, kid.

He'd explained this to her at least three times, but AB was as stubborn as he was.

He grabbed Platypus and tucked it under the covers next to her. She couldn't sleep without it.

"What book do you want to read tonight? Want to try a big kid book? Maybe *Little Women* or *Anne of Green Gables*?" Pearl and Reed had made him swear on his life to read them to Annabelle this year.

"They're boring. They don't have any pictures," she said, snuggling and pouting back into her bed. "Ballet Bunnies."

Shocker, he could probably recite it by now.

"She can stay in AP's old room, or we can get bunk beds," AB offered.

"Remember, goob, it's just temporary. She has to leave after Christmas for her new job." He rifled through the stack of books on the floor beside her bed.

"Why does Olivia have to leave?"

He'd explained it already. More redirection, perhaps? Maybe it was finally time to share his plans with her. They hadn't been secret, but he'd wanted to wait until everything was locked down.

"I have some good news—"

Her face lit up.

"—about my shop."

Her face fell back into a pout.

"I'm moving it down the street. No more long drives."

Her brow furrowed in confusion. *Maybe she doesn't understand.*

"I can go to all your school stuff soon, take you to Girl Scouts. Once I get everything moved, I'll be around a lot more and it'll just be you and me."

His exciting announcement was met with less fanfare than he'd hoped.

AB stared at Platypus. It had a missing eyeball and only half of its tail. She picked at the other eyeball silently.

"Hey," he said, pushing her wet hair out of her face. "What's going on in there?" He bent down to catch her eyes, which were welling up with tears.

"I don't want it to change again." Her voice broke.

It always broke a piece of his heart off when that happened. "You don't want it to just be the two of us?"

She shrugged her shoulders up to her ears, still fiddling with Platypus. Finally: "I want a mom story," she whined.

Ah. It was one of those nights.

Every few weeks, AB would get mom-sick. That's what he called it. Usually after she spent time with her friends and saw their moms do mom stuff.

Despite reading family blogs and every feminist Instagram account Pearl sent him, it always felt like he was playing catch-up on how to do "girl stuff."

He settled against her headboard and pulled her into his lap. She needed some cuddling tonight.

"Your mom had the prettiest hair." He decided to trot out an old favorite because he knew it comforted her. "I decided that I would be a jerk as a kid. Her hair—"

"Looked like spilled sunshine," she said quietly, finishing his sentence against his chest.

"That's right." He cuddled her close and she snuggled in, holding the platypus like he held her.

He told the familiar story of how he'd teased her mom for her long, bright blonde hair in high school because he didn't know how else to say he liked her.

She'd shown up one day with her hair chopped short and dyed bright pink. He'd felt terrible that she thought she needed to change anything about her. He'd admitted she was absolutely perfect just the way she was. And much to his surprise—that part always made AB giggle because she knew it was coming—Marcy had pulled off the pink bob wig on her head, and her golden hair cascaded down her shoulders.

"She was sassy like—"

"—like me," AB finished quietly with a smile.

He kissed the top of her head and just nodded. AB had only been a year old when Marcy had died in a car accident. He wanted to give her as many memories as possible of the funny, sassy woman she'd never know. "And she loved you so much. Every second of every day."

"The other Girl Scouts do cool stuff with their hair," AB said, getting sleepy against his chest. "Sophie's mom had a whale tail."

Luca startled. That was slang for something that had *nothing* to do with hair when he was a kid.

I'll figure it out. "Want me to do your hair like, uh, a whale tail on Saturday?" She had a big Girl Scout event at a campsite nearby.

"I just wanna be like them." She sighed.

He understood. She wanted what she'd never had.

Frankly, he could sympathize. He wanted a partner in all this perfect chaos. *He* also wanted a mom who cared about him. Hell, *any* dad.

Without further comment, he pulled up the ballet book and read it front to back. Her little breaths were heavy and even against him by the time he got to the end of the book.

He gently tucked AB under the covers with Platypus and turned on her night light.

He closed the door and pulled up his phone to google "hair whale tale."

Oh fuck. He almost threw his phone down at the images that popped up. They were *not* about braids.

The warm glow of Olivia's house called to him, and he decided not to fight what felt so good. He'd ask her for guidance.

He'd been so caught up in her body, her smell, finally being able to be a man around her and not a dad or business owner. They could just be two horny people who needed to scratch an itch.

But...his itch still needed to be scratched. He'd hoped that his instincts had been wrong when he first saw her and that their overwhelming attraction would fade.

It seemed to be backfiring as he sighed at a scrunchie she'd left on the kitchen table. He picked it up, inhaled the scent of it like a caveman, and wrapped the silk around his wrist as he texted her.

LUCA

Do you know how to do a whale tail?

OLIVIA

....Exqueeze me?

LUCA

The braid

OLIVIA

So, not wearing a thong above my low rise jeans like it's 2005?

LUCA

Oh, god. No. It's a braid. AB talked about it.

OLIVIA

Ummmmm. Never heard of it.

Whale tail??

OH

FISH TAIL! 😂

She sent him a photo of a braid that looked incredibly complicated, like if two braids had a baby.

LUCA

Yeah, that, probably.

Could you teach me? AB said that she wants to have it for Girl Scouts.

OLIVIA

I will happily show you how to make a whale tail. 🫠

Not going to think about that right now. What Olivia's perfect round ass would look like in the thong she'd left for him.

...That was now in an undisclosed hidden location away from nosy eyes in the house.

Something else weighed on him. AB missing the mom experience was normal, but it seemed to come up more often in the last month or two.

LUCA

Thx

Has AB talked to you about her mom?

OLIVIA

No, it hasn't come up.

Is something wrong?

He thought about telling her that AB had asked if she could stay, but he would never want her to feel guilty about living her dreams. Or like he was using his kid to get what he wanted.

LUCA

She misses her. It comes up sometimes. Especially around Marcy's birthday.

I never want her to forget her, you know?

OLIVIA

Of course not.

AB is the sweetest girl.

Olivia's curtains were open in her dining room, and she walked through in her oversized pajamas with a bowl of something.

A guttural aching at seeing her so cozy hit his stomach.

What kind of mom would Olivia be someday? Did she even want kids? She was great with AB and seemed to have fun with other kids at dance class.

Do you have plans to be a mom someday? he typed out.

Oh, fuck, no, that's a terrible idea—and erased it. *Too much, too soon. Especially because things are in a weird limbo state with us.*

Do you want kids? he typed out.

Shit. Erased.

He stared at his phone, trying to figure out how to phrase: *If by the slim chance of a possibility we end up together in a more permanent situationship, would you want more kids? Would you be okay being a stepmom?*

Olivia's contact filled his screen with an incoming phone call.

He answered it immediately and saw her staring at him from the dining room.

"Creeper," he said with a slow rumble of laughter.

"Seemed faster than waiting four to five business days for you to write whatever you were going to write."

He laughed and bit his lip.

"Everything okay with you?" she said, her pretty eyes clearly filled with worry, visible even from fifteen feet away.

"I like your pajamas," he said.

She was in an oversized sweatshirt and flannel pajamas that looked about three sizes too big for her.

She struck a silly pose. "My lingerie that lures men into my boudoir?"

He laughed. *So fucking cute.*

"So what did you try to ask me four times?" she said, quirking a smile.

I could stare at her lips all. Day. Long.

"What?" she said, looking behind her.

"I just like the way your mouth moves when you talk."

"Lucky for you I talk a lot. Are you wearing my scrunchie on your wrist?" She squinted at him through the windows.

Fuck. He pulled it off and tossed it. "I...thought it was AB's."

"Everything okay with her?"

He nodded. "It just made me realize I don't know what you want in the future."

She leaned on the window frame across from him, smiling wistfully. "Hmm...a pony. World peace. Universal healthcare."

"Okay, good. Simple." He smiled.

"Oh, and nine more leaf costumes made by tomorrow. If you could be so kind."

"*That* seems like a hard ask," he said, leaning against the windowsill too. They smiled like goofballs at one another, giggling.

"What I want…?" she asked, like she needed more information.

"Like, in the future. Your dreams with somebody. Not me, I mean," he added quickly. "But just…someday. When you've achieved everything you want, or when the time seems right, or when you find the right person."

"I'm gonna need a grocery cart for all those caveats." She sighed, staring at him. "I never pictured a specific life for myself. Being in survival mode for fifteen years made it hard to think beyond the end of the month. I just wanted security, and I figured it would all work out once I was successful. You?"

Well, shit. He hadn't expected her to turn the question around on him.

"Liv," he sighed, locking eyes with her and fighting himself. "I can't answer that."

That was as close to the truth as he could get.

"You know," she said with enough sass in her voice to make him smile, "people think it's the short women who are cowards. With the way people talk about women needing protection and 'women and children first' thing on lifeboats, but nooooo." She swiped a hand in the air, emphasizing her point. "It's the big *strong men* when asked a hard question who just turn into giant pus—"

"Fine," he laughed at her pushing, and she laughed with him.

Yes, made her laugh today.

"I can answer." His heart hammered in his throat. "But you're not gonna like it."

Her eyes locked with his, already looking like she knew his answer with her scrunched eyebrows full of concern.

"I want a future where I come home and see..."—*you*—"... my favorite person. Wearing her comfy clothes. Safe and warm in my house where there's no yelling." His voice caught. He'd never said it out loud before. "Where she loves my family as much as I do, and can catch some things I drop. Because I'm only human."

He worried his lip as he pictured her on his couch, in his kitchen, in his bed. How she made everything brighter, happier, because she was there just being herself. The miraculous thought of waking up to her beautiful face every morning. "Where all the simple things seem...magnificent. Because I'm with her."

His eyes misted over thinking of the heart-aching beauty of doing dishes with her. Cleaning up after he'd have cooked her favorite meal, washing pretty dishes they'd have bought together. Lights and water on without worry they'd be shut off.

Soapy dishes as the final result of a hundred happy memories.

"We'd scrub plates from her favorite home goods store. She'd wear those yellow rubber gloves to protect her pretty nails. I'd tease her for it but deep down, I'd love it." His lip trembled but he kept going. "She'd make me laugh ten times. I'd make her laugh once and that would be enough, hopefully. Going to sleep would be the best part of every day because I could hold her against me, safe, all night. My cheek against her silky, long hair. And then in the morning?" He shrugged, fighting tears. "We'd get to do it all over again." His voice caught as a tear track shone on her cheek. "Best day ever," he whispered through the longing clogging his throat.

"She'd need to be pretty special," Olivia said, wiping a tear away quickly.

He nodded, a lump in his throat as he stared at her. "She is."

Her lips twisted with emotion as she blinked fast, looking away and sucking in a breath. "I can, um, come over on Saturday," she said in a too-bright voice, hiding her emotions. "For the hair thing."

"Right." He nodded, wiping a hand down his face and swiping at his eyes. "The whale tail."

Her laugh was watery. "Yeah. I'll see you in the morning."

He waved. "Night."

She flipped off her lights in her dining room, and he did the same.

But he found himself still standing there in the dark thirty minutes later, staring at a picture of dish gloves on his phone with teary eyes for reasons he still didn't understand.

Chapter Twenty-Two

OLIVIA

Two days later, Olivia, her mother, Luca, AB, and Sophie all sat toiling away in Luca's kitchen.

The smell of fresh-cut herbs and simmering broth from Luca's soup wafted toward Olivia as she fought with pinning orange felt fabric.

"Whose stupid idea was it to make giant leaf costumes?" she muttered.

"Yours, dear," her mother said, pins between her pursed lips.

They sat working on costumes while Luca attempted for the third time to braid Olivia's hair.

They'd tried to braid AB's hair, but she couldn't sit still long enough. It was too complicated to explain without seeing what he was doing, so her mother coached Luca while she focused on costumes and sitting still.

The delicious feeling of his fingers running through her hair was a happy byproduct. Given his busy schedule, her busy schedule, and a very nosy six-year-old, they hadn't had any more alone time since their couch run-in. A few sneaky kisses here and there, but spending time with Luca had largely been a looking-only activity.

After another mangled try at a fishtail braid, he brushed out Olivia's hair.

"Maybe try number four will work," her mom said, patting Luca's arm and then staring at it. "What do you do, lift those cars you work on?"

Olivia rolled her eyes. Her mom was as subtle as a car horn. "Mother, I can see you in the window. Stop squeezing his arms."

"What! He's a handsome, strapping young man."

Luca rumbled out a laugh as he ran his fingers over Olivia's crown, gathering two sections of hair.

"Now, gather just a little bit..." Her mother said, coaching him. "That's it, not too big. Now fold that one over the top...and again...good job."

Luca sighed, sounding like he was relieved. "Thanks, Mrs. Maroo-Canon."

"Oh, call me Martha," she said, waving her hand and picking up pieces to pin together for Olivia.

One costume down, nine to go. Olivia had rigged up a series of suspenders and small hula hoops that would give the leaf costumes a big, adorably comical shape without being too heavy for the little girls.

"Now." Her mother looked at Sophie and AB, sitting down at the table across from them. "How are those bats coming?"

They giggled, poking plastic wings into black styrofoam balls. Olivia had decided it was time to decorate for Halloween, and AB's play date was as good a time as any to do it.

Olivia sent her mother silent *do not get attached* mental signals. Her mom had never been a 'when am I going to be a grandmother' type, but astronauts could see from *space* how much she enjoyed spending time with AB and Sophie.

"I made three." Sophie held them up.

"Great job, Soph!" Olivia smiled.

"We're going to go outside and play," AB said unceremoniously. They ran off giggling.

"Shoot, I need to lock the back gate if they'll be out there. Give me five." Luca jogged after them to the back porch.

Olivia sighed wistfully. *God, he's so good at this. Making soup, keeping everyone safe. Looking so fucking hot in that tight long-sleeve shirt.*

Her mother turned slowly to Olivia with a knowing smile.

"Wipe that smile off your face." Olivia narrowed her eyes.

Her mom threaded two more pins into the fabric with a placid look. "So! How long have you been sleeping together?"

"Mother!" Olivia's eyes darted to the door to see if any of them had come back in.

Her mom's wizened face was full of mischief. "Am I wrong?"

"I don't wanna talk about it with my mom, *eughh*." Olivia shuddered.

"You're both grown-ups. He's delicious." She peered over her rhinestone glasses. "Frankly, you'd be a fool not to."

Olivia sighed, finishing the last pin on the side of the leaf costume. "Two weeks." Olivia sighed again. "Just making out. Mostly."

"Ooh," her mother said with a smile, wiggling in her seat. "He seems like a very nice young man. Who can really fill out a pair of jeans."

Luca came through the sliding glass doors looking confused. "They're playing 'ghost princesses'...?"

"Ah, my fault." Olivia raised her hand. "AB and I watched a ballet of *Giselle* online after school. There are...a lot of ghosts." She grimaced. Was that the kind of thing she should have told him? Or *shit*, not done at all?

"Metal," he said with an approving nod.

Her mother smiled wickedly at Olivia. "So—"

Olivia sent her mother a warning look. *Troublemaker.*

"—do you have your auditions lined up?"

Olivia sighed at the small mercy of her mother behaving herself for once. "There are open auditions at Dayton, American Rep, American Midwest, and the Mendocino Ballet."

"Ooh, Dayton could be nice."

Olivia sighed, not wanting to get anyone's hopes up. "I'm working on my audition tape to submit in a few weeks."

Her mother finished pinning the second leaf costume and handed it to Olivia to sew. A beep sounded from the oven, and Luca paused to pull out a loaf of homemade, gluten-free bread he'd proofed earlier in the day.

This all felt so fucking...good? So domestic?

She wouldn't have this in Dayton. Or anywhere else, for that matter.

Her mom stretched. "All right, young man. Show me you know how to fishtail on your own."

The pleasure cascading down her scalp as Luca ran his fingers through her hair was practically obscene. He combed out her hair to start all over again.

"Heard anything from your old coworkers?" her mom asked her.

Olivia shrugged. "A couple friends are in Pittsburgh now. I'm going to see their *Nutcracker* performances in a few weeks."

"That could be fun," Luca said offhandedly as he gently separated her hair into three sections.

Her brow arched in surprise as she tried to turn around, but he held her head in place. "You'd go see the ballet?"

She saw him shrug in the reflection on the sliding glass door as if it was no big deal. "It has candy in it, right? AB would like it."

"That was always my favorite part too," her mother said with a generous smile at Luca.

"Yep, and then you....exactly." Her mother nodded approvingly as he braided Olivia's hair. "Oh, that looks quite nice."

"I want to see," Olivia said as her hair was being gently tugged into place.

"Hold still." Her mother swatted her and turned her megawatt 'I'm an adorable old lady' smile onto Luca. "You and Annabelle should come by for dinner next week. Wells is coming home; Herbert is cooking. We'd love to have you over."

She wondered how much her mother knew about Wells's business investment. Probably nothing, otherwise she'd have heard her mother's lecture at him from three miles away by now.

The end of Olivia's hair was tugged as Luca wrapped it in an elastic band. "Ta-da!"

She used a mirror to see the back of her head with her phone. He'd made a French fishtail braid that looked pretty damn good. "Impressive, Bishop."

"And I cook," he said with a slow smile as he went to stir the soup.

Olivia ran the edge of the costume through the sewing machine that she'd brought over from her house, turning it right side out to see the finished product.

The effect was pretty good. She ran the half hula hoop through each side and swung the sliding glass door open.

"Annabelle, come try on your costume."

The girls both ran inside, carrying the scent of campfire smoke in with them as people had started to burn wood fires in the afternoon.

Olivia's phone pinged.

PEARL

Are you home? I keep knocking.

OLIVIA

At Luca's

Shit, shit, shit. She hadn't realized it was so late. She'd wanted to talk to Luca about her idea before Pearl got here.

Meet me at the back door.

Pearl walked up the back steps with a tray of cupcakes topped with thick purple frosting.

Oh god, maybe this is a terrible idea. Maybe I'm overstepping.

Luca saying he never wanted Annabelle to forget her mom had stuck with Olivia. She'd wanted to do something special for them, to ease his worries in some way.

So, Olivia had put in an order with Pearl for a dozen AB-friendly cupcakes in memory of Marcy's birthday. She held a little 'happy birthday' plastic cupcake topper to stick on top.

She opened the back door quietly and snuck out onto the back steps. "Thank you *so* much," Olivia said, looking at the pretty cupcakes.

Pearl suddenly wrapped Olivia in a hard, crushing hug.

"Whoa." Olivia chuckled as she hugged Pearl back.

"Yeah. I'm a fuckin' hugger now," Pearl grumbled. She wiped her eyes as she pulled away. "Fucking love of my life turning me into a fucking mush."

Pearl shrugged her shoulders, crinkling her leather jacket, trying to brush off any emotion. "Marcy was one of my best friends, so, you know. Thanks. This was a good idea." She handed Olivia the cupcakes.

"Let's hope Luca agrees." Butterflies pirouetted artfully in Olivia's ribcage.

They walked back in as Olivia called for Luca. "Can you meet me in the laundry room?"

"You're in trouble," Annabelle teased him from the kitchen.

"Hey, you," he said with surprise as Pearl walked past him.

"What's all this?" Luca pointed to the cupcakes.

Oh, shit. How do I even start?

"I, uh...wanted to honor Marcy's birthday," Olivia said, bluntly.

His eyebrows shot up in surprise.

Oh no, this is weird. Shit. Too late now. "You were worried about AB forgetting her and I wanted to do something nice to remember her. I mean, she made AB, after all, and you loved her. She was one of Pearl's best friends. She deserves to be remembered. I told Pearl to do it in her favorite color. So, uh, these are happy birthday cupcakes for her." Olivia bit her lip, smiling worriedly, and lifted the tray of purple cupcakes.

Luca's jaw dropped, and he ran a hand over his beard, looking thunderstruck.

"Is this okay? I'm sorry if I'm overstepping."

Luca took the tray from her and set it on the dryer. He pulled her into a hard hug.

The kind where he wrapped himself almost completely around her—his torso bending over her, his head nestling into her neck, her ribs crushing against his with a solidness that grounded her.

She squeezed back, trying to channel all the love everyone had ever had for Luca. She felt connected to Marcy as the only other woman who had fallen in love with him. *She had good taste.*

Luca squeezed tighter, nuzzling into her neck.

"So...this is okay?" she said, her voice coming out muffled against his chest.

Pulling back finally, he angled his body to shield her from the kitchen doorway.

He nodded, swallowed, and his thumb stroked her cheek, her bottom lip. It felt like heaven after a day and a half of behaving themselves in front of Annabelle.

"*You.*" He sighed as she kissed his thumb on her lips. "Just... this is so *you*. Thank you. For being here, and for being you."

Warmth and relief and yearning braided in her chest, matching her hairdo. She leaned into his hand on her cheek, nuzzling it.

He tilted her chin so his mouth could meet hers in a slow, lingering kiss. He tasted like rosemary and freshly baked bread. Warmth, safety, belonging.

Like home.

The sound of footsteps approaching the laundry room grew louder, and he pulled back.

"What's wrong?" Annabelle said in the doorway.

Olivia pulled away, and she saw how concerned AB was for her dad.

"Hey, kiddo," he said, wiping his eyes.

"Why are you crying?" AB's face scrunched in sadness.

Olivia wiped her eyes as well. Having two people in her life who were so amazing was overwhelming.

"Hey," Luca said softly, bending down to AB. "Do you remember how Mom's birthday is in a few days?"

Annabelle nodded solemnly.

"Olivia thought it'd be nice to have some cupcakes in honor of her birthday."

Annabelle's eyes lit up. "That I can have?"

"Made by AP, so they are Sophie-safe, too," Olivia said, knowing Sophie's nut allergies.

AB's eyes sparkled. "We get Mom cupcakes?"

Luca laughed as he grabbed the tray. A few minutes later,

they all sat in the kitchen devouring cookies-and-cream cupcakes. Pearl and Luca swapped stories about Marcy, telling the stories of all of their escapades as Annabelle asked questions about her.

Olivia handed one to her mother at the edge of the kitchen, and her mom squeezed her side. "You did good, kid," she whispered.

"Yeah?" Olivia asked quietly, still not sure. "I didn't know if it was my place."

Her mother nodded sagely as she looked at Annabelle and Luca. "It's always our place to take care of people we love."

Olivia blew out a slow breath and decided not to correct her mother about the fact that she just might be in love.

Chapter Twenty-Three

OLIVIA

"Annnnnd flutter the leaves. Flutter, flutter, flutter! Maddie, bigger! Capital F flutters!"

Olivia coached her older girls' ballet class as they fluttered through the falling leaves the girls were tossing in the studio.

"And then! We *plié, tendu, sauté, chassé,* annnnd lift the leg with attitude."

Olivia clapped along with the music. "*Annnnd* then toss the leaves from your harvest basket," she said, coaching along with them as the girls played their part of autumn maidens.

Vivaldi thrummed through the old studio speakers as the girls did the first run-through of their entire dance. They held hands across their bodies, stepping together in formation. And as the final move, they gathered the leaves up from the floor and joyfully tossed them in the air as Maddie stood *en pointe,* wobbling on tiptoes in her first-ever pair of toe shoes. They all landed in fourth position as leaves fluttered down and the music ended.

Olivia looked at the clock, and time was up. "Excellent job." She clapped.

Parents had their faces smushed onto the glass and burst into applause. *Phew. At least they're happy.*

She would fix the dancers' posture and all the missteps next class. Only two more rehearsals until the fall festival performance.

"Did I do okay in my toe shoes?" Maddie asked. She still had that "first pair of pointe shoes" excitement dancers had after waiting for the satin-wrapped torture for years.

"Yes, but"—Olivia repositioned Maddie's foot that had no weight on it—"make sure you are *over* the box of the shoe, like this, so you don't hurt yourself."

Olivia demonstrated the difference since she was wearing pointe shoes as well, showing how her ankle and body weight changed.

"But good job. You're doing really well." Maddie's eager smile made Olivia's heart melt. Hopefully, Maddie could keep that same excitement after Olivia was gone.

She followed the girls into the hallway to greet their parents. The red and gold light from the setting sun turned the fall trees outside into bright bursts of color. The door opened as the last family walked out, and Luca walked through, backlit by the fiery trees.

By himself.

The clanging doorbell was barely louder than her heart jumping in her chest at the unexpected treat of seeing him.

Every nerve ending pulsed with the beat of her heart. "Hi."

"Hey." His smile was shy.

They couldn't take their eyes off each other this morning, and she'd accidentally poured coffee on Annabelle's cereal.

She could get lost in those eyes of his—ones that looked at her like she was precious and worth something.

She wanted to slide her arms around him, bury her face in his chest. But everything felt so unstable, like they only let themselves have just enough to stave off the hunger of wanting each other.

"No Annabelle?" she said suddenly, flipping the lock and the front lights off and going into the studio to turn off the electronics and room lights.

"She's with Pearl. They kicked me out so they could have girl time. Saw your car, so thought I'd stop by."

Thank you, Pearl.

Luca started picking up the piles of leaves on the studio floor.

"Oh, leave that," Olivia said. "I'll get it with a broom tomorrow."

She walked to join him in the middle of the room because he hadn't listened and continued to scoot leaves together with his foot. She put a hand on his arm to stop him, and he threaded his fingers through hers.

The quiet of the empty, dim studio felt otherworldly as they stood among the piles of bright leaves.

He bit his lip. "I wanted to say thank you, again. For the cupcakes. I don't know why I never thought of it, but AB asked if we could do it every year."

She sighed, happy that she could make him happy and make something easier for him. "I'm glad."

Their dark reflections in the mirrored walls surrounded them. Her hands slid up his dark shirt, and he wrapped his arms around her.

"Hi." His voice was low and slow, greeting her in that quiet, possessive way of his.

As if saying *mine.*

God, I love it.

The inevitability of what was going to happen between them felt predestined. There was no need to fight it.

She was a five-foot-four heaving sigh in toe shoes for this man.

Her lips curved slowly, as she enjoyed the lust-drunk look in his eyes. "You've *got* to work on your pickup lines."

He smirked, nodding as his hand curled around the back of her neck possessively, and captured her mouth.

The lust she'd built staring at him for days ignited like a fireball.

He *devoured* her.

Desire shot straight to her pussy at his needy, claiming kisses. She ran her hands under his jacket, the smell of leather and cedar wrapping around her.

His hand massaged her neck as he licked into her mouth, and she gasped at how good it felt, meeting his tongue with her own. She whimpered as his tongue played with hers.

Her tight nipples brushed against his chest.

She was going to fuck *something* on this man's body in a ballet studio tonight.

Come hell or high kicks.

"Anyone else here?" he gasped between deep, ferocious kisses. He angled her head, each one more deeper, more savoring than the last.

She shoved off his leather jacket. "No." *So please, please, please stay.*

Hungry hands grabbed at her, squeezing her ass over her flouncy dance skirt as he took her mouth. She ruthlessly manhandled the muscles on his arms, ran her hand along his hard cock.

She was wet already, and her pussy pulsed at imagining his cock under her again. Riding him again. Any part of him.

His hand slid up her slick capri tights under her dance skirt. "Security cameras?"

She laugh-sobbed as he bit her earlobe and giggly, lusty

need lit every erogenous zone up like a landing strip. "Definitely no cameras."

His pupils were blown wide in the dark room. Slowly squeezing her ass, he turned her so she faced the mirror with him. Her nipples poked hard against her leotard.

His hand moved under her short dance skirt, sliding around to the front.

Biting her earlobe again, his hand slid under her tights, slowly brushing along the leotard underneath, then down her stomach.

Sucking in a breath, he tugged the bottom of her leotard to the side. "No panties," he said, surprised, taking a ragged breath, the ghost of a smile on his lips.

Her chest heaved up and down as he slowly teased her wet pussy with just one finger, barely touching right where she wanted it, hinting with each brush up and down her slit.

She clutched his head, reveling in his scent when she ran her fingers through his hair.

"Eyes open, Liv," he murmured.

She hadn't even known they were closed, she was so lost in wanting.

Moaning, she watched his hand barely move under her tights. Barely brushing her clit, making her burn for him, tremble with need.

His thick, rough finger started lower, taking its time to reach her clit—but then stopped.

And started teasing again.

She moaned at the torture, tossing her head back onto his chest.

"See how beautiful you are?" he said, grabbing her breast slowly with his other hand. Taking his time squeezing her. Savoring it.

She groaned at how good it felt.

"Say it," he growled, kissing the back of her neck.

She laughed at the thought of even stringing two words together right now while his thick fingers spread her pussy in her tights and he pinched her nipple.

He pulled down her leotard so her breasts were bared to the mirror.

"Beautiful," she sighed, looking at what he did to her. How her tits were propped up by the material and he stared at them hungrily.

"You're gorgeous," he said in a voice that wanted her to repeat after him. Another finger teased a path from her core to her clit.

"I'm—" He finally pinched her clit, and she screamed. "Gorgeous," she said through the agony of pleasure.

He went back to teasing, taking his sweet fucking time.

She loved it and *hated* it. She wanted the cock she'd come against.

"I was tested," she said through a moan, "after my relationship last year. All clear."

"Same."

"No condoms, though," she realized, cursing her planning.

He claimed one breast, squeezing as he raked his teeth across her neck.

"Not what I want tonight anyway." He kissed her hard, backing her across the studio until they ran into the barre mounted on the concrete wall.

He pulled back suddenly and sauntered to the tumbling mats, sucking the fingers covered in her scent. He grabbed two.

What on earth?

He slapped the mats down in front of her. He kissed her hard, briefly sucked on a nipple on his way down, and knelt in front of her.

The width of his shoulders was a gift to behold. The stubble on his beard caught against the fabric of her leotard as he rubbed his face down her stomach, over her skirt.

He yanked off her capri tights. "I plan to be here a while."

Oh.

Oh.

He's going to...

Oh my god. She braced herself on the barre behind her as he lifted her skirt, kissed the tops of her thighs, her hip meat that squeezed out around her leotard. He nipped, making his way to the center of her thighs, biting her muscles.

Guilt weighed heavy on her shoulders. "You... you don't have to."

He froze and looked up. "You don't like this?"

She was lightheaded at his response. "I do, but I know a lot of guys don't." The last two she'd dated. One was grossed out by her, outright. "I want to, but you don't have to."

He wrapped his hands around the backs of her thighs, squeezing them. "Liv." His forehead rested on her belly button. He pressed his face into her, inhaled hard and groaned.

She felt worshipped with every touch.

He rubbed his nose, his mouth back and forth over her belly. "This is all I've dreamed about. For weeks. Months."

He looked up, licking his lips and squeezing her thighs again in his massive hands.

Her knees almost buckled at how much she wanted his mouth between her thighs.

"Please," he whispered, looking desperate for it.

To go down on her after a day of work.

Desperate to taste her and make her come.

A ribbon of power and lust unfurled in her.

She *liked* it.

How much he wanted it.

Wanted *her*. Enough to beg on his *knees*.

"Say it again," she whispered.

He pinned his forehead to her navel. "*Please*," he begged in a shaky voice.

She lifted his chin. His gasping, ragged breaths made his thick chest heave, and his jaw ticked with need.

She bit her lip, wet at the sight of him so gone for her. "*Beg for it.*"

A moan shuddered through him as she cupped his cheek, his eyes squeezing together in pleasured agony. "I never want to stop smelling like you," he murmured against her hand. "Want to coat my face in you. Please. God, Liv, *please.*"

She hooked a thumb on his bottom lip, pulling his mouth down. He looked up, desperately, every muscle tensed. Her world turned inside out as she realized he craved this. Wanted her beyond reason.

Blood hammering in her veins, she wanted to hear him say it. "Tell me how much you need it," she whispered, voice dripping with lust.

Anguish wracked his face as his nostrils flared. "I need to go down on you, eat you out. Can't think about anything else other than what you taste like. *Please*, Liv. Please, let me lick you. Pl—"

He whimpered against her hand as she raised her skirt. Air danced on her pussy, her leotard still pulled to the side.

"Fuck," he moaned, low and slow, at her pussy inches from his face. "I knew you would be perfect."

He grazed a thumb over her, his eyes darting to hers as his thumb connected with her throbbing, swollen clit peeking through.

She bit her lip, wanting his mouth but wanting this... this dance between them more. Feeling so desired and sexy.

His forehead pinned to her hip as his hands wrapped tighter on the backs of her thighs, starting to spread her legs.

He huffed in deep breaths for control as her hands raked through his hair.

He brushed his nose slowly back and forth against the skin of her pussy.

Back and forth, his nose grazed closer and closer until the tip connected with her clit peeking out, and she moaned.

He kissed the top of her thigh. "Your smell alone could make me come, Liv. Every horny fantasy I've ever had came together, and it smells like you. Salty, warm, sexy."

He teased her clit with his nose slowly, enjoying it. She gasped at how good it felt.

Then, she lost her mind because he traced the tip of his nose *straight up her slit, caressing* her with it.

He traced her slowly, mesmerized as their eyes locked. Up and down her pussy with just the tip of his nose, his hot breath on her thighs.

Inhaling her with a shuddering sigh, he begged, "Please," again and again and again.

He slipped it in further, teasing the side of her clit back and forth. She sobbed at how desperate he was that he'd fuck her with anything she'd let him use.

How much he wanted the most intimate, sexual part of her.

She was about to come from his nose fucking her and she finally gave in.

"Yes, eat me," she said, pushing his head down.

His tongue speared her seam immediately as he moaned into her, face pinched in ecstasy. He lapped like a madman, catching every drop of wetness on her thighs, her pussy.

He pulled her legs wider to take what he wanted.

Broad strokes of his tongue from her entrance up to her clit had her leaning back onto the barre as he devoured her, pinning her in place.

The hot, wet heat of his tongue filled her with slippery pleasure that was punctuated by nips and bites. She cried out in shrieks, loud and unbothered, her fingers gripping his hair for more.

The burn of his stubble brushing against her thighs and on her pussy revved her higher and higher.

Growling with need, he lifted one leg, then the other so both legs were slung over his shoulders. He wrapped his arms around each one, holding the weight of her up to his mouth as she pressed into him for more.

He ate with abandon, like she was his last meal, gorging himself on eating her pussy as fast as he could, gobbling every bit down.

He was sloppy, messy slurps and sucking accompanying her shameless moans. Burying his face into her like he couldn't get enough. Like her orgasm was the key to solving his every problem.

He ate her like he needed every drop or he wouldn't live to tomorrow.

Sobs turned into screams as she arched her back. She pushed his face in harder. She bounced on the barre from how hard he ate her, biting and nipping, sucking hard on her clit.

The pleasure felt too good. The sight of him destroying her, face pressed between her thighs and wet with her, was too hot. The combination of his tattoos pressing against her skin and the safety of him holding her down to eat her like a rabid animal was too much for her.

And she still wanted *more*.

He sucked hard on her clit in between licks up and down, savoring every taste. "I want more, Liv," he said against her clit.

"Take whatever you want," she said, pushing his face down into her again, hard, liking how he moaned as she shoved his head down. Ferocious, loud, dirty slurps and moans echoed in the room in between her whimpers. He sucked every part of her he could reach, his tongue teasing her entrance. *Fuck*, she'd die from how good that felt.

He set her down and steadied her legs suddenly. He stood, but she barely had time to register it as he grabbed her by the waist and flipped her upside down.

He held her tight around her waist, her face now in front of his belt—*upside down.*

"What the—*fuuuuck*," she screamed as he buried his face into her pussy, now held open at mouth level.

He sucked and licked, burying his nose at her entrance. Again and again, he pressed his face against her, his tongue licking from clit to entrance. She opened her legs wider, and he moaned when she spread them as wide as they could go.

"Goddamn," he sighed against her clit. "Nothing better than you spreading your legs for me, Liv."

She could only hold on to his hips, the blind pleasure clutching her body making it difficult to think. His tongue traced her entrance, dipping in further and further. She squeezed around it, at his mercy. Her hips bucked against his face, seeking friction. He sucked on her clit hard, then harder and—

A full body shriek of a climax ripped through her, curling into his torso as he kept going and going, eating as if nothing had happened.

She panted as he kept licking and undid his belt, finally gathering her wits. His cock was too far away to reach with her mouth, but she pulled it out of his boxers.

"Liv, I can't last long." He licked slowly around her pussy, teasing her entrance. "I need you to give me one more. Please."

She grasped his leaking cock, and he yelled with pleasure. She slid the precum up and down his head, and he moaned as he sucked on her clit again.

And despite having just come, her slutty clit wanted it.

She clenched around nothing as she licked her lips, imagining what his cock would taste like. She spit on her palms and grabbed his cock as he shifted her in his arms, one arm holding her waist.

Two thick fingers speared her pussy, already slippery and needy. She gasped, clenching around him.

"Fuck, you'd look so good taking it, wouldn't you?" he murmured, sliding in and out of her. He rubbed his stubble back and forth against her clit. "Can you take three, Liv?"

She whined in response, tugging his cock. His fingers stretched her, filled her.

"Please," she whimpered, thinking of how good it would feel. Just like the cock in her hands that might rip her in two if she ever got to ride it.

"Say it again," he said, flicking her clit with his tongue back and forth shamelessly. "Beg for it, Liv."

She moaned at that. Because she *would* beg.

"Please," she whispered, another climax building already from him making her beg. "Please, fuck me," she whined as he teased her with the tip of a third finger. "Please, Luca, please."

She pumped his cock, wanting to show him how much she wanted it.

He sucked her clit hard as he pumped in a third thick finger. She shrieked, fucking his face as best she could, coming all over him, the intensity of it harder and brighter than the first one. He came hard, spilling over her hands.

She ground out every last drop as Luca moaned into her pussy, fucking up into her hands harder and slower, cum sliding between her fingers.

They stilled, catching their breaths, which were echoing in the studio. Luca wiped his face from side to side over her pussy, breathing hard.

He was getting *more* of her on him. Marking himself with her.

Fuck, why do I love that?

But two could play at that game.

He set her down on her feet gently, holding her waist as the blood resettled throughout her body. She locked eyes with him and licked each finger, the taste of him salty on her tongue.

His jaw ticked, and he caught her cheeks with his hands, kissing her as she sucked the last finger into her mouth.

The taste of her on his tongue as he kissed her hard felt primal. Universal.

She pressed against him, feeling safe, treasured, as each kiss was slower, more savoring, until he finally kissed her temple and gently moved her leotard back into place.

They walked on wobbly legs to the stack of tumbling mats in the corner. They collapsed on them, facing the ceiling, gasping for breath.

She collected the thoughts she had screamed all over the room. He tucked her into his chest as they lay together.

"So?" She rubbed her face against his chest. "Why did you come over again?"

They burst into bright, crazed laughter.

"For that." He tucked her head underneath his chin and kissed the top of it. "Wanted to see you."

"You got to see a *lot* of me," she said, squeezing his chest. Laughter rang around the echoey studio as they clutched each other, wheezing.

He traced light fingertips along her hair and around her shoulder.

She could feel herself start to self-sabotage.

Shouldn't he be doing other things? He was so busy. Was she just his favorite hobby?

But, no. She would try to enjoy this.

Whatever *this* was.

"So you said you had a no-dating rule?" She swirled her fingers around on his chest, letting her hand climb underneath his shirt.

He sucked in a breath as her nails toyed with his chest hair. "Yeah, no dating."

She thought about what they'd been doing. Sneaking kisses, mutual mind-blowing orgasms. "But you do this?"

"If you're asking if Georgia and I had a fling, the answer is no." He smiled, pushing a stray lock of hair out of her face with the back of his knuckles.

"I wouldn't put it past her."

His back arched, and he laughed so hard that it made her laugh in return. She loved seeing a lightning bolt of laughter course through him, evaporating the constant frustration in his brows.

He bit his lip, still wet with her arousal. "I've had two one-night stands. Over the last"—he shrugged—"three years."

Her gaze dropped from his, but those fingers tilted her chin back to him.

"That's not what this is," he said confidently, looking straight into her soul.

A question hung unspoken between them, in the silence.

"Oh my gosh, I have to say it," she said, smashing her face into his chest muscles. She felt like the worst cliche. "Then what *is* this?"

"This is… unexpected." His eyes traced her face. "And addicting." He brushed his lips against hers, again and again, lingering longer. Wearing her scent on his skin like a badge of honor.

She curled into him, already wanting him again. Wanting to sleep beside him and wake up in the middle of the night to do it all over again. "For the record, I don't regularly fall for people who pay me."

He smiled mischievously against her lips. "You're falling for me?"

She flopped to face the ceiling and sighed out every frustration in her life. "Like a rock."

He chuckled and kissed the top of her head.

He sat up, leaning over her. His expression was nervous. "Annabelle's getting attached. To you." He pushed the hair out of her face with such care she could have cried. "She had a hard time the other night. Things always keep changing, and people leave her."

Tears sprang unexpectedly to Olivia's eyes in sympathy, and Luca's thumb traced her cheek. It was physically painful to think about ever hurting AB's feelings. "I'm so sorry. Should I stop babysitting?" She'd do whatever they needed.

He bit his lip, shrugged the shoulders she mentally called her happy place. "I don't know. You light her up when you're around. You light up both of us. I guess that has to factor in too." She pulled him down to the mats and snuggled back into her happy place.

Something still felt off. She didn't like the idea of taking payment to be with her favorite people.

"I think..." She traced the stubble on his cheek with her fingertips. "I think you should stop paying me."

"Absolutely not," he said firmly, rolling his eyes.

"I just want to spend time with you guys. It feels weird for you to pay me."

He huffed. "I don't want you to feel weird, but I would also like you to afford groceries."

"How about I start eating at your house three meals a day?" she said with a playful smile.

"Oh, because that's going to be so different from what

happens now?" He nibbled on her neck, the scratch of his stubble causing her to laugh, the sound of it echoing in the studio.

"How about," she said, thinking about her just-have-fun agenda, "we just enjoy each other, for however long I'm here. No labels, no rearranging of anything. Just consensual good times."

AKA this is tomorrow's problem.

He sighed, his eyes roaming over her face and down her body. "This is gonna hurt like a motherfucker later."

She snuggled back into her happy place and squeezed herself against him.

Yes. Yes, it will.

Chapter Twenty-four

LUCA

"Hey, Ritchie," Luca called over his shoulder. "You got the paint guns?"

Luca ripped open another box in his empty new shop in Fairwick Falls.

Jon, his part-timer, lifted up a giant box. "Right here."

"All right, that goes in that cabinet. Hey, where's Braden?"

"Here," a squeaky voice called as the person in question ran through the shop. Luca handed him two boxes.

"You set up the desk like I asked you?"

"Yep." Braden nodded as he held the heavy boxes.

"Young fuck almost put your chair together backwards," Ritchie said as he walked by and tousled Braden's hair.

Braden shifted the boxes with a nervous look in his eye. "I fixed it."

Luca nodded at him. "Good job." The guys ragged on Braden, but frankly, it was a rite of passage in a shop like theirs. And young kids were prone to making mistakes. He'd made a fuck-ton of them when he was young, too. "Go set up those boxes over in that cabinet."

Braden ran with the boxes, almost slipping on the slick concrete. Luca held his breath.

"I said I would do all the unpacking," Angie, his office manager, yelled at him, holding a clipboard.

"I know." Luca pulled another two boxes off the pile. "I just want it done my way."

She shook her head at him. "You pay me so things will be done *my* way. So you can do things like talk to those fancy-ass guys who want all of their vans redone."

Their last big client had recommended them to a catering company in Erie. Their fleet of used vans needed a full custom job. He'd drive two hours tomorrow to secure a deal big enough to pay their shop rent for the next year.

"Why have an office manager if I can't manage the office?" Angie hounded him as he walked a box over to his desk.

He ignored her question. He was too worried that everything would be set up in the wrong place and would cause chaos later. "Can you go check to make sure Ritchie is labeling everything?"

Angie's huff let him know that she was not happy as she turned around.

Bright, happy voices echoed in the empty shop as he unpacked his desk.

Olivia held AB's hand as they walked in through the open garage door. She'd stopped to ask Braden a question.

Luca stopped and stared. Luca fucking loved that she treated even the youngest guy on his crew like they were a professional. He glowed at her kindness, her class.

Braden was melting with pride and embarrassment as he talked to Olivia. He uttered an embarrassed thanks and pointed his thumb toward Luca's office.

Luca smirked at Braden's lovesick stare as Olivia walked away.

Join the club, pal.

"It's looking exciting," Olivia said to him with a bright smile. "Has that new-shop smell."

Annabelle flopped her feet as if she was exhausted as they walked into his office.

"Hey, goober," he said, opening his arms for a hug. AB walked slowly over to him, flopping each foot harder as she went.

"Hey," he said, trying to see what was wrong.

"I'm tired," Annabelle whined.

It was only 4:30. "Long day in first grade?"

Annabelle nodded her head as if it weighed fifty pounds.

"How'd your math races go?" Luca said.

AB shrugged, looking miserable. "I got out on sevens." She laid her head against his shoulder.

She was clingy, and that usually meant she didn't feel good.

He felt her forehead. "You're pretty warm." He leaned down. "Does your throat hurt?"

Annabelle shrugged.

He looked up at Olivia, who looked bewildered. "She hasn't said anything."

He picked Annabelle up and she cuddled against him.

"Cold," she said into his chest.

"I'm sorry, I didn't realize," Olivia said, full of concern, her hand coming to smooth down AB's hair beside him.

Luca rolled his lips together, cursing the bad timing. "I was planning to run by the old shop to do the last sweep tonight." Today was their last day on the lease.

He never liked seeing AB not feel good. It was a wrench in his plans, but she was his number one priority, always. "I'll call the landlord and see if I can extend it to tomorrow morning."

The bullet that was Angie with a clipboard nearly sped past but screeched to a halt as she popped her head in. "Oh, hey, little boss." Angie smiled at Annabelle, who waved back meekly. She loved Angie, who completely spoiled her.

"Why don't you let Angie close up the other shop?" Olivia suggested.

"Yeah, why don't you let Angie close up the other shop?" Angie parroted.

Luca sighed. "She has a lot to do."

"He's nervous for the thing tomorrow," Angie said to Olivia, ignoring him completely.

"I'm not nervous." He rolled his eyes.

"See." Angie pointed at his face as she talked to Olivia. "When the brows come *all the way together*, he's mad. But when they just scrunch like that, he's nervous."

Olivia tried not to smile.

"I just have to go to Erie to pitch to these guys. It's fine. I'll finish everything up in the morning. Sometimes AB just needs a good night's sleep to feel better. Want to go home and put your pj's on?" he said quietly to Annabelle.

She nodded, cuddling against him. He loved feeling the weight of her against his chest.

He really really hoped this was an overnight bug.

But what if it isn't?

What if I can't check the other shop in time to make sure we got everything important?

Lots of people want to help you echoed in his head as he looked at Olivia, who reminded him of this with only her arched eyebrows.

Luca admitted defeat, grinding his teeth. "Ang, can you help make sure everything's gone from the old shop?"

Angie walked over to Olivia and took her by both shoulders. "I don't know you, but I'm in love with you." Olivia burst out laughing. "Whatever witchcraft you're doing," she said, waving a hand at her, "just keep doing it."

A little while later, he and AB made it home. Annabelle fought him putting on her pajamas because she was hot. He settled for a light nightgown and cuddled with her on the couch as they watched her favorite show. She eventually fell asleep as the light turned from a golden orange into a dusky purple.

OLIVIA

How's she doing?

Can I get you anything?

Luca sighed. He wasn't used to having people try to look out for him.

LUCA

Fever of 101. She's asleep. Hopefully, she'll be better tomorrow.

OLIVIA

How are YOU doing? Can I get you anything?

I am very good at reheating soup.

Or I can come over and watch her tomorrow.

He gulped, knowing he could trust Olivia, but still feeling uncomfortable asking.

LUCA

I might need your help if she's not back to school tomorrow.

I hate to leave her, but the Erie client has been hard to schedule. I'd leave and come right back.

OLIVIA

No problem. I'm sewing costumes and happy to take over cartoon and cuddle duty.

He stroked Annabelle's hair and pulled the cover up tighter around her. She clutched at Platypus. He didn't like the idea of leaving her when she was sick, but she'd probably just watch TV all day if her past colds were any indication. AB coughed in her sleep and then stirred. It sounded like she was developing congestion.

LUCA

Let's see how she fares tonight.

Thank you for being someone she'd happily be sick around.

OLIVIA

The honor is all mine 🤍

God, this woman. He needed to come to terms with whatever situationship he was in right now.

They snuck kisses, he depended on her, she made him laugh, and she'd nearly melted his heart out of his body on Saturday with the cupcake thing. And when they actually could find time to...make out? Orgasm their brains out? He felt like a caveman possessed his body, he needed to claim her so badly.

Was he brave enough to potentially lose himself again? He opened a different contact to message.

LUCA

Was I really that out of it? When Marcy died?

SHE-DEMON SISTER

bruh.

yes.

also...whyyyyy??? are you asking me about this????

ooooo

might it perhaps have to do with a ballet dancer
that turns you into luca soup when you look
at her?

LUCA

I don't know how much longer I can fight
whatever this is.

I'm doing a pretty bad job of fighting it now.

But the thought of losing her is terrifying.

I thought maybe I overexaggerated how bad it
had been in my head when Marcy died.

SHE-DEMON SISTER

look, normally i'd make fun of you

because usually you deserve it

but....

.....

i kinda get it now. reed is my soul. my person
outside my body. if anything ever happened to
him....

oh fuck you for making me cry tonight

AND i have you to depend on.

and friends (weird, right??). i know i could get
through it.

you didn't really have anybody to lean on. i was
still hitting you up for money then and was
barely a legal adult.

LUCA

But you came through for us, which is all that
matters.

SHE-DEMON SISTER

look, what happened with marcy was a fucking tragedy. but you have to be brave enough to try again.

olivia is great.

i mean, she could use some tattoos and her knowledge of 1970s san francisco punk is lacking. but! nobody's perfect.

it could all work out.

who knows, you could romantically feed each other pureed prunes in your retirement home

have matching denture glasses on your matching bedside tables.

LUCA

Alright, I get the picture.

SHE-DEMON SISTER

oh! matching bedpans

LUCA

PEARL.

SHE-DEMON SISTER

night buttface

LUCA

Night little monster

And since I don't say it enough

AB and I love you a lot.

SHE-DEMON SISTER

ewwww such a SAP now that you're in LOVE

jkjk i love you or whatever weirdo

Luca tossed his phone onto the couch and bundled AB up to take her to bed.

Brave enough to try again? He sighed, pushing it from his mind for now.

~

HE DIDN'T SLEEP well that night, getting up every few hours to check on Annabelle, giving her more cough medicine so she could sleep, and turned on the humidifier.

By the next morning, her temperature was still at 100, even though she was up and watching cartoons. Dr. Lopez hadn't seemed too worried, but told him to bring her in if it got higher.

It was only 7:30 AM, but he already felt like he'd been through the wringer, running on little sleep.

Annabelle, however, seemed in good spirits as she ate breakfast and played on the couch. He thought about Olivia's offer.

They watched an animated show on the TV, and he cuddled AB closer. "I think you need to stay home from school, kiddo. I might need to run to work for a little while today. Is it okay if Olivia stays with you?"

"Yeah," AB said with a smile.

He texted Olivia, who said she'd be over in a few. He felt nervous. He didn't like this new feeling that potentially felt like overreach.

As he came downstairs, changed for his meeting, he saw her leaving her house. He met her at the back door for a sneaky kiss. She hefted a box of fabric and held her little sewing machine by its handle. There were dark circles underneath her eyes.

He caught her chin and bent down, capturing her mouth in a kiss before pulling back slightly, studying her up close.

"Mm. Good morning," she purred against his lips.

He turned to look over his shoulder, making sure AB was still on the couch, and kissed her again, deeper.

"You should meet me outside in the morning more often," she said, nipping at his lips.

"You feeling okay?" He didn't like the dark circles under her eyes.

"Just slept like crap; it happens sometimes when I'm nervous. I've got a lot to do before the festival this weekend."

"You should go home and sleep. I can move things around." This was why he didn't like asking people for things. It was an imposition.

She smacked a kiss against his cheek and pushed past him. "Won't sleep until I finish two more costumes anyway."

The delight in Annabelle's face at seeing Olivia, despite having seen her only twelve hours earlier, relieved some of Luca's guilt as he grabbed his keys, ready to make the drive to Erie to secure his biggest client yet.

Chapter Twenty-five

OLIVIA

Olivia was a bedside nurse for Annabelle for a day and a half, spoiling her with pancakes and princess movie marathons. When she managed to nap, Olivia made headway on the rest of the leaf costumes and got her workouts in.

But now?

Now Olivia felt like her body's gears were covered in chunky peanut butter. Sticky, slow, and getting slower.

A cough racked her chest, and she took a sip of tea.

I will not get sick.

She sniffed through a stuffed-up nose. She just needed to sleep it off, but there was too much to do. Finish these costumes, dinner with her family, Luca, and AB tonight, not to mention practice for her audition tape. The thing she needed to do most of all and had done so little of in the last four days.

She rolled her shoulders. If there was anything the last twenty years had proved, it was that discipline would get her through most things. She couldn't let her class down, and she *definitely* didn't want to look like managing two kid dance routines was beyond her abilities.

Just work harder.

Luca had offered to grab Annabelle from school since he had been in the neighborhood at the right time, and Olivia expected them back any moment.

She was knee-deep—literally—in tutus. She pinned fabric around the enormous leaf costumes, making them appear like giant leaf ballerinas.

Now just sew it on super fast, she thought, running it through the machine. Holding it up, she admired her work through the haze of her heavy eyelids.

Oh shit. She'd accidentally sewed the entire thing together through the middle, making it impossible to put on.

"Fuck," she said, thunking her head down on the table and closing her eyes for a blissful second.

Her head pounded, but she didn't have time to deal with it.

The door opened, and a tornado burst through. "'Livia, 'Livia. I got a B-plus on my spelling test." AB held the paper up.

Olivia dragged the fifty-pound weight of her head and put it over her shoulders.

"That's great. I'm so proud of you." Her voice came out croaky.

Luca stopped in his tracks when he saw Olivia, eyes wide with concern.

"Hey," he said softly. She wanted to lean against his leg and hip, but she kept her hands to herself.

No need to confuse Annabelle.

His eyes scanned her face. "You look terrible," he said gently.

She laughed, but her chest caught with a cough. "You really know how to talk to a girl."

He grabbed the thermometer gun that they'd used to make sure Annabelle was okay to go to school that morning.

"Holy fuck," he muttered. "One-o-three."

"Degrees?" she said through heavy eyelids.

"You need to lie down immediately."

"I don't have time." She shook her head, pulling up the costume onto the sewing machine.

Wait, no, she thought, looking at it slowly, her head fuzzy. *I have to unpick all the threads and start over.*

Tears pulled at her eyes at the thought of getting even further behind.

"What's your mom's number?" Luca called.

Olivia rattled off the seven digits from her childhood. *Wait, why?* "Think she wants to come unpick threads with me?"

He ignored her question and held the phone up to his ear. "Hey, Martha. We have to cancel tonight."

"What? Nooo," she said, turning. "I'll be fine." She'd looked forward to spending the evening with her family, her not-boyfriend, and her favorite kid.

"Yeah," Luca responded to a question her mom was asking. "One-oh-three." A loud sound on the other end of the phone had him pulling it away from his ear. "She caught a cold from Annabelle."

"I'll take some Tylenol. I'll be good as new in a couple of hours," she said, even as her eyes were closing.

He leaned the microphone away from his mouth. "Do you want to get Pop sick?"

Oh. In theory, Pop was healthy as a horse, but eighty-three-year-olds didn't recover from colds easily.

"No, it's fine, Martha. I'll keep an eye on her. We have a guest room."

"That's ridiculous," Olivia said, standing up and getting dizzy and sitting back down.

"I gotta go, Martha. I'll keep you posted."

She squinted at him through puffy eyes. "I don't like this."

She wagged a woozy finger at him. "Conspiring with my mother."

"People want to help you, Olivia," he said with a smirk. He leaned down and felt her face with the back of his hand. "A little clammy, too."

"Well, *you* don't smell so good after a whole day of work," she said, trying to muster up an insult that hurt as much as *clammy skin*.

"I don't?"

"No, that's a lie," she said, putting her head down on the table and sighing out that ache in her chest that would develop into a horrendous cough. "You smell great."

"'Livia, wanna to come play bubbles?"

"AB, Olivia is sick, so she's going to rest upstairs."

She sighed and coughed. "This is silly. I'll just go home to my bed. I don't need you getting sick, too."

He waved his hand, dismissing the idea. "My immune system is made of steel after getting every cold when Annabelle was in preschool."

"Okay, well, I'm going to go lie down somewhere soft." She stood up and took two steps, closing her eyes as the room tilted.

"And I will be handling this from here on out," Luca said, picking her up in a bridal carry, her legs swept out from underneath her.

"Whoa!"

Annabelle giggled.

"Are you laughing at me?" Olivia flopped her head upside down to look at Annabelle.

She got a giggle-filled "Yeah" in response.

Olivia was too tired to do anything else. She closed her eyes and leaned her head against Luca's chest as she felt him taking the stairs up to the second floor.

"You can stay in Pearl's old room."

"This is such an inconvenience," she muttered, even though she snuggled against his chest.

"I like the inconvenience," he whispered against her cheek, kissing her forehead.

"I'm clammy. Ugh. Don't kiss me."

"I'm made of stronger stuff than that, Olivia," he said, laying her down on the edge of a clean bed.

Luca pulled back the covers, and she climbed into the fresh sheets. "What man keeps fresh sheets on his guest bed?" she muttered, sighing out the aches in her body.

"Lucky timing. I just put this on," he said, tucking the blanket back up around her.

Small, heavy footsteps walked in. Olivia opened her eyes and saw Annabelle holding her ballet book. "I'll read a story to you to make you feel better."

"AB, she needs to rest."

"It's fine," Olivia said, coughing. "It's only fair. I read it to her five times yesterday." She smiled, meeting Luca's eyes.

His tender concern was tinged with helplessness, as if he was worried this was some nineteenth-century consumption and not just a normal cold.

Annabelle sat on the edge of the bed, flopping her legs back and forth.

"Can you read the whole thing?" Olivia said through a stuffed-up nose.

"Yep," Annabelle said confidently.

Luca strode out the door. "I'm getting the humidifier."

Olivia closed her eyes.

Just for a minute. Then I'll go to my house so I don't bother them.

The next thing she knew, Olivia was opening her dry, heavy eyelids in a pitch-black room. The sky was dark, and Platypus was tucked in beside her in the bed.

She smiled through her coughs and cuddled the animal as she turned, every bone aching.

A small pharmacy sat on the bedside table. Crackers, cough drops, medicines, tissues, and water all competed for space beside her plugged-in phone.

The door cracked open as she kept coughing, and Luca walked in wearing pajamas, his hair mussed as if he'd been asleep.

A sight for literally sore eyes.

"Here, take this." His voice was quiet and gentle as he gave her the tiny cup of cough medicine.

Right, medicine could help with the coughing. She hadn't thought about it.

This felt so foreign to her. It had been literally over a decade since someone had taken care of her when she was sick.

"You didn't need to get up," she croaked as she took the medicine.

He aimed the temperature gun at her head. "Take some Tylenol, too." He handed her some pills and a water glass. "Your fever is still pretty high."

"You're sexy when you dole out medicine," she muttered, handing the glass back to him.

The effort to sit up and take the pills exhausted her, and she immediately lay back down, cuddling Platypus.

He sat beside her on the bed, and the scruff of his beard highlighted his smile in the dark room. "See you found Platypus. AB insisted he watch out for you." His hand rested against her hip, and she wanted to curl into him at how good it felt.

Olivia chuckled. "He's been a big help. Pretty much the ideal Platypus, getting up in the middle of the night to take care of me. Insisting I stay at his hou—" She was interrupted by a series of sneezes.

A cooling, Vicks-scented tissue was in her hand by the second sneeze.

"I'm a mess," she croaked.

Luca stroked her hair, an amused smile on his face. "You're the prettiest sneezer I've ever seen."

Oh god. His muscles wrapped in his Henley shirt, the flannel pants, the hair that was a little all over the place.

And those kind eyes that looked at her like she was *special*.

"Stop being perfect," she moaned. She pulled his arm around her as she turned in bed, bringing him with her.

He chuckled as he let himself be pulled down over the covers, spooning her with his delicious body heat. He tightened his arm around her. "Just for a few minutes, then I need to let you sleep."

"Heating blankets have nothing on you," she muttered, her eyes already closed. "Thank you."

"For keeping you warm?" he whispered against her ear.

She sighed, a bone-deep, yearning sound. "For caring."

Hours later, the sun was bright in the room as Olivia woke up. Gentle voices floated up from downstairs in a familiar, clipped, bright cadence. Bowls and cutlery clinked like people were eating.

Footsteps moved up the stairs, and her mom peeked her head through the door.

"Hey, sunshine," she said quietly.

"Mom," she said through her coughs. "I don't want to get you sick."

"Luca said your fever broke this morning. I brought Pop's chicken noodle soup."

"Yeah?" Olivia said, remembering the sound of people eating downstairs. It was a special recipe he'd made every time she'd ever been sick as a kid. It was creamy, filling, and had these amazing dumpling-like noodles—

"Wait!" Olivia pushed out of bed in a panic and stumbled to the door, getting lightheaded after not standing for over twelve hours. "Luca," she yelled through a cough. "Luca, stop. The soup."

She started down the stairs, gripping the banister. "The soup noodles. Don't let AB. Wheat." She coughed through her words on the landing.

"It's okay, it's okay," Luca said, stopping her. "Pop used gluten-free noodles."

Her knees were shaking despite her relief. Stupid tears burned in her eyes.

Pop remembered. AB is safe because Pop remembered, my mom is here at my not-boyfriend's house, who is taking care of me like a private nursing staff. The intense amount of care surrounding her was overwhelming.

Didn't know how starved I'd been for it.

"You're shaking, Liv. Let's get you back to bed." He helped her up the stairs, and she wiped at her cheeks.

"Do you want some soup?" he asked as they walked past her concerned mom back into the guest room.

"No, it's fine. I'll get it later. I'm not hungry." She curled into a ball back in bed as her mom sat down beside her.

"I was going to offer to take care of you, but"—her mother surveyed the row of medicines, supplies, and tissues beside her —"I think I've been outshone." She rubbed her hand on Olivia's back. "Luca is taking very good care of you."

Luca smiled at her mom, grabbing Olivia's empty water glass before leaving the room.

"I know this," she said, coughing, then smiling. "I feel so bad that I'm here. I should be home by myself." She coughed again.

"Sometimes..." Her mother leaned over to kiss her forehead as she stood up. "It's okay to be babied."

"I'm so behind." Olivia sighed, thinking about all the work that waited for her downstairs. "Maybe I could go work for a little bit today."

Her mother was all business now. "Absolutely not. I will be taking all of the leaf costumes."

"Mom, there's too much for you to do."

She tucked the blankets tighter around Olivia. "Honey, I do not have the highest lawsuit settlement rate in the county because I lack tricks up my sleeve." She tapped Olivia's nose. "Just rest and appreciate the handsome, muscular view while you have it."

Some mysterious number of hours later, Olivia woke up in the dead of night feeling more human.

The house was silent, and the room was pitch black except for a bright moonlight filtering in. The cloudiness and heaviness in her head had finally gone, and it had been hours since she'd had a coughing fit.

She realized she'd slept in the same bed, barely getting up for the last forty hours. She stretched, standing up, her muscles creaking from underuse.

Shower, she realized, feeling caked in grossness. Should she go home?

No, she didn't want to deal with getting all her stuff downstairs, finding her keys, and going out into the chilly night and back to a cold house.

But what can I wear?

A chair by the bedroom door held a stack of towels, a large t-shirt, and an extra toothbrush.

Goddamnit. He's going to ruin me for anybody else.

Hot water ran over her body in blissful renewal as she brushed her teeth. Feeling two hundred percent better already, she tossed Luca's shirt over her and crept downstairs for soup.

Heating up and eating the Pop's chicken noodle soup used

more energy than she'd anticipated, so she started back upstairs. She crept down the hallway, avoiding the creaky floorboards.

She spied Luca's bed through his door that was cracked open. It would be warm, and smell like him. Her skin broke out in goose bumps at the idea.

She shut his door behind her. He stirred as she slid underneath his covers, feeling that same flannel warmth and scent she associated with him.

His eyes fluttered open, his sleepy smile lit by moonlight.

"Hey," she said as he pulled her into him, cuddling her body, nearly surrounding it with his own.

"Hey," he said, his voice roughened by sleep. "Feel better?"

"Four thousand percent," she said, snuggling into his chest. "I'm gonna come over and get sick all the time."

Her legs snaked through his, and he wrapped his top leg over hers, locking her in place.

"Good." He kissed her temple.

"Clammy?" she said, smiling.

"Not even a little."

She cuddled into his chest, realizing they had never even napped together before. The room was chilly, but the space under the covers was so warm. The heft of Luca's arm and leg weighed her down, grounding her.

She could *very* easily get used to this.

Too easily.

She turned, getting comfortable, and a snore crept out of Luca's mouth.

I should leave him alone. She tossed and turned in her sleep even on a good day. As she pulled away, his arm tightened around her.

"Don't go," he whispered in her ear. He tucked her into his side, spooning her.

It was going to be hard to sleep with the elation that felt like lightning running through her veins, but she settled in anyway. Cocooned in Luca's embrace, she drifted off.

Hours later, morning light filtered through the curtains. Luca was sleeping on his back, gently snoring. She'd wrapped her arms around him in the night, practically sleeping on top of him.

Part of him was *very* excited at her proximity, and it just so happened to be *so close* to where she wanted it.

She bit her lip, thinking about what they could do with five minutes of alone time now that she was feeling better.

Suddenly, fast, light steps came down the hall, before thankfully going to the bathroom.

Shit!

She shook Luca awake.

He snorted awake from a dead sleep. "What?" he said, slurring his words, surprised.

"It's Annabelle," she whispered, frozen in place.

The only toilet in the house flushed in the next room over, and she panicked.

"Oh, fuck," he muttered. "She always jumps on my bed if I'm still asleep on Sunday mornings."

They both panicked, looking for somewhere for her to go.

"She can't see me in here, right?"

"No." He shook his head quickly.

Footsteps walked to Luca's door as Olivia dove into the only place to hide: Luca's closet. Olivia slammed the closet door closed as AB ran into Luca's room.

"I'm awake!" AB called. An *oof* from Luca made it sound like she'd jumped on the bed.

Luca's closet was a small walk-in, just big enough for her to stand surrounded by his clothes. She petted the flannel shirts on their hangers to soothe her nervous energy.

"Is 'Livia living with us now?" AB asked.

Olivia froze.

"No, goob. She's just staying here until she feels better. It's nice to have other people take care of you when you're sick."

AB hummed in agreement.

"Do you like her?" AB asked suddenly.

Olivia put a hand over her mouth to keep herself from laughing.

"Of course. She's nice and she takes great care of you," Luca said.

Olivia rolled her eyes at the annoyingly right answer. *Cop-out.*

"She smells good, too," AB said with authority. "Sophie *like* likes Sam. He's in Mrs. West's class."

Uh oh. She could see where this was going.

"So, what do you want to do for breakfast?" Luca said.

Olivia muffled a snort, knowing he was desperately trying to change the subject.

Luca and AB chatted over breakfast plans, considering whether to make a feast or go get a feast.

A sneeze grabbed hold of Olivia and wouldn't let go.

Oh no. Oh, fuck.

"Where's 'Livia?" AB asked.

Olivia tried with all her might, but a loud "*Achoo!*" escaped her.

"Bless you," AB said as a reflex, then burst into giggles.

Shit shit shit. Olivia fumbled with whatever pair of pants were on the floor as little footsteps ran to the closet

Olivia yanked on Luca's oversized sweatpants as Annabelle burst the closet door open, belly-giggling. "Are you hiding?"

Yes. "Just putting on clothes your dad is lending me," Olivia said with a *ta-da* motion, spinning around.

"Annabelle, go get changed and we'll grab some breakfast," Luca said.

"Okay," Annabelle said as she ran out of the room.

Olivia heard the bedroom door shut, and the heavy, slow footsteps of Luca walking over to her.

Olivia peeked her head out from the closet. "You *liiiiike* like me."

He laughed, taking his shirt off. Her eyes roamed his chest.

"You liiiiike like me back," he said with an arched eyebrow. He leaned down for a long, slow kiss. "You up for breakfast?"

She kissed him quickly one more time for the road. "Nah, I'm going to go home and take another nap. You're not getting these back, by the way," she said, wrapping his shirt tighter around her.

He ran his hands up through her hair and kissed her hard. "I think we're going to need a one-to-one trade soon."

Olivia waggled her eyebrows. "I'll get started on my part when I'm feeling better. Do you prefer thongs or bikinis?"

He tickled her into the closet where they snuck a thirty extra seconds of happy kissing before going their separate ways for the day.

It somehow already hurt like a motherfucker.

Chapter Twenty-six

LUCA

Luca flinched outside of Fairwick Falls Elementary as a loud, old-timey school bell rang. Kids streamed out, and he looked for his favorite little face.

He and Olivia had agreed he'd do drop-off and pickup to help her catch up from being sick. There were only two more days until the festival, and she was in a rush to finish the costumes for her two classes. Luckily, his shop was almost ready to launch in Fairwick Falls, and the dreaded commute to Cooperstown was over.

"Hey, you," he said as a fifty-pound kid slammed into his leg.

"I touched a frog today!" AB yelled up at him.

"Very exciting." He held AB's bag as she scrambled up into the back seat.

"Can we call 'Livia so I can tell her about the frog?" she yelled as he buckled her seat belt.

"Maybe later." He jogged to the driver's side. This was day two of protecting Olivia from constant interruptions from Annabelle wanting to tell her every third thought.

"When's she gonna be done with the festival?" Annabelle's voice was wistful.

Luca buckled in and waited for the pickup line to start moving. "The festival is in two days. Excited about your performance?"

"Yeah," Annabelle said confidently. They'd been working together on her routine every evening before bed.

"Brought you a snack." Luca handed back a container of apple slices with a glob of sunflower butter.

AB crunched an apple slice. "This feels *weird*. I miss Olivia picking me up."

"Maybe it won't feel so weird if we do it all the time. What do you think about me taking you to school from now on?"

Technically, his need for extra help was nearly done. The shop would open up Monday.

"I wouldn't see Olivia anymore?" Annabelle asked in a tiny, sad voice.

He wiped a hand down his face. *Shit.*

"She'd come over and spend time with us still, like for dinner. You might hang out together if I was busy with work."

"Hmm..." Annabelle thought hard, looking out the window. "No, thank you."

She'd said it politely and firmly, like he'd asked if she wanted more apples.

He chuckled as he looked over his shoulder at her, but it was his turn to finally move in line. "What do you mean, 'no, thank you'?"

"She's better at playing ballet princesses."

"I don't even get credit for the apple snacks?" he said to AB in the rearview mirror. She crunched and wiggled her head noncommittally.

He turned out of the school parking lot. "We're going to the square to run an errand."

"*Ugh.*" Annabelle pushed her body off the back seat in frustration. "I don't want to. Will we have to do that every day?" she said with big, sad eyes.

This is the life you wanted, he thought to himself, *just you and Annabelle. Being there for her and not focusing so much on work.*

They drove through the town square. Hay bales lined the perimeter, and each corner of the square had a decorative stand full of pumpkins. The leaves had finally all turned to bright fall colors. Luca almost let himself smile at how proud he was to give Annabelle a childhood in a place like this.

AB's face was pressed against the window. "Can I go look at the scarecrows?"

"Sure, we'll stop at the scarecrows."

He pulled over into a spot in the town square, and they hopped out. He was sponsoring the pumpkin chucking contest (allegedly a big deal, according to Martha) as a way to get their name out in the community. He needed to drop off the *Bishop Body Shop* sign.

They wandered hand in hand in the breezy afternoon through the small hay-bale maze. A large stage was set up on one side.

"Excited to dance up there?" Luca said, pointing to the stage.

"Yep." AB shrugged confidently, as if it was no big deal. "I'm probably gonna crush it."

"I like the confidence," he said, squeezing her hand.

"Can 'Livia come over tonight? She does really good baby bunny voices for bedtime."

"No," he sighed, hefting the rolled-up sign in his arm. "Remember, kiddo, she's busy right now."

"But I *want* her to," AB whined, pulling his hand hard as they walked around an old-timey wheelbarrow full of pumpkins.

"I'm sorry. You'll just have to deal with my bunny voices."

"You don't even *do* the voices," AB whined, slowing down.

He gritted his teeth and breathed his frustration through his nose. "I'll try harder tonight. C'mon, let's go drop off this sign."

AB let out a very teen-like, "*Ugh*. But you said she was my babysitter!" She tugged on his hand. "What if I need sitting?"

His temper edged near the end of his control. "Annabelle, I'm not explaining this again," he said firmly.

Emotion started to build up in her face. "But I *want* her to come over. I miss her."

Jesus, it had only been three days.

And yeah, he missed her too.

But this was everything he'd wanted to avoid.

While he'd been falling more in love with Olivia and enjoying how good she was with AB, AB had quietly gotten attached to Olivia.

His worst nightmare had happened right under his nose.

He sighed and bent down to talk with her. "I know you miss her. I do too. We'll see her soon, okay?"

AB sighed. "Can we go see the scarecrows?"

Luca kissed her head as he stood up, and they walked through the decorated scarecrows each business in town had created. The Bloom scarecrow was covered in flowers, while Reed and Pearl had worked the night before on their Bookish scarecrow with a sweater vest and had sent him photos. The hardware store, the Maroo law office, and heck, even the Thirsty Beaver had made one with an old-school beer t-shirt. He made a mental note to sign up for next year. *AB will have fun decorating it.*

Luca dropped off the sign at the pumpkin chucking station as AB hung on his arm with boredom. She'd already mentioned Olivia two more times as they walked through the square.

Luca spied Bookish across the street. "Let's go get a new book." AB jumped and chattered in excitement.

Maybe I can find one where I can actually do the voices. He'd been *trying* to do a baby bunny voice, damnit, he was just crap at it.

They walked into Bookish, the scent of old and new books wrapping around them. Pearl walked by with a stack in her arms. "Hey, you two. No Olivia?"

AB turned to him with a deadpan look. "See? It's weird."

He finally let himself say what he'd felt all afternoon—yes, it felt weird without her.

~

OLIVIA

OLIVIA SHUSHED the little girls in giant leaf costumes behind her as Gerald stepped up to the mic to kick off the fall festival.

"As chairman of the festival board, I'd like to welcome you to the Fairwick Falls Fall of Fairwick Festivities Festival." Polite clapping greeted him. "This year's theme is Leaf All Your Worries Behind at the Fairwick Falls Fall of Fairwick Festivities Festival."

"Really flows off the tongue," Olivia muttered, fixing Sophie's costume as she wiggled in line.

A crowd gathered in front of the stage as the chairman spoke, thanking their sponsors.

They were up next—the opening act. Olivia got them in the proper order to walk out on stage.

She'd had to cancel her coaching call at the last minute to get the final costumes ready for the second number. She'd be late sending an audition tape to the Dayton Ballet, but she couldn't let the kids down.

"'Livia, where's *your* leaf costume?" AB asked as she flapped her hands up and down in excitement, standing in line.

"I will be right here watching you dance," Olivia said, bending down on her knees so she was eye level, "just like in class, and you guys are going to crush it, okay?"

AB looked up at the stage with big, surprised eyes. "You won't be on stage with us?"

Uh oh. "I'll be right here, okay? You're going to do great. Now, girls, what do we remember before going on stage?"

"The audience can smell fear," they answered in unison.

"And how do we cover up that stinky fear?"

"Have fun!" they yelled together and giggled.

"And now," the man on stage said, "let's welcome Olivia Maroo's first-grade ballet class, The Leaflets."

"All right, go, go, go," Olivia whispered urgently.

The little girls toddled on stage to an audible *aww* in their giant leaf costumes with the pink tutus. The audience started clapping even before the dancing started. Olivia's heart skipped a beat at the reaction. She still lived for it.

She cued the sound guy, who started playing a famous Carole King hit that always reminded Olivia of autumn.

This was it—the big reveal of whether she should have been entrusted with small children for the past eight weeks.

The first eight counts went well as Olivia held her breath. The girls danced and twirled just like they were supposed to, going up and back, side to side.

She spied Luca in the front row. Her eyes drank him in. It had been two whole days since they'd seen each other, and she was thirsty for a glance.

He mimed along to the dance subconsciously. Had he practiced with AB at home, and she'd missed it?

Oh my god, I will never recover from how perfect he is.

Suddenly, Annabelle stopped dancing, looking unsure. She

stood as the other girls kept dancing and walked up to the front of the stage, where Luca was.

Oh no.

AB bent down to talk to him, and his face got worried. They exchanged a few quiet words, and AB's leaf shook at her top point as if she was saying no.

Luca darted his eyes to Olivia beside the stage as she made a *what's going on?* motion.

AB held out her hand to him, and he shrugged and, holding her hand, walked up the front steps of the stage.

Oh. My. God.

He joined the girls onstage to a considerable chorus of *awws.*

Olivia's hand flew up to cover her mouth in shock.

Holding AB's hand, Luca waddled side to side, skipping in place and turning around with his arms held up over his head like a ballerina.

Her ovaries were practically climbing out of her body to get to this man. All she could do was press her hands to both cheeks at the adorable sight.

As they all hit their final pose, uproarious applause made Olivia's heart jump. She clapped along with them, looking straight at Luca.

AB turned to Luca and gave him a high five, but then Sophie wanted one too. A chain reaction started, and all the girls lined up for a high five from him as he laughed and then shepherded them off stage toward Olivia.

They ran to her in their bobbling leaf costumes. The buzz of dopamine Olivia always got from applause in the audience hummed through her veins as she congratulated each dancer. "Good job, Harper. Good job, Sophie," she said as they all passed her. "Annabelle, I am so proud of you for finishing, even though you were nervous."

"My dad helped me," Annabelle said, beaming up at her dad, not embarrassed in the slightest.

Luca's ears turned pink.

"You did a very good job, too, Luca," Olivia said in the same voice, trying to hold back her giggles. "Really nailed that last *pirouette*," she said with a wink.

Her heart could have melted at the fact that he didn't think twice about being ridiculously cute in front of the entire town when his little girl needed him.

He lifted AB up into his arms. "Your grandparents are here." AB gasped. "Let's go say hi."

"Yeah!" AB said loudly.

"We'll see you after?" Luca said to Olivia.

"Yeah," she said with a quiet smile. She could feel herself and him holding back from the quick goodbye kiss they could usually sneak in.

The older girls in their leotards and graceful autumn-colored gauzy skirts lined up next as they waited to go on. Someone on stage was playing a guitar and singing some fall song about sticks.

They all held baskets of leaves in hand and smoothed down their ballerina buns. Olivia hairsprayed flyaways as they stretched in line, keeping their muscles warm.

"You are going to be great," Olivia said, trying to hype them up and calm their nerves. "Everyone's got their leaves?"

They all nodded enthusiastically.

The festival chair introduced them, and the girls prettily dance-walked across the stage. Olivia sighed, feeling proud.

A familiar clanking of bangles and bracelets came up behind her.

"The kiddos did marvelous, darling." Georgia enveloped her in a crushing hug. "This was always my favorite part," she said, with an arm around Olivia as they watched the girls start to dance. "I love seeing the dancers' progress. Maddie was terrified of toe shoes last year, and look at her now. She's really blossomed with you. Sure I can't coax you to stay past December?"

Olivia sighed, looking at the girls doing an excellent job *pirouetting, jetéing,* and then the gasp in the audience as two girls went *en pointe.*

Yes, she was proud of them, but it didn't *fit.*

Didn't feel like it was what she was destined for. "I don't think I'll be a teacher long term," Olivia said with a sigh.

"You miss being in the corps?" Georgia asked.

"No." *I miss having potential.* "I want to be a success, still. At something."

At least one time in her whole life.

But maybe the time for success has already passed me by.

Maybe it was time to just be happy.

Georgia hummed in understanding. "I *loved* teaching dance. It's why my classes always ran over; I was having too much fun. Wherever you lose time, that's what you're meant to do, I say."

Olivia considered the idea. Where did she lose time?

Her eyes scanned the handsome face making his way through the crowd while he held a happy little leaf.

She lost time with Luca and AB, in just being happy.

Maybe it's okay that I don't know what else is next, but I do know I want to be happy, whatever I do.

After the performance, she found Annabelle and Luca in the spun-sugar-scented crowd. They stood in line at the face-painting booth, talking with two older people. AB's grandparents were cheerful, smiling, and petite.

Uh oh. Maybe she shouldn't bother them. AB rarely got to see her grandparents, who were usually in Florida.

As she started to change course, however, AB saw her before she could pivot away. "Come get your face painted, 'Livia!"

Luca's eyes met hers, and he nodded her over. "Olivia, meet Marcy's parents. Ed and Carol, this is Olivia. She's—"

What's he going to say? Nanny? Neighbor? Dance teacher?

"Oh!" AB's grandmother interrupted Luca, face full of excitement. "We've heard *so* much about you on our weekly calls." Olivia was wrapped in a firm hug, which she barely registered enough to return. "Our Annabelle is taken with you."

Olivia breathed out a sigh of relief. "It's mutual," she said, running a hand over AB's hair.

"Those older girls danced *so* beautifully," Carol said. Olivia chatted casually with them as they waited in line.

She finally let herself look back at Luca. The wanting inside her body was so bad it felt like a physical ache. She wanted to interlace her fingers with his, rub a hand on his back, and just *be* together.

It was AB's turn in line, and she hopped up into the face-painting chair.

Luca leaned past Olivia. "Carol, can you watch AB for five minutes? I need to talk to Olivia about something."

I really hope it's what I want to talk about.

Specifically, his face on my face.

AB and her grandparents chattered away about Halloween, not even blinking when Luca stepped away.

Luca placed his hand on Olivia's back as they navigated through the crowd.

Even just that contact made her physically relax. "Where are we going?"

"Some place very important," he said into her ear. When they were out of sight of the face-painting booth, his fingers threaded through hers, and her body felt like it was back in the right place, grounded with him.

They beelined from the middle of the festival out to the edge.

"Why, Luca, are you taking me somewhere to have your way with me?" she whispered, smiling wickedly.

"Behave," he said, but it had come out as a stilted growl, as if he was holding something back.

She bit her lip to keep from laughing.

Several food vendor trucks faced a row of trees on the outskirts of the town square. They walked between two break-fast food trucks that had closed up for the night, and he tugged her behind one.

He pulled her to him and—*finally*—his hand threaded through her hair as his lips met hers. The warm, soothing taste of what felt like safety danced on her tongue as she kissed him back.

Her hands slid around his middle, squeezing him tight against her. She sighed at his kiss, at the comfort of his lips on hers because everything was okay when they were together.

It felt like their souls clicked into place, two puzzle pieces that just fit and felt better together, as he kissed her, slow and savoring.

She buried her face into his chest with a groan. She caught her breath, feeling like she was a fawn who was finally safe after *running running running*. "There isn't a strong enough word for how much I needed this."

He kissed her forehead and squeezed her. "I missed you so much. I know we should get back, but it's been driving me crazy." A ragged sigh of contentment in his chest made her nuzzle in further.

"The good news is"—she caught his eye, and his slow, amused smile made her want to turn into a puddle—"no more costumes. No more cold. No more festival prep."

"No more commute either," he said, running a thumb along her lip.

"Maybe"—her tone was flirty—"we can play hooky soon and actually, you know…"

You could fuck my brains out, please and thank you?

"AB's grandparents want to take her to the house they still have in Cooperstown for her long weekend." Luca's eyes sparkled.

"You don't need to join?" Olivia asked, not wanting to get in the way.

Luca shook his head. "They like spoiling her and want to give me a break."

Olivia kissed him, letting some of the need bleed through at how much she wanted to ride him right here in the open. She smiled against his lips. "Then consider my weekend booked for our very first sleepover."

Chapter Twenty-seven

LUCA

Luca sped over the country roads from Cooperstown, pushing his normal speed limit of five miles over. He'd dropped AB off with her grandparents to stay the night.

Next, he'd have to swing by the festival to grab his only shop sign since the pumpkin chucking contest had been last night. Tiny, the bouncer from Thirsty Beaver, had won and already emailed photos of his cats for his custom auto-body-job prize.

But Luca wasn't speeding for a sign.

The clock was ticking on how much free time—and free house—he and Olivia had until AB came home tomorrow.

And I'm going to use every second.

Being with Olivia, even when she'd been sick, was torture if he couldn't hold her the way he wanted.

Taste her again like I did in the studio.

A call from Olivia came through on his SUV. "Hey, Liv." He had a dopey grin on his face just from picturing her calling him.

"How'd drop-off go?"

"Fine. She barely even turned around to wave at me. I'm fifteen minutes out from home."

A *hmmm* purred through his SUV. He straightened in his seat as it set his blood on fire.

"I wish it was more like five," she said in a teasing voice. "I've been working out, and I'm *very* sweaty." Her pouty voice was teasing. "I might have to take a shower."

"Don't you dare," he said, gritting his teeth, imagining licking every part of her.

A low, sultry laugh echoed around him, teasing his cock. "I guess it's okay since I'm not wearing much," she said with a sigh. "Just a workout bra and panties."

He growled as he hopped off the highway and slowed to a stop at a stop sign, letting himself picture her for one second. "What kind?" he rasped.

"Thong," she answered playfully. "Easier to see my ass bounce that way."

He threw his head back, and his cock went rock hard as he pictured her ass bouncing like it had when he'd eaten her out upside down, becoming the animal he usually kept caged away.

"Did I lose you?" she asked, a smirk in her voice.

"Almost. Christ," he murmured. "All my blood went to the fucking steel in my pants, Liv."

She hummed into the phone again. "I cannot *wait* until you get home."

"Touch yourself," he ground out, driving into town.

"Way ahead of you," she sighed.

Fuck. Me. He squeezed his hard cock over his jeans for relief.

"I want you wet when I get home. Gonna fuck you in the kitchen first, bent over the island." A moan wrapped around him from his car speakers. "Haven't stopped thinking about it since I first saw you stretched out over it."

The animal he normally kept locked away rattled in its cage. "Liv, I'm gonna warn you. I—" He faltered, taking an extra second at a stop sign, trying to gain composure. "I need to fuck you first, hard. I'll make love to you later."

"Good. I want it so bad. But... can I make a request?" she asked, breathless.

He pulled into the town square. "Anything, other than not coming home."

"Can you..."

He could *hear* her smile as she paused.

"Can you pull my hair? Like you did when we first kissed?"

His brain went blank, and he choked on a breath.

Fuck the sign.

"Gotta go. Be home soon." He pulled a U-turn at an intersection and hit a button on his console to call the shop.

"I *told* you, don't come in. Almost done with final inventory," Angie answered amiably.

"Can you pick up the shop sign at the Fairwick Falls square today?" he asked, beelining to his house.

"Sure—"

He hung up. He'd apologize later, but he couldn't multitask beyond getting home safely as soon as possible.

The condoms he'd stashed in his wallet and pockets were burning holes in his brain. He screeched to a halt in his garage, threw the SUV into park, and leapt out.

Stalking through the backyard, he pulled out his wallet with trembling fingers. Grabbing a condom, he took the stairs two at a time. He gripped it in his teeth as he pulled open his belt buckle. Shoving open the door, he tossed his wallet and keys on the floor as he unzipped his fly.

The scent of cinnamon and nutmeg—that goddamn lotion she wore—catcalled him as he entered the laundry room.

Olivia was in the kitchen, bent over with her hair loose and spilled onto the island. Her tits pushed against the top of her sports bra.

A blush pinked her cheeks as she held her ass in the air and a hand between her thighs. Every limb glistened, covered in sweat.

Not breaking his stride through the hallway, he pulled out his cock.

"Wet?" he growled, resorting to one-word sentences.

"Too wet," she moaned, biting her lip, looking needy.

"*Good*." Need made his hulking movements fast and possessive. "Need to fuck you. Claim you."

She nodded, arching her back as she rubbed herself harder. "Do it," she whispered.

Stalking across the kitchen to her, his eyes only on her blushed ass and the sound of her wet pussy being stroked, he tore the condom open with his teeth and rolled it on.

In three swift movements, he yanked her thong over, kicked out her foot to make room, and thrust into her.

Hard.

They gasped, frozen in the moment of *finally* joining.

Finally.

The hot, tight heat of her made his eyes cross. He breathed through it.

Bending over her, he threaded their fingers together as they sighed in relief. He thrust into her like that, sliding in further.

Where I belong.

"Oh," she panted, "god." She moaned as he thrust hard again, pinning her to the island. He bit her shoulder, tasting the salt of her. He nipped at the cord of muscle on her neck, squeezing her fingers threaded through his as her muscles squeezed hard around his cock.

"Fuck," he yelled, trying to keep it together. He licked up her spine, tasting the salt from her workout.

He bent her back down over the counter, savoring the view as he slid his cock out of her, slowly, seeing her stretched around him. He gripped her hips, slamming into her again, her ass bouncing.

She squeezed around him again hard, and he saw stars.

"Fuck, Liv," he gasped. "It's too good."

He bent over her and pulled her face back to him. This wasn't going to last long, and he needed to kiss her at least once.

Tongues and lips met in messy, grasping kisses as he held her jaw, twisting her face toward him. She grabbed his arm for leverage, sucking on his tongue, making him need her even more.

Let me out, his animal raged, and he growled.

"Touch yourself," he ordered.

She kissed him harder, her teeth drawing blood from his lips. "No, you have to come first. I"—he thrust hard, and she moaned—"I want you to use me."

He kissed her hard, tasting the lust on her tongue.

She panted, meeting his eyes. "Like you dreamt of. I can take it."

The animal burst out of the cage, and he roared out a sob of need.

He shoved her back down, savoring the view of her ass bouncing as he fucked her at a punishing pace like a beast, claiming her. He ran his hand up into her hair and grasped the roots, tugging her hair back.

"Yes," she sobbed, grabbing a nipple.

He leaned over, tugging her hair back harder so he could whisper in her ear. "I love that you're like me." He fucked her harder, and she whimpered, bouncing from it. "Depraved and dirty and shameless for what you want." She moaned, and the animal inside him liked it.

Liked that she was at his mercy and wanted to be used.

"More," she gasped. Her tits brushed against the island as he slammed into her. *Can't wait to suck them later.*

"Fuck, Liv. That's it, louder. You love it like this, don't you?" he growled, grabbing her waist, pulling her hair hard.

She screamed as he slammed into her, his belt clanging with every thrust, her cries getting louder. His control slipped as her hips chased and bucked against the counter's edge for friction, willing to use anything to get off as he fucked her.

Needy. Desperate. Like me.

Lightning shot up his spine, tightened his balls, as that sight of her fucking the counter pushed him over the edge.

He bent over her as he lost control, coming hard in thrust after thrust, roaring out his climax as she squeezed her muscles around him.

His heart was floating somewhere outside his body, pleasure coursing up his legs and into her.

Until they stilled, panting over the counter.

God.

Damn.

He held her head, kissed her cheek, the edge of her mouth as she leaned into him. Blushing cheeks warmed his lips as her hands held on to his arms, stilled in savoring the moment together.

"That was..." he said through ragged breaths.

"Perfect," she said, arching against him.

There weren't words he could think of other than *I'm so fucking gone for you.*

So, instead, he slowly slid out of her, tugged off the condom, and tossed it in the trash. She was wobbly, leaning against the counter.

He bundled her against his chest, needing to take care of her, and tilted her face up to his with concern. "You okay?"

She nodded, melting against him. He palmed her head, kissing her temple, holding her safe.

Pieces of his brain started to come back online.

She hasn't come yet.

And you're just getting started.

He swept her into his arms.

"What are you doing?" she said in a confused, lusty haze.

He carried her into the living room. "Liv, I just fucked you hard, pulled your hair. Being treated like a queen is the bare minimum for aftercare. And during-care, I guess. You owe me two more orgasms."

She curled into his neck, placing a kiss there and practically purring. "Mmmm, two?"

He kissed her as he sidestepped a pile of toys. "Two-to-one ratio, Liv. For as long as we're doing this."

It was selfish, really. Imagining her coming under him, over him, *anywhere*. It had been how he'd finished every handjob since the day he'd seen her at Bookish. *I just want to see it as much as I can in real life.*

Time to indulge his fantasy.

"Your little panties trick on the stairs made me realize what I wish I'd done instead," he said, taking her upstairs.

He made it halfway up before he sat her down. Slowly, he tugged the zipper of her sports bra down and slid it off her shoulders. Pulled her thong off.

He stood back for a second, drinking in the view.

Completely naked in front of him, back arched on the stairs as she looked at him, radiant. Her breasts were perfect handfuls, her hips flared out and were smooth with those hip dips that drove him fucking *crazy*.

Her skin was flushed from head to toe, pink glowing where he'd grabbed her while he'd taken her in the kitchen. "See anything you like?" she said, eyes dancing.

He kneeled two stairs below her, pushed her legs open wide, and stared at her pussy, salivating. "I'd go to war for what I see."

It was impossibly perfect. Pink lips, a clit just peeking out for more, wet from earlier. He stared up at her above him, the cascade of hair falling around her breasts as her pretty hands cupped them, squeezed them.

Sliding his hands up her strong thighs, he licked his way up as he locked eyes with her. He shamelessly inhaled, leaning against her as the pleasure of it made him weak.

The warm skin of her panty line glowed against his cheek. "You like being used earlier?" With a barely there lick, he teased her clit.

"Yessss," she moaned, sounding so close already just from that one lick.

He teased her again, wanting her to agonize—to *beg* to come.

"Just want to be wanted," she said, scratching her nails through his hair.

He huffed a laugh into her slit, pulling it wider so he could enjoy the view. "Liv, I want you so badly I can't think straight."

He sucked on her clit, slid a finger in her. "Have to make myself come twice sometimes at night after I see you…" Licked a line from her entrance to her clit with the wide flat of his tongue. "…so I don't barge into your house, throw you over my shoulder, and take you to my bed."

He sucked her clit, and she pushed his head down, fucking against his face.

He reveled in it. It had been too long since his beard, his face, *anything* had smelled like her.

He lifted her up, helping her with the work of grinding against his mouth. She came on his tongue, hot and fast, riding his face.

His cock stirred at her screams as he pressed his mouth harder into her pussy, wringing every last drop from her.

He lifted his head, panting as he set her down. She lay boneless on the stairs. He spied something over her shoulder on his door.

"Is that..."

With confused, lusty eyes, she looked over her shoulder. "Brought it from home. Thought we could... try it out." She bit her lip with wicked delight.

The straps that Olivia used to stretch were on *his* door. The sex swing ones he'd pictured her in a million times.

A primal growl slipped out, and he pushed himself up the stairs, grabbing her in his arms as he went. She shrieked with laughter.

The bedroom door was closed so the straps would stay in place, and they hung in the hallway. There were footholds on each strap, handles at the top, and a small cushion in the middle to hold her weight.

"Can you give me another one so soon?" he said, pausing. She slid a graceful leg into the foothold in response. "You are magic," he said through deep, lusty kisses.

She grasped the handles, her arms pinned to the top for balance. He pushed her legs so they were spread wide and her pussy was stretched on display.

"Gorgeous," he whispered.

He couldn't get to his knees fast enough to put his mouth where it belonged.

He feasted, taking his time to build her desire back up. Teasing, experimenting to see what made her buck into his face and moan. His Liv liked to be teased, it turned out. *And I get to enjoy the view of her wet pussy while I do it. Win-fucking-win.*

She screamed as he ate her, tongue sliding into her

entrance, nipping and biting. Then sucking so hard she threw her head back and shrieked. Her hips bucked against his face.

He liked that she was needy, pinned where he wanted her so he could give her as much pleasure as she could take. His hands traced up her thighs, spread out on each side, grasping her calves as he sucked her clit, smoothing over every part of her he could reach.

His cock was begging for attention again, leaking from the tip.

Not yet.

She was a moaning, sobbing mess as he pressed his face into her; he moved back and forth, soaking up her scent. "Louder, Liv," he demanded. He wanted her aching moans etched into his memory.

Every muscle.

Pressing a second finger into her, he teased her clit back and forth with his tongue as he moaned, using it as his personal lollipop. "Best thing I've ever tasted." He looked up at her as he sucked, her tits heaving with sighs as she arched into him.

He sucked, licking every last bit from every angle of her clit until she crashed through her climax, screaming and thrashing, bucking against the restraints. He catalogued every movement, soaked up every drop of how she wrung her pleasure out.

It was so much better than he could have imagined. She was graceful normally, but he liked this messy, sweat-soaked, desperate version of her. The real her.

Who fucks my face like I've dreamed of.

He grabbed a condom from his pocket as she panted, catching her breath. "You can give me one more, can't you?" he said, belt clanging as he pulled his cock out.

She looked at his cock with a needy bite of her bottom lip and nodded.

That's my girl.

He lifted her hips, taking the pressure off her arms in the swing. He thrust against her wet pussy with his bare cock as he kissed her, teasing them both.

"I like it when you taste like mine," she muttered against his lips.

Crippling yearning *speared* him.

"Christ, woman." He moaned against her. "You can't say things like that if I'm going to fuck you properly. It'll be over too soon."

They moaned together as his bare cock hit her clit. Jesus, he couldn't wait to come in her raw. Bend her over and fuck her any time he could.

Couldn't even *think* about getting her pregnant or he'd come right now.

He rolled on the condom before they did something stupid and slowly pressed into her.

"Ah!" She threw her head back with a cry as he pressed all the way in, even deeper than before.

His mouth couldn't leave hers for even a second. Their tongues couldn't lose touch; it was too important. Too life-altering not to keep licking, kissing every part of each other's mouths, chins.

"So full," she panted.

She let go of the handholds and let him carry her weight as he fucked her with her legs spread open wide against the door, grinding against her clit as much as he could.

She reached between their bodies, stroked her clit.

Does she need more stimulation? I should—

But as she lifted her glistening fingers, he realized it wasn't that.

Her eyes were on fire, looking fierce. "Open."

He sucked her soaked fingers into his mouth with a mewling whimper, thrusting harder into her.

"Mine," she whispered in a ravenous voice. He nodded against her hand, sucking and licking every bit off.

"More," he demanded. His thrusts grew harder, longer.

She shoved her fingers down and got more but held the fingers from him. Her eyes were alight with possessiveness, waiting for him.

"Yours," he whispered. She gave him what he wanted, and he licked every bit off.

"Yours," he panted, grabbing the top of the door frame for leverage. "Yours, yours..." he kept moaning as he pinned her against the door until she came again in a ragged cry as he ground against her clit. Her pussy tugged in her climax, squeezed around him until he came with a shuddering moan, harder and fiercer than before.

Claiming her, being claimed *by* her.

After his last thrust, he immediately unwrapped her from every restraint and let her stand, stretching and resetting her muscles.

They wobbled as they stood, catching their breath.

Her smile was relaxed, almost drunk-looking, but her face looked pale. "We should get you some food and water."

"Just want to cuddle." She sighed out her displeasure, and he realized she was shaking as she leaned against him.

"Hey," he said, suddenly worried. "When did you eat last? Lunch?"

She grimaced, thinking. "Dinner last night?"

"Then, food first." He picked her up into his arms.

"Luca, I can walk," she laughed, though she rubbed at her wrists where the straps had dug in. Her limbs still shook.

"Liv. Please," he said softly, making her meet his eyes. "Let me. Let me show you how I feel about you."

She seemed surprised that he wasn't joking but relented. She cuddled into him as he slowly took her downstairs.

Chapter Twenty-eight

OLIVIA

Time moved in slow motion for Olivia in Luca's arms as he slowly carried her to the kitchen. His words echoed in her ears.

Let me show you how I feel about you.

This quiet man never ceased to completely blow her away with how much he cared.

He laid a kitchen towel out on the counter, then set her down on top of it.

"It's too cold," he said, taking his shirt off.

He'd somehow stayed completely clothed during their entire sex marathon, which honestly had only made the whole thing hotter for her.

But she *was* chilled. He helped her into his pre-warmed Henley, and she shuddered at how good it felt.

"Stay right there," he said, giving her a quick kiss. "Grilled cheese sound okay?" He started pulling out butter and hearty slices of cheese from the fridge.

"Sounds amazing," she said, trying to figure out if maybe she'd died during the third orgasm and this was just heaven now.

He picked up an extra flannel shirt from a kitchen chair and tossed it around her shoulders.

"You know," she said, leaning on her hands and smiling as he fussed at the stove. "You really should try to *care* a little more for the people that you sleep with. Do something nice for them sometimes."

She winked at him as he smiled softly at her, buttering the bread.

"I've always been bad at making these," she said offhandedly.

"The secret," he said with a flourish, "is water. Learned that from Mrs. Brown, my babysitter."

"You had a babysitter?" she asked, surprised it had never come up.

He smiled to himself. "Sort of. She was a very nice lady who also lived in the trailer park and taught me how to make a home nice, even if you didn't have a lot."

She looked around his kitchen and into the living room. His house was nice, tidy. Things were worn but clean. She'd always loved being here.

"She would take pity on Pearl and me sometimes. Feed us when we were running wild. Gave me my first job," he said, the bread sizzling in the pan. "Picked weeds out of her potted plants. Earned a whole dollar. I still have it," he told her with a smile.

Her heart. What had he looked like as a little kid? Probably as cute as AB but with that earnest, sweet look that was always hiding behind his eyes. "She sounds like a really nice lady."

He nodded. "She was. She was pissed at me when I first got my tattoos. Said no one would hire me." He chuckled. "She came around, though. Right before she passed, I got this one." He pointed to a winding branch of weeds on his rib cage.

Olivia's fingers traced along tall cattails, bushy wildflowers, and spiky leaves.

He tossed the grilled cheese in the pan.

"Do the rest have a story?" she said, taking in his chest, the complicated patterns and scribbles. She let her eyes linger there, kissing his shoulder when he moved close enough to her.

"Yes and no," he said, pointing to a list of numbers. "Annabelle's birthday in Roman numerals. Some flash tattoos some buddies and I got after high school on a dare. One that Pearl and I got together when I lost a bet." He pointed to a lyric.

He turned and reached up, and she spied a tiny unicorn tucked in between spiked vines along the sides of his back.

"Wait a minute," she said with a laugh. "Did you lose a bet with Annabelle?" She tapped the spot on his back.

He laughed. "Pearl *and* Annabelle. Want anything to drink? Water?" he asked.

"Oh, I can get it," she said, scooting to hop down.

"Don't," he said seriously. "Liv, don't put a foot on the floor. Please. I'll get it." He stared at her until she relented and scooted back into place.

Let me show you how I feel about you.

He overwhelmed her with how much he cared. How special he made her feel. How beautiful a soul he was under all those muscles and that handsome face.

He got her a glass of water and squeezed her hip as he walked back to the stove.

Taking a chef's knife, he carefully sliced the gooey grilled cheese exactly diagonally. Hunched over one of the rare ceramic, non-kid plates in his cabinet, he plated it just so.

He handed it to her with a kiss on her temple—a little heart drawn in ketchup sat next to the sandwich, with a neatly folded napkin under the plate.

And then he just... *casually* walked away.

As if he hadn't just done the sweetest, most precious thing she'd ever seen.

Hadn't been the kindest, most considerate person every day for the past two months.

She bit into the grilled cheese. Buttery, gooey love gushed out of the sandwich and into her soul, healing the last crack in her heart she hadn't even known was there.

Oh my god.

She stared at the plate in her hands, thunderstruck.

Dizzy from the now very obvious truth on her tongue and unable to run from it any longer.

I'm in love with him.

Her heart beat faster as she stared at him in shock.

He stood on one side of the double sink, washing a dish.

She knew in her *bones* she was supposed to be in the open spot beside him.

As long as we both shall live.

I'm in capital-L, he's-the-one, have-his-babies love.

How had it taken her so long to realize it?

The warmth and kindness in those deep brown eyes, the care in his every movement. How she wanted to protect him *and* be protected by him.

Luca turned around with a dish towel slung over his bare shoulder. She gulped, a feral *want* tugging at her.

Their gazes caught. "Do you need another one?" he asked.

She hadn't realized she'd eaten the whole thing while ogling him. She slowly shook her head no.

She set the plate down slowly, never taking her eyes off him. An ache hummed in her core.

She *wanted* him.

Grasping the waistband of his jeans, she pulled him between her legs.

He looked smug as he yanked the towel off his shoulder. "Take it you liked the grilled cheese?"

"Buddy." She shook her head in disbelief, her fingers tracing the dark stubble on his face. "You have *no* idea."

He swept her up from the counter and carried her upstairs. The buckle of his open belt clanked as he walked, stoking her lust higher and higher.

She studied *just* how much pressure was needed to make him shudder as she nibbled his neck while he carried her upstairs.

He laid her down on his bed. The flannel comforter that smelled like him puffed up around her.

She pushed up to watch him push off his jeans, his boxers.

She took him in, seeing him naked for the first time. Thick, meaty thighs with more tattoos made her clench her inner muscles.

"Want to lick them," she said, reaching out to trace the snaking thorns and patterns. His cock hung down, heavy with wanting her again.

She licked her lips at seeing it, but instead of giving her what she wanted, he caught her lips in a needy kiss. Never breaking it, he pushed her back onto the bed with a sigh, crawling over her until he surrounded her.

Thick arms wrapped around her, heavy thighs bracketed hers, and his kisses pushed her further into the blankets that smelled like cedar and felt like home. She savored each kiss like sips of champagne, dragging each one out on her tongue as they went to her head.

He pulled the shirt up over her breasts. A moan sighed out from them both as he licked and sucked her nipple, rolling the other with his hands.

She scraped her nails down his back, and goosebumps appeared on his thick arms.

Oh my god, I even love his goosebumps.

The sweet, aching sensation of his sucking and licking was intensified by all the love she had for him.

He stayed there, licking broad strokes around her breasts, moving from one to the other, pinching and teasing with his thumb.

Squirming for more, she sighed at what was becoming torture. "Luca, please."

He pressed her breasts together, his jaw ticking as he handled her. "I've wanted to take my time here for months." He licked a path between her breasts. Licked the crease under them. "Show you how I feel about you, and them." He sucked harder, and she arched into him.

When he repositioned himself, she took the opportunity and rolled him over.

Show him how I feel about him.

She shimmied down his body, kissing every tattoo she found along the way. Kissing the cattails and the weeds, loving his soul and ambition. Kissing each silly flash tattoo because she loved that this serious, dependable man had been a carefree kid once too.

She licked and kissed each one on the way down his solid, soft core, trying to put as much love into each kiss as possible.

"I've never felt more safe than when I'm with you," she said, brushing her lips across his hip bone.

A stuttering sigh wrenched out of him.

"How you make me melt, and laugh." She brushed her cheek against his thigh as his cock brushed her other cheek. She stared up at him, her hands clenching his thighs, squeezing.

She inhaled his scent as she kissed her way across his hip bones, licking up the track of precum that had dripped there.

He stroked her cheek.

She leaned into it, eyeing him. "I don't know if you're mine to keep, but I wish you would be."

"Liv—" Her name was sighed out, like his heart was leaping out of his chest.

Licking up his cock from the base, she slowly ran her tongue up to the head. He arched off the bed with a moan. Sucking on the head of his cock, she licked up the precum like a lollipop as his hand ran into her hair.

Yes.

She sucked him down deeper and felt him tremble under her. His muscles trembled but he never took his eyes from hers.

The power of him in her mouth while he restrained himself made her blood pulse.

She licked him playfully, enjoying it. "Tell me one of your fantasies."

"This." His ragged breaths caught on the edge of control as she sucked him hard. "You."

He looked down as she smiled around his cock. "Oh fuck, that too. I can't look at you. It's too good."

She climbed up his body and grabbed a condom from the bedside table, rolling it on. He squeezed her thighs as she straddled him.

She kissed his chest, wanting to know him more, wanting to know everything about him.

Wanting to make this so good for him.

"C'mon," she teased breathlessly.

"Can't," he said, sitting up and kissing her breast, her neck.

"Too dirty?" she said with a wicked grin.

"No," he said, his eyes connecting with hers, swallowing. "Too real."

Now she *had* to know.

"Please," she said, sliding down onto him. They sighed together as she seated herself onto his cock, feeling full.

A sudden, desperate urge to know every part of him urged her on.

"Please," she begged into his mouth. He held her head as he kissed her, and she was lost momentarily in how perfect it was with him.

He lay down, rocked her hard against him, and a moan ripped out of her.

"Luca, please," she sighed against his mouth, staring at him as they slowly moved together.

He looked so tortured, holding something back.

"Tell me," she said, tracing his bottom lip with her tongue. "I want it all."

She pinned her forehead on his as he grabbed the back of her neck, and they moved together on the bed, noses nuzzling, breathy kisses drifting back and forth.

"Please," she sighed, begging.

His breaths were shaky. "It's you, in the morning. In our bed."

Their eyes met and the nervous, vulnerable look in his made her realize just how *real* he meant.

He closed his eyes, looking pained. "It's bright, and I've made you pancakes and orange juice. And..." His voice shook.

"I can take it," she whispered. "Trust me. It's me, Luca."

His eyes burned with raw desire. "It's morning, and," he sighed out as she clenched around him. "And... god, you're pregnant, and my head is between your thighs, eating you."

She clenched hard around his cock in surprise at the visual, wanting it so bad.

A groan ripped out of both of them as they grasped and clutched at each other, each thrust becoming more intense, more needy.

"You look like a goddess," he said against her cheek as she moved faster over him. "Gorgeous and round and safe. Your hair is everywhere, and you fuck my face, taking exactly what you need."

"Yes, yes," she panted, lost in the fantasy with him.

"Not too much?" he said worriedly as his eyes found hers.

"About to come," she moaned, looking helplessly at him as the fantasy tugged at her secret desires.

He held her jaw as she rode him harder and harder. "That's it, Liv. Give it to me. Give me all of you."

"You have me."

You have my heart.

All of it.

The rhythm of their hard thrusts sounded like *love you, love you, love you* to her ears.

"I... I..." The pleasure of him holding her, treasuring her, was too much. Too good. She might explode from the clenching need if she didn't have him.

He squeezed her, pumping into her harder. "I want it all with you, Liv."

Her climax pitched up through her clit and ripped into every limb as she grasped him. He rocked harder up against her, coming with a shout as both of their muscles seized, still at the apex with the pleasure of it, until finally, they sighed out on the other side.

Her forehead rested against his neck, sweaty and delicious.

"So beautiful when you come," he sighed.

"So hot when *you* come," she said with a smile, and he chuckled.

He wants it all with me.

They finally caught their breath.

"I think..." He nuzzled her into him and wrapped a thigh around hers, sighing like what he was about to say was heavy. "It's time we go on a real date."

Her mind raced.

He stroked her hair. "I can ask Pearl to babysit. She's been encouraging me to, quote, 'finally get your shit together with Olivia.'"

She bit the inside of her cheek, feeling nervous. "What about the no-dating rule?"

He shifted so she looked at him and ran a thumb over her lips.

"The rule was created in a universe where I didn't know you existed. Simple as that. Had I known, the rule would have been: I don't date, except for Olivia Maroo. If she were to ever feel the same way about me."

Falling a little more in love with him, she nodded and then kissed him.

They fell asleep, with his arm wrapped tight around her middle. He lay on her hair and nuzzled the back of her neck.

As Olivia fell asleep tucked into him, a quiet murmur behind her of "Best day ever" made her smile before she drifted off into a dream that could never compete with the day she'd just had.

Chapter Twenty-nine

OLIVIA

Hot Girl Group Chat (17 Unread Messages)

BESTIE LIL

SooooOOOOoooooo how'd your sleepover go Olivia?????

Oliviaaaaaaaaaaaa

Are you alive???

ALLISON (NEW FRIEND)

She's probably still cocked out

CONKED.

I meant conked.

BESTIE LIL

Almost spit my latte out on these hothouse peonies Gray ordered for Rose for their anniversary. WARN A GIRL.

PEARL (AB CONTACT)

the best kind of slips are freudian.

but also please don't make me read about my
brother's sex life barrrrrrrrrrrrrrrf

ALLISON (NEW FRIEND)

I mean, just because she slept over doesn't
mean they HAD to have sex.

PEARL (AB CONTACT)

sure. i'm sure they spent a quiet evening
organizing their receipts.

and NOT borking each others brains out during
precious kid-free hours. have you SEEN them
together? eye fucking for days.

BESTIE LIL

organized their receipts all over his face!

PEARL (AB CONTACT)

lily! blaaaaaaaaaaargh

ALLISON (NEW FRIEND)

Maybe we should use a code word for starting /
stopping so Pearl knows when the sexy coast
is clear.

PEARL (AB CONTACT)

might i suggest BLEACH PEARLS EYEBALLS

OLIVIA

.....Hiiiiiiiiiii

This is not at ALL an insane thing to wake
up to.

ALLISON (NEW FRIEND)

Yay!! You're here. How'd it go??

BESTIE LIL

Spill it, sister (BLEACH PEARLS EYEBALLS
::rolls lily's eyes::)

OLIVIA

He's in the shower. It was…oh my god. Rough.
Amazing. Sweet. Mindblowing. Dirty. Perfect.

BESTIE LIL

YAAAS

ALLISON (NEW FRIEND)

Yaaaaaaaaaaayyyyyyy! Omg I'm so happy
for you.

BESTIE LIL

What's the count?

ALLISON (NEW FRIEND)

Of what?

BESTIE LIL

I bet her lunch at Fox & Forrest that she'd have
more than 3 orgasms. She doesn't see the way
he luuuuusts after her when she's not looking.

OLIVIA

You know what? I'm not even mad I have
to pay.

BESTIE LIL

HA. What's the coooooount

OLIVIA

Six 😌 Four last night, two this morning

ALLISON (NEW FRIEND)

Dammmmmmmn. Some people really are out
here living my dreams.

BESTIE LIL

Did you hear that? Me yelling WAHOO out of
Bloom's door?

Though in really unfortunate timing, your mom
walked by and I had to lie and say it was
because I won $500 in the state lottery. She
told me congrats 😌

OLIVIA

Oh god. She would be THRILLED to be part of this conversation

ALLISON DO NOT ADD HER.

ALLISON (NEW FRIEND)

::slowly deletes numbers::

I just love her so much!!

OLIVIA

She is STILL talking about dyeing her hair orange since the last Bitch & Stitch.

BESTIE LIL

I can't believe sweet angel baby Allison is going to be Martha's bad influence.

OLIVIA

Well, lunch is on me at Fox & Forrest.

What's the code word again?

ALLISON (NEW FRIEND)

UNBLEACH PEARLS EYEBALLS

PEARL (AB CONTACT)

why hello

i take it things went well.

OLIVIA

He um…asked me on a date? Maybe in a few days.

ALLISON (NEW FRIEND)

Finally!!!!!!

PEARL (AB CONTACT)

awwwwww hells yes. bring my lil bestie over any time.

ALLISON (NEW FRIEND)

I have *such* a good feeling about this.

OLIVIA

I'm trying not to get my hopes up too high

But man...

I do too.

LUCA

Luca and Olivia picked up Annabelle from her grandparents' house late the next morning. He loved seeing how kind Ed and Carol were with Olivia, how excited AB was to see her.

After they'd all gotten home, Annabelle took off her Girl Scouts hoodie, and Luca realized her favorite shirt didn't fit anymore. The long sleeves ended above her wrists, and her tummy stuck out the bottom.

The passage of time couldn't have been more obvious if it had blinking neon bar lights on it.

She was growing up so fast. Just six months ago, it had been loose on her.

"Hey, goob," he said gently. "I think you've outgrown that shirt. Why don't you go pick out another one?"

"No!" She scowled at him.

Carol had said she hadn't slept well the night before. She'd been grumpy all the way home.

"Isn't it a little tight?" he asked, trying again. *Maybe she'd be less grumpy if she was comfortable.*

"I like it," she said, stomping her foot. He looked at Olivia, who looked confused as to where the attitude was coming from.

"Hey, sweetie," Olivia said breezily to AB. "Why don't you change into Ballet Princess Supreme's dress, and we can play for a bit?"

"Ugh, fine!" Annabelle ran out of the room.

"Why doesn't she listen when *I* say it?" Luca asked her, confounded.

Olivia squeezed his arm. "Because she needs you to love her just like she is. She might already be self-conscious of being taller than the other kids."

That's true. She is *almost a head taller than the other girls in her dance class and Girl Scouts.*

"Hey Annabelle!" Luca called as tiny feet stomped up the steps.

"*What?!*"

Olivia mouthed "attitude" with an impish smile.

He winked at her. "I love you, okay?" he called to AB. "Just like you are. Even when you're grumpy."

Tiny footsteps stomped back down. Annabelle shoved at her hair, which had fallen into her face, as she walked back across the living room. "I'm not *grumpy*. Everything is just annoying... and stupid... and... and it's all crap and shit!"

He couldn't stop himself from smiling at how cute she was. He crouched down so he was at her eye level. "Crap *and* shit?" His mouth tugged into a smile.

"Yeah." She laughed a little, feeling better at talking it out, apparently.

They both giggled as he tickled her tummy. "Hey, when everything feels annoying and stupid, that's what being grumpy means. Sorry to tell you, but you got a bad case of the grumps, kid."

"No I don't." AB giggled as he pulled her into his hug.

Olivia popped in from the kitchen and struck an exaggerated thinking pose, wearing AB's toy stethoscope around her neck. "I'm a vurld-renowned profezzer of grump-ology. I sink za only known cu-ore for za grumps is being attacked by za Hug Monsterz!"

She hugged Annabelle from the other side as Luca played along, squeezing Annabelle on his side. Her belly laughs turned into shrieks as they all fell onto the ground.

AB scrambled up. " 'Kay, I'm gonna change, then we can play."

Luca watched her run up the stairs and kissed Olivia soundly. His thumb lingered on her chin.

What were they going to do without her? She made everything better.

"Stop overthinking," she said, kissing his thumb. "We said no thinking."

He nodded at the reminder as they sat up.

"Ready!" AB called from the top of the stairs.

"Want to come join the kingdom of Ballettopia?" Olivia said, stretching as she hopped up elegantly.

"Nah." He shook his head. "I should work on the leaves outside."

Olivia ran upstairs after AB hounded her again. Their giggles and chatter floated down the stairs.

He debated. Soon AB would be too big for playing. Who knew how much she'd grow up in the *next* six months.

What was he doing all this for if not to enjoy the tiniest love of his life and the woman he'd take a bullet for?

He knocked on AB's open door. Olivia and AB looked up from their pretend game.

He took a big inhale, not believing what he was about to say. "I need you to teach me how to play Ballet Princesses."

Olivia and Annabelle looked at each other skeptically, like they weren't sure he could handle it.

"There's a lot of lore you need to know," Olivia said, grimacing.

AB stood up, now in charge of the situation. "Yeah, Dad, like a lot. Like how we taxed the frog kingdom because they… they gave the juice to the bad guys who wanted to steal our slippers."

Olivia sat on the floor smiling at him, wearing her tiara. "And how we ensure the kingdom is fairly taken care of through a basic universal income. Not to mention our trap-neuter-return program for the wild caticorns. Part cat, part unicorn, of course."

"Their population was exploding and hurting the magic dragonpixies!" AB said, jumping and swinging her arms out wide.

Luca nodded, psyching himself up. *I can do this.* "I'm… gonna go get a notebook."

"Oh, let me." Olivia popped up. "I've got one with our notes." She ran downstairs.

He sat on the floor of AB's room, and she flung her body at him, hugging him.

"I like it when you play," she said with a shy smile. "I missed it. Even though I've never had it." She laughed at that idea. "Guess I've been missing it a lot."

The world screeched to a halt.

He felt like he'd just missed a step on the stairs. Heart-seizing panic at AB's words gripped him.

I don't play with her? How is that possible?

He mentally replayed the last two months, searching for clues.

The last two years.

The last *four* years.

He played with her... right? They went to the park some-times. *Shit, was the last time during Easter?* They'd done lots of sightseeing in Florida over the summer.

Four months ago.

He was overwhelmed with so many feelings at once. How had he missed this on the checklist of Being a Dad?

Being silly was the missing row he'd forgotten to add. He'd never had the bandwidth.

He needed to fix this. "Hey." She stood eye to eye with him since he'd sat on the ground. "I'm sorry I'm not always the best daddy. I didn't know I wasn't playing this enough."

Her face was unsure as she stared up at him with her cute little button nose twitching in thought.

He straightened her off-kilter tiara. "I didn't have a dad, really. So, I've tried to be a good one without knowing what that is. Kind of like playing pretend and making it up as I went. I'm sorry if I missed some things. I'll do better."

He'd never talked about this with her. Didn't want to bring her down or put his worries on her shoulders.

"You didn't have a dad?" she asked, picking at her sparkling cape.

He shrugged, wanting to not make it a big deal. "Nah."

"But who tucked you in?" Her brows drew together.

Good question. "I guess... I tucked myself in."

Her head tilted, trying to understand. "Who fixed your dinner?"

"Sometimes I did."

"But who... who..." She struggled to express herself and flopped her arms. "Who took *care* of you?"

The concept was so confusing and foreign to her that it felt like he'd done something right.

He shrugged, choking up. "I guess I took care of me."

She wrapped her arms around his neck and patted his head like he did to her. "You're a really good daddy. I can tuck you in."

His vision blurred as he hugged her little body against his. Finally, in that moment, he realized maybe he was doing okay at this parenting thing. To raise someone who had such kindness.

Now as a parent, he realized just how easy it was to love your kid. It would have cost his mom nothing to be kind.

He needed to prioritize himself, he realized, and not enable his mom. She hadn't reached out since their fight in the yard, but that didn't mean he didn't need to have a plan when it happened again. No amount of trying to save his mom would make her love him, he realized. Not really. She'd just be using him, if the last thirty years were any indication.

He'd come clean to Pearl. He didn't like hiding things from her. *But I'll need to find a place without breakable objects to tell her, first.*

"You're the sweetest, Annabelle, but it's *my* job to take care of *you*." He looked her in the eye. "I want you to let me know if there's something I'm not doing enough of, okay? You have good ideas."

She smiled. "Like playing?"

He nodded. "Like playing."

She jumped and grabbed a light-up wand. "Okay, we should play more. Here, you be the security guard."

Olivia walked back in holding a notebook covered in pink stickers. "Found our constitution!"

Luca looked between them. "I thought you said you were princesses? Isn't that a monarchy?"

"We've got to have a constitutional monarchy; otherwise, we'd be drunk with power, Luca," Olivia said with a laugh. "Duh."

AB rolled her eyes. "Duh, Dad. I mean Security Guard Dad."

Olivia handed him a toy sheriff's badge and sunglasses.

They looked expectantly at him.

"Oh, right." He clipped the badge to his shirt and put on the sunglasses. "Now what?"

"Okay." AB waved her light-up wand. "Here are the rules…"

Luca took copious notes as his daughter, who was full of what Pearl would call *leadership potential*, told him *exactly* how to play Ballet Princesses.

OLIVIA

O livia drummed her fingers on the container of rolls Luca handed her as he got Annabelle out of her booster seat.

"Now remember," Luca said as Annabelle hopped down, "we need our best manners today."

"Oh, don't worry about him," Olivia said, holding out her hand for AB. "I once saw my mom covered head to toe in barbecue sauce after eating *really* good ribs."

"I got my fancy dress on, so I can't have those probably," AB said, hop-skipping up the cobblestone walk of Olivia's childhood home.

They'd finally rescheduled the dinner they were all supposed to have before she'd gotten sick. Her heart had melted when she'd walked over to Luca's house to ride together and saw them in their "fancy meal" clothes, as AB had called them. Luca wore a charcoal-gray button-up shirt with slacks, and Annabelle had on a cute plaid dress.

Luca put his hand on the small of Olivia's back briefly. "Nervous?"

She stopped drumming her nails against the Tupperware.

"No, that would be silly. I grew up here, and it's my family, and they already love you, and it's fine that you are the first, uh, people I've brought home for dinner in a really long time."

"Great," he said quietly, his hand now resting on the small of her back. "So, clearly not nervous."

She sighed and squeezed AB's hand.

Annabelle knocked hard on the door, and Wells opened it with a surprised sparkle in his eye. "Well, hello!" he said, sweeping his arm dramatically. "Our most honored guests have arrived, including the two extra special Princesses of Balletland. Or was it Ballettopia?"

Annabelle giggled and looked up at Olivia, who rolled her eyes. "He never remembers the important stuff. Topia." Olivia wrapped her arms around her pine tree of a brother.

"Hey, Freckles," he said, lifting her up in a squeezing hug. He'd gotten his height from their father, whereas she was a carbon copy of their mother.

Wells bent down to AB. "There are some crayons and coloring pages for you." He pointed to a coffee table in the living room. Annabelle ran in.

Wells narrowed his eyes. "Luca," Wells said, throwing a hand out, which Luca grasped. "Nice to meet you, officially."

Wells could be a charming guy when he needed to be, and downright frightening when he *had* to be. That second part seeped in as his Penn-Law-School-Alumni eyes hardened at Luca.

Wells stepped onto the porch and let the door close behind him, still shaking Luca's hand. He towered over Luca's six-foot-something frame. "So! You're fucking my sister. Pretty interesting given you are also *technically* her employer."

"Wellesley Maroo," Olivia gasped and smacked his arm.

Luca just smiled and shook his hand. "Nice to meet you too."

Olivia yanked her brother's shirt until he was at her eye level. "You will behave yourself, or"—she gave him an eyebrow raise—"I will make your life a living hell for the next two hours."

Wells straightened up and yanked his hand back from Luca, shaking it a little to get the blood flowing back into it. "I'm just looking out for you."

"I will *let* you know when I need looking out for," she said, patting his cheek and smacking it a little too hard.

"Come in," Wells said, smiling widely now as he opened the door. "Pop's still working on the food. Mom made cocktails."

Luca helped Olivia out of her coat.

"Sorry for my idiot brother," she whispered as Wells moved to the kitchen.

Luca smiled and calmly shrugged. As if her enormous brother accosting him before dinner was no big deal. "It's okay; he doesn't know me. I'm glad somebody's looking out for you."

Olivia's mouth dropped open at his reaction. Unbothered with a capital U was how he looked right now. *Fascinating.*

"And," Luca whispered in her ear as he walked by, low and close, "he's not wrong. I *am* fucking you."

A thrum of pleasure squeezed at all of her favorite parts at the reminder.

"Ah, you're here!" her mother called.

She hugged her mom, still never having gotten over the thrill of seeing her every few days. In the kitchen, she gave Pop a kiss on the cheek as he sautéed vegetables on the stove. "There's my girl," he said, leaning into her hug.

"It smells good," she said, peeking at the stove.

"Uh-ah!" He shooed her away. "It's almost finished."

"I made cocktails." Her mother brought a tray over. "Including a special drink for AB, my own concoction," she said as they wandered into the living room.

"I get one too?" Annabelle said, looking up from her coloring.

"I call it the ballerina special," Olivia's mother said, pulling out a cute, clear cup with a lid and swirly straw. "Sprite with a dollop of cranberry juice, making it sparkly and pink, just like you were at the festival last week."

"That's very nice. Thank you, Martha," Luca said. "I brought the rolls I told you about on the phone."

It thrilled Olivia that he just... called? her mother??

Like it was totally normal for her not-boyfriend to call up her mom to talk about their family dinner plans that week.

"Your *professional* ballerina specials," her mom said, handing the tray to Wells, Olivia, and Luca. "Tonic, cranberry juice, and a *whole* lot of vodka."

Olivia sipped. "Shit, is it *ninety* percent vodka?"

"Language," Wells said, nodding at Annabelle.

AB shrugged while she colored. "Oh, I can say that word once a week."

Wells choked on his drink as he laughed.

"So, my dear." Her mother sat across from Olivia in the comfortable, warm living room. "How are things going now that the festival is off your plate?"

"Well..." Olivia cozied into the couch and found herself leaning against Luca's leg. "I finished my audition clips, finally. Dayton had a rare spot open up before January, so I sent in my audition." Polite claps filled the room as she cheersed them. "So here's hoping that somebody wants these old bones that have excellent technique."

"Luca," Wells said in a friendly voice that Olivia didn't trust one bit. "I saw your business sponsored part of the festival. Things must be going well."

"Luca smiled confidently. "They are. We're excited to be in Fairwick Falls now."

Wells leaned forward, his face full of concern. "Is there a need for a body shop in a town of a thousand people?"

Olivia glared at him.

Luca smiled to himself. "I'm lucky that many people have referred us for custom work around the area."

Wells shrugged. "Seems like a fussy business if the economy went south."

God, she hated this bullshit male posturing.

Luca shrugged. "Unfortunately, there are always fenders that need unbending."

"Wells!" Olivia interrupted him before he could get out another word, not liking how he was interrogating Luca. She put on a mock-confused voice. "Why are *you* here? Gosh, I've been seeing you around a *lot* lately."

Her mother looked attentively at Wells as she sipped her cocktail. "That's true, dear. You have been around a lot. Five hours is a long drive just for Pop's pancakes."

"Maybe we should all go to the *diner* while you're here," Olivia said, narrowing her eyes at Wells, taunting him into submission.

Wells glared at her. "My business trip was canceled. All the flights on the East Coast are down with a computer malfunction. So I came here for a long weekend instead."

"Martha?" Pop called from the kitchen.

"Coming! Annabelle, do you want to help me set the table? We need to put your art right in the middle for our decorations."

Annabelle popped up, grabbing her coloring pages of fall leaves, and walked into the kitchen.

Wells swiveled to Olivia. "I told you—"

"*I* told *you*—" Olivia said, interrupting Wells.

"—I'm just saying a guy who sleeps with his nanny is probably trying to get the cow with all the milk for free," Wells hissed.

Olivia gasped indignantly, throwing a pillow at him. "I am not a *cow*. There is no *milk* involved," she said as Luca tried to speak up, but she held out her hand to his chest. "*And* I've told him not to pay me while we're together."

"*What?*" Wells yelled. "That's literally *free milk.*"

"Everything all right, dear?" her mom called from the kitchen.

"Fine!" Olivia and Wells said, glaring at each other.

Olivia stood up, all five feet four of her in front of him with her eyes on fire. "I love you, but I *will* throw you under the bus without a second glance if you cross me."

Wells threw his head back with a surprised laugh. "See, I always knew there was a part of dad somewhere in there. I just hadn't looked hard enough yet. Fine. Truce."

"Truce," she echoed. "And stop calling me *milk!*" She smacked his arm.

"Food's ready, kids," Pop called from the kitchen.

They set down platters of food so the dining room table was nearly covered. Her mom had decorated the center of the table for fall, mixing in evergreens and leaves together with low twinkle lights.

"*Whoa*," Annabelle said in awe, looking at the table. "That's a lot of food. It's like a commercial."

"This does look amazing. Thank you so much for having us," Luca said politely.

"Oh"—Olivia's mom waved away the compliment—"that's so nice. You're welcome."

"We never eat food like this," Annabelle said as she stared down the table at the sparkly table runner laden with heaping platters of food.

Luca chuckled. "I do feed her, I promise," he said, and her

family smiled at him. "We just usually don't make a meal with lots of sides because it's just me cooking."

Her mom started passing dishes around. "You're welcome to join us for Thanksgiving if you don't have any other plans."

"Oh. Uh..." Olivia said, panicking. *Is that too much? Too soon?*

Her mother continued, unbothered. "We love having lots of people join since our family is scattered around the U.S."

Olivia tried to read Luca's expression across the table. "Marcy's family is nearby, right? Do you normally spend it with them?"

Luca smiled at Annabelle beside him. "We don't usually do big holiday celebrations with Marcy's family because they bring food with wheat in it. It's hard to avoid," he said, running a hand down Annabelle's hair, "and she's still too little to not eat something accidentally. I wouldn't want to intrude, given Annabelle's allergy. It can make it hard, and it's not fun for her. Thanks for being so kind to make sure that everything was okay for her today."

"Oh, my goodness!" Olivia's mother said, as if shocked and disgusted. "It was no trouble at all. We can easily skip wheat for Thanksgiving."

Pop ate a slice of the buttered rolls that Luca had brought with them. "I'll ask Pearl for this recipe," he said, gesturing. "It's real good."

Pop was at the end of the table, and Annabelle was seated at his right hand. "We don't need that pesky wheat anyway, do we, darlin'? Now make sure to put some butter on your roll. I handmade it for tonight." He helped her navigate the butter knife onto her roll.

Luca had gone silent. He looked like he was fighting through emotion, though no one else seemed to notice. Pop and Annabelle chatted about her schoolwork as Wells and her mother chattered about his business travel.

"You okay?" Olivia whispered, putting a hand on his thigh underneath the tablecloth and squeezing his knee.

He gulped and nodded as he fought to keep his face neutral. "Yeah," he said. It came out a husky whisper. "That would be really nice," he said finally, replying to Martha. "We'd love that."

"Ooh," her mom said, getting an idea. "We could invite Reed and Pearl as well, and the Parker sisters, and all their hunks. Make a whole party of it. Oh, my goodness." She clapped her hands. "My house is going to look like a firefighter calendar."

She giggled as Pop chuckled at her and leaned over to place a kiss on her cheek. "You can be January, Herbert. All these handsome men mashing potatoes, pumpkin-ing pie, and gravy-ing our dressing," she said, throwing a subtle wink at Olivia.

"Oh my god," Olivia muttered, dragging her hand down her face.

They passed plates around, and an overwhelming feeling built up at how amazing it would feel to be home with her family, surrounded by her friends and the man she'd fallen in love with.

It had been over a decade since she'd been home for Thanksgiving. She'd forgotten what it could even feel like. She'd had Friendsgivings that were casual, wine-infused events the one day off they'd have between rehearsals. Nutcracker season kicked off in earnest the day after Thanksgiving, so there had been no time to travel back and forth.

She got misty-eyed thinking about a home-cooked Thanksgiving again, with her two favorite people, and Pop cooking in their house like he always should have been.

"Are *you* okay?" Luca asked her, surprised.

"Yeah," she said. She looked at her phone camera to check if her mascara was running and saw a text come through from

Henri, an old colleague from Salt Lake. It had been ages since they texted.

HENRI

Hey, sorry, this is super random. Do you have five minutes to talk ASAP?

OLIVIA

Everything okay?

HENRI

Yeah, just too busy to text. Call when you have a minute.

She excused herself from the table and called Henri. He picked up within one ring.

"Oooliiiviaaaaaaa," he dragged out in his French accent. "Oh, my god. I am so glad to talk with you."

"Hi," she said, bewildered as to why an old coworker would ask her to call urgently on a Thursday night. "You need bail money?" she said, laughing.

His laugh was despondent. "I wish. I am desperate for your help."

"Name it."

Henri had always been very kind to her when she'd understudied the Sugar Plum Fairy. The role had a duet dance with a prince-like character that Henri had played for many years. Most dancers found it beneath them to practice with an understudy, but he'd gone out of his way to be kind. It had been a rare commodity in her career, which she'd treasured.

"You said you were in Pennsylvania, right?" Henri asked.

"Yes, I'm so excited to see you dance soon. Pittsburgh is just a few hours away."

"Well, my fucking fairy is grounded," Henri said, in a tizzy.

Olivia squinted in confusion, trying to keep up.

"All the flights are canceled, and she cannot get here in time for tomorrow's performance. The new director here *insists* on doing the Gregorovitch version of the choreography. There was a miscommunication, their understudy only knew the Ivanov version, lalala, you get the picture."

That was code for *she got fired.*

"Oh, no," Olivia said, putting all the pieces together.

"Marie cannot get back in time, and we started performing *The Nutcracker* last weekend."

Olivia looked at the calendar on her mom's kitchen wall. "It's barely after Halloween!"

He huffed out a sad laugh. "They wanted to cash in and be the first to do performances, so we started doing every weekend in November. Marie thought she'd do a quick trip to LA, but now here I am, Sugar Plum Fairy-less. It's a nightmare. Truly an *epic* disaster," he wailed dramatically.

All right, Olivia thought, *maybe not a disaster. I mean, this is just ballet we're talking about.*

"You are the only one I trust within driving distance. Could you go on tomorrow?" he said in a pleading voice.

"*Oh.*" Her heart leaped out of her chest. It hadn't even occurred to her that he'd ask *her.*

"And," he continued, "can you send me a video so I can show the director? You'd need to rehearse tomorrow morning with us if he says yes."

"Uh, yeah," she said, scrambling. "I just filmed an audition for somebody else."

"Perfect. You are an absolute lifesaver. Can you *imagine* if we did *The Nutcracker* with no Sugar Plum? *Quelle horreur*! I knew I could count on you."

"Yeah, I'll send it right now."

"Olivia, I will name my firstborn child after you."

She laughed, and they hung up. She texted the video link to him.

"Everything okay?" Luca said, walking into the living room.

"Yeah, I think..." She stared at her phone, dumbfounded. "...Every one of my dreams just came true?" she said, laughing as if it was ludicrous. "I might have to move our date tomorrow, though. A friend might have me fill in for the Sugar Plum Fairy in Pittsburgh."

"Just tomorrow?" he said, confused.

"There's a flight issue, the same thing that Wells is dealing with. I feel so bad—I know we were really looking forward to it."

"Olivia, I will wait until the dead of summer when no one can even *think* about the Nutcracker ballet if it means having a date with you."

What even *was* this? A man who was perfect standing in front of her, her family laughing with the cutest little girl in the next room, getting to dance out her most treasured role ever after feeling like she was the sludge at the bottom of the ballet barrel.

"You'd be shocked how many men do not agree with you," she said, wiping a tear from her eye, feeling overwhelmed with everything in her life right now. "Thanks." She leaned up and kissed his cheek. "I should... go? No, that's crazy." She shook her head. "I need to finish dinner. And then if they say yes and want me, *then* I'll go home and pack."

He hugged her, but his eyes were sad. "I'm really proud of you."

She laughed, and she squeezed him back. "Let's see if I get —" Olivia's phone buzzed.

HENRI

You're in. See you tomorrow at 9:00 AM.

Olivia felt lightheaded looking at the text.

HENRI

Paperwork and details will be emailed.

OLIVIA

Thank you.

"I got it," she whispered, trying to process it.

"Yeah?" Luca laughed with her, a loud booming laugh that filled her up. He wrapped her up in a hug and spun her.

"What's going on?" Her mom peeked in from the dining room.

"I think we're going to have to cut dinner short," Olivia said, the smile bursting on her face.

Chapter Thirty-one

OLIVIA

"Again!"

Olivia's muscles hummed with the warmth of a good workout. They were thirty minutes into the rehearsal, but her unease about being back in a professional ballet studio hadn't gone away.

It felt *weird*, she realized. She'd loved dancing from the minute the music started playing, but there was an uneasiness at being among the dancers.

Like when animals pinned their ears back right before they bit.

Don't be silly; it's just your nerves.

"And then you come in," the artistic director said, beelining in a fast walk through three dancers who looked at her with bored faces. "And then present—*ah*," the director said, facing the audience. "And then... we begin."

"Sure." She nodded, following his direction.

"Let's look at your costume." She'd brought her tutu with her from home since she was a different height and size than Henri's partner.

She rolled down the zipper of her garment bag and pulled it out. "Ah, beautiful." The director nodded approvingly. "Who made?"

"Oh, I mean, I took an existing one and, you know, added flair to it." *I do love a bedazzler.*

"Perfect."

They went onto the stage. It was a beautiful, old, ornate theater dating back to the nineteenth century.

She looked up into the balcony and tried to forget just how many people would be staring at her.

The uneasiness lessened as she walked onto the stage. Just her, and three thousand of her closest friends.

They'd done a quick run-through of her solo, which none of them were worried about. It was the duet that she, Henri, and the director were nervous about.

Their *pas de deux* was a two-person, intricate dance, full of lifts and trust between partners. She was grateful she had five years of rehearsals with Henri under her belt.

I just wish they weren't two years ago.

Henri marked his routine, showing where they would hit in key points around the stage.

"It's going to be great, okay?" he said with a hopeful smile.

"Yes." She did some quick moves from the Sugar Plum solo to get a sense of the grit of the stage against her toe shoes. She'd broken these shoes in the best she could, beating them against the cement wall outside the dressing room, but they still needed just a little bit more.

She fiddled with her toes in her shoe, getting the cotton padding just so.

The director queued up the music. He stood to the side on stage. "Let's take it from the back half, where the lifts start. From the greet into the shoulder lift."

Getting the timing right on the lifts would be the most important thing to nail. Her footwork could be sloppy, but no one wanted a Sugar Plum dropped on the ground.

The music started, and Olivia did her run-up to where she would jump and twist in midair so she would land facing out on Henri's shoulder. It was a complicated lift to seat right, and though she jumped, his hand fumbled, and he grasped at her hip, and they gently came out of it, not able to hold the move.

The director turned off the music. "Again."

"Sorry," they both said with an embarrassed laugh to each other. Henri wiped his hand over his face.

"You've been eating extra Halloween candy." He laughed, a kind smile reaching his eyes. A pit formed in her stomach, and she laughed like it was a reflex.

And then swallowed it as she caught her breath.

No. Not anymore.

"Your hand slipped, actually." She said it kindly but firmly.

Henri registered her frustration. "Oh, my normal partner is lighter. That's all," he said, laughing nervously, trying to smooth things over.

What did she have to lose? She wasn't staying here. She didn't need to be agreeable.

They needed *her*.

She gulped. "I'd rather you not compare my body to hers again," she said, her heart beating fast, the most nerve-wracking thing she'd done all day.

Not doing fifteen *fouettés* in a row, not walking into a room full of people who didn't want her there, but standing up for herself.

Henri's face was full of genuine, surprised concern. "Oh. Olivia, I'm so sorry. I didn't mean to hurt your feelings. I'll do better, I promise."

She smiled faintly. "Thanks," she said, forgiving him. His comment was a love tap in comparison to the truly heinous comments she'd heard as a professional dancer.

It's just been a while since someone has made me feel bad about myself, that's all.

It hit her like an iron glove in the face.

She'd *forgotten* that this... this feeling had been normal.

Feeling bad about myself was just... normal.

The realization thundered through her body, zooming through every nerve ending at how *good* she'd felt before she'd come in.

How different it felt being in a place like this that wanted to keep her *small*.

Figuratively. *Literally*. Hungry for praise, for scraps of attention, and sometimes, yes, for Halloween candy.

She liked being in a place where she felt good about herself every day. Where everyone she talked to, Luca, AB, her mom, Lily, made her feel like the best version of herself.

"Again," the director called as Olivia walked back to the place to reset for another try at the lift. She felt a little taller, walking back to her spot.

Fuller.

They nailed the lift in the next take and finished the back half of the duet. They ran through it all again and again, finally doing two full run-throughs where everything worked out.

They took a five-minute break, and she went to grab water. She checked her phone, hunching over her bag as she caught her breath.

A video came through from Luca of Annabelle saying, "Break a leg!" with her cheesiest smile.

She'd said good night to both of them quickly last night, needing to get her head in the game immediately after dinner.

The husky laugh from Luca recording the video was her favorite sound.

LUCA

How are things going?

We're thinking about you.

You're going to crush it today.

She sighed, looking at the letters on the screen. *And to think he used to just type K.*

"Places in two."

Jesus, she forgot how strict everything was. No time to type with her fingers shaking from the adrenaline.

She hit record to send an audio clip, talking into her phone. "Oh, my gosh. AB is the cutest thing ever. Now I'm *definitely* going to do a great job. It's been tough, but I'm feeling really good. I can't wait to tell you about it. And I miss you. Is that weird to say?" She laughed.

"Places!"

"Oh shoot, I've got to go. I love you, bye!"

She sent the audio clip and tossed the phone into her bag.

She walked two steps to rehearsal before a full-body panic gripped her.

"*Fuck!*"

She dove for her phone, tapping furiously on the audio message to delete.

"Why isn't the menu coming up? *Why isn't the menu coming up?*" she panicked.

She called Luca immediately.

"Olivia, let's go!" Henri called.

"One second!"

"Hey, everything okay?" Luca's low, rumbling voice coming through her phone felt like velvet.

She waved at the new flop sweat under her arms. "Hey, real quick, uh... no big deal, but... could you delete that audio note before you listen to it?"

"...Why?" he said with confusion.

"I, um..." She gulped. *Actually, I said I love you at the exact wrong time.* "Uh... I farted really bad. It's very embarrassing."

A roaring laugh sounded in her ear, and she bit her lip, loving him even more. "I mean, most things you do are cute. Are you sure it wasn't cute?"

"Look, I have to go, please, just please promise me?"

Oh my god, oh my god, oh my god, oh my god, oh my god—

A laugh rumbled out of him. "I promise I won't play it when we hop off. Go break some toe shoes."

"All right. Thanks." *Don't say I love you.* "Bye."

And suddenly, a new wave of things to be nervous about gripped her body, and she hustled to the stage to do one last run-through.

~

LUCA

LUCA GAPED AT THE ENORMOUS, old-ass theater as he and Annabelle sat down in velvet, cushioned seats.

Annabelle's jaw had dropped when they'd entered the lobby. Every piece of trim was lined with tinsel or evergreen, and the lobby ceiling reflected back a gold-frosted version of themselves. Life-size prop nutcrackers stood around the lobby. Giant snowflakes and sugar plums were dotted around the merch tables. They'd both been flabbergasted that this was what ballet could be.

They were seated in the nosebleed section, behind Martha

and Pop, who sat beside Wells with his long legs stretched out into the aisle.

"Oh, I'm so nervous," Martha tittered, wiggling about. Pop patted her hand, and Wells clenched his jaw as he typed furiously on his phone.

They'd all decided to get tickets secretly so they wouldn't make Olivia more nervous. The season had already started to sell out, and they didn't want to promise her they could be there if they weren't able to scrounge up tickets.

Annabelle bounced up and down hard in her seat, flopping shiny patent leather shoes back and forth. She'd worn her sparkliest dress—it was a little too short on her, Luca realized now—with her pink ballet tights. Pearl had come over to put her hair in a pretty updo. She'd wanted to look pretty for Olivia's special night.

He pulled Annabelle up into his lap to talk to her. She was still too jazzed. "This is like a test at school for Olivia. She has to concentrate. Okay?" he said, squeezing her to him.

"And we can't yell," Annabelle said. They'd practiced that last part for an hour and a half in the car. "*And* we can't dance."

"That's right." He kissed the top of her head. Originally, she'd wanted to wear her ballet leotard today. Her reasoning had been flawless—why *wouldn't* she wear her ballet outfit to the ballet? But he'd had to clarify that there was no dancing involved for her tonight.

The lights dimmed, and Annabelle sat on his lap in awe. He felt the same childlike wonder he saw on her face as the colorful, bright ballet unfolded.

Luca's heart was in his throat as he followed along with the program, waiting for Olivia's numbers.

Suddenly, the scenery changed, and beautiful, big sugar plums lined the stage, held by dancers.

Olivia slowly and elegantly walked out to center stage.

His heartbeat thundered outside of his body as he realized she was wearing the tutu from Bookish.

The one she'd worn when he *knew* she was going to be his.

A brutal ache almost made him laugh out loud at how right he'd been.

And here she was on a stage in front of three thousand people. Miraculously, everyone around him looked at her expectantly, instead of leaping to their feet and applauding at the mere sight of her like he wanted to.

He sat on his hands, just to make sure.

Martha clutched a tissue to her lips. Bright tear tracks of pride shone down her cheeks, and she clutched Pop's hand, both of them looking nervous.

Luca snuck out his phone and took a quick photo of them watching the performance. *Olivia would want it.*

Familiar music started to play that he'd heard in every TV commercial during Christmas.

Olivia was impossibly beautiful. Achingly breathtaking. She had such joy in her dancing. The audience had started smiling at the sight of her.

People lined the stage, acting as part of the scenery.

Olivia had to do this for eight years? Watch while somebody else danced the solo she'd never gotten to perform? Torture.

His brain tried to take it all in. Her hand gestures, her foot that flounced sometimes, her legs stretching up so her calf was by her ears by some miracle of gravity *while she stood on a single fucking tiptoe.*

Why weren't people screaming? Cheering? Wearing face paint and jerseys with Olivia's name on them?

The sheer athleticism was brain-scrambling.

Then, just as it was over and he almost clapped like an idiot, she kept dancing and did what looked like turn after turn after turn. Five, ten, twenty—it had to be thirty turns around the stage, like a snowflake dancing on a spinning top. Halfway around the stage, the audience broke into applause as she was still spinning. Ten more turns, then ten more.

Those perfect cheeks broke into a genuine, blinding smile that was reflected back to her three thousand times.

The applause grew as the tempo got faster and faster. She was still spinning until suddenly she stopped on a dime, her head angled just so, to thunderous applause and shouts.

Pop whistled, and he saw Olivia blink in recognition but not move a muscle at the sound as her stage smile widened into a laughing, joyful one.

AB was on her knees on her chair, clapping as hard as she could. "THAT'S MY—" Luca covered AB's mouth as he dragged her onto his lap with a laugh.

More random dances came through, then a while later Olivia was back on stage.

A handsome, prince-like dancer was escorting her. Their warm, intimate smiles with each other made Luca's teeth grind.

The music started, and they danced together as if they had known each other all their lives.

The music—a familiar, romantic, aching melody—hit him in the heart and squeezed, twisting it.

It was the perfect encapsulation of what he'd felt when he'd first seen her—inevitable longing.

Olivia *was* this music.

Beautiful, devastating. Sweeping out the sadness and emptiness in his bones and filling them with an insatiable yearning for her.

Like he'd never fully live without her.

His eyes devoured every move, trying to remember it all. Trying to live in the moment with her.

At least he could always be with her in this music.

Pretending *he* was the one basking in her smile on stage, holding her waist as she spun like pink cotton candy.

Radiance beamed from her as she elegantly, yet with military precision, did the complex choreography.

As the music gained steam, she leapt into the man's arms. They danced together as if they were birds in flight, joyful, carefree, miraculous.

Grand.

That was the only word he could think of to describe her.

She was so much bigger than the small life he led.

As big as this three-thousand-person auditorium. As grand as a sparkling tutu in a million-dollar production.

So much bigger than the small life he could give her.

Years of work in every pose, in every movement, the sureness, athleticism, and grace, and all while standing on the edge of a few toes.

He shook his head back and forth, unable to comprehend it. The bright, bubbling woman who snorted when she laughed and danced with his kid in the kitchen was also the work of art capturing the hearts of the other two thousand nine hundred ninety-nine people in the room.

The music approached the end. Luca sat on the edge of his seat, holding his breath during the drumroll. They hit pose after pose after pose, finally landing on the last beat with Olivia in the air, wearing a blindingly bright, happy smile.

Applause shattered the short silence in the room, and people in the front row stood up. He whistled along with Pop and Wells's shouts. Annabelle shouted too. They could be as raucous as they wanted now that Olivia wouldn't be distracted.

She held her pose on stage, drinking it in. He could see the happiness of it running through her veins.

His heart broke for himself and the little girl beside him, knowing they'd never keep her in their lives now.

She brought so much joy into everyone's life. Even if it meant his life would be dimmer and hollower without her, it was a sacrifice he would happily make if it made her happy.

He only wanted the absolute best for her. She was finally living her dream, as she should.

It was a consolation, though, that she was so fucking good at it.

Chapter Thirty-Two

OLIVIA

Olivia's hands shook from the adrenaline as she and Henri made it into the wings.

She exhaled a long breath. They'd landed every lift, every turn. It had been nearly flawless.

She'd heard Pop in the audience, which meant her mom was there. She had a sneaky feeling that maybe a couple of other people were there, specifically a man with a little girl who wouldn't let two senior citizens drive two hours back home at night on the highway.

She swallowed the emotion, trying not to cry. She still had the last dance, where the entire company was on stage.

She looked up to find Henri and congratulate him, thank him for this amazing opportunity, and saw he was already across the wing, hugging Marie, his usual Sugar Plum Fairy. She was in street clothes and had been watching from the wings. She waved at Olivia with a smile.

Olivia waved sadly back, realizing her time as the Fairy would end tonight.

That went so well. She'd never danced better professionally. She was going to talk to the director.

If there was any time to see if they had an open spot for her someday, this was it.

She found the director on the computer in his office. She knocked on the door.

"Yes?" he said quickly.

"The *pas de deux* went well," she said. "Thank you for your help."

"I saw. The lift—good." He shrugged. "The back leg needed to raise."

"Oh." *Not what I wanted to talk about.*

"Marie is here, I heard. So nothing more needed for you. You'll be paid in two to three weeks." He turned back to his computer.

"I'm not sure if you know, but I'm looking for a new role."

"Henri mentioned," the director said, taking his glasses off again. "You can put this on your resume."

She nodded, thrown off by his comment. *Of course I would put it on my resume. What the hell?* "I was curious if you had any open corps roles?"

"We'll have one in January. Not posted yet."

"Well, I would love to apply."

"Hmm," he said, looking her up and down. "Maybe... too old? But you can try." He shrugged and went back to his work, dismissing her.

Right, she remembered. That was how this game was played.

You were a favorite until you weren't.

They cared about you until they didn't.

She went to reapply her makeup for the final waltz number.

A clawing ache she'd remembered for so many years was back with a vengeance. It was *want*. Wanting to be part of something, wanting to be included, feeling like she'd made it, like she wasn't teetering on the edge at all times.

The best performance of her life, and it *still* hadn't been good enough to make all those feelings go away.

The final waltz went off without a hitch. She'd always liked this part. It was joyful with the entire company on stage dancing together.

She basked in the glow of the company bows, trying to savor the feeling of being special, stave off any emotion, and just smile brighter.

Given *The Nutcracker* was a children's ballet, the cast members were encouraged to go out into the lobby to meet and greet families. She had many pictures taken at the photo station, and eventually, one of the other dancers subbed in for her as she saw her tall brother over the top of the crowd.

She met her family in an alcove away from the rest of the crowd. Wells gathered her up, swinging her around, squeezing the life out of her. "I'm so proud of you, Freckles," he said with a big kiss on her cheek.

"Oh," was all her mother could get out as she started crying —what looked like—*again*. "We're just so proud of you," her mom whispered as she gathered her in a hug, and then Pop squeezed the life out of her as well.

Although Olivia savored the moment of hugging the two best people on this Earth, her eyes were drawn to the bouncing six-year-old and the quiet man holding a huge bouquet of flowers behind them.

Her eyes locked with Luca's, and he gathered her up, crushing her to him. "You were stunning."

A small sob escaped her in the comfort and safety of that hug.

"'Livia, 'Livia!" Annabelle said, bouncing up and down. "That was *so* cool! I *saw* you."

"Yeah?" Olivia said, wiping her eyes carefully. "Did you have fun watching it?"

Annabelle nodded her head up and down so hard it might have almost fallen off. She could see AB was overwhelmed.

"Yeah, I had fun too." Olivia's lip wobbled at that last part.

"Let's take pictures," Wells said.

Olivia shuttered her emotion behind a stage smile. As she was flanked by her brother and parents on either side, the smile turned genuine.

The crowd had thinned out as they all stood and talked about her performance. Before long, Wells left to start the long drive back to Philly.

Luca leaned down to her mother. "Hey, Martha and Pop, could you take Annabelle to meet the characters?"

"Ooh, let's look at the merch too," Martha said, holding Annabelle's hand. "I think you're a size *fabulous,* same as me." She winked at Annabelle. Annabelle giggled as Pop grabbed her other hand and they walked to the other side of the lobby.

"Hey," Luca said, now that it was just the two of them. The look of concern in his eyes had only gotten more intense the longer he'd looked at her. He pulled her farther around the corner, away from other people. "Talk to me."

She smiled and blinked, overwhelmed. Couldn't process it.

"I'm good. I'm just... It felt so good," she said, breathless, remembering the rush of the feeling onstage.

"But?" he said, a questioning look in his eyes.

A tear plopped onto her cheek as her lip twisted down. "But it wasn't enough," she said, her voice catching. "It'll never be enough. I loved finally showing what I've been preparing for, you know? Just dance and show the joy that I've always had in performing this amazing choreography, but... it didn't solve all my problems," she said with a laugh, wiping her eyes. "Which is a ridiculous thing to think anyway."

He handed her his hanky, and it only made her want to cry more. He enveloped her in a hug, and she finally let herself sob.

There was a low from it not feeling like she'd always imagined.

Not feeling like she belonged and not *being enough.*

It's an endless pit. It'll never be full. The job can't love you back.

"I've given so much of my life," she said, pacing now. "Given my time, sweat, tears, social life, joints, relationships, time with my family. Given so much that there's... there's this emptiness now. All I have to show for it is an empty airplane hangar where my life should be. I thought this would be the thing that fixed it, you know?" she said. "Even if I keep trying..."

"It might still feel this way," he said, understanding.

She nodded, biting her lip.

"Wherever you go..." he said.

"There I am," she sighed, "in toe shoes. I don't know what I was expecting—a red carpet to join a company or what? But they didn't seem interested."

He wrapped her in a hug again, and she finally relaxed. "Thank you for coming," she said. It meant so much that he'd come at the last minute. "It means everything, actually."

"Olivia, you were breathtaking. I don't even feel fancy enough to talk to you right now."

A smile grew on her face as she took in his dark sweater layered over a charcoal button-up, dress slacks, and dress shoes. Tattoos peeked out above the neckline and onto his hands, which somehow turned the hot outfit into scorching.

"I like your outfit," she said, looking him up and down as they held hands. *An understatement.*

"You mean my fancy-meal clothes?" His eyes danced but stared at her ruby-red lips. "I like yours. I have fond memories of this tutu. But this time, I can ask: will I mess up your makeup if I kiss you?"

"Definitely," she laughed, her heart fluttering. "But more

importantly, I will leave bright red lipstick all over your face. Annabelle might be six, but she is *not* a dummy."

"Hmm," he said with a warm smile, nodding in agreement. He hugged her hard and kissed her temple.

"I can't wait to be home with you," she said. He squeezed harder in response.

"Look what we got!"

They turned around to see Annabelle, Pop, and her mother all in matching bright red sweatshirts, carrying bags of merch.

"Martha," Luca said, "you didn't need to—"

"Oh, nonsense. I have no grandbabies to spoil, so you just let me." Annabelle had a commemorative sweatshirt, a book, a doll, and her own sparkling pink tutu.

Her mother looked genuinely thrilled to have spoiled Annabelle. And to her credit, Annabelle looked like she really loved to be spoiled. Martha, Pop, and Annabelle chattered with each other.

Oh, god. A realization hit Olivia. *What are Luca and I doing?*

Their families were becoming entangled with each other. They'd completely lost control of the situation.

She looked up at Luca as he seemed to realize the same thing.

Uh oh.

"Do you want us to wait for you?" her mom asked. "You can follow us home."

"No, it's going to take me a minute to get everything. And to de-"—she gestured at her face and her hair—"-sparkle."

Annabelle giggled. "I'll take your sparkles."

"I will save some for you," she said, booping Annabelle's nose. "Thank you for coming to see me."

"I'm going to be a ballerina like you."

Well, there's the road to heartbreak, kid. She mentally started saving for Annabelle's therapy someday.

No, she would drive back alone because she had many hours of thinking to do.

~

At 1:00 AM that night, Olivia quietly snuck up the stairs of Luca's house. She just needed to feel him. The empty darkness of her own house next to his felt chilling in comparison.

She gently closed Luca's bedroom door and locked it. They'd just get up early together, she decided. She tugged off her yoga pants and sweatshirt. He roused as she climbed into bed.

"Good," he said, holding up the cover so she could climb in. "I was worried about you," he mumbled sleepily into his pillow.

She smirked at his sleepy face. "You seem very distraught," she said, snuggling into the cocoon of pre-warmed flannel sheets that smelled like him. Her whole body melted back into feeling okay once she was in his arms.

"I can worry and sleep at the same time," he muttered, eyes closed and squeezing his arms around her waist. "How'd your thinking go?"

"Inconclusive," she sighed, staring at the ceiling. He tugged her closer, so that she was flush against him, being the little spoon.

"Stop thinking so loud," he said, nuzzling the back of her neck.

She leaned back into him, enjoying how her mind finally stopped spinning when he did that. "Can't stop my brain."

A heavy leg hooked around hers and tugged her legs back flush with his. He squeezed his arm around her, and she could have died from how good it felt. His mouth moved to the curve of her neck with slow, lazy kisses.

She sighed. "That helps."

She pushed back against him, needing to feel even closer, until he angled her jaw for a slow, gentle kiss.

Just warmth and nuzzling. Taking their time. The scratch of his beard against her cheek made her smile.

She turned so they were nose to nose. For the first time, they were in no hurry. Just savoring each kiss as if it was a gift.

His hand cupped her jaw and ran up into her hair as his lips danced with hers in their own duet. Slow and sliding. The sensation made her feel like she was precious, perfect.

She ran her hands along his back, down to his ass, and squeezed.

He smiled against her lips. "Bunhead," he whispered with a chuckle. An unexpected snort of laughter escaped her as he sucked on her earlobe.

He laughed harder and moved over her, his charming smirk making her weak with lust and love. "I'll never get tired of your laugh," he said, dipping down to kiss and bite along her jaw.

She loved the pinning weight of him against her hips. He was hard, and she spread her legs so he landed at *just* the right spot, wrapping her sore legs around him.

Propped up on his arms, he took his time as each kiss grew longer and deeper. He held her head with both hands, and the romance of it, how treasured she felt, was almost too much for her.

She loved him so much she might break in two.

"Luca, I..." she sighed, not even knowing how to say every-thing she felt. *Can't say "I love you" right now.* Not during the lead-up to sex, like it was foreplay instead of her soul finding its twin flame.

He clenched his jaw, looking hungry. "I know, Liv."

Their kisses became more desperate, more grasping. His hand slid under her shirt and grabbed her bare breast. They moved against each other at the pleasure of it.

He breathed against her neck as he wrapped an arm around her waist. "That music you danced to with the prince."

She smiled in surprise as he locked eyes with her. *The pas de deux?*

"I... I knew it somehow." He faltered, kissing her briefly. "I hear it when I touch you. In here," he said, swiping a thumb over her heart.

He looked pained, as if he'd admitted something terrible.

Tears of longing filled her eyes. The most romantic melody ever. She understood him exactly. "You do?"

He nodded, kissing her, stroking over her heart again, the heat of his hand burning into her. Her eyes filled at the impossible sweetness of him. How much she loved him.

"Let me show you how I feel about you," she whispered.

She pushed his sweatpants down as her lips never left his. Had to show him how much she loved him since she couldn't tell him, for now. She had to make sure that when she finally told him, it was perfect, just like he always made her feel.

He reached for the drawer beside the bed as she tugged off her panties, her t-shirt. She didn't want anything between them, wanted to feel every part of his heat against her.

As he rolled on a condom, she had to keep touching him. Kissing his heart where the music came from, nuzzling the chest hair there. Licking along the waves of his tattoos that covered his teddy-bear heart of gold.

Breathing against him, inhaling the cedar soap and sleep-warmed skin, she wrapped her arms around him and pulled him down.

Thick fingers slid into her easily. Luca whimpered, her favorite sound, she realized, as he slid his fingers in and out. Her legs itched to wrap around him, but she threw her head back as his thumb strummed her clit. They breathed through their noses hard, feasting on each other's mouths.

He threaded his fingers through hers and pushed his cock into her, so slow, so sweet. Needy and clinging to one another as if they'd finally found the place they belonged.

"This," she gasped against his mouth, wrapping around him and pushing his head into the curve of her neck. "*This* is my fantasy."

His thrust back into her was jagged, roughened, as if his muscles were fighting his control.

"Just like that," she sighed. "Like you need me."

"God, I do, Liv. I do." His tortured face above her looked at her like she might sail away forever, never to see him again. "I do."

She loved those words.

Wanted to hear them again and again.

While standing in front of everyone they loved, in a white dress, across from him.

"I do," she echoed back to him. Their kisses were more urgent, more desperate as he reached between them and rubbed her clit in just the right way as he thrust.

"Coming," she whispered through a hissed breath, trying to be so quiet. He kissed her hard, cradling her head as he destroyed every last defense around her heart.

As his tongue met hers, she climaxed with a gasped moan into his mouth and came around his cock, pulling and clenching it until a wrenched, whispered *Liv* had him coming in her.

Live. The word echoed into her as the sizzling, white static pleasure of her climax fizzled through her.

That was how it felt with him. Like she was finally living. *Finally* living a big, full life she'd never thought she could have.

Wrapped around each other, they stilled, and Olivia held him tight. *The best gift he hasn't even realized he's given me.*

Luca finally pulled back, his jaw moving like he was looking at a feast as he stared at her. "Go on our date tonight?" he asked suddenly, urgently. "If Pearl is free."

She smiled. *I want to go on a date with you for the rest of my life.* "Is there a rush?"

"I just don't want to miss whatever time I have with you."

The reality of her life came back into focus. Her decisions to make, the people she might hurt, the potential she might lose.

Still, she nodded and kissed him as they cuddled back in bed, spooning as they'd started.

Chapter Thirty-Three

OLIVIA

Olivia sat in her mother's house the next day, savoring the warmth of her favorite mug against her hands.

It was a hearty, ugly, purple mug she'd painted in freshman art class, sitting next to Lily. She'd used it every time she'd come back home, from junior year onward.

So many years away.

Olivia had really only lived in Fairwick Falls for about ten years. She'd spent almost double that time away, yet it still was home.

How is that possible? That some places and people just stick with you? That some things just feel right, even though they make no sense?

A handsome face she'd kissed until her lips bruised last night came to mind, and she smiled over the memory.

"I *said*, will you go back to Pittsburgh to dance again?" her mom said, trying to catch her eye across the kitchen table.

Olivia blinked out of her thoughts. "Sorry, distracted. I don't know."

"Something bothering you?" her mom asked with a knowing smile.

Olivia rested her hands on top of the warm coffee and set her chin on them. "I just feel... unsettled. I mean, my life." Olivia shrugged. "What even is it? I feel like the random stuff at the bottom of a purse. Sort of a dancer, sort of a teacher, sort of a nanny. I'm not sure if any of it fits anymore. I *want* to stay here—"

"For an obvious, handsome, beefy reason," her mother chuckled into her coffee.

Olivia rolled her eyes but nodded in assent. "Obviously. But also seeing you and Pop, seeing Lily when she's in town, and Wells. But I'm not cut out to teach dance classes to small children for the rest of my life."

Her mother straightened her omnipresent rhinestone glasses and got down to business. "Tell me what you like about your job now? Dancing, I mean."

Olivia twirled her mug, thinking. "I like discipline and working hard. Making things that bring people joy. I always liked the technical aspects of ballet, getting them *just right*. Meeting the challenge of finessing and perfecting something. It's a lot easier for me than wrangling classes of young kids. More fulfilling."

Her mom shrugged. "Then you make it work long distance with Luca."

Olivia shook her head, feeling so torn. "This is bigger than him. Dancing in front of the audience felt great in the moment, but that's ten minutes of the week. Being back in the studio felt so... lonely. After the performance, I thought I'd finally feel like I belonged. Turns out... not so much." She fought to keep her lip from quivering.

Her mother squeezed her hand and nodded kindly. "Sometimes the worst thing that can happen is you get exactly what you always wanted. And it turns out you wanted horse shit this whole time."

Olivia laughed and blinked away the tears in her eyes. God, she'd missed her mom so much. The number of days she'd seen her since coming home two months ago was more than she had in the last ten years combined.

That realization made her stomach plummet. How much had she missed out on already?

Her mom shook her head. "The real question is: Is dance all there is to your life? Being a success?"

She'd never thought about it like that.

"I just wanted to be good enough for you and Dad. I needed to be amazing at dance to feel like I belonged in our family."

Every six weeks, as a kid, she'd feel sick to her stomach knowing what was coming when report cards came out. Her father would call and yell, her mother would scold her for not trying harder. They'd tell her, "You're a smart girl, just try harder," which only made her feel worse.

Her mother looked surprised.

Hadn't she known this on some level already?

"It was so hard to follow in Wells's straight-A's, advanced-classes footsteps. You didn't notice me unless I danced, and I was *good* at that. It felt like the only thing I had to give myself a chance in the world. I'm dyslexic, it turns out. That's why I had trouble in school."

Her mom was surprised. "No," she said, dismissing it as if that couldn't be true.

Olivia stared at her, waiting for it to sink in. Her experience wasn't up for debate.

Her mom put a hand to her lips in shock. "You are?"

Olivia nodded slowly. *And I dealt with it on my own.* Olivia thought about a little kid, tiny like Annabelle, braving it on their own, and her heart broke for how lonely she'd felt then.

"I am so, so, so sorry, Olivia." Her mom leaped up and walked around the table to hug her hard, yanking off her glasses. She sat next to her and held Olivia's face. "I didn't care if you danced. I cared that you had friends. That you were healthy and happy. You never had to earn my love, sugar pea. I'd be proud of you if you... well, if you poured shots at The Thirsty Beaver." They both laughed, and Olivia squeezed her mom's hand. "I just wanted to see you happy, and I thought dancing made you that way. Turns out I had it backwards."

Saying goodbye to dance felt scary. "Ballet is all I've ever known." A tear dripped down Olivia's nose. "You sacrificed so much for me. I feel like I should have done more with all that potential. Had a bigger life."

"Sweetie. All that matters is if you're happy. So, are you?"

Olivia thought about it. About the stark difference of being with her people, doing things that had nothing to do with dance, and how happy she'd been. How happy Luca made her.

"Yes," she sighed. "Really, really happy. I feel good about myself here. Loved."

Her mom squeezed her hand. "Honey, being loved completely is the biggest life there is. You can't ask for anything better than someone shining love in all the places you need it. Now." She smacked the table and popped up to flutter around the kitchen. "What does Olivia Maroo look like when you take away the dance? You took it so *seriously*, sweetie. At eight years old, you had your eyes set on being a professional. That's *twenty-five years* of dogged determination. I never saw a teenager who showed more discipline." She chuckled as she gathered ingredients in the kitchen.

Dance would always be part of her. It was sewn into her DNA now. Every muscle and joint would remember it until the day she died. But what else was there to her? She didn't even know. "What if I waste my time and pick the wrong thing?"

Her mother shrugged. "If it makes you happy, it's not wasted. Being happy is what time was made *for*, dear. Speaking of!" The front door closed, and Pop toddled in wearing his newsboy cap and flannel coat.

"Well, why didn't you *tell* me there was a beauty pageant this morning?" He chuckled as he kissed her mom.

"Hi, Pop." Olivia leaned into his quick hug. "Brought your shirts." He'd needed some dress shirts taken in because he and her mother had started playing competitive pickleball.

"Ah, thanks. Your mom's always so busy, and there's no tailor in town. I hate driving on the highway to Elliotsville for a few old shirts."

"No problem," she said back, but he was already lost, staring at her mother with a lovestruck look as she flitted about the kitchen.

A spark of an idea hit her.

I like sewing. Most dancers had to learn to sew a little out of necessity. They took care of their costumes in small ballet companies and did repairs as needed, sometimes custom fitting things like leotards or undergarments. She liked that it was creative and technical, and she made something beautiful in the end.

Maybe I could even study costume design.

Or heck, redo my twenties and take gen ed college classes and see what I've been missing this whole time.

She'd gone down a rabbit hole listening to YouTube videos about forms of government preparing for Ballettopia with AB. Maybe *that* was what she might want to do. It turned out she really liked to learn once she knew how her brain worked.

I could live in the world of possibility, rather than only try for perfection. She rolled the idea around in her head.

It sounded scary, but she'd be here where she'd be loved, so that had to be better, right?

Find my next adventure and myself. The purple mug in her hands reminded her where her home had always been, and may always be.

Right where I belong.

~

LUCA

LUCA'S HEART beat hard against his ribs as he walked Olivia through the diner door with his hand over her eyes. *Please god don't let this be the dumbest idea I've ever had.*

"Eyes closed, no peeking," he said over the clanging of the bells on the diner door.

She looked confused. "Are those the *diner* bells?" she said, sniffing the air but keeping her eyes closed.

"Tada," he said, wincing.

But her eyes went wide as she saw his surprise: Pop in his old apron and uniform, waiting beside a table.

"What?!" Olivia yelled in surprise.

"It's just for tonight," Luca said, relieved at her reaction.

"Hello, my girl," Pop said with a laugh. "I'll go get your drinks."

"How?" Olivia asked as Luca helped her out of her coat.

"It wasn't hard to convince the manager to let me have the diner all night because no one comes in anymore. I figured if you kept coming back, even though the food was terrible, there had to be some bigger reason. Maybe I could give you what you were looking for one more time."

"A memory of my favorite place from my childhood?" She kissed his cheek, looking like she was going to melt. "This is an *amazing* first date."

Phew.

Luca pulled out her chair for her, and they sat down at a small table where Pop had added a little vase and a battery-operated candle.

"Wells, my mom, and I would come here every day after school. Mom with her legal briefs, us with homework. Pop would make us eat some fruit first, but then we'd share this big plate of cheese fries. It was our place, our home away from home. Is that how you fell for her, Pop? Because we came in so often?" Olivia smiled, charmed by him as he walked up with a tray.

"Nah," Pop chuckled in his gravelly way. "Fell for your mom the minute I saw her. Just was an idiot and thought I'd ruin everything if I told her. Took me too long to fix that mistake." Pop eyed Luca with a subtle arch of his brow as he slid a platter between them.

I get it, I get it.

"Cheese fries for the lady, and two cups of coffee that taste halfway decent."

"Thanks," Luca said to Pop, who winked and slowly toddled back to the kitchen.

Olivia's mouth was still open in surprise. "You got my favorite cheese fries that don't technically exist anymore *and* good coffee."

That warm, happy, gooey feeling radiated in his chest as he took in her pretty face. "The first time I saw you was right here last Christmas. Carol and Ed took Annabelle to this Christmas train thing in Cooperstown after we did presents. I was dreading coming here, but Pearl had made me promise. And then I saw you. I couldn't stop *staring.* I turned around for *one second*, and you were gone. Poof. Couldn't find you anywhere. I looked in the parking lot only to see your car drive away. I'd always look for you when I came into the diner. So, this is sort of our place in my head."

He gulped at sharing all that, and her eyes went dreamy as she adorably chewed a cheese fry.

"Our place?" She puffed out her lower lip as if he was adorable. "We've had a place this whole time? What did Pearl say when you told her after the Christmas party?"

He smirked and rolled his eyes as he held her hand from across the table. "I kept it to myself. It sounded crazy. *'Hey, there's a woman I saw briefly as I walked through a room, and can you help me find her, please?'* She'd have probably slapped me."

Olivia snorted as she sipped her coffee. "I was *so* out of it that day. I'd performed two shows the day before, caught a red-eye, and got home at 10 a.m. for Pop's last Christmas party at the diner. Then drove *back* to the airport for a flight to perform the next day. I assumed I'd hallucinated *you*, honestly."

Luca laughed and grabbed her hand, interlacing their fingers.

"For our main course." Pop delivered two heavy diner plates with burgers and salads.

Olivia's eyes widened. "Did you cook these here?" Olivia said, poking the burger hesitantly.

"Brought it from home." Pop rolled his eyes in disgust. "It's a mess back there." He untied his apron and patted Luca's shoulder as he walked out. "Hey, kid, key's by the door. Lock up when you leave."

Olivia's phone buzzed in her purse. She checked it briefly. "I'm still getting messages about the clips I posted on social media."

In the very last number, he'd recorded some of her dancing so she'd have the memory.

"You still riding the high?" he said, savoring the delicious burger he'd missed so badly.

Olivia took a bite of her burger and sighed over it. "I mean, it's hard to compete with the high of this burger," she said through a mouthful of food.

He could have leaped over tall buildings at making her so happy.

She sighed as she chewed. "I've decided the bravest, best thing I can do is be honest with myself. That dancing will always be part of me, but I still feel empty."

Anxiety wracked his body at what might be coming.

She continued. "I've been searching for what's next, and what's next has been greeting me in the mirror for thirty-three years. Finding out what *I* really like, beyond dance. Not because it'll make me worthy to love. But because I *really* just... like it. Giving myself permission to try new things. To have hobbies, and drink too much at ladies' night with my friends, and see my mom and Pop every day if I want to. I'm giving myself permission to live out my sloppy twenties, find what I want to do, find myself, and surround myself with as much love as I can take in. It turns out I've been running on a love deficit for fifteen years, and I have a lot of catching up to do."

Was she staying here? *Don't push her. Just support her.*

He smiled. "Would you try going to college?"

"Maybe." She munched a cheese fry contemplatively. "Reading would be different now. I could ask for help."

"I talked to Annabelle's teacher last week, by the way. Apparently, she had the same concerns and gave me some tips to help her at home. We're going to keep an eye on it. Maybe follow up with a specialist after Christmas. She'll get whatever help she needs because of you."

Olivia had worn her hair down in loose curls, and it swung to the side as she cocked her head, giving him a sappy smile. "Good. That makes my heart happy."

God, she is gorgeous, inside and out.

They chatted about their days as he asked even more questions about her dancing. She'd been surprised that he wanted to know absolutely everything. How did she know all of that choreography? What had it been like to rehearse, and more importantly, was the guy she'd danced with in a loving and committed relationship with *somebody else* so that Luca didn't have to worry about it anymore? *That* had made her almost choke on her pickles with laughter.

It had been a long time since he'd had a grown-up conversation over dinner, losing track of time and enjoying somebody's company.

He hadn't thought it could get better being with her, and yet here they were, chatting away until he realized he was late for the next part of their date.

After putting their plates in the sink and locking up, Luca told her about the rest of their evening plans. "There is a part two," he said. "Annabelle is staying with Pearl for a girls-only slumber party."

She smiled, and the simmering heat of it went straight to his cock. "Well, *whatever* shall we do with a house to ourselves?"

Just you wait.

LUCA

Five minutes later, he pulled up to his house and escorted Olivia to the back, where Reed sat tending a fire pit. He'd asked him to come start one so he and Olivia could enjoy it rather than fuss with building a fire.

"Thanks, man. Say hi to your parents for me," Luca said as Reed walked past, patting Luca's shoulder and waving at Olivia.

Twinkle lights crisscrossed through the backyard. A cozy fire pit crackled beside two chairs. Warm blankets, a packet of marshmallows, a bottle of whiskey, two glasses, and new marshmallow roasting sticks for her with a bow on them had been carefully laid out.

She looked as if he'd given her a shiny new Corvette.

"What?! What?!" She clapped, looking as enchanting as a wide-eyed Disney princess. "When did you do this?"

He laughed and squeezed her against him. "Turns out, people want to help me when I ask for it. I wanted to *finally* have you on my lap while we roast marshmallows and drink whiskey. And get you some better sticks for your house."

"Oh," she said, looking disappointed by the metal roasting sticks. "I like the ones you made. Because *you* made them."

His heart melted. She made everything he did feel special. "I'll go get the ones I made last time. Why don't you cozy up by the fire?"

Her eyes and smile full of warmth, she gave him a quick kiss. "See? That's why I love you so much."

Her eyes went wide as she froze, looking shocked at what she'd just said.

He froze, too, trying to understand what was happening.

"*Shoot,*" Olivia said, squinting her eyes together, cursing herself. "I wanted to make it a *whole* thing."

He gulped, still not believing what was happening.

She looked at him nervously, twisting her hands. "So, um. It turns out... I'm in love with you. Like, a lot. An embarrassing amount."

She grimaced as if she was sorry, rather than it being the most astounding thing he'd ever heard. "And I'm sorry for not making it more special when I told you, and now I've forgotten the speech I had, and you don't have to say it back, but you *do* deserve to feel special. You know when I sent that audio message and said not to play it? I, um, accidentally said it then too."

He nodded, trying to follow her rambling, fast speech. "I know," he said with an apologetic shrug.

Her eyes went wider. "You *knew*? You said you wouldn't play it."

He smiled through his panic as he looked at her. "*Technically,* I promised I wouldn't play it... again. You freaked out, and I thought it was like when a cab driver says, 'Have a safe flight!' and you say, 'You too!' Just... muscle memory. No meaning."

The firelight danced in her wide, pretty eyes.

He gulped as he brushed the backs of his fingers against hers. "Couldn't get my hopes up," he whispered.

She looked touched and surprised. "You hoped I loved you?"

"Liv." He sighed out her name, as if that alone didn't make his feelings obvious.

His hands were shaking, but she had to know. *Had* to know how much she was loved.

"The first second I saw you in Bookish, I knew you were kind."

He fought past the emotion in his throat. "The next second? I knew you were *gorgeous*. Stunning. So far out of my league I shouldn't even be allowed to look at you."

His thumb stroked over the freckles he'd memorized that night, the smile lines. Impossibly lucky with his good fortune of finding her.

His heartbeats thundered in his ears from the adrenaline.

"That third second, though?" He blew out a breath as his lip trembled.

He shook his head helplessly as he shrugged at the obvious truth. "That third second, I fell in love with you. Hook, line, sinker... rod... boat... heart."

She stared open-mouthed in shock.

His thumb stroked her soft bottom lip. "As soon as I saw you, I knew you were mine. Like I know these veins are mine. I have no idea how they came to be or why I deserve them, but I know I'd die without them. Without you."

Her cheeks had gone pink in the cold, and the firelight shimmered on her pretty hair. "This whole time?" she whispered.

"Yeah." He laughed at the ironic misery of his life the last two months. "This whole time."

She shook her head slowly in disbelief.

"The thing you don't see, though," he said, cupping her cheek, "is that everyone falls in love with you. My kid, my shop team, my sister who doesn't like anybody, your ballet kids, every person in the theater when you danced. How could anyone *help* but love you when you shine like you do?"

He pulled her hand to his heart, needing her to know it beat for her. "You bring light to all the spots that need it most. Like me. You never notice it because it's always light where you are. You've luckily never known how dark and lonely life feels without you in it."

He gulped, miserably laying *everything* he felt for her at her feet.

"I love you, Olivia Maroo, with every molecule in my body. My fibula, my right pinky nail, my carotid artery. They're all yours if you need them."

"So." He inhaled a shaky, big breath at how overwhelmed he was. "Yes. I hoped you loved me three days ago. Because... I might die of whatever this is otherwise."

His face was pained as he looked at her, afraid she'd bolt like any reasonable woman would after hearing how desperately he loved her.

"Cool." Her voice was watery with tears as she bit her lip. "We'll just keep things casual, then," she said, a teary, snorting laugh escaping her as she wrapped her arms around him.

He laughed with her at the shared torturous honor of loving someone so much. He held her tight against him, savoring the silk of her hair against his cheek. Marveling at the miracle of her loving him back, even after he told her how he felt.

She sniffed into his chest, rubbing her face against him as they cuddled. "How did you keep all that inside for so long?"

He wheezed with aching laughter. "Practice."

She stared up at him with those pretty eyes that he now knew loved him.

Amazing.

She shook her head. "I felt like I'd been punched in the gut when you glowered at me in Bookish. Like there was *something* about what we were supposed to be to each other, but I couldn't figure it out."

He smiled indulgently as he kissed the tip of her nose. "I did not *glower*."

She kissed the corner of his mouth, smiling impishly. "Mmm, you did. But I wasn't enough for someone to want. I was a mess. Or... *more* of a mess. But you felt all that for me for *two months*?" She still looked confused.

As if he'd somehow mixed her up with some other drop-dead gorgeous, thoughtfully kind, and strong woman in his life.

He tucked a lock of hair behind her cute ear, brushed the earlobe he'd fallen for. "I don't know why it hit me like a ton of bricks, but all I know is that I love you. Just as you are. Snorts while laughing required." He held her chin with his thumb. "Toe shoes optional."

"I would never want to confuse AB or upset your dynamic. But I want you both in my life for as long as you'd like to be in it. Since I'm staying here, we can take things slow—"

"What?" He blinked, his mind coming to a screeching halt. That had been key information he'd missed somewhere along the way.

"Since I'm staying here—"

"*What*? Since when?" He replayed their conversations.

She'd talked about college. Doing something other than dancing.

Not that she was staying.

Olivia laughed at his expression. "I told you, I'm going to explore what makes me happy."

"Here?" he asked, the word coming out in a ragged whisper.

She looked at him like he was an adorable lunkhead. "Obviously. I don't know if you heard me earlier, but I'm in plan-shattering love with you."

He gulped as she turned away from him, reaching down into her bag. "Speaking of, I have a present for you."

"Liv, you staying is the best present I could ever hope for."

She handed him a thin, rectangular gift box with a shy smile. He shook it close to his ear.

"Ah, you're a shaker?" She grabbed for the box with a smile, but he evaded her. "No, I take it back, not in love with you." She grabbed again as he laughed, catching her around the waist and kissing her instead.

"We can negotiate gift-giving protocols." He kissed her cheek, laughing as he opened the lid.

His laughter fell as his heart stopped.

Yellow rubber dish gloves, laid tenderly in tissue paper.

The same ones he'd stared at weeks ago, imagining a perfect life with her.

"Size XL for you," Olivia said nervously. "So we match." She pulled out yellow gloves in her size from her bag.

Soapy dishes as the result of a hundred happy memories.

He reached for her, untethered to reality without feeling her in his hands.

She nuzzled his hand against her cheek. "I want to do dishes with you. Buy plates we like, and eat the food you cook. Take care of AB. Argue about whose turn it is to take out the trash—"

"Mine, forever," he interrupted, feeling overwhelmed at how much he loved her. How lucky he was.

She laughed. "Okay, or vacuum—"

"I love vacuuming," he added, not letting her imagine a future where they wouldn't be happy.

"Well, we'll figure something out." She smiled, her eyes dewy. "In our house, where there's no yelling." She brushed his cheek with her soft fingers, and the beauty of it shattered through him.

He closed his eyes, savoring this perfect moment in his life.

Instantly, he saw a road map of the next ten, twenty years of amazing things that would happen. The house they'd eventually buy. Maybe another kid someday. One with Olivia's pretty eyes. A wedding somewhere in there. The vacations they'd take AB on, seeing her graduate and do whatever made her heart happy. The nights they'd fall asleep together, tangled up after making love.

"I'm gonna restart therapy," he said suddenly. The future was too shimmery with potential. He couldn't mess this up. "I went after the accident, but I thought I'd fixed everything. Or... enough. Now, I want to be better because I have an amazing life to live."

Her eyes were wistful. "We'll take things slow for AB, but otherwise, I want it all right now too."

Yes, she was so smart. They'd be careful with AB's heart, but he'd abandon all fear with his own. He finally kissed her, and they sighed into the safety of it.

The miraculous warmth of someone who loved you.

"I love you," she murmured against his lips as he kissed her.

Need ticked at his jaw as it reverberated through him. He captured her mouth, letting himself show how much he wanted her.

"I love you," she gasped as he licked into her mouth. Wanting her clawed at him, hot and needy.

She pulled away suddenly, panting, putting a hand on his chest. "I don't know what I'm doing with my life in four months, but I know one thing, and that's that *I love you*. You carry *so much* for everyone else. All alone. Let someone take care of you, love you. I'd like it to be me. That's..." She wiped her mouth with the back of her hand, gasping. "That's what I meant to say earlier."

He nodded and stalked to the bucket of water beside the fire pit, then dumped it onto the flames.

"What are you doing?" Olivia asked in shock.

"Going inside," he said, grabbing her hand and tugging her with him to the house. "Because I'm not getting a public indecency charge while I fuck the woman I love."

He pulled out his keys as she laughed, climbing up the steps.

She kissed his cheek while his shaking hands tried to unlock the door. "She loves you back enough to get one."

"I'll keep that in mind for the future," he said, kicking open the door and kissing her on the way through it.

Slamming the back door behind him, she pushed him up against it as she kissed him back hard.

Jesus, fuck. He was weak for her.

They made it as far as the laundry room before shoving off each other's coats, never leaving each other's lips. He tugged off her big scarf, and she pulled at his gloves.

"I love you," she gasped as his hands grasped at her. "I love your body that's hot as *fuck*." She bit his arm as he raked his teeth across her earlobe. "I love how thoughtful you are, love how good a person you are."

His cock pulsed with every *love*. "Fuck, Liv. I'm gonna come if you keep talking," he growled.

She huffed a laugh as she captured his mouth. "Did I find your kink? Loving you?" He licked into her mouth, kissing her mindlessly as he grabbed her ass, squeezing it as they stumbled until they hit the washer.

"Yes," he whispered, pushing a leg between hers and rocking her on it. She'd worn a cute plaid skirt, leggings, and boots for their date. He could feel the heat of her against his thigh through her leggings and pushed her harder against his thigh. "Fuck, I need to taste it, Liv."

He spun her around, yanked her leggings down, and bent her over the washer. Falling to his knees, he spread her ass and buried his face in her pussy.

He feasted on how wet she was, licking and sucking up every drop as she moaned. He inhaled gulps of the salty, bright scent that made his cock leak. If he angled just right, he could bury his nose deep into her as he licked her clit.

He squeezed the hips in his hands, moving her how he wanted as she grabbed at the washer for stability.

Olivia pushed back into him, panting. "I love you, I— I love —" she screamed as he sucked hard on her clit, coating his face in her.

This was how they'd spend every date night, he decided. Somewhere he could bend her over and fuck her brainless with his tongue. Hopefully for years—decades.

He pushed two fingers into her as he teased her clit. "I want to do *everything* with you," she moaned.

He pumped two fingers into her and dragged another slippery finger to her ass, circling the tight hole there.

"Even this?" He teased it, and she fluttered around his fingers, grasping at him. He chuckled as she curled over in pleasure on the washer.

"Yes," she sobbed, "more." He spat on her and gently, slowly slid his pinky into her ass as he fucked her with his mouth.

Her cries echoed in the small room, and his cock was about to blow.

She grabbed her breast. "Need this," she panted. "In every room of every house we have. Except the kids' rooms."

Oh fuuuuck me. He moaned hard and long against her and squeezed his cock over his jeans with his free hand.

Imagining her in his fantasy in their bed. Being a family with her.

The vibrations of his moans pushed her over the edge as she came in squealing thrashes, pumping her hips against his face.

She panted as he stood and pulled her up to him, wanting to hold her, but her hands yanked his belt open, unzipped his fly.

"Liv, we can take a break—"

Her feral eyes were on fire. "Wrong. Two to one, my love. I want my other one right"—she stroked his weeping cock hard—"now."

"Fucking hell, I'm never letting go of you," he muttered against her mouth.

He pulled his wallet out of his back pocket and handed it to her as he knelt to take off her boots.

He yanked, but they didn't budge.

"They're tight," she said, tossing his wallet and tearing the condom foil with her teeth.

"Fuck it."

He pulled her leggings down as far as they would go, lifted her onto the washer as she yelped, and, tossing her legs over him, stepped into the open space between her legs.

She rolled the condom on, and one half-second later, he lifted her up with one arm and, fisting his cock with the other, thrust into her.

A guttural moan sighed out from both of them at the relief of it.

She wrapped her legs tight around him as he moved them to the wall, lifting her up and down on his cock.

Surrounded by her limbs, her scent in his nose, his tongue met hers in greedy, claiming kisses. Silky hair teased his hands as he thrust into her, pinning her against the wall.

So strong, so soft, and able to take it all.

Begging him for more.

"Mine," he panted against her cheek as he pumped hard and fast into her. "Say it."

"Yours." She tugged his hair toward her for emphasis. "I love you."

He moaned at that. "Always—"

"Forever—"

Every thrust, every kiss, every touch was punctuated with the word they'd both craved for too long—love.

They came against each other with a crushing kiss that would—now and forever— feel like home.

Chapter Thirty-five

LUCA

After reading fifteen blog articles, four Reddit posts, and one book—okay, he'd skimmed the book—Luca still wasn't sure he was going to do a good job explaining his relationship with Olivia to Annabelle.

He and Olivia had prepped, discussed boundaries of what to do and not do in front of AB, how she'd handle any parenting-adjacent territory if it came up. She'd never dated someone with kids, and he'd never dated someone since he'd had one.

Had a whole fucking rule about it and everything, like an idiot. He wiped a hand down his face as he watched Olivia nap on the couch in the living room.

He sighed at how much he fucking *loved* this woman. He needed her in his bloodstream—scent, taste, all of it.

The books all said to wait until the relationship was solid to introduce them.

That ship? Sailed. Trusting the new partner with the kid? Done. Ensuring the kid likes the partner?

Sometimes AB likes her more than me.

It would only get harder to hide their relationship now that Olivia was staying and he was a giant fucking sap for her.

Cracking his neck, he knew that the time had come. AB was up in her room, and now was as good a time as any.

I can do this.

He knocked on the open door, and AB looked up from her coloring. "Hey, goob. Have a minute to talk?"

She held up two papers. "I made this one for you, and this one for 'Livia." His paper was a house and car, all black. Olivia's was two blob figures holding hands with a little blob.

Maybe this won't be so bad after all.

"Thank you, these are great." He patted her bed, and she scrambled up next to him. "You remember how I said Olivia was going to move away for a job?" AB nodded, looking a little sad. "Well, things have changed. Olivia is going to stay in Fairwick Falls."

AB's face lit up, and she popped onto her knees with excitement. "Will she be my babysitter still?"

"Good question." He held her still while she bounced on the bed with growing energy. "That's what I wanted to talk about. Olivia and I are dating." *Oh god. Do kids even know what dating is?* "We, uh, *like* like each other."

AB bounced harder, completely unfazed. "Will she still be my dance teacher?"

"I'm not sure; you can ask her."

"Is she moving in?"

Oh god. "No. Maybe someday, but not right now."

AB frowned. "Why not?"

He sighed. *Investigative journalism, your brightest star is six years old.* He pulled her into his lap. "We want to take things slow. We both love you a lot, and we want to make sure there aren't too many changes at once."

"That's dumb." Her *you're an idiot* scowl nearly made him laugh.

"Your opinion is noted, thank you. Do you... have any questions?" *This seems too easy.*

"When do we get a baby?"

Holy fuck. He blinked hard, hoping he'd misheard her. "... What now?"

AB shrugged, as if it was obvious. "Harper's getting a new sister because her mom has a boyfriend."

"Oh, it's... uh... not a package deal for everybody." This seemed to satisfy her for now. "Olivia and I might hold hands sometimes and hug. Is that okay?"

"*Ewwww.*" AB squirmed but looked happy about it.

Luca laughed with her. "We don't have to." *At least not around you, kid.*

AB shrugged, now looking grown-up. "It's okay. Are you in looooove?" AB teased him, but he could see a question in her eyes.

He swiped a hand along AB's hair. He was so lucky to be her dad.

"Yeah, I am in love, kid. I love Olivia a lot. I love *you* a lot, too, and that won't change, ever. No matter what happens with Olivia and me. Okay?"

AB's happy smile started to look overwhelmed. Tears welled up in her eyes as she tried to smile through them.

"Hey." He was caught off guard. "What's wrong? Talk to me."

Her mouth turned into a frown. "I wanted her to stay really baa-aad." Her voice cracked into a cry on the last word, breaking his heart.

"Oh, kiddo." He gathered her up, and her cries turned into big, full-chested little-kid sobs, with big gasps in the middle.

What is happening? He patted her back as he stood, rocking her. "Olivia *is* staying," he clarified, making sure she understood.

Her sobs turned to wails.

Are these... happy tears?

He kissed her temple and rocked her. He tried to untangle what was happening in her head. "Were you worried she'd leave?"

AB nodded against his shoulder, her face a red mess of snot and tears. "I wanted... her to... sta-aa-aa-aay," she ugly sobbed through hiccups.

His heart ached. God, this whole time he'd been in his head with his own stuff, and she'd been worried. *Still fucked this up even when I tried to protect her.* "Honey, I'm so sorry you were worried. That must have been really hard."

She nodded, her sobs quieting down.

"And you're... happy she's staying now?" he clarified, to make sure he followed.

A pitiful, ragged "yeah" broke his heart.

Olivia burst through the open door, arms reaching out for AB and sobbing twice as hard. "I was eavesdropping, I'm s-s-sorry."

Annabelle immediately reached out for Olivia, who took her from him.

AB ugly sobbed into Olivia's neck, wrapped tight around her. "I'm so sorry you were worried, sweetie," Olivia whispered through hiccuping sobs as she swayed back and forth, soothing Annabelle. "But I'm so happy I'm staying and I still get to see you. I'll be right next door."

AB wailed harder in, apparently, happy tears.

God, he'd fucked this all up. Even though he'd tried to protect her, AB had been worried for weeks, maybe months, and could finally show it.

Poor, sweetest girl of his.

Luca blew out a long breath, looking at the two crying

hearts outside his body, hysterically sobbing with joy as they clutched each other.

He was going to need more tissues in this house.

I'll just have to make it up to AB and marry Olivia as soon as I can.

~

OLIVIA

THE BARRE'S STUDIO PARTY, celebrating their performance at the festival, was underway. Olivia weaved through students and their parents, all enjoying snacks in the studio as they played games.

Luca and AB walked in, with Luca holding a gorgeous, big bouquet.

"Hi, you two." She hugged both of them, having not seen them for an entire day, prepping for the party. "Nice shirt, sweetie." She winked at AB, who giggled.

Olivia had figured out a way to thoughtfully add more material in a contrasting color to the sleeves, length, and width of AB's favorite teal unicorn shirt. Now it had sort of a vintage striped vibe, and AB wore it constantly. "These flowers are gorgeous. For moi?"

Luca smiled indulgently at her; she'd never get tired of looking at his handsome face. "Sorry, Liv. These are for the most important woman in my life this year. Georgia."

Olivia was confused, but then gasped, following his logic. "Oh my god, you're *right*. If she hadn't conned me—convinced me," Olivia corrected with a glance at AB, "then..."

"I'd still be looking in the diner for you," Luca said with a wistful sigh.

Olivia's face turned pleading. "Put my name on the card?"

Luca squeezed her waist as he passed. "Already done."

Georgia fluttered and flirted outrageously across the room with Luca when he handed her the flowers.

A dance party broke out as the music turned more upbeat into holiday music, and the students coaxed her into dancing with them. She bounced and jumped, swinging her arms with theirs, looking silly and not caring even a little.

She was having *fun*.

Georgia winked at her from across the room, seeming to understand the realization Olivia'd had. "He's mine now," she mouthed to Olivia while pointing to Luca, and Olivia belly-laughed so hard she almost took out Sophie when she bent over laughing.

What a difference two and a half months could make.

She'd agreed to teach at The Barre for one more semester as she got herself organized to take a gen ed class at a community college and try her hand at more sewing. Georgia had insisted that she continue to house-sit until she and Luca decided everyone was ready to try living together.

As the afternoon party wound down, Luca managed to untangle himself from Georgia and the other parents and helped Olivia start to clean up.

One by one, Olivia waved goodbye to her students and promised she'd see them in January for the next round of classes. Luca, AB, and Georgia all helped her clean and lock up.

"Hey, I need to stop by your mom's house. Mind if we make a detour?"

Olivia shrugged as she squeezed his hand. "Pop will probably make us eat *dessert*," she said, rolling her eyes at AB comically. "Oh nooo, how *terrible*."

AB giggled in the back seat.

Luca drove down the familiar cobblestone streets as warm, cozy lights glowed from the houses on both sides.

How different life seemed from the first time she'd driven down the street after coming back. Each bump had felt like failure, dread sloshing in her stomach. Now she couldn't wait for each day, spending it with her favorite people.

The street was unusually full of cars, but Luca managed to find a parking space. *Maybe the neighbors are having a family thing.*

As they walked up the stone steps to her parents' house, she realized the noise was coming from inside.

"Is your mom throwing a kegger?" Luca asked.

Olivia snorted. "Honestly, it wouldn't be the first time." But then he turned, and she saw the way his eyes danced. *Wait a minute...*

They walked in the door, and all her favorite faces—Lily, Georgia, Pop, her mom, Pearl—turned to clap and yell, "Surprise!"

What the f—

More heads popped into view from the adjoining rooms—Reed, Lily's sisters, Nash, her mom's friends, and Allison all shouted, "Surprise!" at her with bright, happy smiles.

Utterly baffled, she looked between Luca and her mother for an explanation.

"Because you finally chose where you wanted to stay, dear," her mother said, giving her a kiss on the cheek. "So, we're throwing you a welcome-home party. Finally."

Olivia was overwhelmed at the happy faces smiling at her, giving her hugs.

"Are you *so* surprised?" Lily said, bouncing with excitement. She wrapped her in a tight hug. "I can't wait to see you any time I want." Olivia settled into her friend's hug.

Everybody looked at Olivia as her mom raised a glass to toast her. "For the incredibly kind, smart, talented girl who had to leave too soon, may the rest of your days in Fairwick Falls be as happy as we are when you're here."

Olivia sucked in a ragged breath and hugged her mom, trying not to cry.

"Speech!" Pearl called from the corner, and Allison elbowed her, laughing.

"Can't take her anywhere," Allison said with an eye roll.

"I... I just forgot how good it felt." She looked at her friends. "To be with people who were kind, and loyal, and considerate." She saw her mom, Pop, and Georgia. "Who looked out for me and loved me despite me not being perfect." Finally, her eyes landed on Luca and AB. "Who made me so happy, just by being themselves. I forgot how happy I could be until you helped me remember."

"You've got gifts!" AB shouted. They cheersed, and AB dragged her to the table. Olivia was blown away. A gift card to Fox & Forrest cafe, chocolates from Bloom, a "Come & Get Your Beaver Wet" t-shirt from The Thirsty Beaver—from either Pearl or her mother, it was anyone's guess.

A framed photo of her and Lily as kids stood at the back, beside a physical calendar with festivals circled on it and the committees she'd be joining (ah, *that* one was from her mother). Luca handed her their gifts.

"Just a little something I thought you'd like," he said, looking nervous. It was a framed black-and-white photo of her mom and Pop watching at the Pittsburgh performance. The awe and pride in their faces made Olivia's eyes mist. "Since you couldn't see them," Luca said.

She hugged him, and he squeezed her tight. "I love you so much," she whispered.

"I love you the most," he whispered back into her ear, and she nuzzled against him.

"I have a present," AB said politely and handed her a

picture. It was a crayon drawing of what Olivia imagined was the three of them between two houses, and a heart over the top. She hugged Annabelle tight. "Don't tell the others," Olivia said in a whisper, "but this one is my favorite." AB giggled.

Olivia stood and met Luca's eyes, who bit his lip. Putting a hand over AB's eyes, he pulled Olivia in for a kiss, firm and claiming. A wolf whistle sounded from somewhere, and Pearl yelled, "Get a room!"

"He has one!" AB yelled back as Olivia pulled away and Luca finally removed his hand.

Everyone laughed but, thankfully, went back to their conversations.

AB got distracted by completing her complicated hand-shake with Reed, and Luca pulled Olivia into a hug.

"This okay?" he asked, rubbing her back but checking in.

Olivia laughed, still surprised with the turn her life had taken. "A man that smells like my personal catnip loves me, more friends than I can count, Pop's apple-pie pancakes are over there in bite-sized servings so I can have as many as I want and no one will know." Luca laughed, his eyes dancing as he held her face. "And I'm in love with the hottest man in the room. I have literally—quite literally—never been better."

Olivia Maroo spent the rest of the night—the first in what would be a decades-long string of nights—surrounded by people she loved and who thoroughly loved her back.

Just as she was.

Epilogue

THREE WEEKS LATER

LUCA

A giant printout of a complicated van wrap design rolled across Luca's desk as Lily emphatically pointed at it.

"So the Cooperstown Bloom van needs *this* color, Elliotsville Bloom van needs this color, and the Philly van needs this one. And make sure you add on the 'cute as fuck' Farmers Market package."

"I think we can do that," he said with a smile, excited to take on more work for a trendsetting business that was growing.

His shop was running smoothly, and business had picked up as people had discovered their new location.

He stood suddenly as he saw the clock. "I've gotta run to Annabelle's Thanksgiving program. Angie will finish up any logistics with you."

"Adorbs," Lily sighed. "Go be the best dad ever."

He waved to Angie as she walked in.

"Tell Little Boss to break a turkey leg," Angie said as he grabbed his coat and walked out.

With ten minutes to spare, he walked into the elementary gymnasium. It was AB's first school program ever, since kinder-gartners didn't participate.

Children sat on the floor; parents sat in the bleachers. Olivia waved to him, patting an empty spot between her and Pearl, who sat next to Marcy's parents.

He took the steps two at a time to the very top row. "Hope-fully AB doesn't get stage-fright again," he said, kissing Olivia on the cheek hello. "I don't know this choreography."

Olivia laughed and squeezed his knee, and they chatted as the first class filed onto the risers on the gym floor.

Excitement bubbled in Luca's chest. He closed his eyes, savoring the moment and the hum of chatter around him, as Olivia and Pearl talked about holiday plans. The woman he loved, his sister safe and sound, his heart was about to go on stage, and he was right *here* where he should be.

He'd thought about this moment for so long—over twenty years. On the outside, this was just a normal Thanksgiving play, but to him, it was the culmination of a lifetime of good choices, luck, and hard work. He'd made it out of his past, with only a few scrapes along the way.

Annabelle stood on the risers with her class. She looked for him in the audience, and he waved his arm high up so she'd see him. Her eyes sparkled suddenly, and she waved back, not even a little self-conscious.

He sighed, a grin bursting on his face. *Life goal achieved.*

Forty-five minutes later, after several first-grade turkeys sang songs about gratitude, he, Olivia, and AB walked hand in hand in hand to his car. Pearl and Marcy's parents had *oohed* and *aahed* over Annabelle's stellar performance as Tailfree, the turkey with no tail feathers.

"Now that I have taken in the thee-ah-tah," Olivia said

dramatically, "it's time for me to go start the Thanksgiving prep marathon."

"Sure we can't help?" Luca said, squeezing her hand.

"Nah." Olivia shrugged, giving him a smile. "It'll be fun. My mom and I get wine drunk and creative with seasonings. Lily and Violet come over; it's a whole thing."

She hugged him goodbye hard as they stood beside the car, then bent down to hug AB goodbye with an *oomf* squeeze and a kiss on the head.

"You won't be there to tuck me in tonight," AB said sadly.

"No, kid," Olivia said with a wistful sigh but a mischievous smile. "But a certain platypus is back in action with two arms *and* two legs. He's on your bed. Can you cuddle him for me instead?" She swooped a boop onto Annabelle's nose, making her giggle through her "yeah."

"I'll miss you both, but I'll see you tomorrow afternoon at my mom's house." She squeezed AB's cheek as she walked away.

"Love you," Luca called, placing a quick kiss on her lips.

"I love you too!" AB echoed loudly at Olivia.

Olivia laughed and blew them both dramatic kisses as she walked to her car.

Luca sighed. Turned out, there was no end to the pit of falling deeper and more helplessly in love with Olivia every day.

He popped AB up into her booster seat.

"*Pleeeeeeease.*" She stared at him like he was an absolute moron.

This was the seventh day in a row she'd campaigned for Olivia to move in. Patience had never been either of their strengths.

He glanced at Olivia hopping into her car across the parking lot. "I will take your input under advisement."

He'd barely opened the driver's side door when he heard—

"Her bedtime stories are better."

He smiled. "I've been working on my Canadian accent for Anne of Green Gables."

"She smells nicer."

"Fair, she does smell nice."

Out of ideas, AB flopped her arms. "Ugh, I just don't like it when she's not at home. 'Cause it doesn't feel like home if she's not there."

His eyes caught AB's in the rearview mirror.

That was it. The slip of the tongue he didn't know he'd been waiting for. That AB thought Olivia's home was *with them*.

Because it is.

And I really, really hope it always will be.

THE NEXT AFTERNOON, they stood outside of Olivia's childhood home. "Remember, we use our nice manners today," he said to Annabelle, squeezing her hand.

"Pleases and thank yous and no cursing, even if I want to real bad," AB said, parroting back the list.

They'd brought kid-friendly, cut-up vegetables, a peanut-butter pie, and he'd added flowers for Olivia's mom. He raised his hand to knock on the door, but Olivia swung it open. "Hey, you. I missed you."

AB ran in and hugged her, wrapping her arms around Olivia's legs. She'd already run into the house by the time Luca stooped down to kiss Olivia.

"I missed you too," Olivia said, lingering on their kiss with a sparkling smile.

Chaos was already underway as plates of food lined the large kitchen island. Pop was elbow-deep in five dishes on the stove.

More and more people piled into Martha and Pop's house. Allison was talking with Nash in the dining room. Lily and Olivia and Annabelle were trying to do something with parsley, but it wasn't working out well. Lily's sisters, Rose and Violet, and their husbands had been put to work by Martha and Pop. Pearl and Reed would join them after the meal since he hated the sound of people eating.

"Hey, you." Violet patted Luca's arm. "Could you reach up there?" She pointed to a high shelf with a bunch of sheet pans.

"Here you go," he said, feeling in the way in the kitchen with all these people. "Happy to be of help."

Rose squeezed past him, and she and Violet bickered playfully about the vegan cheese ball Violet was making, while Olivia reached in to grab a bite from the bowl.

"It needs more dill, right?" Rose asked Olivia, who shrugged.

"Tastes like it always does," Olivia said, licking her fingers, all of them perfectly at home in Martha's kitchen.

Lily shoved in between them and mimicked Olivia, grabbing a sample as the three sisters started arguing.

"Having fun?" Olivia said with a smile over the chatter that, apparently, she was used to.

This is so nice, but overwhelming.

"Yeah," he said, looking for Annabelle and seeing that she was sitting at a table with Martha doing a craft. "I'm going to step outside for some fresh air."

"Okay," Olivia said, kissing his cheek and smiling as she went back to stealing a bite from Violet's bowl.

Luca stepped out onto the small patio of Martha's pretty house. The chaos and noise of a happy family slowly quieted as he closed the door. It was so different from what he'd known when he was Annabelle's age.

Warm and happy, bursting with love. His brain needed time to calibrate.

He sipped the cocktail Martha had shoved into his hand and choked at how strong it was, laughing at himself.

Wells walked from the little carriage garage in the backyard, and an expensive-sounding beep echoed as he locked his car.

Luca waved in greeting, and Wells returned it.

He loved that Wells didn't bullshit around. He liked people who were straight shooters.

"Escape the crazy in there?" Wells said with a friendly smile.

Luca sighed, leaning against the deck fence. "I'm not really used to it, but it's nice."

Wells sighed. "Yeah. Me either, really. I didn't come home that much until... recently."

"Liv told me—"

Wells's eyes flashed.

"And swore me to secrecy," Luca said, crossing his heart. "It's a nice thing you did."

Though he was pissed at Wells for ruining one of the only two good restaurants in town, he had to admire that his heart was in the right place.

Wells shrugged it off, looking uncomfortable with Luca's words. "I just didn't imagine I'd be so bad at it. Pop made it look so easy. It's one of the first things I wanted to be when I was a kid," Wells said, smiling ruefully.

"A diner owner?" Luca asked, genuinely curious.

Wells laughed. "A line cook. Wanted to be just like Pop."

A roar of laughter sounded from inside, and Luca realized he probably wouldn't get a quiet moment with Wells again.

Wish me luck, universe. He gulped, looking over his shoulder, making sure no one inside would hear.

He squared his shoulders as he looked at Wells. "I had

someone do this for me, so I'm returning the favor. I'm going to marry your sister. Not right now, but... someday. Soon, I hope."

Wells looked at him appraisingly, like a shark, but his eyes softened as he saw Olivia dancing with AB inside.

But maybe one who's on my side?

"Good," Wells said definitively. "She's never been happier. She's had a rough go. There were a lot of tears in our house when we were kids. And then"—he whistled to emphasize how terrible it had been—"she spent two years living with our dad. He's an excellent lawyer, and a terrible father," he said with a humorless laugh. "And yet? Still, she's Olivia."

Luca nodded. "She's the best."

Wells nodded and sighed as he looked at Olivia and Annabelle playing. "This dad thing," he said wistfully. "You recommend it?"

Luca couldn't tell if he was joking or not, so he just decided to be honest. "Best thing that's ever happened to me. Easy."

Wells scrunched his brows together and nodded to himself. He patted Luca's shoulder a little too hard as he walked away. "Welcome to the family. Hope you like festivals."

And he opened the sliding glass door to a chorus of surprised yells.

Luca chuckled into his cocktail glass.

He realized with a shock that he hadn't even considered what else he'd gained beyond the miracle of finding Olivia. As Annabelle fit right in with their motley crew, he realized they maybe just got a much bigger family than they'd ever hoped for.

❧

OLIVIA

"HEY, YOU," Olivia said, hugging her brother in surprise. "I thought you had to be in Philly tomorrow morning. A heads-up would have been nice."

So I could send Allison one county away.

He squeezed her into a gentle headlock. "I'm not welcome at Thanksgiving anymore, pipsqueak?"

Olivia poked his side. "Not fair, you're nine feet tall."

His mom waved them in to sit down. "All right, kids. Pop's finally got everything out of the oven!"

Olivia stuck her head out and waved Luca in. They walked by her favorite sight—the front entrance piled high with shoes. All her favorite people were safe and snug inside.

The extended dining table was comprised of her mother's dining table for three, two card tables, and a large sheet of plywood on sawhorses, all draped creatively with tablecloths and décor so no one was any the wiser.

Violet and Rose were making themselves at home in her mom's kitchen like they had since Olivia was a kid, getting extra spoons for serving.

This was home, and these were her people.

Food started being passed back and forth. She grabbed potatoes from Violet's husband, Jack, plopped some on her plate and Annabelle's, and handed them to Luca as she talked to Rose beside her.

But through very unfortunate luck, her brother and Allison sat across from each other at the end of the table.

"What are *you* doing here?" Wells said, taken aback.

Allison sat up straighter. "My parents are on a cruise, and when your angel of a mother—who you're *somehow* related to —heard I'd be spending Thanksgiving alone, she insisted I come because *you* wouldn't be here."

"You mucked it all up, darling," her mom said, patting

Wells's head as she kissed his cheek. "But it's fine. Should make for a good story." She winked at Olivia.

"Oh god," Rose murmured to Olivia. "Maybe I should trade spots with Annabelle," she said, looking concerned. "It's not fair for a six-year-old to get caught in their cross-fire."

"They're adults," Lily said with an eye roll.

"Well. *She's* an adult," Olivia said, looking at her brother skeptically.

Allison simmered across from Olivia's brother for most of the dinner. Luckily, Violet's husband held an easy conversation with her. AB was also very curious about Allison's pink hair, which was a happy distraction for a solid ten minutes.

Olivia grabbed the bowl of green beans from Luca and spooned some onto Annabelle's plate. A sappy, love-drunk look was in his eyes as he met her gaze. He winked, and she smiled, trying to memorize the moment in the middle of all the chaos and conversation around them.

Maybe the rest of her Thanksgivings would look exactly like this.

Her and Luca, Pearl and Reed, the Parker sisters, her idiot brother, and all of their spouses, their babies. All sitting at this table that was supposed to hold three and had expanded to hold so much more—into a world so much bigger than she'd ever thought possible for herself.

She was pulled out of her dreams by Allison's heated voice.

"Not all of us can make a fortune out of the *misfortune* of others," Allison said. She tore one of Pop's wheat-free rolls in half fiercely.

"As I recall," Wells started in.

Ah shit—that was his lawyer voice. Condescension mixed with a highbrow sneer. *As if he didn't grow up washing the inside of his Ziploc bags like the rest of us.*

Wells leaned toward Allison and grabbed a deviled egg from

between them. "You were *just* as excited to sign the dotted line as he was. Doesn't sound like misfortune to me. I did the world a service by setting you free." He popped a second deviled egg in his mouth.

"The only thing that's free," Allison said, her cheeks burning pink, "is the money that *was* in my bank account that my ex-husband now has."

Wells popped another half of a deviled egg into his mouth. "Should've had a better lawyer."

Allison yanked the deviled egg plate away from him, and Wells flinched. "I'm *not* going to throw it at you," she said, rolling her eyes.

"Then why'd you move it?" he asked through a mouthful.

"Because I don't want your fingers in my *eggs!*" she said, throwing down the other half of her roll and storming to the kitchen.

Chatter died down at the table as everybody stopped to stare.

"Would you like to share with the class?" their mother said with a pointed look at Wells.

Wells stretched his arms out with his hands behind his head, confident and cool. "We had an unfortunate run-in a few years ago at…" He stretched, cracking his neck. "Divorce court. I represented her ex-husband. Unfortunately for her, I was the better lawyer. Per usual," he said with a smirk as he reached across the table with his long arms for another one of her deviled eggs and popped it in his mouth, glaring in the direction of the kitchen.

"Question for you, Wells," Nash said with a smile at his old friend. "Can your big head fit *in* the sports car when you drive it, or does it poke out the sunroof?"

Wells rolled his eyes, smiling as everyone laughed at his expense.

"This is fun!" Annabelle said loudly, laughing with everyone.

Luca met Olivia's eyes with a shared sparkle of "Isn't our little human the best?" The tension was broken, and everyone went back to their conversations.

"You having fun?" Olivia asked Luca. He kissed her cheek.

"The most," Luca said, winking at her and making her all fluttery.

As they finished up, Pearl and Reed walked in.

"Just in time for cocktails and charades," her mom said, popping up. Olivia loved seeing her mom in her element with all her favorite people.

"What's a charade? Is it chocolate?" Annabelle asked.

Olivia laughed. "It's a game. It's where you—"

A loud crash sounded from the kitchen. Olivia darted in, worried about Pop or her mom.

Instead, Allison stood covered head to toe in mashed potatoes, an empty catering pan rattling on the floor.

Wells looked horrified on the other side of the island, frozen in shock. Everyone gasped, holding their hands to their mouths in the two doorways of the kitchen.

"I swear—I *swear* it was an accident," Wells said.

Olivia and Luca dove for the paper towels as Lily grabbed a tea towel and handed it to Allison.

Allison wiped one eye. "How... could that possibly have been an accident?"

"I would never waste the world's best mashed potatoes on *you*," he said, emphasis on the word you. "The world's most miserable divorcée."

"Okay—" Olivia said, needing to step in and put him in his place.

"I have literally"—Allison cut her off, wiping mashed potatoes out of her eyes—"*never* been happier than I am right now —except for being covered in..." She looked down. "Vegetables."

"Is everything—" Olivia's mother entered the kitchen, and her mouth fell open as she clocked the situation in one second. "Wellesley Maroo. You will clean this all up, and everyone else will leave him to it." Her mom took Allison's hand. "Come on, deary. I think I have a nightgown you can use as a mini-skirt with those gams of yours."

"AP! AP!" Annabelle said as she ran into the kitchen, thankfully avoiding the mashed potatoes. Pearl caught her around the middle.

Luca handed Olivia her coat, looking overwhelmed. "Want to take a breather?"

Olivia smiled as he helped her into her coat. "I'd *rather* watch Wells on his hands and knees in the kitchen." Wells stuck up his middle finger, wiping up globs of potato from the floor.

"Pearl—" Luca called.

"Go," Pearl shooed them. "I need the play-by-play of the potato situation from our resident journalist here," she said, pointing to Annabelle.

The quiet seemed to echo around Luca and Olivia as the front door shut.

The neighborhood had wasted no time on Thanksgiving evening in turning on their Christmas lights.

"How was your first Maroo holiday?" she said, looping her arm through Luca's.

"Pretty fucking great," he said with a loud laugh.

"Dinner *and* a show," she said, squeezing his arm as they chuckled together.

They held hands, debriefing about the drama and talking about each other's days, as they wound around the block. Hers —being Pop's sous chef and nicking her thumb; his—fashion consultant for AB as she tried on literally eleven outfits for the gathering.

"Maybe next year, we swap responsibilities since I'm no good with color palettes," Luca said, kissing her finger, which had a band-aid on it.

Next year.

What an amazing thought.

The simplicity of it thrilled her. That she'd have next year with him, and maybe the year after that. On and on.

They ended up at the town square, already covered in Christmas lights.

"The festival committee wasted no time," Luca said with a smile, fixing a dangling red bow on the corner trash can. Decorations were on every lamppost and door front. The gazebo on the edge of the town square was covered with lights, glowing gently in the dark. Clouds of their breath rolled out in front of them as they walked across the square.

"Oooh, I've always wanted to do this," Olivia said, tugging him up the gazebo steps to the hanging mistletoe. Big, fat flakes started twirling down outside the gazebo.

She pointed up, and Luca smiled.

"I never need an excuse to kiss you," he said but still bent down and swooped her up into his arms for a firm, happy kiss.

She pulled back, about to tease him, but he looked concerned.

"What's wrong?" she said.

He gulped, holding her hands.

Maybe this is all too much. It was their first holiday together, and they'd only dated for weeks, technically. "If it was too intense back there, we don't have to spend every holiday—"

"Will you move in with me? With us?" he said, finally meeting her eyes. "Whenever you're ready—tomorrow or the next day or..." He shrugged, gulping. "Whenever."

Her heart beat hard in her chest.

"What does Annabelle think?" she said quietly, worried for her favorite little girl.

He sighed out a relieved "I love you so much." His hand cupped her cheek, and he kissed her slowly, a reassurance.

His eyes traced her face as he stroked her cheek. "She's been campaigning since I told her we were dating. Before that, honestly," he said with a laugh. "But now she understands you would share *my* room and not bunk beds in *her* room."

A hard snort of laughter escaped her, which made Luca chuckle even harder. He pulled her against him, and her arms wrapped around his waist, snuggling in.

I practically live there now anyway. She cuddled into his chest. "Don't the parenting books say to wait a year?"

He sighed, nuzzled her, and kissed her forehead slowly. "The books didn't know about you, Olivia. You tuck Annabelle in half the time now, and sometimes you're there again when she wakes up in the morning."

She smiled wickedly, remembering *why* she was usually there before Annabelle woke up in the morning. Luca had turned into an early riser because, thankfully, the laundry room was far away from the bedrooms and the door locked, which meant they could spend some quick, sexy quality time together.

Everything. He was offering her everything on a silver platter that she'd ever *really* wanted—a home with people she loved, who made her happy.

"We might have our first fight if I live there," she said, nervous she might mess it up.

"About what?" He smirked, as if she was adorable.

"I don't know," she said, exasperated. "How I load the dishwasher." She threw it out as an example.

"Easy, there isn't one. Next."

"Okay." She pointed, coming up with a good one. "How I leave water bottles and tea mugs everywhere."

He laughed, kissing the tops of her cheeks dotted with freckles. "That's not any different than now."

"Well," she said, "I'll keep thinking."

He smiled. "I look forward to it. Because then, we can make up in *our* bedroom."

It all sounded amazing. Perfect.

Maybe too good?

"This is too easy," she said to him, confiding her fear.

He nodded, looking as concerned as she was. "I know. Maybe... it's supposed to be?"

She bit her lip, weighing her next words.

They felt scary, but she was brave.

"If I move in," she whispered, finally looking up at him, "I might not move out."

He sighed through a smile, hovering over her lips. "I'm *kind* of counting on that."

Snowflakes blew onto their faces as he kissed her—the warm safety of his body against hers, the perfect taste of him. Her softest, strongest man.

She was so happy to have fallen *right* where she belonged.

THE END

THANK you so much for reading Falling at the Barre! Pre-order Allison & Well's book (Book 6) out next summer!

Not ready to leave Luca and Olivia's epic love story yet? To read a free bonus epilogue for this story and other stories, sign up for my newsletter at elisekbooks.com

. . .

ALSO BY ELISE KENNEDY

LOVE IN FAIRWICK *Falls* Novels
Accidentally in Bloom (Rose & Gray)
Wallflower in Bloom (Violet & Jack)
Conveniently in Bloom (Lily & Nash)
Unexpectedly Bookish (Pearl & Reed)
Falling at the Barre (Olivia & Luca)
Book 6 - Summer 2026 (Allison & Wells)

~

COZY NIGHTS *in Vermont* Novellas
Fall Inn Love
Falling in Vermont

~

ONLY ONE COZY *Bed* Novellas
Pumpkin Spice & Pour-overs
Apple Cider & Subterfuge
Hot Cocoa & Mistletoe
Snowed In & Snuggle Weather

POP'S CHICKEN NOODLE SOUP

This is my family's go-to dish when someone needs some extra love. It's a crowd pleaser that's gentle on the stomach and so very cozy!

Pop Canon's Chicken Noodle Soup

3-4 chicken breasts
1 package (16oz) of Reams Egg Noodles (*Note: you'll find these in the frozen food aisle, and yes, you **must**! use this type of noodle. It makes for delicious, doughy noodles. Note: they are not wheat-free* 🥴)
Boullion cubes
1 Campbells cream of chicken soup
13oz of Evaporated Milk
Poultry seasoning to taste
1 cup of chopped celery for extra crunch

1. In a large pot, combine the chicken with 7 cups of water, 4 bouillon cubes, and pepper. Cook until the chicken is fully cooked and tender.

2. Remove the chicken from the pot and pull it apart into bite-sized pieces. Set aside.

3. Bring the broth to a rolling boil.

4. Drop in the egg noodles a few at a time and cook for about 20 minutes, or until tender.

5. Once the noodles are done, stir in the cream of chicken soup and the evaporated milk until fully combined and creamy.

6. Return the shredded chicken to the pot.

7. Sprinkle poultry seasoning over the soup to taste and stir well. Add celery if desired and let simmer.

Note: this will be better the second day, and the noodles will soak up most of the liquid!

Pairs best with comfy pjs and a blanket warm from the dryer.

ACKNOWLEDGMENTS

Thank you as always to my fantastic beta readers, my editors, and dictation transcriptionists!

A special thanks to Mr. Kennedy, who took me on such a memorable first date that some of our conversation made it into this book. I hope to *just keep talking* with you for decades and decades more.

Thank you as always to my amazing ARC team!

Kristina Holmes, Reed Towne, Sara Rawson, Persephone Hawker, Meagan Vogus, Amanda Brown, Kaylee Holland, Jennifer Gibson, Alexus Smith, Kailey Huber, Rachel Kent, Kelsie Wheeler, Terryn Winfield, Stephanie Toot, Katie Anne Ranney, Jenna Rhiannon, Melanie Granata Egan, Nicole Scarborough, Tiffany Amber Schwartz, Laura Jones, Kelly King, Bianca Sevidal, Rania Laham, Alizae Cratch, Grace Casteel, Laura Lee, Amanda-Jane Savage, Kaylene Ledger, Božena Stojanovič, Nicola Butler, Allison Thommen, Sarah Gwerder, Janina Majeran, Mary McCabe, Melinda Mauro, Thuy Cu, Chloe Simpson, Lisa Christensen, Oasis Donnelly, Jenny Ellis, Jen Williams, Jenna Baker, Shaafia Kasmani, Kailyn Glassmacher, Eva Bower, Caitlin Timm, Trish Meade, Cristie Lynn, Lottie Sheppard, Caitie Parker, Marianne Kay, Ashley Babineaux Medina, Susan Dara, Heather Kelley, Rachelle Leblanc, Cynthia Cabrera, Lyna Nguyen Stanley, Riley Collins, Jennifer Castillo, Celeste Velocci, Chelsea Higley, Sam Nelson, Melissa Letts, Kimber Kennedy Alexander, Sasha M Fountain, Ashley Marie Vaccaro, Karli

Jordan, Jane Litherland, Amanda Preece, Sarah Elyse, Julie, Jenna Coulson, Christine Fass, Lauren Giacalone, Shannon Shimada, Chloe Eggers, Rudi Hilson, Heather Hull Hallberg, Joe Kendall, Andrea Jones Graham, Laura Harnish, Dana Kriston, Katrina Gardner, Joslyn Beltram, Tracy Presse, Jo Bolton, Rebecca Hoch, Gabriela Trad, Jessica De Sa-Mota, Annabelle Hurtt, Jennifer Jansen, Erin Genoe, Sarah Reads, Christine Madigan Fass, Lauren Nicole, Jodi Barnes, Dawn Wilson, Danielle Watts, Chantel Van Dyk and many others!

(Interested in being an ARC reader? Fill out my general interest form!)

About the Author

Elise Kennedy is an author of cozy, spicy, heartfelt small-town romances. She lives in the midwest with her (very) patient husband and two perfect pups.

Join Elise's private Facebook reader group to chat, vote on future books, and make general romantic merriment the small town romantics or her Instagram channel the small town romantics. Å